Malignos

RICHARD CALDER

EARTHLIGHT

LONDON · SYDNEY · NEW YORK · TOKYO · SINGAPORE · TORONTO

www.earthlight.co.uk

First published in Great Britain by Earthlight, 2000
An imprint of Simon & Schuster UK Ltd
A Viacom Company

Copyright © Richard Calder, 2000

The right of Richard Calder to be identified as author of
this work has been asserted in accordance with sections 77
and 78 of the Copyright Designs and Patents Act 1988

Simon & Schuster UK Ltd
Africa House
64-78 Kingsway
London
WC2B 6AH

Simon & Schuster Australia
Sydney

A CIP catalogue for this book is available
from the British Library.

ISBN 0-671-03720-X

1 3 5 7 9 10 8 6 4 2

Typeset in Melior by SX Composing DTP, Rayleigh, Essex

Printed and bound in Great Britain by Caledonian International
Book Manufacturing, Glasgow.

For Joy Centino

'In public we were cocksure, in private superstitious, and everywhere void and empty.'

St Augustine, *Confessions*

Part One

Chapter One

'You will recall,' said Gala, 'that you are to meet with a client at eight o'clock.' But at that moment the gross, impertinent antipodean who I had called out the previous evening chose to lunge at me, and all business, save that of despatching my opponent with the utmost effect, was banished from my thoughts. *'Sus,'* continued Gala as the arc of the Tasmanian devil's *itak* came near to shaving off a portion of my nose, 'you really must bring this present affair to conclusion. We're not so flush that you can afford to pass up on a *client.'* Gala had only underscored, of course, what was already uppermost in my mind: that I needed to wound, otherwise incapacitate or kill my man *now.* My new client – my first in many months – promised to provide much needed revenue. I could not afford to keep him waiting.

I brought my own *itak* down against my opponent's weapon, driving his arm towards the sand. The world knows me for a swordsman of surpassing excellence. But the weapon I had been constrained to use that day continued to refuse the sophisticated swordplay I demanded of it (the *itak* is but an excuse for a sword; indeed, it is little more than a machete), and I found myself forced to fall back on certain dirty-fighting skills that, if neither excellent, surpassing, nor even skills I liked to readily own up to, had nevertheless kept me alive whenever my own beloved blade, *Espiritu Santo*, was beyond reach.

With my *itak* deployed in keeping the Tasmanian's pointed towards the ground, I stepped forward and kicked my opponent in the solar plexus. It was a nonchalant, indeed, rather dignified kick. Not one imbued with the kind of grace that, I like to believe, characterizes my essential nature, whether I be wearing the mask of an artist, scholar, lover, or (most particularly) an ex-captain of the armies of the Darkling Isle. But it had the desired effect.

With a grunt the uneducated savage who had besmirched the reputation of the woman I admired above all women, both inhuman and human, retreated to the nearby shoreline, surf lapping about his thonged feet. I laughed.

The rush of self-congratulation I felt was short-lived. It was dawn, the sun was low in the sky, and my opponent's back had been turned towards its bright disc. As the Tasmanian doubled over with delayed shock, my eyes were assaulted by a barrage of furious early-morning light. Stopped in my tracks, I let my arms fall to my side and stood stock-still, dazed, defenceless. Pain filled my head, and then found its way to my stomach. My hangover, which had dogged me during our boat ride to Snake Island, became disproportionate, truly monstrous.

'Ritchie, put up your guard!' cried Gala. I spat. What remained of last night's complement of liquor had filled my mouth and demanded instant disemboguement. Silhouetted against the sun, my opponent grew dim. The duel which I had called for but six hours previously no longer seemed, on this too-bright morning, such a good idea.

'Ritchie!'

The sun's evil eye was inescapable. Its light was everywhere, glittering on the sea and burning away the mist that scudded over the Zambales mountains across the bay. The inadequate filter of the clouds was suffused with rashes of cruel brilliance.

'*Ritchie*!'

The Tasmanian had recovered and was again advancing. His face was flushed from exertion and nightly binges at my favourite bar; the bar he had once-too-often blighted with his presence. For a fat man, he was disconcertingly agile. I lifted an empty hand in a gesture of parley, keeping my right hand and the *itak* close to my side.

'Wait,' I said. 'I am discomposed. I am unfairly disadvantaged. This is not gentlemanly, surely. First, you choose to fight with weapons only louts and oafs are familiar with, and then you have me up at an hour only schoolchildren, milkmaids and insomnious maiden aunts can tolerate. Is this fair?'

'Popinjay!' he said, with a taunting sweep of his blade.

I shrugged. 'The dawn,' I said. 'It is absurdly dramatic. I refuse to walk the boards of a stage that is illuminated by such vulgar, demotic light. Look! That sun-inebriated cloud: it is enough to have Turner leaping from his grave to say "I was wrong, the sun is not God, he is the very *devil*!"' My rhetoric was unpersuasive. The only real devil I faced that morning was the Tasmanian.

'Charlatan! Impostor! We all know the measure of *you*, my man. Now listen: you chose to call me out, and now you're going to have to count the cost of your idiocy.' The unsympathetic brute's coarse, antipodean vowels exacerbated my already considerable discomfort. But my obvious state of helplessness had, at least, checked his homicidal momentum. He stood as I stood now, his hands at his sides. 'And don't talk to me about *gentlemanly*,' he continued, glancing at Gala, 'we agreed upon a *recontre*. There should be no seconds.'

'She is the object of this quarrel,' I said, passing a hand across my throbbing brow. 'She has a right to be here.' The truth was I had been unsuccessful in dissuading her. Not that I had pitched my arguments with any great conviction. I fight honourably, but I believe in having insurance, and Gala – I had discovered over the years – would do her best to indemnify any hurt I might sustain by swiftly revenging me. She was no mean fighter herself.

The Tasmanian smiled. It was a fat man's smile, the smile of a colossal baby, a smile both ludicrous and sinister. The smile broadened as he allowed himself the luxury of gloating over my imminent demise. 'Do you still feel I insulted her? I merely gave you a friendly warning. Girls like her,' he nodded towards Gala, 'are trouble.'

'You called her a *malignos*.'

'I called her a *malignos whore*.' I raised an eyebrow.

'Well, it's true she's a whore,' I said, unable to gainsay his assertion without seeming the blindest of fools, 'but *malignos*? That shows a lack of civility.'

'But she *is* a *malignos*!'

Malignos

Gala pulled back the cowl of her silk cloak. She shook out her hair. A thick mane cascaded down her back, each lock, curl and ringlet having the appearance of a shaving found on the floor of a silversmith. The mass of hair caught the rays of the sun, as did the silvery bone of the two elliptical horns that protruded from the white thatch of her pate; the mica-encrusted fingernails; the scales that covered her face, neck and half-exposed shoulder. How palely she shone. With what fire. The fire of hell, and the fire of heaven.

'I've been called many things,' said Gala. 'In the Darkling Isle the term *teratoid* is, I believe, still in vogue. An improvement, I suppose, upon *goblin* or *orc*. I feel, however, that we are not so much here because you called me a *malignos* – it's good Tagalog, and besides, Ritchie and I use the expression all the time – but that we can no longer tolerate seeing your ugly face at my place of work.'

'A place,' I said, 'which also happens to be my watering-hole of choice.'

Her hand vanished into the folds of her cloak; reappeared. I saw, then, that she clutched the hilt of that length of Toledo steel for which I held an esteem that – barring she for whose honour I fought – had no parallel. It was my rapier, *Espiritu Santo*. 'Ritchie, I think you'll be needing this.' She tossed the sword towards me. It wheeled through the air, lazily it seemed, as if to say Relax, take it easy, don't worry. I knew then that all would be well, that all manner of things would be well.

'But I have choice of weapons!' said the Tasmanian. On sighting my rapier – that blade Gala had had baptised in my stead in the hope that my own baptism

7

might follow – I felt my hangover-induced clumsiness disappear. I dropped the *itak* and caught the sword by its spinning hilt. 'I have choice of weapons!' he repeated. 'It is the custom! You challenged *me*!' He would, of course, have heard of my reputation amongst the habitués of the barrio's *salle d'armes*. Why else had he chosen to fight with the *itak*, a weapon that, in my classically trained hand, would be a handicap to my technique as much as an affront to my dignity?

'The *itak*,' I said, kicking that crude implement contemptuously aside as I swung my own blade in a circle above my head, 'the *itak* is so vulgar.' I brought *Espiritu Santo* down to the level of my waist. Made a few passes at the vacant air. 'It belongs,' I continued, 'in the hands of peasants and *banditos*. Not a creature such as myself. Custom, you say? You are right to remind me of custom. But when custom defies elegance, custom must go.' The light teeming across the sea seemed muted now. Concomitantly, the pain behind my eyes no longer had the power to distract, the feel of that finely balanced rapier – heirloom that had been in my family for six generations, but had been nameless until I had come to the Pilipinas – concentrating my attention on the task before me. 'Yes, yes, custom must go, and so, gross antipodean, must *you*.' I went into a crouch and, daintily, but with supreme confidence, began to edge towards him. As before, he retreated to the shoreline, though this time propelled by no toe punt, but by an apprehension that had transformed his gloating face into a twitching mass of blubber. 'Ah yesssss,' I whispered, indulging myself in a little melodramatic sibilance, 'you see this blue steel? You see its holy fire? Let me introduce you to *Espiritu Santo*.'

I was about to go into a running attack, or *flèche*, when the Tasmanian looked down at his feet and cried out.

A pair of hands had emerged from the wet sand and grasped him by the ankles.

I looked over my shoulder. 'Gala!'

Her mouth was frozen in a rictus. Unable to speak, she seemed equally unable to move.

I turned my attention back to the Tasmanian. He was hacking at that pair of disembodied hands with his *itak* and, though he had managed to sever several anonymous fingers, he had, in the process, inflicted deep wounds upon his own flesh. 'Help me!' he cried, looking up. 'Please, as one human to another—' And then, as his eyes glazed with panic, he stared down once again at the two bloody, alien appendages, that, despite by now being almost completely diced, still clung to him tenaciously. He put a hand to his heart; gasped; then let go of the *itak*. The beach had cratered about where he stood. And into that soft, yielding circumference he sank, pulled partway down until the oozy sand was level with the tops of his thighs. His gaze fell upon Gala. 'I don't deserve this! I don't deserve to be taken by your filthy cousins! Oh damn you, help me! Don't let me die at the hands of *malignos*!' And then with a soft sound of ingestion that melded with the soughing of the waves, the rest of him disappeared, the sand closing in over his head. Gala crossed herself.

'There must be a tunnel under there,' I said, pointing to where my fellow duellist had been swallowed up. It had been an effort to keep my voice level.

'There, here, everywhere,' said Gala, her eyes darting about the panorama of the beach. 'Many tunnels, probably. Humans don't come here often. It would be a good place for my people to live. Near enough to the barrio to steal food, but isolated enough to provide safety.' It was true: Snake Island's notoriety as a venue for the settling of quarrels did not make it a popular destination. And where there were no humans, you might expect to sometimes encounter *malignos*. The peace treaty prohibited the arrogation of arable land and forbade encroachments on centres of human population. Wastelands and deserts, these days, were the only places Netherworlders dared surface when they tunnelled upward into the light and air. 'We should leave, Ritchie.' Gala turned away and walked towards the jetty.

I hesitated, looking around me, wondering where other *malignos* lurked. Behind the rocks, perhaps, or in the thick vegetation that sprang from the cliff-face, or, more worryingly, directly beneath my feet. I scrambled after Gala, stooping to pick up my jacket as I proceeded, all the time casting glances about the beach, *Espiritu Santo* held at the ready.

'I could have taken him,' I said to Gala. 'I hope you realize that. If it hadn't been for—' But I checked myself. *For one of your friends*, I was about to say. But Gala, who had betrayed her people, no longer had any friends. Not in the Netherworld, at least. 'I could have taken him,' I repeated, lamely. As I trotted along, I brushed the sand from my clothes. Of late, I had been unhappy at the state of my wardrobe. With only rags left to me I would soon have to get my old army uniform out of mothballs, loathe as I was to have its glory soiled by everyday wear and tear.

Our *banca* was anchored where we had left it. The elderly sailor, his skin as dark and wrinkled as a burnt walnut, held out a hand and helped Gala into the little boat. I followed, clambering along the bamboo outrigger with such haste that I nearly slipped into the sea. The old man brought up the anchor, cast off, unfurled the sail, and then settled himself by the tiller. The sea was choppy, but we had a good wind – a typhoon, it was said, was closing on the archipelago from the Sea of Cathay – and the *banca* clipped towards the mainland at a rate that soon left Snake Island far behind.

Despite the morning's heat, Gala shivered. 'Do you think they might have been coming for me, Ritchie? Do you think they just got that antipodean by mistake?'

Quickly, I shook my head. 'No; of course not.' But I was unsure. I looked back at the island. 'Three years after the armistice, and it seems we still have cause to fear them. Ah, this is how it all began, hundreds of years ago: terrorist incursions, guerrilla raids, *camisados*.'

'Followed by demands that *malignos* be given their share of the Earth's surface,' said Gala. 'Was that so unreasonable?'

'Unreasonable or not,' I said, 'it's difficult to negotiate with creatures that seem determined to fulfil your every nightmare. What will stop them?'

'Nothing will, Ritchie. They still dream of living like we do. Beneath the sun and the sky.' The sea spray had covered us with a patina of brine. Gala pulled the cowl back over her head. 'If my kind did not feel such a longing for the open air, then this *malignos* would

11

never have been driven to turn her back on her own people and fight on the side of humanity. Then where would you be, little boy?'

'Where would *you* be,' I countered, looking back at the little island we had recently left, now framed by a mountainous headland. Gala had been given little choice: Obey the Darkling Isle's directives, or else be returned to the depths.

'And yet,' said Gala, 'there are times when I can't help feeling that my freedom to walk beneath the sky is a curse. Humans hate me, even though I helped them win the war. I can't go back, but neither can I expect to be accepted here. I'm exiled from both worlds.' I put my arm about her shoulder.

'When we have some money—'

'Oh Ritchie, how many times have I heard that before?' She leant her head back against me, fingers slipping under my shirt and across my chest. I winced as she petulantly plucked a hair from its follicle. From a brassy young woman who knew too much of the world she had become suddenly childlike. Quietly, she began to cry. 'Don't leave me, Ritchie,' she said. 'Promise you won't leave me.'

'Of course I promise.' I looked into her face; touched the ferronnière suspended about the forehead, its silver crucifix matching the metallic texture of her skin. She reminded me, when she wore that particular item of jewellery, of an illumination I had seen, a copy of that celebrated lost masterpiece of the Ancients, Leonardo's *La Belle Ferronnière*. Certainly, she was as beautiful as that belle, if twice as strange.

I passed my hand under the cowl, massaging that area

of the scalp between the smooth, polished bone of her horns. I retracted, slipped the same hand under the folds of her cloak and stroked her long, white mane, its damp locks and strands plastered to the tiny plates that scaled her body. I caressed her knotty spine; felt her great, folded wings – bat's wings that had the aspect of steel beaten so thin it had become limpid – and, lower down, felt, too, the root of her tail, the arrowhead of which poked from under the cloak's hem and swished negligently against the boat's slim hull.

'When we have some money we'll get away from this place,' I said. 'You won't have to work in a bar any longer. You can open that little *carinderia* you always talk about.'

'Ah, people will always make trouble for us.'

'Then we'll make trouble for *them*,' I said, smiling at her. 'So much trouble that we'll be given some space of our own, our own island, yes, our own country,'

'Our own world,' she said, with a child's seriousness. 'Yes, Ritchie, that would be nice.'

We were in shallower water now. To either side of us protruded the masts, jib-booms and other identifying markers of half-sunken wrecks: junks, sampans, schooners and barquentines – all victims of a centuries-long conflict that had almost wiped humanity from the face of the Earth. I looked ahead. A ruined church – its steeple half blasted away – jutted above the low skyline of Barrio Barretto, the shacks and hovels lining the shore standing out in relief against the whitewashed tenements of the town proper. We would soon be home.

Quite suddenly, Gala's presence had begun to make me feel uncomfortable. The feel of her cool skin beneath the black silk mantle became unsettling. And then it became vile. The flesh seemed to fibrillate beneath my hand, as if hordes of insects were engaged in furious copulation beneath the chain mail of the epidermis. She was 'the woman I admired above all women, both inhuman and human.' Empty words, I thought, which neither came from the heart, nor had any hope of finding one. What was wrong with me? But it was redundant to ask myself such a question. I knew too well what was wrong. The malaise was one I had contracted in the Darkling Isle. The prognosis? The prognosis was that I would, in time, find it impossible to touch another, or to be moved by their want. All I would be left with would be the ability to *curse*.

I broke free of her embrace. Hurt, she looked up at me. At such times as this, in the fever of affectlessness that, like malaria, attacks but in fits, I knew that I was a creature unsuited to company, that humanity and I would be better served by a tacit agreement that each should exclude the other. The war, doubtless, was much to blame. It was almost as if, in delving deep, and then deeper into the Earth to engage with the enemy, we had overreached ourselves and come upon, amongst the remains of those weird, buried artefacts of the ancient world, some terrible and still operative machine designed for the destruction of 'the intimate' and, inadvertently, had turned it on.

The *banca* was nearing the shore. Let silence reign. Let vacancy triumph. Let me end my days staring at the blankest of walls. At all costs, I thought, keep that skyline with its hordes of chattering men, women and children away! But soon a boy was running across the sand to assist us in our disembarkation. Life had me in its maw again.

I pulled my half-hunter from my waistcoat pocket. I hoped my new client was not a stickler for punctiliousness.

It was nearly eight o'clock.

Chapter Two

The balcony of my apartment overlooked a road that ran the length of Baloy Beach. The balcony did not exactly provide a 'sea view' – a series of obstructions, such as tin roofs and a profuse, almost manic outgrowth of coconut trees that were entwined amongst the road's tall, wrought-iron oil lamps, obscured all but a sliver of the bay – but, as long as it was not raining (and that day, the rain had held off, though the skies were darkening by the hour), it was the place where I always conducted interviews with those who sought my services. Not because I expected them to be impressed with the ambience, but because the interior of my apartment was so threadbare as to suggest that here lived a PI for whom the P stood less of *Private* than *Privation*.

I handed the boy a drink and sank back into my chair, slapping at my neck as I felt the tingle of a mosquito. (I had had a bad case of dengue only six months ago and had since developed something of a neurotic obsession with the antics of the dengue-carrying *Aedes egypti*, that fickle mosquito which will only bite during the early hours of the day.) 'Tell me about yourself,' I said. 'Tell me about your problem. And tell me what you want me to do.'

But as the boy talked I found my attention drifting. I let my gaze travel across the rooftops. From the poverty of my vantage point, I spotted, in a corner of that sliver of blue which was all one could see of Subic Bay, the tiny mound that was Snake Island. To the other side of the bay rose Cubi Point, where, they said, a man, if he could dig deep enough, could make himself rich on the remains of the spaceport that had stood there thousands of years ago.

My lack of concentration mattered little, I knew. I had heard the boy's story from a dozen other clients, some of whom I had been able to help, some of whom I hadn't. His mouth opened and closed, the words buzzing about me like a swarm of insects. That drowsy music carried me to the borders of dreamland.

I was a child again. I lived in a place called Greenwich. Above the town, there was a hill I would climb, surrounded by parkland and river. From its top I could see all of London, and beyond its walled periphery, the hills. Out there, they said, were wastelands populated by shades and goblins. My father, finding me one night crying in my bed, took me in his arms. 'Goblins aren't going to hurt you,' he said. 'They live underground, far, far away. Once, we traded with them. They provided us with those fragments of the ancient world upon which our science is based. Without their help, our country's renaissance would have been still-born.' And he told me that the war was a tragedy. But I shouldn't cry, because goblins would never invade London. They terrorized us sometimes, yes. They crept from the sewers at night and thieved and murdered. But the army had the threat under control. Goblins would never emerge from the Netherworld in sufficient numbers to make our lives intolerable. And he kissed me goodnight. For a moment, I had been comforted. My father held a junior position at the Naval College. He was a *maître d'armes*. One of the best duelling masters in London. And he was, I felt, sure to know about such things. But I would still see, in the shadows that swarmed about my bed, the faces of goblins smirking malevolently at me. Still imagine that, at any minute, a pair of scaly hands would reach under my bedclothes and grab me by the legs. Those shadows were a presentiment of the intensification of the war, the invasion that, despite my father's reassurances, shortly followed.

A shouted exchange between the owner of the *sari-sari* store downstairs and a drunken customer snapped me out of my daydream. After-images of smirking goblin-faces haunted my eyes.

I sighed. I was no longer able to defer making a mental précis of the boy's case. Dredging up the details my mind had managed to register while the thrust of my thoughts had been elsewhere, I came up with this:

Fourteen years old, he too was from the Darkling Isle. At ten he had been orphaned and become the responsibility of the state, the army soon after pressing him into service as a tunnel rat. Whey-faced, malnourished and a little crookbacked, he was small for his age. At the age of ten he would have been capable of wriggling his way through passages which regular troops, such as myself, had had no hope of negotiating.

He had been lucky to survive. I knew few who had. His name was John Defoe. And the little *malignos* who had rescued him when he had become lost underground, stranded in the dark tunnels and caverns beneath London, was now in the easternmost part of the

Netherworld. Or so he had come to believe after acquiring information from teratoid traitors who, like Gala (and indeed, his own goblin girl), had purchased the right to live on the surface of the Earth by selling out their own people.

Defoe's story shared more than a few elements with my own. I had, like the boy, once lain wounded in the Netherworld. And, like the boy, I had been rescued by a *malignos* recruited by the Darkling Isle who, after tending to my wounds, had dragged me to the surface. It was Gala, of course, who had been that *malignos*; she who had saved my life.

The boy's story had struck a chord.

But even if it had not, my impecuniousness would, of course, have compelled me to accept his fee, whatever the hazards.

'When I was underground . . .' He put his head in his hands, unable for the moment to continue. I had, it seemed, brought my concentration to bear upon the boy's words at the very moment he had been lost for them.

'A *malignos*, in such times as these in which we live,' I said, in an effort to loosen his tongue, 'is often the only prospect we have of intimacy. Of being touched. It is ironic, is it not, that so many ex-soldiers should discover, in their former enemies, a panacea for their ills?'

Like other damaged humans who had knocked on my door he was of the world but not in it. He existed in a windswept limbo, blown hither and thither and unable to connect with that parallel universe of laughter and tears that lay just beyond his reach. His hopes, now, lay in turning from the human altogether and embracing the alien.

'I suppose,' said the boy, 'that my quest must seem, to most people, a somewhat odd one. An immoral one, perhaps. When I heard about your own exogamy—'

'My *exogamy*?'

'Your liaison with a teratoid.'

'I'm not married,' I said, wondering at his boldness, but indifferent to what he thought of me. 'Gala Diaz Garcita is my mistress.' The boy nodded, seemingly a little embarrassed, even though he had already outlined his own circumstances. 'Though some day . . .' But what, I thought, am I doing explaining myself to this pup? Why on earth should I be making excuses?

'Marriage to a *malignos*, of course, carries certain legal penalties. Even out here, you would still, I believe, lose your human status?' I nodded. 'Yes, yes. It is not a thing to be taken lightly. You and me, Dr Pike: we are fellow travellers. It is on that basis that I decided that you were the man best suited to lend me assistance.'

'I've taken up cases like yours before,' I said. 'I'm glad to have won your confidence. But tell me, where did you learn of my abilities, here or—'

'Back home,' interrupted the boy, 'in the Darkling Isle.'

'Home?' I waved my hand to encompass the scene beneath the balcony. Gigs rattled along the dirt road; pedlars of fish and seaweed, their eyes momentarily brightening as they misinterpreted my gesture as one portending a sale, gritted their teeth and passed by; and raggedy urchins, sighting the unwashed Europan leaning over the stone balustrade, his lips compressed with pernickety distaste, giggled. 'This is home now,' I said. 'But am I still spoken of in London?'

'Indeed, your exploits are spoken of all the time. You are known as a great goblin killer. Of course, you are also known as—'

'Go on,' I said. *A great goblin fucker*, he might have concluded, if he'd had the courage. Yes; I knew what people said back 'home' when they spoke of Richard Pike, the noted miscegenist. But the boy refrained:

'Suffice to say, you are notorious. Yet you still have friends.'

'And enemies too, doubtless.' The boy knotted his brow and shifted in his seat. 'Have you been to the Pilipinas before?' I continued, eager to get back to the business at hand.

'No,' he said. 'I've never been outside Europa.'

'Then you have done the right thing in calling on me before you proceed to do anything else. The archipelago is a dangerous place.' The boy sipped at his drink, his eyelids bruised with sleeplessness. It had grown hot. Sluggishly, the boy stared up at me, a glint from the ice-blue depths of his regard seeming to echo something in my own soul, something bright, infinitely self-serving and quite, quite dead.

'Dr Pike, I can well believe it is a dangerous place.'

I walked through the barrio. Lamps cast their lurid light over shop-houses and cheap hotels, leaving the whiff of whale oil in the air. Shirtless young men gathered about *carinderias* and *sari-saris* drinking *tapuy*. And the passing gigs sprayed me with muddy water whenever they rumbled over a pothole. The palms swayed in the gathering wind and a rain, heavier than the one that had fallen that afternoon, beat upon the corrugated iron of the rooftops, filling my ears with susurrant clamour.

There were a handful of pretty women on the streets that evening. Human women. Women of quality. And for a time, I found myself following this one or that, forgetting the downpour in contemplation of a trim waist or well-turned fundament. The sheath dresses common to the archipelago accentuated those aspects of female anatomy wonderfully. But I think the women, as is often the case, must have felt my eyes upon them, for sometimes an amber-skinned, sloe-eyed visage would peek from beneath a painted parasol to look backward with agitation, or disdain. Then I entered a part of the barrio when such women would never be so audacious as to set foot.

I pulled my cloak about me, holding the cowl in place with my hand. 'Pssst!' called a voice from a doorway. 'Why so much make-up, *Inglés*? You are not in the Darkling Isle now. Come, *amigo*, show some respect.' I didn't usually respond to these unimaginative insults. I was well-known about town, and suffered the scurrility of the locals with that measure of good humour and detachment that is expected of a foreigner. But the continuous anxiety I felt, of late, over the emptiness of my purse, had frayed my nerves and primed my temper. It was only after I had swept back my cloak and reached for my sword that I had remembered I was unarmed; that here, in the barrio, there was an ordinance that forbade the bearing of edged weapons in public; an ordinance that it would be foolish to contravene. The iron fist of the law came down more heavily on foreigners than locals.

Cursing, and wishing that *Espiritu Santo* was buckled

to my side and not languishing in my apartment, I walked on, with the muted laughter of my tormentor in my ears.

When I had turned a corner, and was sure I could not be observed, I walked up to a shop-house window. The shop was unmarked, but lay between *Regina's Lovely Place* and *Edward's Hair Wax Boutique*. From what I could establish from the wares displayed behind its murky panes, it seemed to belong to a ship-chandler. I pulled back my cowl and examined my reflection.

My mascara was tasteful, I thought (it had been expensive), and my eyeshadow neither excessive nor otherwise contrary to the standards of my, or indeed any other of my countrymen's toilette. These locals: they did not understand that, for a gentleman and officer of the Darkling Isle, appearance is of much importance as martial accomplishment. Unwilling to pass by a reflective surface without giving other aspects of my appearance a cursory inspection, I studied myself more closely. A few grey hairs, a somewhat lean but by no means unattractive face – not bad, I thought, for a man of middling years. I turned away as my gaze fell upon my attire. The raggedy suit I had been condemned to wear was beneath contempt. I refused to award it notice.

I walked on. Five years I had lived in this town – five years of poking about in other people's sordid lives – and more often than not with little more than a pocketful of pesos to my name. The cases I investigated brought in enough to pay the rent, but if it had not been for the money Gala made from taking various lowlifes into our bed, I would have starved long ago.

I stopped outside the bar where Gala worked and where I did my drinking: *Nightriders*. I entered, passing through a haze of dragonflies that flitted about the porch. Inside was a vestibule, its black walls and ceiling illuminated by a single taper.

'Good evening, Dr Pike,' said the guard in the wheelchair. A long dagger lay across his polio-wasted thighs.

'Good evening, Bong,' I said, raising my voice so that I might be heard above the music emanating from beyond the connecting door.

'No loud man to annoy you tonight I think, Dr Pike?'

'I think not, Bong,' I said, treating him to a thin, ironic smile. 'Such a pity. I do so enjoy stentorian company. But tonight, I am fated to suffer only loud music, it seems.'

'Ah, I think you throw the Tasmanian a good *despedida*. Yes? Ha, ha, I think that crazy, fat sea gypsy *deserve* it.' I nodded. The Tasmanian's going-away party on Snake Island had gone well. He had indeed got what was coming to him. Bong returned my smile, his lips curling themselves into an obsequious imitation of my own. 'First time I meet you I think you are a stuck-up man, Dr Pike. Very stuck-up. I think, maybe, that you are a *faggot*. But you have a way about you, I think. A way I like. That Tasmanian. It was he who was the queer. He who was the Benny boy, I think. Not you.'

'You're too kind, Bong,' I said. 'Thank you for having faith in my machismo.'

He reached up and opened the door and I proceeded into the bar's interior, a narrow, low-ceilinged expanse decorated with great swathes of primary colours. The candelabras that stood on each table sent shadows dancing across the walls.

The four-piece band – harpsichord, guitar, drums and gamelan – was knocking out a *kundiman* with some degree of abandon. The tune had an Iberian flavour, and a girl, somewhat drunk, I suspected, spun about the area immediately before the little stage. A thigh flashed from the hip-high slit in her skirt, and her hands wove sinuous patterns as she worked her castanets. My left eardrum, perforated during the war, made its usual complaint, its pain receptors fired up by the gamelan's chimes and peals, so like tinnitus; the castanets' staccato, so like stiletto-heeled shoes on marble tiles.

The shadows danced; the girl danced. But they were not alone. Down the centre of the bar, on a long catwalk, three forms strutted and jiggled, their nakedness partly obscured by a gauzy curtain of smoke. Though the blue-grey haze blurred the differences between human and inhuman, one of those forms was certainly a *malignos*. As I made my way amongst the half-empty tables I could swear that the creature smiled at me. I looked up. Her flesh was configured in a manner that, as well as setting her apart from humanity, also set her apart from Gala. *Malignos*, of course, have racial characteristics far more marked, more various, than humans. The flirta-tious creature who shimmied before me had Gala's horns, but she was as green as a lizard, possessed stunted, non-functional wings, and had an extra set of eyes where her nipples should have been. I gave a desultory salute and passed her by. I had other matters to attend to.

I hissed and caught the attention of a waitress. She

was human and had only one set of eyes, but they were eyes that distinguished her from humanity as effectively as those of the *malignos* that danced nearby. The bleak, incurious way in which they surveyed me immediately identified her as one who had been simplified. How, I wondered, had she obtained permission to enter within the confines of the barrio? The simplified were cheap labour. Perhaps the bar's owner had thrown some pesos in the way of the *barangay*, or otherwise pulled strings.

'Is Gala out back?' I asked. Her face grew pained, as if the electrical activity I had demanded of her brain was too much for her to bear. Then, summoning all her strength, she gave a curt affirmation and resumed her work, placing a jug of beer on a table where a group of local men sang along with the band, unconscious of anything but the music, and, not too far off on the horizon of their inebriated perception, the joyful possibility of violence. I had had enough fighting for one day. I gave them a wide berth and walked through an open doorway leading on to a patio overlooking the beach.

To one side of the patio stood a cage which housed two forlorn monkeys. A small girl teased them, jabbing at their ulcerated hides with a pointed stick. The child looked up as I approached and then pursed her lips towards a party of bar girls who congregated about a table at the patio's farther end, smoking and playing cards. Amongst their number I spotted Gala.

I hallooed, catching her attention. She put out her pipe and strolled towards me. 'Let's go down to the sea,' I said. Gala at once understood the need for private

26

conference and followed me across the sand until we stood near the edge of the surf. There, we sheltered under one of several beach umbrellas that, despite the incoming typhoon, the staff had failed to stow away. The gaily-painted canopy shuddered with each gust of wind, its upright bamboo moaning and creaking.

Gala drew her peignoir tightly about her body. Though the night was hot, each drop of rain pricked the skin with the severity of a miniature piece of hail. Looking up at the dark sky, avoiding those eyes that were darker, more mysterious, than any stormy, cloud-covered firmament, I briefed her on the nature of our new assignment.

'Familiar story,' I concluded. 'Soldier enters into a liaison with a *malignos*, loses her, seeks her again. The boy seemed to think she's in this part of the world, though, by all accounts, she originally lived beneath Europa. She's a traitor, like you. But unlike you, she couldn't take the pressures of living with a human. Anyway, seems she left him and travelled East. And now he wants us to help him track her down. Curious thing is, he says she's in the Netherworld.'

'In the Netherworld?' said Gala, with some surprise. 'Why should she have gone back to the Netherworld? If she's a traitor, she risks losing her life.'

'Perhaps the Netherworld is not so eager to wreak revenge as you sometimes make out, my sweet.'

'No, Ritchie. The Netherworld does not forgive. I can only suppose that, coming from Europa, she does not expect to be recognized out here.'

'The boy said as much.'

'All the same—'

'So we take the assignment?'

'We've certainly done similar things before,' she said. 'But I'm never happy going underground. You know that.'

'The boy insists,' I said. 'And he's already given me a retainer. Enough pesos for us to live in the style we richly deserve.' I shrugged, conceding the hyperbole. 'Well, enough at least for us to be able to eat out for a couple of weeks.'

'Enough pesos for you to spend on books, on canvases, on clothes or on that stuff you plaster your face with.' I looked away, a little put out, my attention given to the bar girls on the patio, and in particular a young human called Esperanza who had the plumpest lips you could possibly imagine. Lips that were always set in a becoming pout.

'Our client,' I said, distractedly, 'won't be happy if we try to fob him off with anything less than a *full-blooded* investigation. If the trail goes underground – and according to the boy's information, it does – then so must we.' Gala turned about and stared at the rows of *banca* anchored in the shallows. The sea was more turbulent than this morning, and though the band, at this distance, no longer had the power to inflict the kind of aural discomfort it had made me suffer inside the bar, the crashing of the waves made it necessary for me to again raise my voice. 'Remember our plans? The little restaurant, a home, a *real* home we can call our own, and—' I checked my tongue. My knowledge of what constituted domestic bliss was severely limited, and I did not know if, in attempting to seduce her in this manner, I might simply sound like a crooked horse dealer checking off a list of tarted-up old nags.

'I've always stood by you, Ritchie. And what have I got? Nothing. I just get kicked in the teeth. All your life you've set yourself up on a pedestal for your own admiration. I'm sick of it. Sick of your vain, selfish concerns, your dilettantism and your, your' – she turned; caught me looking at the girl on the patio – 'your philandering!' I laughed and put my hands up, as if to ward off a blow I knew would never come. The laugh stuck in my throat like a chicken bone. I did not care for Gala when she was in this mood. She frightened me. 'And just look at this suit!' she said, reaching out and taking the lapel between her long fingers. 'How many men did I have to sleep with to buy this? It's barely two months old and already you're saying you need another!' Gala, tonight, was less a revelation – we had had these little set-tos before – than a reminder of my inadequacy. And I could do without such memoranda. 'That Tasmanian was right. You're a charlatan! A popinjay!'

I removed her hand from my jacket and tried to compose myself. 'Gala, I know I haven't given you much—'

'*Walanghiya*! You haven't given me *anything*.' Her eyes had grown misty. Damnation, I thought, let me be spared this. Let me be spared a woman's tears.

'If we just do this one job, then I promise you—' But now the tears were in full flood. Her head was bowed and she gulped at the air, her body shaking. Nervously, I looked about. But seeing we were unobserved I took Gala in my arms and held her, swaying back and forth as if I might be rocking a baby.

'Oh please, honeyko,' she said, as she choked and shuddered. 'Please look after me. You said we would get married.'

'Just this one more time,' I said. 'And then I'll make everything right. I *promise*.'

'You know what would happen to me if I was captured?' I knew. But there was little hope of navigating the Netherworld without Gala's help. Was my conscience perturbed, at times such as these, by the fact that I made money only because a young woman, as much an outsider to the world of her birth as her adopted world, was willing, for my sake, and my sake alone, to put her life in mortal danger? I was a sham. I was worse than a ponce. For I lived not just off immoral earnings, but off money tainted by the callous disregard in which I used Gala in my investigative work. She should have been better served. Better served by one such as myself, a man who clung to her because she was the only person in the world who had ever moved him, who had ever stirred him from his state of chronic affectlessness.

'No harm is going to come to you,' I said, wishing I could summon up a degree of shame. 'I won't let it.'

'Do you promise, Ritchie? Do you really promise?'

'I promise.' I held her more tightly.

'I sometimes wish we'd never left the Darkling Isle,' she said.

'But we had no choice,' I said. 'No human army will tolerate a soldier consorting with a *malignos*, even if she's gone over. Besides, it was you who suggested we come here.' Gala had been born in the archipelago, in the worm-eaten innards of the Zambales mountains. As a child she had joined her mother on an expedition to the surface world to look for food. The light and air had had a bewitching effect, and, while her mother looked the other way, she had wandered off, chasing sunbeams and butterflies. Lost, she wandered many days, and at last came to Barrio Barretto. Friendless, she had lived beneath the city walls. The church had discovered her, taken her into its fold; and she was given a new name, a new life. My own government, at that time, was looking for teratoid children whom they could turn and train to serve in their armies. And Gala – discovered in a Carmelite priory and kidnapped at gunpoint – was one of many such children transported to the Darkling Isle. There, she had been trained to infiltrate the depths beneath London and spy on her brothers and sisters. The Darkling Isle desperately needed intelligence of what transpired in the deepest parts of the Nether-world. Tunnel rats like John Defoe could never survive such descents. For such work, the army needed the talents of a *malignos*.

'It was you,' I continued, 'who thought we would have more of a chance of prospering here, in a country familiar to you from your childhood.' But I was being somewhat disingenuous. I had come to hate the English. Hate them as much as they had hated me. Even now, with a treaty between the Netherworld and Earth-Above, there was, in the Darkling Isle, still too much hostility towards *malignos* for Gala and I to be able to set foot in that country without incurring the general population's wrath. Five years ago, after I had been stripped of my commission, and while the war still raged, I had forced Gala's hand, eager to travel as far from the Darkling Isle's shores as possible. It was only

out here, in the East, amongst the outcasts and vaga-
bonds of the Pilipinas, that we were partially accepted,
and could live without fear of being stoned by street
urchins, or having our house set fire by a screaming
mob.

'You could have been discreet,' she said. Gala the
little girl went into hiding, and Gala, the tough,
streetwise survivor, became predominant. But still she
held on to me. 'You needn't have been cashiered if
you'd been more careful. But you just had to show off.
You had to tell everyone how unafraid you were. You
had to tell everyone that you slept with a *malignos*. You
always show off. You're so *selfish*.'

'Well, I'm *sorry*,' I said, like an automaton. I avoided
her eyes; looked up at the night sky. I felt as if I had lived
my life on one of those hard stars that peeped through
chinks in the clouds, so far away and surrounded by
such cold immensities. I receded into myself. Gala
continued to talk. As earlier, when I had interviewed
John Defoe, I saw her mouth open and close but heard
nothing but a distant buzz. My mind was elsewhere.
Like an astral body, it had travelled many miles. But in
an inward, rather than outward, journey.

I glided above the streets and towers of London,
winding through a dark cityscape decimated by three
centuries of war; a city, a country, that had borne the
brunt of the last, great invasion from the Earth's depths,
whose soul had been perverted and deadened by terror.
Sorry. The word echoed through the darkness of my
soul, echoed through the emptiness of my existence, as
if I were the Darkling Isle itself, ruined, bereft of any
emotion that might qualify me as human. It was as dark

as the depths which, over the centuries of turmoil, it had come to mirror, with only the reverberation of that one word to remind me that once here had been life: *sorry*.

Call it emotional blackmail, but no sooner had I told Gala that I would venture into the Netherworld alone, if need be, than she readily acceded to my demands. I have always enjoyed a flair for manipulating people. Indeed, in my work as a private investigator, it has often proved of paramount importance. I felt uneasy of course. I think even some of that rare commodity 'shame' percolated through the dead stuff that armoured my conscience. But I really did intend that, with the money we should make from this case, Gala and I should make a new start.

We lay in bed. Shadows raced across the walls and ceiling. The typhoon had arrived, and the rattle of roofs, the whiplash of wind-lashed trees, mixed with the commotion of the sea.

I was tired, but I could not sleep. The flotsam of my life's shipwreck surrounded me. A broken easel, upon which stood a half-finished study of Gala, a study that was a pathetic attempt to combine Turner's lighting effects with Leonardo's anatomic precision, testified to my failed ambitions as an artist. A row of mildewed books on a rickety shelf reminded me of what I might have been if, instead of enlisting, I had pursued my academic career as a professor of antiquity. My old uniform hung from a peg on the door, its epaulettes and brass buttons reflecting the ghastly light that streamed in from the bedroom window. What a reminder *that* was of failure, disgrace and exile.

My gaze fell upon Gala's dolls' house. The tiny lead figurines that Gala liked to collect, sculpted into semblances of human women from around the world, stood and lay in the cheap, cardboard habitation I had bought for her last Easter. How was it that such a hardened character as Gala could find comfort in those children's toys?

Gala was asleep, but dreamily, unconsciously still ran her hands through the hairs of my chest, sometimes idly plucking at them. Pinned to the wall opposite, and livid in the glare from outside, was a picture of the Virgin; beside it, a few miniatures of Gala, which I had sketched inside *Nightriders*. And on the night table beside me was the little king of heaven: a doll in velvet robes, carrying an orb and sceptre and wearing a tin crown: *El Niño Santo*. I turned my face to him, and, in my worthlessness, whispered *Agnus Dei, qui tollis peccata mundi, miserere nobis*. Despite not being able to believe in either your grace or your person, out of the depths into which I will soon plunge, I thought, O Lord, let my cry come unto thee.

Chapter Three

The next day our party hired horses and rode through the barrio until we came to the wall beyond which lay the wastelands of central Luzon. As we passed through the gates the boy, Defoe, gave a start of surprise.

'The simplified – you have them here too!' Camped along the length of the wall were men, women and children who all had the dull-eyed look of the waitress I had encountered the night before. Some lay insensate, bivouacked under scraps of canvas. Others, grinning, laughing, shrieking, scavenged for food amongst steaming refuse, or else clawed, thirst-crazed, at the oozy soil in the hope of discovering a cracked water pipe. Amidst the laughter, the shrieks, a general cry of *uh, uh, uh* preponderated and rose into the insect-filled air. These wretches represented those amongst the rural population who had been coerced into eating the noxious herb that, in the local dialect, is called *manggagawa*, and which in the Darkling Isle we familiarly name *Tom o'Bedlam* or *Zany's Delight*. The narcotic contained in that herb induces a persistent mental state that allows human beings to bear their poverty without rancour. And, more to the point, without causing civil unrest.

'In the Pilipinas, those simplified are called the *masa*,' I said. I regarded them with an equal measure of pity and contempt, but more than anything, with relief. On leave in London, I had been denied my sword.

(There was an ordinance in the Darkling Isle, just as there was in the barrio, that forbade the bearing of arms in public places.) And without my sword, certain kinds of urban scum who had *resisted* simplification had often made life uncomfortable for me.

I would not be denied a sword here. No; not now I had passed beyond the city limits. In London, going unarmed in the dark lanes and alleys by the Thames had turned me into a resourceful pugilist, if a somewhat unconventional one. But fighting with fist and foot was not my *métier*. I was a swordsman, not a common brawler.

I detached *Espiritu Santo* from where it hung beside my saddle and unwound the oiled rag that swaddled it. Then I sheathed my beloved blade in the scabbard that I had buckled on in preparation for this moment when we would again be together.

Defoe geed his horse so that it came level with my own, all the time surveying the *masa* with stoic distaste. It was an attitude typical of my countrymen, who employed beast-people as labourers, even, sometimes, as servants, but who, nevertheless, could not rid themselves of a deep-seated disgust for the beings they themselves had created; yet I saw, to my surprise, that the boy's eyes also glinted with fear. Few of the Darkling Isle actually feared the simplified.

Defoe noticed that I was watching him and, after clearing his throat, seemed to feel obliged to offer an explanation.

'After I lost my parents, the authorities tried to coerce *me* into undergoing simplification,' he said. 'Unless, that is, I chose to become a tunnel rat. They said they would—' He closed his eyes. 'There is a passage from the writings of the Ancients,' he continued, rather more quickly, as if eager to have all said and done. 'It perfectly describes the contempt in which I would have been held if I had consumed *Tom o'Bedlam*.' He took a deep breath and then began to recite. ' "*He possessed no power of thought, no depth of feeling, no troublesome sensibilities: nothing, in short, but a few commonplace instincts, which aided by the cheerful temper that grew inevitably out of his physical well-being, did duty very respectably, and to general acceptance, in lieu of a heart . . .*" ' He paused; studied me to see if I had understood. And again he spoke. 'After simplification, there is barely enough intellect left to prevent a man from walking on all fours. And that, Dr Pike, is why I shudder to look upon these human cattle. But for lady luck, there go I.'

'The Ancients,' I mused, 'they seemed to have understood the price of losing one's humanity. But we . . .'

We passed a roadside shrine. On a plinth, a statue of the Virgin stood, garlanded with pale *sampaguitas*. Gala crossed herself as we continued on our way.

'Are you Christians?' said Defoe, a note of embarrassment informing his query.

'*She* is,' I said, nodding towards Gala. We rode parallel to each other now, with me in the middle. 'Does that surprise you?'

'I suppose it shouldn't,' he said, directing his voice across my steed. 'You were born in these parts, were you not, *Señorita*? Christianity is in your blood. Besides, when the transcendental is lost, and in time of war, people turn to all manner of things for comfort, no matter how outlandish.'

'Outlandish?' said Gala.

'Christianity is a dead religion. It is forgotten,' said the boy.

'Not out here,' I said. 'Here, in the archipelago, it has never been forgotten.'

'But I would never have thought,' he said, still talking across me, 'that a woman from your background—' But I answered before Gala could reply.

'If she embraces old superstition, Defoe, it is because the new superstitions that have currency in our world, superstitions that inhibit and finally destroy our sense of empathy, will lead us all to destruction.' Gala frowned. She did not seem to like the equation of her faith with superstition. Neither, perhaps, did I. But I was too damaged by war to be able to lift my face to heaven and put all my hope in the love everlasting. The only thing I feared more than the mummery of my own existence was the possibility that God also was an ostentatious fake.

'Dr Pike,' she said, 'entertains the notion that there is an essential grace to his being, a grace that has to do with what he would call his gentlemanly virtues. That is what he believes in. That is *his* faith. But one day he will have his worthless life transformed by *true* grace. That day, I fear, is some way off. So far I have only succeeded in converting his sword.'

'My sword flourishes under its new dispensation,' I said with a dry laugh, 'though whether I would likewise thrive, of course, remains part of the divine mystery.'

'The only mystery,' said Gala, 'is whether you, my dear, have more of a soul than your rapier.'

The boy averted his gaze from Gala and looked straight ahead, as if trying to descry some end to the dusty road. 'It is difficult for any of us who come from the Darkling

Isle to know whether or not we have souls,' he said.

'Indeed,' said I. 'Our religion is nihilism. The only thing left to my countrymen after three centuries of war is the ability to *curse*. It is not a philosophy to live by.' But I still cursed those who had precipitated our exile. And cursed much else besides.

We rode on in silence. By the wayside, nipa huts sheltered those amongst the *masa* who, despite the invidious effects of *manggagawa* on their brains, had mastered the art of constructing crude, bamboo dwellings. We passed, then, into the uninhabited wastelands.

The muddy fields that surrounded us had once been rice paddies. And the ghostly remnants of the villages that we passed through had once sounded with the prattle of peasants and the lowing of carabao. But the incursions from the Netherworld had, over time, had the effect of depopulating the countryside. Those that could afford to had withdrawn within the walls of Barrio Barretto. Those that could not had been co-opted into what, by the closing stages of the war, had become a planet-wide system of cretinization of the poor and dispossessed. Only birds and *banditos* now populated this place, the birds occasionally landing to perch upon the exposed ribs of those of the *masa* who had wandered into the wastelands and died. The *banditos*, thankfully, were nowhere to be seen. I flexed my sword hand, apprehensive of a chance encounter.

An hour into our journey we were following the road as it serpentined up the Zambales mountains. The going was rocky, and our horses often stumbled, the ascent made more difficult by the blinding light of the overhead sun. Yesterday's storm had blown itself out. With no cloud cover, the sun was merciless. Soon, my brain began to reel. I pulled my sombrero down and hunched over my saddle in a futile effort to minimize the effects of the grilling. But the heat was relentless. It was with considerable relief when, after attaining a point where we had a clear view of Mt Pinatubo, Gala signalled for us to halt.

We all dismounted and withdrew to the shade of the vegetation that swarmed up the nearby escarpment. Immediately below lay the lahar field that had been created during Pinatubo's most recent bout of activity.

'It's safe to descend here?' asked Defoe. 'We won't be scalded?' I looked down, surveying the lahar, that grey porridge of ash and mud desolate but for sprigs of hardy greenery.

'There is a fumerole over there,' said Gala, pointing across the tangle of vegetation to where the lahar was pockmarked with vents. 'It's one that no longer emits gases. It will allow us to descend without threat of being poisoned or burnt.'

'Trust her,' I said to the boy. 'She lived here—'

'Beneath here,' Gala corrected.

'*Beneath* here, when she was a child.'

'The purpose of our expedition,' said Gala, anxious that Defoe understand that she was unprepared to take unnecessary risks, 'is to reconnoitre the area directly beneath us and then resurface so that we may draw up a plan of action.'

'I'm sure we'll run into some of Gala's contacts down there who'll give us leads on where to find your friend,' I said, as anxious as Gala was, but only to keep my client happy.

We tethered our horses beneath the shade of a tree and gave them some feed. Then, after we had all strapped on our backpacks, Gala led us down an obscure path that led us through the escarpment's undergrowth. It was a steep descent, and my feet slipped several times on wet grass. Despite the heat, the dense vegetation had prevented last night's rain from completely evaporating. The air was so humid I almost choked.

The trail wound through a small, deserted village. A few dogs snarled and snapped at our ankles as we passed. A little way past the village a carabao, startled from its grazing by the sudden appearance of humans where, these days, few humans roamed, jumped into the air – its massive bulk incongruously gymnastic. I kept my hand on the pommel of my rapier, anxious about what the next turn in the trail might reveal.

After descending perhaps half a kilometre, we emerged from beneath the jungle canopy to find ourselves at the edge of the lahar. Without hesitation, Gala proceeded onward, confidently walking across the moonscape until she came to a vent that lay within the shadow cast by Pinatubo.

After the boy and I had caught Gala up, we unburdened ourselves of our backpacks. Then we took from each pack ropes, lamps and other paraphernalia, laying out on the ground all that we would most immediately need, but no more. Once underground, we would be travelling light.

'Do you think I might actually find her *today*?' said Defoe. Using chocks, Gala and I secured three lengths of rope into the rocky ground at the fumarole's lip. About us, all was desert, a grey expanse dotted with lapilli. A slight breeze carried little clouds of dust across the plain where, once, giant pyroclastic flows had annihilated whole villages.

'I doubt it,' said Gala. 'Today, we're just going to find out how things might have changed down there. It's been nearly a year since Dr Pike and I ventured into the depths. But, as he has stated, I still have a few contacts below. If possible, I'll talk to them to see if we can glean any information. And then we must resurface. It's dangerous enough for humans down there, but for a *malignos*, such as myself, who has betrayed her own people, it is especially dangerous.' Gala sighed. 'I have not, and can never be forgiven.'

She took off her cloak and let it fall upon the ground. In the barrio, she seldom wore more than that cloak; and despite the cold, it had been the same in London. Like all *malignos*, she was happier when naked. Today, only her argent scales would separate her from the rocks; rocks with which she had been too long denied voluptuous communion. For despite her craving for sun and air, she could not, so near her former, childhood home, deny the dark, atavistic call of her blood, the generations before her for whom shadows and slime were the stuff of life.

Her tailed curled, its fluke-like tip snaking about her thigh. Her wings extended and beat at the air, the veined silver of their membranes scintillating in the sunlight. But the fumarole was too narrow for her to descend by way of flight. With a sound like rice paper scrunched within a fist, the wings folded themselves, cruciform, across her back, the pinions curling about her ankles.

She picked up a rope; dropped over the side; vanished. Tossing my sombrero onto the ground, I too grasped a rope and, with more caution but no less determinedly, followed.

My rope went taut. I kicked out as my feet met the rock wall. And then I began to abseil. Below, Gala had already reached the ledge which was our first objective. Soon, I had joined her, Defoe only seconds behind. The ledge was as it had been one year previously. There was even an old, rotted length of hemp beneath our feet, where we had discarded a rope from our previous expedition. Most importantly, the adit remained free of hindrance, allowing us access to the Netherworld.

I detached an oil lamp from my belt, lit it, and handed it to Gala. She gestured towards the dark opening in the rock face. And then, walking in a slight crouch, she merged with the shadows, the entrance enveloping her, so that only the flicker of the lamp could be descried.

'We're fortunate,' said Defoe, his eyes trained upon that naked flame, 'that there's no firedamp.'

'Don't worry about that,' I said. 'Gala and I know this tunnel.' But I wondered then, not only at the confidence but at the prescience of his statement. It was almost as if he had been here before. 'Come,' I continued. 'You'll see.' I took him by the arm and followed the tongue of flame as it wove through the darkness.

We had walked perhaps no more than fifty metres when, turning a sharp bend, we were confronted by a finely chiselled arch which opened on to a stairway. Graffiti had been scored into the soft stone of the arch's perpendicular sides, hieroglyphics that I recognized as constituting the written language of the *malignos*. Gala snuffed out the lamp and handed it back to me. I re-secured it to my belt. The lamp was superfluous here, for the stairway was illuminated by a faint blue light. It emanated from the bioluminescent fungi that the *malignos* habitually planted in the veins of rock that they had hewn.

The extreme gradient of the stairway meant that, as soon as we had put foot upon its timeworn steps, both myself and the boy tottered, then windmilled our arms in an instinctive bid to correct a headlong fall. Gala suffered no such problems of adjustment. This, for her, was a home-coming, if an unwelcome one. She blew out her lamp, then reached out and steadied me. The vertigo passed.

'Ah,' said Defoe, gazing about him, 'if only life could have been so simple during the war. Many's the time I've had to crawl miles through tunnels and passages scarcely big enough to admit a greased piglet before I'd stumble upon anything like this.'

'The stairway is seldom used,' said Gala. 'This small part of the Netherworld is abandoned. But we must go quietly. Sound conducts through the rock and our approach may be picked up several kilometres away.' Framed portraits hung from the rock wall on either side of us. Composed in what seemed a limited palette of blues, these gloomy paintings depicted long-dead *malignos* who had obviously exercised some authority in the Netherworld. They looked at us askance, or else brazenly met our eyes. I edged forward and took my first tentative steps down the stairway.

Gala led, the silvery scales of her lithe body corus-cating like sequins, each one of which captured the shaft's pale-blue luminosity. It seemed as if we were descending through a coral sea, Gala a fantastic sea creature, and we two humans clumsy hunters of the deep, doomed never to add her to our catch. The violence of the shaft's gradient, as Gala had explained to me on a previous occasion, was due to that fact that it had originally been designed, not for *malignos*, but for human traders whom Gala's ancestors had enjoyed putting at a disadvantage.

My legs began to ache. We seemed to have descended hundreds of metres. And still we lurched downward, striding, tripping, almost falling into endless space. As we descended, the blueness of the light intensified, though without hampering our vision. At last the staircase bottomed out, and Defoe and I were able to rendezvous with our guide.

It was a monochromatic world we found ourselves in, but one with many shades, cyanic, azure, cerulean, sapphire and cobalt. I knew, from past experience, that it would take several days before my brain rearranged those shades into approximations of other colours. We planned, on this trip, to be underground no more than a few hours. I would have to accept that a variegated spectrum would be denied me.

We stood in what might have been an antechamber, or lobby, of a country house in the Darkling Isle. The area formed a semicircle before a door, the lintel of which supported a bust. I recognized it. It represented the old Roman god, Pluto. The inscription above it – the hieroglyphs of the *malignos* replacing, in the Netherworld, Roman script – was, though untranslatable, still able to confer a sense of ominous forewarning. Small pieces of furniture hugged the antechamber's contours: a card table, an escritoire, a few high-backed chairs.

Gala strode across the checkerboard floor, her scales

rustling like voile, organza, mousseline-de-soie, or any of the other fabrics she disdained to wear. Apart from the beat of my own heart, that swishing, alluring music was the only sound to break the silence. 'Come,' she said, looking at Defoe. 'We're at the outskirts of an old Netherworld city. The one my people call Aeta. Beyond the door is a terminus where many tunnels and passages converge. In some of those forsaken tunnels live discontents and criminals, those amongst my people who have been condemned to live apart. It is they who I hope may give us the information we seek.'

'You trust such creatures?' said Defoe.

'Not entirely. But they have a proud tradition of exchanging gossip for hard cash. You have money with you, of course?'

'Gold,' he said. 'I believe that will be acceptable.' He flushed, and added, with a little bitterness, 'The one you Christians call Judas certainly found it so.'

'Indeed he did. The *malignos*, hereabout, will also find it acceptable, I assure you.'

Gala opened the door and we passed through into an immense cavern. Though it was something I had been ready for, the sight of glossy walls curving towards a ceiling lost to a fathomless dark again precipitated the vertigo I had suffered when descending the staircase. As on the stairs, and in the antechamber outside, the illumination here was blue. But unlike outside, the light in the cavern emanated not from fungi, but from petrified vegetation lodged in the rock face's cracks and fissures. Seething with luminescent micro-organisms, those dead flowers and plants glowed with cold intensity, allowing me to see at once that we were not alone.

Chapter Four

Above us, on a gallery that ran about the cavern's circumference where the light gave ground to the shadows that obscured the vault, were a company of *malignos*. Hundreds of forms, sometimes misshapen, sometimes beautiful, stared down at us, their eyes sparkling like stars against the backdrop of a dark blue night. Their silence was infectious. How long Gala and I stood tongue-tied, staring into each other's face, I do not know, but when I looked about for Defoe, he was gone. And then, breaking that suffocating quiet, came a man's voice.

'Good day, prodigal daughter.' The man, or rather, the *malignos*, had emerged from behind the crumbling structure of an old building, such as the Ancients had inhabited, and which was set partly into the glistening rock face, as if it had been uncovered by a landslide or treasure hunters. Other such buildings projected from the cavern's wall at various intervals, or burst through the ground, the floor of the chamber scattered with the remains of mighty superstructures and those mysterious engines and machines that had driven the old world's cities. As much as the stairway, the cavern reminded me that, before the war, trade between the Netherworld and Earth-Above had been commonplace. 'Good day, good day. If it *is* day up there, that is. It is so hard to tell, now that we are once again condemned to the depths, with so little hope of enjoying what humans take for granted. I think *you* took it for granted that you might find only inhuman scum in these parts, hmmm, my dear? Some of those undesirables who would sell out their own people. Not totally unlike yourself, yes?'

Beside the *malignos* stood Defoe, the long, taloned hand of the Netherworlder placed on the boy's shoulder. 'Gala Diaz Garcita,' said the *malignos*, his mouth opening to display rows of pointed teeth, 'I believe that is what you call yourself now? I remember when you were called Aberattzia. Aberattzia de Profundis. But don't you remember *me*, my chick? Don't you remember your Uncle Nimrod?' His wings unfolded, and, after beating at the air, were brought flush against his side, the tips flexed slightly so that the pinions might scratch at the scarlet lamellae of his pot belly. As if at that signal several *malignos* threw themselves from their eminence, their own wings, bat-like, transparent, and criss-crossed with veins that were like frets of wood, extending as they fell and swooped towards us.

'I am no longer one of the family!' cried Gala, her voice carrying throughout the chamber and reverberating off its cavernous walls. 'I am no longer of the house de Profundis!'

I reached for my sword. '*Who* is he?' I said.

'*Sus*, he really is my uncle,' she said. 'Don't you know that a Netherworld family must assume responsibility for the crimes of its members? It's our law. That little creep' – she pointed at Defoe who was taking pains to avoid her eyes – 'that *rat* who bought your services is a *malignos* agent. He's stitched us up.' She took a few steps towards uncle and his human protégé; stopped; looked heavenward, her attention drawn by the beat of wings and a shadow cast from something that passed overhead.

Above her, two *malignos* carried a net. They hovered for a moment, and then let it drop. The net – made of finely woven steel and weighted at the corners – smothered her and, screaming, she was borne to the ground. I drew *Espiritu Santo*.

Several other *malignos* glided past me. I slashed at them, and was showered with atomized scales, each fragment twinkling in the monotonous blue air like a mote of fairy dust. The one I had wounded yelped, but continued his trajectory, his face briefly registering a flicker of anger and reproach. Landing where Gala had fallen, he and the *malignos* that swiftly followed began to drag the net and its burden towards Nimrod. Gala writhed within the confinement of her steel prison. 'Devils!' she cried, incipient hysteria translating itself into high rhetoric. 'Spawn of Satan! I walk with Christ now! I've seen dawns and noons and sunsets! *Real* sunsets! I've tasted fresh air and felt the monsoon! I won't have you take me back to the shadows!'

I began to run towards her, but was almost immediately thrown onto my face by a blow from behind. *Espiritu Santo* was knocked out of my hand, and, helpless, I watched it skitter across the obsidian floor. A webbed foot, its hooked nails digging into my shoulder blades, prevented me from rising. Defoe disengaged himself from his patron's arm and retrieved my rapier from where it had come to rest.

'I'm sorry, Dr Pike,' he said. 'I didn't lie about

everything. I really did get lost in the tunnels beneath London. But I had no Gala to rescue me. I've often dreamt about how things might have worked out if, like you, I'd met a beautiful *malignos* who would have taken me back to the surface. *I* was fated to stay below. Alas, the story I told you was, for the most part, no more than wishful thinking.'

'You modelled that story on my own, didn't you?'

'I was envious, Dr Pike. But what use is it to dream? After I was captured by the *malignos*, I knew I had to put away my dreams. My new friends had plans for me.'

'They turned you,' I said.

'They made me see the truth: that I no longer belonged on the Earth's surface. One survives as best one can, Dr Pike. It's nothing personal. When I was asked to travel through the tunnels and caverns that link West with East, I consented. But it was not as if I had any great choice. I have never had many choices, Dr Pike, not in all my fourteen years. Become a tunnel rat, or be simplified; become a *malignos* agent, or starve. What kind of choices are they? When I arrived here and was asked to help bring in *malignos* traitors, then—'

'You've done well,' said Nimrod, tiring of his protégé's soliloquy. And then he trained his eyes upon Gala. The net was wrapped about her so tightly that blood trickled from beneath her scales where the steel mesh bit into the unprotected flesh. 'So: you call upon Christ. And we are devils, hmmm? You learnt, it seems, not merely treachery when you entered the human world. You learnt the rankest of superstitions, too.' And then choosing, for the moment, to ignore his captive niece, he took a few steps towards me, stooping so that he might study my face. Pressed against the ground, I grimaced. The bitter, volcanic ash that carpeted the obsidian had found its way into my mouth and nose. Nimrod smiled, the scales that hung from his cheekbones so heavy that they jingled at the tensing of his muscles. 'We always find them in the end,' he continued. 'The ones who betray us, who go over to the humans in exchange for a little sunlight. The ones who forget their own proud history.'

'What history?' I said, pining for my sword and unable to skewer him with anything but limp words. 'You don't have a history. You're as ignorant of the origins of the *malignos* as are humans.' Nimrod's smile withered, and then was reborn as a smirk.

'Some say,' he said, 'that we buried ourselves beneath the Earth some two thousand years ago to avoid the persecution of mankind. We were different creatures then, they say. We were called the children of the perverse. A great catastrophe had occurred in a parallel universe, and the spiritual radiation from that cataclysm infected our own. That was when some human beings began to change. They looked as others looked, but their souls were alien. But the day came when they made other bodies for themselves, bodies expressive of the perversity of their spirit: cat bodies, rat bodies, snake bodies, shark and spider bodies. And thus they set themselves apart forever from mankind. And for centuries they thrived until human jealousy at last drove them into the Earth's bowels. Human jealousy, and human hatred. In the darkness, they became what mankind had claimed they had always been: hobgoblins, demons, *malignos* . . . They became us.'

'Two thousand years ago,' I said. 'Sure.' I knew I had to filibuster until I could find a way of getting my hands on *Espiritu Santo*. 'Listen: I used to lecture in history, and I tell you that you are talking of the interregnum we call the Dark Ages. A time of which next-to-nothing is known. Just as next-to-nothing is known about the Ancients.' I had chosen, as the subject of my doctoral thesis, a manuscript I had discovered in the National Archives. Its illuminations – which represented copies of copies of copies – were inscribed *Turner, Leonardo, Giotto, Bacon*. But there had been little to give context. No text, apart from enigmatic incantations and spells, that might have provided clues that would have allowed me to decipher the age to which those illuminations referred. 'One might as well speculate about the machinery which litters this cavern,' I concluded.

'Speculate?' he said. 'I do not speculate. The Netherworld, by trading in such machinery, will one day be rich. That is certain. And that is all I *need* to know. We will not allow humans to steal from us like before.'

'Indeed,' I said. 'The war is over and the peace treaty concedes your people the right to trade in artefacts. So how does it profit you to hold Gala like this?'

'It profits my sense of rectitude. It profits my sense of proportion.' Nimrod gestured to one of the *malignos* that attended him. The servant walked forward and delivered a goblet into his hands. 'What do we have after three centuries of war? Nothing. Only the shadows that have been our lot for millennia. Many of us are so hard-pressed that we have to surface at night and enter human towns to steal food. Yes; there is every need to punish those amongst us who helped condemn the *malignos* to this half-life below ground.'

He moved towards Gala, the goblet held before him. 'Perhaps you are right about our mutual ignorance of the past. The time of the Ancients is a time of mystery. And all we know of the Dark Ages that followed is that it was a time of blood and sorrow. A time when men forgot how to use the machines that had sustained the ancient world, the machines that gave men new bodies, the machines that took them to the stars. Perhaps the notion that we have evolved from those we call the "children of the perverse" is a myth.' He glanced at me, a tight-lipped smile again precipitating the jingle-jangle of his scales. It was a sound that reminded me of wind chimes. Wind chimes outside a haunted house. 'Indeed, we may have simply evolved from those you call the *masa*. The deliberate cretinization of those unable to work precedes the war between the Netherworld and Earth-Above. It precedes, in one form or another, known history. For they say that even in the time of the Ancients those they called the "information poor", who huddled outside the walls of the world's greatest cities, were pacified by cheap pleasures and drugs. In which case—' A *malignos* took Gala by a hank of hair that had spilled through the interstices of the net. He jerked her head from the floor. Another *malignos* pushed thumb and forefinger through the netting and pinched her nose until she was forced to open her mouth. 'In which case my errant kinswoman will be joining our ancestors, in spirit if not in body.' Kneeling down, his genitals dangling amongst guano and ash, his pot belly squashed against his knees, he held the goblet above Gala's lips. And then he tipped it, so that the murky liquid within poured into her mouth. She choked, spat, but inevitably I saw her throat contract as she was forced to take some of the stuff down. 'Oh yes, there are many things in the Netherworld which we will again sell to mankind. We even have an antidote to this drug. What confusion that will sow when we distribute it amongst the *masa*. Ah, when those cretins wake, they will burn down your cities!'

Two little *malignos* girls danced about Gala. They must have been about the age Gala had been when she left home. 'Simple sister,' they sang, 'simple sister, tra-la-la, simple sister, ha-ha-ha!'

Defoe took a step forward; stopped; placed a hand over his heart; took another step. 'This thing you do,' he said, quietly, 'this thing isn't right.' His breathing was laboured and he had spoken with considerable effort. Each word had had to be squeezed out of vocal cords constipated by a lifetime spent parroting the psychopathic sentiments of the Darkling Isle. He hurried to his patron's side and put his arms about the creature's midsection. 'Don't you understand? Humans were going to simplify *me* unless I spied for them. It's why I hate mankind. It's why I sided with the Netherworld.' Nimrod grunted and shook the boy off.

'Oh no,' I said, my voice breaking as I realized what had been done. 'No, no. Please no.' I began to sob. 'You take the only thing she ever truly possessed. Why, why do this to her? Oh God forgive you, and God forgive me.'

My anguish became convulsive. It was as if I had just inhaled a whole bottle of *sal volatile*, or gulped down a gallon of tisane. I bucked, turned, and, with an agonized moan, flipped onto my side, got a grip on a scaly leg, and twisted, so that the *malignos* who had pinned me to the floor, big as he was, fell sideways. I got to my feet and kicked the one I had just felled under the chin as, less readily than me, he began to rise. 'Defoe!' I shouted. Nimrod, with the dart of his eye, had ordered his guards to attack.

'I'm sorry,' said the boy for the second time that day. Sorry, I thought. I too was sorry, had always been sorry, but not as sorry as I planned to make him. 'They told me that I would never be accepted by humans,' he continued, 'that I belonged here, with them.' He stepped towards me, looked once over his shoulder, and then threw me the rapier.

There was a pure, infinitely satisfying sound of razor-sharp steel cutting through air as *Espiritu Santo* wheeled towards me. How my sword sang! It sang for Gala. It sang like a choir of pitiless angels. It sang, *Sanctus, sanctus, sanctus, Dominus. Osanna in excelsis*! I jumped and caught the spinning blade, and, as my fingers closed about the hilt, I too sang, my sword and I, as ever, in perfect harmony. I hit the floor, went into a crouch, ready to advance on my foes.

Some of the *malignos* drew long daggers from sheaths buckled to their thighs; but most were unarmed. One such – the largest of their number – charged, in an attempt to catch me off guard. Tauntingly, I lowered my sword, bestowing on him a few extra seconds of life. He was a brute, twice as fat and ugly as the man I had faced yesterday, and a hundred times as deserving of an unpleasant fate. His trunk-like legs were scaled, but above the waist he was covered in greasy, matted hair. The hair, which reached his face, coupled with his prognathous jaw, gave him the appearance of a hornèd blue gorilla. As he closed in, I flicked my sword before his eyes, distracting him; then, after debating momentarily with myself whether I should attempt to scientifically stun or indeed kill the creature, chose the only real option a gentleman, faced with such repulsive hideousness, can take, and, in keeping with my original intentions, lunged and skewered, the tip of my sword passing between the shark-like teeth and through the back of the thing's mouth. The *malignos* fell. The only blue that mattered now, in this chamber of blue, the steel-blue of my flashing, blood-slicked rapier.

Two others closed in a flanking manoeuvre. Built like rhinoceroses, with long, single horns projecting from their brows, they hunched and ran at me with the seeming intention of punching holes through either side of my ribcage. I jumped back; they collided, the silvery horns connecting with a shower of sparks. And then I side-stepped, pinked one in the carotid artery and jabbed the other in the gut, turning the blade with a cruelty somewhat wanton, but, nevertheless, wholly amusing, as I felt it encounter the vitals.

No hangover, today, to offer the enemy a fighting chance; I was not only on form, I was at my most exquisite. I went up on my toes and began to dance like a teenage pugilist. But then, the sight of Gala spread out on the ground, so pinched by the embrace of the steel net, brought me down smartly on my heels. With slow, flat-footed determination – a pugilist, now, who had outgrown his salad style and was opting to go for power

– I closed in on Uncle Nimrod. The pot-bellied fool had not moved since the moment I had sprung into action.

Most of the *malignos* now backed away, and, as soon as I had sunk the tip of *Espiritu Santo* into the solar plexus of their astonished chief and watched him drop to the ground, those that were left followed suit.

I ran to where Gala lay. 'Get over here,' I said to Defoe as I struggled to free her. With the boy's assistance I soon peeled back the mesh and had her sitting up. Above us, *malignos* circled, leaderless and unsure of how to proceed.

I looked into Gala's eyes. They had dulled, and yet at the same time were curiously focused, though upon something I had no inkling of, as beneath my understanding as certain abstruse areas of hermeneutics were above it. Saliva dribbled from her chin. 'Ritchie,' she murmured, thickly, as if her tongue had suddenly swollen and filled her mouth, 'I'm late for mass. The sisters will be angry. Help me, Ritchie. I don't want to go back on the streets. The barrio's a bad place. Oh, what's all this darkness? Tunnels. Corridors. Passages. If only I could breathe the fresh air. I saw the surface once. My mother took me. We were looking for firewood and food. It's so beautiful, all the flowers and the trees. And the sky, Ritchie, how blue it is! Not like the blue in the Netherworld, no not like it at all!' Her head lolled forward, and, behind her eyes, the tiny flame that had struggled to blaze, the flame that was Gala, was extinguished. '*Uh, uh,*' she moaned. '*Uh, uh, uh.*'

I turned to Defoe. I was tempted to kill the little shit there and then and let his bones lie with those of his *malignos* friends, four of whom were already sprawled face down on the ground, despatched with that elegance and grace which, I like to think . . . No, no, I felt no grace at the moment. Nothing to convince me that my essential nature was anything but black. 'We have to get her to the surface,' I said, deferring my plans to slit him from nave to chaps. I needed his help, and he, whatever his motives, had shown himself ready to give it.

Between us we hauled Gala to her feet and walked her towards the door by which we had entered the cavern. A *malignos* swooped. I flinched at the wake of air as he passed over our heads. He turned, came back at us, long taloned fingers stretched before him. Slashing, I felt my sword connect just as the speeding form became a blur. Blood arced and spattered my face. The wounded enemy flew upward, his hand to his throat, and, with a desperate flapping of his wings, made his way back to the gallery. His comrades maintained their distance.

'I know this one,' said a *malignos* hovering a little way off. 'He's from Europa. He has killed many of our people.' Now other *malignos* retreated to the gallery. Some disappeared into holes and cracks in the rocks – tunnels, I knew, that led to the city of Aeta and beyond.

'You know me, eh? The *world* knows me!' I shouted after them as we passed through the door, my voice echoing about the cavern's great expanse. 'The world knows me for a swordsman of *surpassing* excellence!'

On crossing the antechamber and seeing the stairs, something prompted Gala to unfold her wings. When travelling from the surface to the depths, *malignos* more often than not choose to fly. But *malignos* wings, while capable of sustaining a prolonged glide, are not suited to ascents, especially of the near-vertical kind that lay before us. Gala's clouded reason might well, I speculated, get us killed.

I was not allowed time to speculate further. Gala grabbed me by my collar. And then she grabbed Defoe. Her wings beat frantically at the air.

Though she could not support both my weight and the boy's, by holding on to her both Defoe and I were dragged upward, our feet trailing over the steps. She flew, or rather half flew, almost standing up, her own feet raised but a few centimetres from the stone gradient, until, after long minutes, we reached the entrance to the tunnel.

I disengaged myself from Gala's grasp and, with trembling hands, detached my lamp from my belt. As soon as I had lit it I pushed Gala into the tunnel's shadows. And then I followed, Defoe in my wake.

Retracing the route that had brought us to the Netherworld, Defoe and I found it necessary to hold Gala under her arms. Her wings could not extend in that confined space, and she was so confused and exhausted by her recent flight that she was unable to walk unaided. Slumped between us, her feet trailing over the rough, rock-strewn ground as ours had over the stairway, we dragged her towards the light.

We reached the adit. I ordered Defoe to climb to the top of the fumarole. I then looped a rope about Gala's shoulders and secured it. Leaving her supine on the ledge, I ascended. With the boy and myself at the lip of the fumarole and able to share the work, we hauled Gala onto the surface.

When I had lain her down upon the lahar, Defoe walked a little way off and sat with his face in his hands. I bent over Gala, anxious to spot some sign of intelligence in her half-closed eyes. But there was none. '*Uh, uh, uh,*' she continued to moan. I took her in my arms and gently rocked her.

Oh, I did have a soul. To my cost, I knew that now. For I felt it writhing in agony, a raw, flayed thing that had been sprinkled with salt. At the moment Gala had lost her soul to the drug *manggagawa*, my own soul had been discovered. I felt it extend its wings, just as a *malignos* might, and prepare to take flight. It was too cruel. Too cruel that whatever God or Demiurge ruled this universe had chosen to sacrifice Gala for me.

'You'll have to take her to where there are others who are simplified. She'll have no other chance of surviving,' said the boy. I took off my jacket, folded it, and used it to cushion Gala's head. Then I got up, walked over to the spot where Defoe hunkered, and took him by the hair, just as one of Nimrod's *malignos* had earlier taken Gala.

'You are going to escort her back to where we left the horses,' I said, pulling his head back and looking down into a pair of pain-filled, rheumy eyes. 'You will then proceed to the barrio. Get her inside the walls. Make sure of this, hear me? The only reason I don't kill you now is because I am probably as guilty as you for what has happened. Perhaps more guilty.' A sob caught my throat. I snarled, frightened that this was mere self-pity masquerading as grief, one more example of my sham existence. I had persuaded her to come here with hollow promises of a future life; a life together. Poor girl, I thought, all life with me has brought you is this great insult, this catastrophe to your being. 'You will take her back to the barrio and have her decently lodged until I return.'

'Return?'

'I have to go back. Your friend Nimrod said there was an antidote.'

'But it's hopeless,' said the boy. 'Even if there is an antidote, some kind of elixir that will reverse simplification, it will, in all probability, only be found in the Netherworld's capital, where the great magi and alchemists live.'

'Pandemonium?'

'Yes; and no human has succeeded in penetrating so deep into the Earth. You know that.' Pandemonium. Where every passage, tunnel and highway from all the Netherworld's cities converged. 'It lies too deep,' Defoe continued. It was true. It was one reason why the war had ended in a conditional peace. We had not been able to take the enemy's chief city; rumour said it lay near the Earth's core, protected from the searing heat by ancient machines that the *malignos* had managed to restart. I released the boy's hair, unbuckled my sword, laid it upon the ground, and then walked over to where I had left my backpack and, bending over, rummaged inside.

I brought out my old uniform, the uniform of a captain of the Darkling Isle. I took off my grubby white suit and assumed the aspect of one who had battled *malignos* in the depths beneath London; one whose deeds, both bloody and amorous, were still spoken of in palace and slum. Smoothing out the creases, pulling on doublet and hose, I found the uniform still fitted. Years of poverty had corrected my tendency towards corpulence. If I had crow's-feet about my eyes and a little rheumatism in my joints, I was compensated for it by being lean as a greyhound. I ran my hands down the doublet's skin-tight black leather, its polished brass buttons and puffed shoulders surmounted by gold epaulettes; the leather hose with matching, studded codpiece, also in black. And then I pulled on my black calf boots, newly polished; my black leather gauntlets, the fingers cut away so that my flesh might enjoy more intimate association with the hilt of *Espiritu Santo*. Lastly, I re-buckled *Espiritu Santo* itself. And I was again a black knight of the isle of darkness.

I retrieved several other items from the backpack, chief amongst them a compass, water bottle, a bag of jerky, pipe, tobacco, a little opium, a money belt and a pair of field glasses. But I also found a small cracked mirror. I took out the gentleman's mascara and eyeshadow that was in the top pocket of my uniform. (It was an emergency supply that I kept there for occasions when, cut off beneath the Earth, I might not be panicked by finding myself without means to re-fix my face.) Slowly, deliberately, I touched up my warpaint.

I slung the strap of the water bottle over my shoulder, buckled on the money belt and used its spare utility pockets to stow my compass, jerky, pipe and tobacco. Then I hung the field glasses about my neck.

I knelt and held my sword before me, so that it substituted for a holy cross. I lowered my head, but could not pray. All I could offer the dust-filled air were these mumbled words: 'I am not like Gala. I cannot see beyond this mean world and its petty hatreds and villainies. I am a selfish man. A conceited man. I am a man whose heart has been poisoned by long years of war, by the enmity of his own country, the Darkling Isle, whose people believe in nothing, because they themselves are nothing, only shadows of the Nether-world, weaned on darkness and matured in spite. But I swear that I will reach Pandemonium or die. And if I live, I will return to give my poor Gala new life. Let my existence remain as barren as the lives of my country-men if I do not achieve this.'

I rose, adjusted my rapier's scabbard so that it was more comfortable, then stepped to the edge of the fumarole and once more took up the rope.

'Mind you do as I say,' I said, looking behind me. 'I *will* be back. You have gold. Make sure you use it to take care of her.' Defoe got to his feet. I saw that he too had been crying.

'I betrayed you,' he said. 'How can you trust me?' How indeed. Had his *sorry* been as my own had been the other evening (ah, it seemed a lifetime ago), a mere echo reverberating about the ruins of his conscience? I did not know. But, down below, the cavern that had been the venue for our ambush would surely not remain empty for long. It was imperative I seize the opportunity that now presented itself to pass through it and into the passages beyond, where I could begin my quest proper.

'We've all been traitors in our time, we three. Gala to her people, you to ours. But I've been the worst traitor of all.'

'I will take care of her,' he said. 'I promise.'

'You had better,' I said, thinking of my own promises to Gala, and how they had brought about her ruin, but knowing I had no other choice.

And then I again descended into the fumarole.

Into the darkness I went, thinking of *malignos* that fly, *malignos* that fling themselves on you in the darkness, *malignos* whose hands surface from the ground you are walking over, grasp you by the ankles and pull you to your doom. But I thought pre-eminently about Gala. I knew now her life was my life; that if either of us should perish, then so would the other. And so into the shadows I went, the clear blue sky growing smaller while another, eerier sort of blue awaited below. And Gala went with me. For as I descended, I think I descried truly for the first time in my life, a light. From out of the pitch-black depths it seeped into my soul, if soul I should have. It was as if the sun had broken through the dark clouds that always swathed the Darkling Isle, splinters of light invading the streets and towers of London. And it was not like Snake Island; this light did not make me ill; its rays did not prick my eyes like white-hot gimlets. This light was cool, it was beautiful, it was Gala. Let God fulminate in his heaven. If I should be lost, or come to lie bleeding as I did when you first came to me, in the darkness, and in my despair, then I thought, out of the depths, Gala, my own goddess, my divine:

Let my cry come unto *thee*.

Part Two

Chapter Five

The freakshow had drawn a big crowd. I adjusted my field glasses, focusing on a human who eased himself through the press of bodies. He was a small man, thin and pale. To my surprise, the crowd ignored his progress. What was he doing here? And why did the *malignos* suffer his presence? When he had reached the penultimate row of townsfolk that separated him from the marquee, he stopped. He seemed to have decided that it would be prudent not to get too near and contented himself with peering through the crooks of elbows and other physical interstices offered up by the crowd's restlessness.

I laid my field glasses down and reclined behind the boulder. I did not know if it were entirely necessary to skulk. The shadows were thick about me and the crowd was over three hundred metres away. In such circumstances, even the keen eyes of the *malignos* would have had difficulty descrying a human form, whether standing, cocking a snook, or performing semaphore. But since leaving the tunnels and coming upon this inhabited area of the Netherworld, I had been happy to be one with the shadows. I turned to my guide.

'Do they really have human prisoners down there?' I said. 'In that tent?'

'Freakshow,' said the *malignos*, not for the first time. 'If my people cannot claim victory in the war, they can at least still gloat over those humans they hold in captivity.'

I handed him one of the gold coins John Defoe had given me as a retainer. The *malignos* stared at it. His face was transformed. For a moment, he seemed oddly human, the gaping mouth and cunning eyes expressive of a greedy peasant, such as might be found in the archipelago. I gave him another. He looked up and grinned, mucus strung from tooth to tooth like a broken spider's web. The pseudo-humanity vanished and his face again became demoniacal. Without offering a word or even a gesture of farewell, he crawled away on all fours, traversing the bluff and then vanishing into the shaft from which we had emerged ten minutes earlier.

I had been underground, if my half-hunter could be trusted, for two days. The cavern where Gala had been simplified had been deserted, and I had proceeded directly to a stairway that lay at the cavern's far end. It took me to the gallery that ran about the cavern's circumference. There I had chosen a tunnel that I knew would lead into what had once been the old human city of Aeta, long eaten up by subsidence and larva flows. In a few hours I had passed through the city's ruins. I had then wandered through regions which I had never before encroached on, relying on my compass and that sixth sense developed during my career in the military to maintain a westerly bearing. I had heard Gala say that a great underground highway lay to the west. Such a highway would doubtless lead to a Netherworld city, from which the way to Pandemonium might, perhaps, reveal itself. Walking through a maze of blue tunnels I had begun to despair that I was lost. It was then that I met

one of those outcasts whom Gala had hoped to bribe
when we had sought news of John Defoe's fictive lover.
And, following a brief period of distrust and con-
frontation – the wisdom of striking a bargain edging out
my inclination to run the creature through – *malignos*
and man had come to the mutually beneficent agreement
by which I had been led here, to the outskirts of a
Netherworld settlement. No highway was in sight, and
the settlement was a minor one, certainly no city. But it
was my first indication that I might be on the right path.

The settlement's name, my guide had informed me,
was Wormwood.

I picked up the field glasses, put my head above the
boulder and surveyed the town. The bluff I occupied
sloped downward until it reached a dusty plain whose
dimensions made the floor of the cavern I had left two
days earlier seem like a tennis court. The plain might
well have been endless, for the rock face opposite was
obscured by ink-blue shadows. But at what I intuited
was its centre lay a huddled mass of mean, gloomy
dwellings. Looming over those habitations, and rising
from an overhang in the rock face, was a castle.

I trained my glasses back on the beggarly settlement of
Wormwood, and in particular, on the periphery road
beside which the marquee had been erected. The crowd
had grown larger, people spread out so that they encom-
passed the wagons that lay to either side of the tent, as
well as the tent itself. I refocused on the small man. He
stood, as before, peering through the row of *malignos* in
front of him, as if he were eager to be one of the first to
enter the freakshow. I noticed that he wore a steel collar
about his throat; that an attached leash, snaking over his

shoulder, trailed behind him on the ground. What was a human doing here, amongst *malignos*? Was he one of their pawns? An agent? A slave? Some kind of *rara avis*?

As if to answer these questions, a woman rode into my field of vision. Mounted side-saddle, in black riding habit, with the veil of her bonnet pulled down and hiding her face (only the plump, ruby lips were visible), she urged her black steed into the crowd, regardless of the cries of fear and protest that greeted her. The crowd parted. The woman moved on, looking down haughtily at those who, recovering from their shock, went down on one knee as she passed by.

Despite the heavy weeds that enshrouded her, the woman was undoubtedly a *malignos*, though seemingly one for whom human clothing exerted a perverse fascination.

The small man ran to meet her. As he drew alongside, she said something – I saw only those red, red lips moving under the gauzy veil – and handed him her quirt. Then she turned her mount about and, at a walk, again proceeded through the townsfolk, who by now had formed two orderly rows to either side of her, each *malignos* kneeling, with his or her head bowed. The little man, using the quirt to beat himself about the shoulders and back, followed the woman, the avenue of scaly bodies closing as the grande dame and her plaything left the crowd's perimeter and took to the road.

I watched them as they travelled along the outskirts of the town to then take a path that zigzagged up the bluff. They were at a point some distance from me, heading towards the promontory upon which stood the castle.

Malignos

The castle, at the remove from which I viewed it, seemed made of children's building blocks, so simple was its design. Its keep was a tall, thin oblong of flawless stone, with three windows facing me, and one window, on a side oblique to my line of sight and bathed in the same ink-blue shadows that obscured the horizon, lit with a phantasmagoric flame. From its flat roof four turrets rose, each one a perfect conoid.

The woman tied the human's leash to her saddle and spurred her horse into a trot. The man ran haplessly behind. As they neared the drawbridge – it lay across a deep chasm – she reined in; the castle's portcullis rose to greet her; and at a more sedate pace, she entered into what I could just make out to be a courtyard. The drawbridge, closing, prevented me from seeing more.

I put the field glasses down. Even without them I could see that the freakshow had opened for business. The crowd was gradually filing into the marquee. My pocket watch told me that, on the surface, it was night. But I knew I would have to wait some time before the *malignos*, keeping to their own circadian rhythms, would retire to their paltry dwellings to sleep. Only then might I risk making my way across the plain.

I snapped awake. Blinking, I cursed myself for having succumbed to exhaustion. I put my head above the boulder. *Malignos* no longer crowded about the marquee. Neither did I spot any *malignos* in the town, at least, in that part of the town visible from my vantage point. I stood up and, half walking, half sliding, descended the bluff, eventually coming to the grey horizontal of the cavern's floor.

Grey. My brain's organizational powers had outshone themselves. It usually took far longer before I started to be able to differentiate the monotonous light of the Netherworld in terms of the available spectrum. Soon, the universal blueness of my surroundings would reveal itself in reds, yellows and greens.

I dusted myself. Then, in the knowledge that the barrenness of the plain would make any attempt to camouflage my movements futile, I strode forth towards the town, back erect, chin up. To put a little steel into my spine, some fortitude into my step, I entertained the idea that I was leading a company on parade, a ghost company perhaps, such as might be comprised of men who had served with me but who had not survived the war. I wondered if I were soon to join their number. My water bottle was empty, and I had consumed nearly all my jerky. No, I thought, ridding myself of the conceit that the undead followed in my footsteps; no, I was not ready to die. I would ape the *malignos*, and become, below ground, a scavenger, such as they were on the surface. But as I neared the marquee, the inquisitiveness I had earlier felt began to outweigh not only hunger and thirst, but also good sense. Rather than circumventing the marquee, and entering the outskirts of the town, I began to close upon it.

When I stood outside the big tent, I struggled with myself, undecided whether to enter or, as shrewdness demanded, proceed straightaway to Wormwood. Pulling back a flap of canvas, I went inside, curiosity triumphing over sound judgement.

I was confronted by rows of cages, such as might have been designed for lions, tigers, or some other variety of rare, feral beast trained to perform for the public. Some cages were caparisoned with gaudy tarpaulins. Some were as they might have been when the marquee admitted its customers. And of these cages that were open to view, each contained a man, woman or child asleep on top of a filthy bed of straw. The interior of the marquee was otherwise bare.

I walked up to the nearest cage. Of the two cages that flanked it, one contained an unconscious woman cradling a dead infant, her half-open eyes revealing two meniscuses of white, the other an old man, his arms locked about his knees, his lips a burr of gentle, incontinent babble. But in the cage directly before me was something that had induced an unwelcome thrill of recognition in the pit of my stomach. The imprisoned man's face, though turned my way, was partly masked by the matted hair that fell over his bruised eyes. But there could be no doubt: he was the Tasmanian.

My gross adversary, my fat antipodean devil, was even now, perhaps, discovering for himself whether contact with the *malignos* offered a cure for the fifty-third century's primary affliction: the death of intimacy.

I was about to reach through the bars and shake him when the erectile hairs on my nape alerted me to danger. I unsheathed my sword. As I began to turn about, my peripheral vision registered the threat's physical dimensions, or at least, enough about its height, width and breadth or enable me, once my turn was complete, to deploy *Espiritu Santo* not only in a position best suited to defence, but in one that would allow me to conduct an interrogation.

Leaning backward to avoid the sword tip that

brushed against his Adam's apple was the human I had spied earlier amongst the crowd. Though otherwise enviably composed, his gaze flitted up and down the length of steel that extended from beneath his chin, *Espiritu Santo* evoking more than casual interest.

'And what,' I said, 'is a human doing running freely about the Netherworld?'

'Oh, running freely, am I?' he laughed. 'Might I ask what *you* are doing here?' He spoke in English, but his accent, as much as his demeanour, identified him as Pilipino.

'You might indeed ask,' I said, 'if you were to have a rapier at my throat. But it is I who have a rapier at yours. Now, if you would be so kind – *answer*.'

'There is a peace treaty in effect. Why shouldn't I be here?' His foolishness seemed premeditative, and, as such, tried my patience. Nevertheless, I awarded him a response.

'Because for humans the Netherworld remains a realm of terror.' He put a finger upon the flat of the blade and tried to push it away. I gave him a tiny jab, just above the steel collar. It was executed with enough force to break the skin, but with sufficient delicacy to spare his life. A thin stream of blood ran from the wound and stained his unlaced shirt. 'You are wise not to scream,' I said.

'It wouldn't matter if I did,' he said, his eyes darting hither and thither. 'These captive humans are drugged. They will not wake until morning. And we are too far from Wormwood to rouse any *malignos*. But did you know that when you pinked me? And, not knowing, were *you* wise to do so?' He was, I would have guessed, in his early twenties. I didn't like being twitted by a younger man, but there was truth in what he said. And I could not, in my present situation, afford to be pig-headed. I lowered the sword, intent on proving I could be polite as well as impulsive.

'Let me introduce myself. My name is—'

'I'm not sure I want to know anything about you,' he interrupted. He put a hand in his trouser pocket and pulled out a handkerchief with which he dabbed at his wound. 'I am equally unsure if I want you to know anything about *me*.' He started to back away.

'What *should* I know, except that you're a *malignos* agent?'

He laughed, contemptuously. 'I'm a slave to the *malignos*. Or rather, a pet. Does that frighten you, brave adventurer? Does that make you tremble, does that make you quake?' I raised my left eyebrow and at the same time, my sword. I could be politic, it is true. But patience has its limits. Mesmerized by the sword whose tip still showed evidence of his blood, he stopped dead in his tracks.

'Let me introduce myself,' I said again, 'if you will be so kind . . .'

'Very well,' he said, his gaze wholly upon *Espiritu Santo*.

'Richard Pike,' I said. 'Ex-captain of the armies of the Darkling Isle. And you?'

'Nothing so glamorous. Above, I was just another Juan de la Cruz. By trade, a cobbler.' He paused; frowned. 'Here I go by the moniker of *Boot*.' He stepped to one side of the drawn, minatory steel and presented me his hand. I ignored it.

'I saw you,' I said, 'earlier, when you were outside the tent. The woman—'

'My mistress,' said Boot. 'The Countess of Suspiria. She rules here, by the authority of Pandemonium.'

'Pandemonium?' At the mention of that city's name the discretion that I had promised myself would inform all my encounters underground (and which I had already compromised by giving my name) disappeared, utterly. 'That is the city I am seeking. That is why I am in the Netherworld.'

'Are you mad?'

'The woman,' I said, immediately regretting my out-burst, and slapping his still outstretched hand away with the flat of my sword. 'The countess. How did you come to belong to her retinue?'

'The same way,' said Boot, pursing his lips towards the cages, 'that these unfortunates came to be carnival fodder. By being kidnapped. By being dragged below ground.'

'Your mistress does not seem like other *malignos*,' I said.

'You mean—'

'I mean she chooses not to go naked.'

'Ah yes, she has a passion for clothes. She has a passion for all things human. You might say she has a passion for *mankind*. Once, there were nine of us in her retinue. But the others died. Died long ago. She would take one to her bed each night, you see. Not me, you understand. I am regarded as little more than a dog, a bagatelle. That is why I've survived.' He gazed at the humans in the cages. 'I like to come here, sometimes,' he continued, 'to be with other humans. Even if they cannot talk.' He stroked the bars of the cage that held the Tasmanian. 'They leave tomorrow. They leave for another town down the highway. And they shall not come back for many months.' He turned away from the cage, bitterness chasing the sentimentality from his face and replacing it with calculation. 'You say you seek the great city?' I tilted my head to one side, regretting my former outburst and unwilling to commit myself. 'The mistress might, perhaps, be able to assist you. I mean, you're not going to tell me you know how to travel all the way down, are you? All the way down to Pandemonium?'

'*How* can she help me?' I said. 'And *why* should she?'

'How? Because she has a library filled with many, many maps. Why? Because, my friend, you are *human*. She would doubtless enjoy a night of your company.'

'Do you seriously expect me to believe she would lend me her assistance?'

'She lives a life apart. Her habits are somewhat frowned on. Aristocrats, you know, do as they please. Yes, I believe she *would* help.'

'And what would you get out of this?'

'The chance, perhaps, to come with you? I have often daydreamed about leaving this place. With a map, navigation would be simple.'

'So why haven't you taken one?'

'Her library is always locked. But even if I did steal a map, what use would it be? I would not get very far. I am no fighting man, as you can well suppose. Before a day had passed, I would be killed in the tunnels. But with you to protect me—'

'Quiet,' I said. 'Let me think.'

I wondered if it were worth hazarding. My whole endeavour, of course, was a fantastically hazardous exercise. And I felt then, that if I were too fastidious about the best way to proceed, then my quest would end up taking me nowhere.

I sheathed my sword. 'I will come with you,' I said.

Chapter Six

We sat at opposite ends of a long dining table. In one corner of the room was a stairwell, which led to the castle's lower floors. The room was exceptionally plain, with little more than a mullioned window set in each wall to disturb the uniformity of the unornamented plaster. (A bell-rope, which, I suspected, was used to summon servants, hung from the room's cornice, and supplied the only other relief to the room's vapidity.) My impressions of the castle's interior had conformed to those I had had when first seeing its bulwarks and fortifications through my field glasses: it seemed made of children's building blocks, and was, in essence, a toy castle. I felt as if I had suddenly become one of the tiny figurines in Gala's precious dolls' house.

We ate off lapis lazuli. I was uncertain of the fare. Rat? I skimmed off a little of the mushroom sauce and brought a forkful of meat to my lips, all the time trying to keep my gaze from re-establishing contact with the side dish of sautéed cockroach. I knew I should consume as much as I could. For the last few days I had eaten only jerky, and, in the lower depths, food would be scarce. But after a few mouthfuls, and despite my hunger, disgust prevailed.

I lay down my fork and stared at the Countess Suspiria, intent on fulfilling the task I had set myself. The candelabra that stood midway between us seemed to surround her face with a nimbus of gold. I stared hard and meaningfully. I had enjoyed, in London, the reputation of a lady's man, and had had my share of whores and hymens. I stared harder, my eyes half hooded, a personification of lust. But I needn't have exerted myself. It was she who was to do the seducing.

'That is a captain's uniform, is it not?' Like her slave, Boot, she spoke in English. We were near enough to the surface for the World Language to enjoy equivalence with the language of the Netherworld.

'You are perceptive. Have you visited the Darkling Isle?'

'No; but I have heard stories, of course. Many stories of heroism and sacrifice. Many stories of triumph. Perhaps you find it strange to hear a *malignos* praise humanity?' She lifted a wine goblet to her lips and studied me over the rim. She set the goblet down, circled the rim with a finger, and put the finger to her mouth. 'All Wormwood finds me strange. And I don't give a damn! If I choose to entertain humans then that is my affair. I must have *something* to alleviate the tedium of living so far from a major city, amongst bumpkins, dullards and woodenheads.'

She was, I thought, not an unattractive woman, though somewhat past her prime. She had lost some of the scales from her cheeks and brow, and I noticed that she had resorted to cosmetics to promote the illusion that they were still in place. Her hair was bountiful, though. It was almost as massive and argentine as Gala's. And the horns had been well tended, carved, as they were, into long, graceful flutes. I did not think it would be too difficult to summon up the requisite passion to satisfy her.

'Would you mind, captain,' she said, 'if I asked you to

rise, for a moment, from your chair?' I shrugged and complied. 'Thank you.' Her gaze travelled from the top of my head to my groin. 'Is this then the current fashion in London? Or merely one adopted by you military men? Either way, I approve. A codpiece is so *distinguished.*'

'I'm glad you approve, countess. You have a fine, and, if I may say so, unusual taste for clothes yourself.'

'Oh,' she said, waving me back into my seat, 'you refer to the fact that I choose to embellish myself with silks and satins, like a human woman?' I smiled; nodded. 'I do go naked on such occasions when I meet a man whose company I find exhilarating.' She looked at me from under a fringe that seemed constituted of fine metal wire. Her eyes, hooded as my own had lately been, also twinkled with amusement. 'And, of course, when state business so dictates.' She wore a black silk evening gown, cut low to reveal a bosom as opulently scaled as it was fabulously proportioned. 'But on all other occasions I like human clothes next to my skin. It reminds me of what my people desire, but have been so long denied.'

'The light and air? Good farmland? A chance – ' I looked down upon my unfinished repast – 'to consume something vaguely edible?'

'Oh you understand me *very* well, captain. But as you see' – she extended her arms to indicate the breadth of her hospitality – 'I do not harbour useless resentments.'

That my smile became lopsided was, perhaps, attributable to the wine, or more likely to my ungovernable propensity for archness. The result was the same. I began to hold forth like someone auditioning for the villainous lead in a melodrama. 'I am glad you so like human apparel, countess,' I said, out of the corner of my mouth. 'You look magnificent. But is it all you enjoy having next to your skin?' Her own mouth opened, its corners turning upward, but in a manner insufficiently licentious for me to feel confident about pressing matters home. But I knew her coquetry must eventually lead *somewhere*. I would let her continue to set the pace.

'Boot tells me you seek Pandemonium,' she said, playfully refusing to acknowledge my latest advance. The rows of pointed teeth glinted in the candlelight, and then, a forkful of meat demanding their attention, her mouth closed, and she chewed, slowly, as if meditating upon some issue as obscure as the shadows that were her home. 'Why?'

'I seek the antidote to *manggagawa*.' She raised an eyebrow, her mouth once again turning upward, but this time threatening to convert what had been an imitation of sexual congress into a full-blown smile of derision.

'I see. You are one of those who take pity on the *masa*? You may change your tune if the antidote is ever used. The *masa* would surely turn on such privileged creatures as yourself.'

'I do not seek the antidote for the *masa*. I seek it for . . . a friend.' The countess narrowed her eyes.

'A *lady* friend?' She had stopped chewing on her meat. A long-fingered hand reached out for the goblet. 'I see, yes, yes, I *understand*. It was you who was responsible for that little fracas beneath Pinatubo? That little encounter with the family de Profundis? We are related, you know, the family de Profundis and I. Albeit distantly, I admit. They live some way off. You will not reach *that* city so easily, I can assure you.' The name of

Gala's city of birth was Sibma. On the occasions when Gala and I had descended beneath the surface of the archipelago, we had, at her behest, taken pains to avoid it, though I often complained – it stung me now to recollect – that circumventing Sibma added hours, sometimes days to our itinerary.

'It is not my intention to reach it, countess. It never has been, and it never will be. Pandemonium is my goal. I have no wish to quarrel further with the house de Profundis, or indeed any other *malignos* family.' I trusted that things stood as she had said: that she was only a distant relative of Gala's, and as such, would not feel obliged to revenge the sullying of the de Profundis family honour.

'If I were to turn you over to the authorities, you would reach Pandemonium soon enough, I think. Certain people would wish to talk to you. Not as I wish to talk to you, of course, over wine and supper. But in far more unwelcome conditions. What do you think, captain? Would these travel arrangements suit you? Would you, in such circumstances, still entertain such fond thoughts of your treacherous little *malignos* friend?' her tone had surprised me. Her concerns, it seemed, were far removed from those surrounding 'family honour'. This was a woman seized with unreasonable jealousy.

'Indeed, those travel arrangements would *not* suit me. But I had heard that, in your library, you have certain maps—'

'They have a price.'

'I have gold.'

'Do not insult me.'

'Then what price?'

'Forget about your friend. For this night at least.'

'I have forgotten,' I said, with somewhat too much celerity; enough indeed, to perhaps have her think me sarcastic. But she had her mind on other things. She stood up, knocking over her chair. Anger, it seemed, had thrown oil upon her fire where, previously, it had only smouldered.

The long, curving fingernails tore at her gown's lacing. Silk, stays and chemise, falling to the ground about her feet, left her as naked as the room's bare wall; as naked as her brothers and sisters; as naked as the Earth's hot core.

She hopped upon the table and came towards me on her hands and knees, her tail sweeping from side to side, upsetting silverware and crockery. I stood, less in enthusiasm to meet her than in a state of comprehensive alarm at the rolling eyes, the gnashing teeth, and the tongue that would sometimes loll out of her mouth and make an elaborate orbit of her lips. But it was too late to make my excuses and leave. I had sown the wind, and now I was set to reap Countess Suspiria's whirling, stormy lust.

She sprang and, with a single beat of her wings, was upon me. We tumbled to the floor, my scabbard clattering against the flagstones. My hands smarted as I made a futile gesture at breaking my fall. And then she was astride me, snarling and spitting in my face. She jerked my codpiece to one side, and, I suppose, by so doing, gave notice that she now considered our relationship – such as it was – to have evolved into one where the little courtesies that grease the social machine were deemed unnecessary. The sex act that followed lasted no more than perhaps five seconds, but in that time my head was banged repeatedly against the floor, my ears were scored through by her small, but pre-eminently sharp teeth, and my chest and thighs pummelled and raked by her taloned hands. I do not know how I managed to perform. But perform I did, and, more to the point, survived.

She rolled off. Her eyes closed. Her chest heaved. And I wondered if she had taken any pleasure of me, or whether she had simply given me up as a poor lot.

I wiggled my toes to check that my spine had not been snapped. Ran my hands down my body, seeking to establish whether I had other structural damage. Found none. Brushed off a few scales. Spat out a clot of blood. And then:

'The maps, countess?'

'Your post-coital pillow talk leaves much to be desired, captain.' I peered down at my penis, conscious, for the first time, that I had an erection. The rainbow-hues refracted by the wet, detumescing shaft betokened that the coupling had had, at least, one positive outcome. Due, perhaps, to the blows my head had sustained, I now saw in perfect colour. That is, the blueness about me was demarcated into shades upon which my brain superimposed violets, indigos, greens, yellows, oranges and reds.

'You have my gratitude,' I said, 'for a most memorable experience. But is it such an unwarranted hope that your feelings of tenderness towards me might extend to giving me the help I have requested?' I pulled my codpiece back into place, sucking the air between my teeth as the studded leather came into contact with abrasions and friction burns.

'Maps, you say. Maps, maps. You cannot wait? If you

cannot wait, you will not be happy here, my pet. Listen. You shall have your maps, but not tonight, and perhaps not even tomorrow.' She turned her head and looked into my eyes. 'Perhaps, captain, not for a long, long time. I have exhausted my stock of human men, and have need of you.'

I struggled to my feet. 'Your man, Boot, has done me the service this evening of reminding me that a scream, in an out-of-the-way place such as this, is often ineffectual.' I drew my sword. Lazily, like a great lady awakened by her maid at noon after last night's *liaison dangereuse*, she levered herself up on to her elbows and studied me with understated scorn.

'I have guards.'

'I think not, countess.' I looked over at the bell-rope. It was safely out of her reach. Even if she were to employ the agility of a *malignos* and, with a beat of her wings, attempt to fling herself upon it, I would skewer her before she was halfway across the floor. I made a few swaggering passes, *Espiritu Santo* cutting through the air and singing its cruel, familiar song. 'But if you do, now would be the time to call for them.' As if to oblige my overconfidence, she screamed. I stepped back, a little rattled.

'Stop it,' I said. Again, she screamed. But when the door opened and only Boot stood there, the relief was so great I laughed.

'And what are *you* going to do, little man?' I said.

'This is not the way to go about things,' he said. 'This is really not the way at all. You should not antagonize the mistress.'

'It's a little late for that.'

'If you proceed in this manner,' said Boot, 'I fear we shall never leave the Netherworld.'

'Never, eh? I got *in* to the Netherworld, didn't I?'

'And you will *stay* here,' said the countess, who, by now, had risen to her feet. I saw that she was edging towards the bell-rope. I looked on. Boot had been the only one of her retinue to respond to her scream. Should I worry if there were any other slaves or servants lurking in the castle's byways? During our walk to the castle, the diminutive cobbler had assured me that the countess was impoverished, her retinue small. If he was the most gallant of their number I would have no trouble in despatching the few poor specimens likely to come running at the bell's summons.

'That will raise the whole town,' said Boot. 'It is connected to the castle's bellcote.'

I shot the countess an angry glance; ground my teeth, angrier, by far, at my own insouciance; skipped towards her and put the rapier to her throat. She took a step backward. I pursued her, the tip of the rapier positioned under her chin. Soon, I had her against the wall.

'I have no intention of staying here, countess. Shall we proceed to the library?'

I had unrolled the parchment so that it covered most of the table. 'And this here?' I queried, resting my index finger upon a pair of narrow, parallel lines that led away from Wormwood. 'What is this?' The room we occupied was identical to the one we had recently left, three floors above, except that its walls, far from being unornamented, were lined, from floor to ceiling, with books and rolls of parchment. And where, upstairs, a dining table had stood, here stood the bureau upon which I had spread the map.

'That's the highway,' said the countess. My heart rose. It was surely the highway that Gala had spoken of. 'It stretches for hundreds of kilometres,' she continued, 'across the Great Plain, until it reaches Tophet, on the banks of the Sea of Sammael.' The countess could not use her hands to indicate the route I should take – I had tied them behind her back with strips torn from her clothes – and so employed the arrowhead of her tail as a pointer. It swung across the map and came to rest upon the subterranean sea. Upon the sea was a symbol which, according to the map's legend, indicated a great whirlpool. Next to the symbol was a pointer upon which had been stencilled a large, decorative hieroglyphic which I knew to be the equivalent of a P. 'Yes, that will put you on the road to Pandemonium. The maelstrom, at least, will take you to the necessary depths. You will still have a long way to travel.'

'A ship may survive such a descent?' I said.

'I have heard that it is possible,' said Boot, looking to his mistress for corroboration. 'The maelstrom, as I understand it, leads to the place the *malignos* call the Torrid Zone.'

'Yes,' smiled the countess, somewhat nastily, 'the Torrid Zone. There you will find the Naphtha, a waterway that passes through many of the Netherworld's great cities: Cheos, Sheol, Tammuz, Eblis, Mulciber—' The countess nodded, as much to quiet him, I thought, as in acknowledgement of his geographical prowess.

'I need another map,' I said. 'This one only illustrates passage to the *maelstrom* that you speak of. I must have something to guide me through the regions that lie beyond. To the *zone*.'

'Classified,' said the countess. 'No maps of such details are allowed so near the surface. You will not, at least, discover such a map in *my* library. My tastes have left me somewhat isolated from my peers. My fellow patricians do not altogether trust me.' I drummed my fingers upon the parchment. What she said was likely true. I had no option, it seemed, to follow the map until it delivered me to the maelstrom, and then to blunder on towards my goal aided by whatever fortune should present.

Boot knelt before me, as I had seen the townsfolk kneel before the Countess Suspiria. 'You are the one I serve now,' he said. Now that his mistress was antagonized beyond measure he no longer seemed inclined to criticize my strategy. 'You remember your promise. Take me with you. Take me back to the surface.'

'I made no promise,' I said. I rested a foot upon the armillary sphere that stood on the floor next to the bureau, rocking it idly to and fro. 'And besides, I'm not going to the surface. You know that. I'm going to Pandemonium.'

'Ah yes,' he said. 'But take poor Boot home first, master. Take him back into the light and air!' He grovelled at my feet. I kicked the sphere across the floor. The skeletal ball rolled across the flagstones until the ecliptic and horizon of its celestial hoops bounced off the wainscot. The sharp rattle of the sphere's trajectory set my teeth on edge. I reminded myself that it would be unwise to linger. I stepped over Boot's prostrate body, walked across the room and scanned the bookshelves to see if there was anything else I could steal that might help me in the days ahead.

The books were grimoires, the catalogued fragments of ancient texts handed down generation after generation as spells, charms and incantations. The linguistic and symbolic detritus of dead religions, half-remembered lore. During the Dark Ages, books – real books – had been preserved by Cathay scribes. But those books, like the knowledge they contained, were now hopelessly lost.

I sauntered along a row of shelves, running a finger over leather spines. I had made such tomes my study when I had been an academic, sifting through millennia of accumulated rubbish to try and find a phrase, a formula, an illustration, a series of musical notes, that yielded some truth about the human spirit, or veracity of the natural world. I had tried to arrange these scraps of ancient knowledge in chronological order. They terminated, as all other historians had discovered, at the end of the twenty-first century. That was the time when something peculiar had happened to history; a time when, according to myth, the 'children of the perverse' had come into the world. Gala's kinsman, Nimrod, whom I had skewered below Pinatubo, encapsulated the moment when he had talked of how '*a great catastrophe had occurred in a parallel universe,*' and of how '*the spiritual radiation from that cataclysm infected our own. That was when some human beings began to change. They looked as others looked, but their souls were alien. But the day came when they made other bodies for themselves, bodies expressive of the perversity of their spirit: cat bodies, rat bodies, snake bodies, shark and spider bodies. And thus they set themselves apart forever from mankind.*' Whatever that 'great catastrophe' had really been, whatever the reality behind the myth of the 'children of the perverse', that convulsion in time had brought technological progress to a halt. More than that, in the succeeding centuries, it had also ensured that mankind forgot, or rather, refused to understand, anything approaching a rational interpretation of his world. We are only now beginning to learn how to again perceive the world truly, and not see it through the warped lens of the perverse.

So many grimoires to choose from! Most were tomes that you would expect, of course, to find in a *malignos* library, but fascinating nevertheless. Very rare, and, on the Earth's surface, very valuable. There was the *De Conceptu Et Generatione Homines.* The *Monstrorum Historia.* The *De Animalibus Natis Ex Sodomia.* And the *Curiositatis Eroticae Physioligiae.* Latin had come into widespread use at the end of the twenty-first century. One theory held that it had been an artificial language invented to defend human tongues against corruption. The alien and altogether monstrous new discourse that informed the age had, so the theory went, necessitated it. Another theory held that it had been resurrected from another Dark Age, now lost to the vagaries of Time. I was less sympathetic to this approach. All my studies had indicated that the people called Romans had spoken a language closely related to English. Hadn't they invented our own, human alphabet? Weren't they credited with prophesying the coming of the *malignos*, their temples filled with images of strange, hornèd gods?

So many grimoires. But I reminded myself that I was committed to travelling light. Turning my attention from the countess's library, I walked over to the bureau, rolled up the map, put it under my arm, and crooked my finger at Boot. He came to me, almost salivating with expectation, like a dog recognizing his true owner.

I kicked his legs out from under him. Then, placing my hands upon the countess's shoulders, I pushed her, so that she joined her slave on the floor. With some of the leftover strips of material that I had used to tie up his mistress, I secured the little man's hands. And then, in a fit of fancy, I tied mistress and slave together, quite tightly, so that their lips were compelled to touch. I stepped back and evaluated my handiwork.

'Farewell, sweet lovers,' I said.

'No, master, please!' said Boot, trying to pull his face away from contact with the furious reptilian countenance before him. 'I told you about the maps! I brought you here! If it weren't for me, then—'

'This evening I have, of necessity, been unfaithful to the woman I love.' I frowned. It had not, I reminded myself, been the first time. 'The abominableness of that act, I'm afraid, quite overwhelms any thought I might have for the injustice I am presently meting out to you.'

'You will never reach Pandemonium,' said the countess. 'No human has ever been so far, or so deep. Besides which, I shall raise the hue and cry! You are a dead man captain.'

I gave her a cursory salute. Then I spun on my heels and departed.

I walked away from the castle, down the winding road

that connected it to the plain, and then across the plain itself, all the time glancing over my shoulder, and wondering whether the countess had found a way of raising that hue and cry she had boasted of. But all was quiet. The *malignos* were asleep, and the town remained deserted.

Again, rather than circumventing the marquee, I closed upon it. But this time it was not mere inquisitiveness that distracted me from pressing on to the town and beyond, it was the memory of something Boot had said when I had first encountered him. '*They leave tomorrow for another town down the highway.*' If I could secrete myself in one of their wagons, I thought, then I should have passage not just to the next town, but perhaps all the way to the sea and the maelstrom. And if, during the journey, I should be questioned at a roadblock, or otherwise detained, I might pretend that I too was a freak, just another sideshow attraction. Pretend, that is, until a suitable opportunity should provide means of escape.

I scanned the periphery road. All was quiet. At random, I picked a wagon and began walking towards it. I would hide beneath its low-slung chassis until those *malignos* who ran the freakshow awoke and ordered the packing away of the marquee and the cages. When they were ready to depart, I would clamber inside.

I walked on, hunched over, as if heading into a storm. Then I broke into a steady run, the marquee's dimensions growing until they dominated my line of sight.

Chapter Seven

I squinted through a tear in the canvas. A grey, barren plain extended in all directions, bathed in permanent twilight.

I had never before seen such a cavern. Certainly, not one that was anywhere near so vast. I strained to take in its limits. Several days ago, shortly after I had left Wormwood, the rock walls which bordered the Netherworld had begun to recede. Several hours ago, they had disappeared altogether. Now, at the edges of the featureless terrain, I perceived only a mountainous horizon. Beyond its peaks the shadows which had long been banished from the cavern's floor clustered together as if about to defend their last stronghold.

This desolate expanse was surely not natural. It must, I reasoned, have been hewn millennia ago in jealous imitation of Earth-Above. Despite the incalculable man-hours doubtless expended on its construction, we had passed no settlements. The cavern was abandoned, its original function, perhaps, as forgotten by the *malignos* as it was incomprehensible to me.

I withdrew, leaning back against the vanward panels. I took out my pipe and stuffed its bowl with tobacco. Then I took a length of straw and held it over the oil lamp's flame, brought it to the bowl and lit up. Sucking meditatively, if not with any real sense of contentment, I filled my lungs with warm, voluptuous smoke. Then,

trying to ignore the sound of the iron-rimmed wheels –
like boiled sweets ground between molars – I turned my
attention to the Tasmanian.

'So, you still refuse to offer me an apology?'

'If you do as you've promised, then—'

'Stop!' I put a finger in each ear, taking particular care
to plug the damaged, hypersensitive left. Having to
suffer the insistent racket of the wheels was bad
enough, but to be also asked to cope with the strident
inflection of the Tasmanian's voice was nigh intolerable. Here, as much as in *Nightriders* and on Snake
Island, those antipodean vowels caused me immeasur-
able grief.

When his lips stopped moving, I unplugged the right
eardrum and wagged my finger with grave reproach. The
Tasmanian retreated to the back of his cage. He could
not have been more intimidated if I had threatened him
with an edged sword. His days as a freakshow attraction
had ruined his nerves. It was, I must admit, a condition
I had done little to ameliorate. I despised him still, even
though he was the only human in Madame Tetrallini's
show who had been less than utterly bestialized by
captivity. Soon, I knew, he would be like the other
attractions: somewhat above the *masa*, but as far
beneath men as men were beneath the Ancients.

'Now,' I continued, addressing the naked, filthy,
tremulous creature who hunkered against the cage's
bars, 'proceed, and if you'd be so kind, try to speak with
a degree of mellifluence. Five days we've been together.
Five days. The ride has been rough, what with having to
eat the slop that gets pushed through that hatch' – I
nodded towards the wagon's farther end – 'and having

to sleep in such circumstances. I have no wish to further test my powers of endurance by submitting to the *peine forte et dure* of your scandalously tortuous intonation.' I removed my finger from the other ear.

'Ah, give it a rest you foppish, over-precise weasel. I *said*, if you do as you've promised I'll apologize readily enough.' He had, in part, swiftly recovered his composure. I wondered if his fear would now give way to fury. During the early days of our confinement he had reacted with some violence when I had thought fit to upbraid him, whether it be for his murderous designs upon the English language, his snoring, or his dismal conversation. Sometimes his tantrums had been so terrible I had thought he would break free of his cage.

'No, no,' I said impatiently, 'I'll do as I've promised – I'll release you – but only if you first apologize.'

'We've been over this a million times.' It was true. For days we had fenced about the same paradox: I would free him only if he showed good faith by apologizing for the insult that had been the *raison d'être* of our duel; he would apologize only if I showed good faith by freeing him.

I stretched out a leg; groaned. The wagon was box-shaped, small, with barely enough room for me to squeeze between the cage and the panelling, and I had been periodically inflicted with attacks of cramps.

'You still don't trust me, do you?' he said.

'It wasn't so long ago that you were trying to kill me,' I replied.

'I didn't blow the whistle on you when you crept in here, did I? And every time that hatch opens—' He nodded, as I had done earlier, towards the farther end of

the wagon, where a hatchway was set into the bolted
door. Nearby, where a sawn-off segment of steel bar
allowed the prisoner access to his daily nourishment,
lay a tin pannikin smeared with gruel. 'Every time that
hatch opens and they bring me my feed, haven't I
shared it with you? And haven't I kept mum?'

I did not remember ever asking his permission to eat.
But I could not deny that he had maintained his silence.
'Yes, I admit that, at any time during the last five days,
you might have turned me over to the *malignos* if you
had so chosen. But how much has that to do with the
fact that I am your only chance of escape? If I should
free you now, how do I know you wouldn't find some
way of betraying me before making off? An apology for
the way you treated Gala would at least give me some
indication that you are willing to regard escape as a
cooperative venture.'

'It will take two of us to assume control of this
caravan. Why shouldn't I want to cooperate?'

'Why shouldn't you, in that case, offer me an
apology?' Our conversation had reached a kind of crisis.
It was as if we had chewed its substance, first to pap,
then to water, and now, to such a hyper-attenuated state
that it was inevitable that it would disappear.

'Oh, the hell with it, I *apologize*,' he said. I smiled. At
that moment, our childish quarrel should have been
resolved. 'Now will you let me out of here?' But despite
my avowals I hesitated to accept his apology. There
were many reasons why. Disgust for his gross, antipodean personhood had something to do with it, of
course (though I would have welcomed his hand in a
fight). But what truly made me prevaricate was the

practical aspect of fulfilling my end of the bargain.

'It's hardly as simple as that.'

'You gave your *word*.'

'You forget. Madame Tetrallini has the keys.'

'So go get them. Kill the old bitch. You shouldn't find it difficult.'

'There's the small question of her dogs,' I said.

When I had left the Countess Suspiria's castle and prepared to leave Wormwood I had waited until the last moment before secreting myself within the freakshow. It was fortunate I had done so. Though I had not known I would be sharing the journey with the Tasmanian – his cage, when loaded, had been covered with a tarpaulin – I had, by virtue of my time spent loitering in the shadows, been able to identify the lead wagon, that is, the one used by Madame Tetrallini. The old *malignos* woman who ran the freakshow kept six enormous wolfhounds. To have tried to secrete myself within *her* itinerant domicile would have entailed not merely discovery, but an extremely unpleasant mauling.

'Dogs? What're you worried about *dogs* for?' he said. 'A swordsman like you should be able to fend off a handful of dogs.'

'There are her sons as well, of course,' I continued, referring to the good Madam's six offspring, each of whom was as proportionately gigantic as her hellhounds. I had first set eyes upon them when they had packed away the marquee. I had since used my spyhole to study them further whenever the caravan had stopped to make camp. They seemed to spend what remained of their waking hours eating. The huge quantities consumed teased my ever-shrinking stomach. But what concerned me most were their postprandial activities, the way they would sit about the fire, sharpening their scimitars and engaging in casual swordplay. They were, I could tell, experienced fighters, veterans, probably, of the war. And they would doubtless prove formidable in combat. 'No, far better to wait until we near Tophet. Here, in the middle of the Great Plain, hundreds of kilometres between towns, we must accept that, for the time being, escape is impossible.' He began banging his head against the bars. 'I suggest, since it is likely that, for several days yet, it will be necessary for us to suffer each other's company, we do so with as much fortitude as we can muster.'

'You, you, you gave your *word*.'

'When we are within walking distance of Tophet, I shall burglarize Madame Tetrallini's wagon while she and her sons are asleep, and thereby gain the keys. The dogs?' I waved my hand dismissively. 'I shall deal with the dogs in a manner yet undetermined. Suffice to say, after I have freed you we will, if possible, help ourselves to the caravan's provisions, and then, leaving the caravan behind us, enter Tophet by night. There will be no need to "assume control" as you put it. No need for violence. All shall be done by stealth.'

He looked dubious. Well he might have been. Nearing Tophet, the most sensible thing for me to do would be to slip out of the wagon and leave the Tasmanian to his fate. With untold billions of tonnes of rock above his head, what hope had he, anyway, even if I *should* free him, of making good his escape and finding a way to the Earth's surface? I was too consumed by the task of finding Pandemonium to be much concerned about how or when I might see sun and sky. But if I had been in the Tasmanian's position, I think I would have so despaired of resurfacing that I might well have become resigned to the life of a caged animal.

Again, I put my eye to the rent in the wagon's covering. 'Be patient,' I said, keen to verbalize and add the balm of words, weasel words, to my conscience's hurt. Damaged, scrawny, pathetic, wounded thing that my conscience was, I was surprised at how successfully it defied my attempts to ignore it. 'I mean, even if I should set you free immediately, where exactly would you go?' Though it glimmered, shadow-less, with micro-organisms, the dusty plain seemed dead, a lifeless desert surrounded by jagged mountains and the umbrageous vault that substituted here, in the Netherworld, for sky.

I took the pipe from my mouth and exhaled. Then, putting my lips to the rent, tried to breath in a little fresh air. But the air outside was not much of an improvement on the fetid stuff that had become trapped within the wagon. I sat back and put the pipe back in my mouth. The toffee-flavoured smoke filled my lungs.

I spread my legs. At least, as much as I was able. And then, checking to see that my scabbard was not so arranged as to make the drawing of my sword impossible, I let my gaze settle upon my obese travelling companion.

He had abjured striking the bars with his crown and sat, head between his knees, staring at the cage's floor. The bruises on his face had largely healed, but the gashes on his shins, sustained on Snake Island when he had been panicked into belabouring his own body with an *itak*, still looked horribly raw.

'Men should never fight over a woman,' he slurred, as if a little punch-drunk.

I thought to remind him that our duel had only ostensibly been over a woman, and that the real reason I had wished to cut him to pieces was to rid the world of his loutishness. If fatigue and fatalism had not wormed themselves so deeply into me, I would, I think, still have felt like cutting him. But instead I merely said: 'I don't really want to talk about Gala.'

Gala. Saying her name evoked a whole iconography of women. Women who had been badly served, women who wait for letters that never come, whose prayers are forever unanswered. They called to me, '*Come home, Ritchie, come home.*' I had betrayed Gala just as I intended to betray the Tasmanian.

'We shouldn't have fought,' he added.

'Gala's *worth* fighting for,' I said. I had, some days earlier, told him of Gala's fate and how I hoped to redress it. He had surprised me by openly weeping.

'I thought you didn't want to talk about her?'

'Yeah, well—'

'That night, I was drunk,' he said.

'Drunk? Me too,' I said, a little surprised at myself for agreeing so readily. 'Anyway, you didn't really insult Gala, you know. Even if you had, I should hardly have taken you to task when I myself have insulted her so many times, in so many despicable ways.'

'Best all forgotten,' he said.

'Yeah,' I said, 'best forgotten.'

For a time we sat in silence.

'It was life at sea that led to my downfall,' said the Tasmanian, just when I had begun to relish the quiet.

Oh no, I thought. I had been treated to the Tasmanian's maudlin recollections before. 'If I had not taken to piracy—'

I switched off, as I have the ability to do when my boredom threshold is taxed. Seeking escape, I took a pellet of opium from my money belt. I had brought the substance along as emergency medication. But I had spent what seemed an eternity cramped inside the wagon. I needed a holiday from space and time.

I took a few puffs, then put the pipe aside. After a minute or so I turned my head and retched, the inevitable stream of clear, watery vomit splashing onto the straw-covered boards, with a few droplets sizzling as they hit the oil lamp. I hoped I had not inhaled too much. When I took opium for recreational purposes, I usually introduced the pellets into my body as a suppository. The effect was easier to control. But my backside was sore with sitting for so long. Besides which, I had no wish to present the Tasmanian with a sight that might provoke him to mockery.

I resisted the temptation of sleep. Instead, I concentrated and sought a favourite memory, so that, with the opium's help, I could relive it; enter, in effect, a virtual world, such as they in the ancient world made out of numbers and the lightning that flashes across the sky, a world constructed from engrams, the bric-à-brac of the past. I closed my eyes. On schedule, the visions came.

I open my eyes. A malignos *leans over me. Where am I? And then I remember. I am in the tunnels, the maze of shafts, mines, potholes and cavities that the enemy have constructed under London. I try to reach for my sword, but my arm refuses to obey. I seem to have lost a great deal of blood. The* malignos *is a female. I see that she is young, no more, perhaps, than sixteen or seventeen. In the blue light that fills the shored passageway, she seems to be praying. 'Who are you?' I say. 'What are you doing?'*

'Don't worry. I'm not one of the enemy,' she says. 'I serve humans. Been in the army for five years now. I've been sent in to get you.' I prop myself up on one elbow. About me lie the bodies of several malignos. *She seems to notice the look of sullen pleasure in my eyes. 'You've been busy.'*

'I was cut off from my men. I got lost.'

She brings her face close to mine, looking into my eyes, I think, to make sure the pupils are the same size, or do not otherwise betray signs consistent with brain damage; and then she runs her hands down my body. The cursory examination seems to satisfy her that I am fit to travel. As she supports me under the arm and lifts me into a sitting position her face comes close to my own. I feel her breath on my cheek and smell the musky scent that is peculiar to the malignos *female. I have smelt it before, of course, but at that moment I recognize its import for the first time. It is the scent of the alien, the perfume that sometimes drifts into this world from those that lie on the other side of life. It is, I know at once, something I have been seeking for a long, long time. I put an arm about her neck and draw her close. Her eyes are black, their sclera yellow, but not as with jaundice, but canary yellow, like a snake's, perhaps, or some other kind of reptile. The facial scales are tiny – diminutive versions of the silvery plates that cover her torso, arms and legs. They coruscate in the blue light so that she seems a piece of fanciful costume jewellery, a sapphire-encrusted charm. The hair falls over my chest, its strands soaking up a little of the blood that dribbles from my punctured doublet; and as the hair cascades down, the horns, the beautiful horns are the better displayed, the better to drive me crazy.*

But then the face undergoes metamorphosis. It is no longer the face of a beautiful, female malignos, *it is the face of a bat, small, dark and baleful, and the wings, which formerly spanned several metres, are now truly bat-like, scaled to match the face and compact body. All is suddenly a convulsive blur of fluttering membrane, a chaos of squeals, a confusion of snapping fangs . . .*

I shook the fumes from my head. Above, a hole had been chewed through the canvas. *Malignos* children, some no more than infants, flew about the wagon, buzzing like a congestion of bluebottles above a latrine.

One of their number clung to my chest, the hooks that extended from the leading edges of its wings snarled in my doublet. The child's face was only a few centimetres from my own. As it opened its mouth to try to bite me, I was almost overpowered by the stench of rotten meat. I grabbed it by one of its horns and ripped it away. There was a scream, followed by a tear of leather.

I held it up before my eyes. The child was begrimed with such a thick layer of dirt that it took a good few seconds before I could ascertain that my attacker was a little boy. With a spasm of disgust, I threw him across the wagon.

By now, at least a dozen other *malignos* children

weaved and circled about me. Wings clattered against
metal as they occasionally collided with the cage. The
children would collide with me, too, and, before I could
beat them off, often managed to sink their teeth into my
flesh. The Tasmanian cowered on the cage floor, protected, for the moment, by the steel bars. Through the
hole in the roof I could see others eager to join the fray.

I groped for my field glasses. Finding them, I slipped
the strap about my neck. Then I patted the front of my
doublet to check that the map – tightly folded into a
square and stowed under my clothes – was accounted
for. I drew my sword.

My sword-arm, I noticed, bore evidence of several
sets of bite marks, some of which welled with generous
beads of blood. If I had had the time, I would have
begun to worry about the chances of infection. The cage
was by now completely enshrouded by small, scaly
bodies. From within their compass I heard the muffled
cries of the Tasmanian.

I was conscious that we had stopped. I thrust *Espiritu
Santo* through the tear in the canvas that I had
employed as a spyhole and sawed downwards. Then I
sawed to one side. Pulling at the flap I had created, I
rolled out into space. I do not like to think I panicked. I
prefer to think that I took the only prudent option.

To have remained inside the wagon would have
surely proved fatal.

I hit the roadside and continued rolling. When I came
to rest half in, half out of a culvert, I saw that the air,
until recently suffused with mellow light, was now
black with *malignos*, a swarm that must have totalled in
the tens, perhaps hundreds of thousands. Though they

RICHARD CALDER

seemed at first an undifferentiated mass, I could tell, by
the faces that hurtled by and the cries of those farther
off, that they, like the *malignos* that had invaded the
wagon, were children, infants; some – it seemed all the
more horrible – grinning, malicious babes-in-arms.

The caravan extended along the road. It was over
thirty wagons long. Each wagon was harnessed to the
next, with only the foremost wagon harnessed to a team
of horses. On that wagon stood the crone, Madam
Tetrallini, attended by her sons and dogs. In response to
the present crisis, the whole family, mutant and canine
alike, was either sprawled on the roof or crowded about
the driver's seat. Madame Tetrallini had risen in order
to use her whip. The children were attacking the horses.

Three of her team of twelve had already succumbed,
their hides picked raw. *Malignos* swarmed over the
fallen, quivering bodies like flies. One horse had been
disembowelled, and several infants played in the
steaming innards that spilled across the road.

The murderous children had, for the moment, forgotten me. But I knew that if they succeeded in killing
and eating the entire team of horses then, even if I were
to survive this encounter, I would be stranded in the
wilderness. With little water or food, I would have no
hope of reaching Tophet.

Waving my sword above my head to dissuade the
attacking *malignos* from getting too near, I ran alongside
the caravan, my shoulder chafing against its contours.
What did I care, now, if I were discovered by the family
Tetrallini? The question of whether I should attempt
escape while travelling over the plain, or wait until
reaching Tophet's outskirts, had become ridiculously

academic. I had to find a mount. I had to get out of this slaughterhouse. And I had to do it now.

I closed upon the lead wagon. The swarm thickened about me. Ahead, two of Madame Tetrallini's sons had jumped down onto the roadside. Their scimitars cut impotently at the air, children darting between their legs, circling about their heads, as if teasing them for their ineffective swipes and thrusts. I ran past them and positioned myself amidst the traces, determined to salvage a steed.

Almost blinded by the density of the swarm, I slashed to right and left, sometimes feeling a thrill of satisfaction as *Espiritu Santo* connected and sent a dark shudder through my forearm. The old woman's horsewhip snaked and cracked. I assumed that her ire was concentrated upon the children. But then I felt the whip cross my cheek and leave a burning weal in its wake. At seeing a human materialize before her, she had instinctively reverted to her role of freakshow proprietress.

'Madame,' I cried, 'look to the children!'

'Back to your cage!' she cried, 'back to your cage!'

One of the little old woman's sons put his hand upon her shoulder. 'He's got clothes on, Ma. And they're soldiers clothes, too. He's not one of ours, Ma, he's not one of our *freaks*.' I saw that he had hold of a dog. As his inbred features compressed themselves into a grimace, his big meaty digits fumbled with its leash.

'The children!' I reiterated. 'If we don't stop them savaging the horses, we'll be stranded! We'll die!' Still the whip snaked at me. I put up an arm to protect myself, weals now criss-crossing the bite marks that I had incurred earlier. 'Help me,' I screamed, 'you incestuous bunch of pinheaded bumpkins, or suffer the consequences!'

The whip curled about my arm. I managed to grab it. Pulling, I jerked its stock out of the old woman's hand. At that moment, a pack of *malignos* fell out of the sky and fastened themselves upon her. Others followed, their numbers such that she was soon enveloped in a seething mass of scaly flesh. Her son tried to leap clear, but both he and his dog were overwhelmed before they hit the ground. One after another, the remaining members of Madame Tetrallini's brood succumbed, clawing hopelessly at the infant bodies that knotted themselves about them.

I was so distracted by the sight of the family's sudden and awful demise that it did not occur to me why I should be spared.

The swarm dispersed. It regrouped high above, skirting the blackness that obscured the cavern's vault. Doll-like faces flitted in and out of visibility.

Apart from a few infants who scavenged amongst the remains, and a handful of older children, I was alone. The older children hovered above the wagon. During the war, *malignos* children were often used for special operations. Their wing-to-body ratio was superior to adults. It allowed them to take off from a stationary position, and also to hover. They formed a line, the youngest and smallest at either end, and in the middle a boy of about nine or ten years, who seemed to be their chief. He stared down at me with vacant, tranquil eyes.

'We have had word of you,' said the little chieftain. 'It is Captain Pike, is it not?' Though he spoke English, it was heavily inflected with the sound-shape of the *malignos* tongue, and it was necessary for me to pause a while to decipher what he had said.

'I am Richard Pike, captain of the Darkling Isle, yes.'

'Well, how do you do, captain. I am Delville. They say that you were involved in a disagreement with the family de Profundis?'

'If killing four of their number constitutes a disagreement, I stand guilty.'

'You admit it?'

'It would be redundant to deny it, since you are undoubtedly apprised of the situation. Of course I killed them. After what they had done to Gala, that is, Aberattzia de Profundis, I *had* to kill them.'

'They made her drink *manggagawa*. We know.'

'Are you here then to avenge those I killed?' I made a few insouciant passes with my sword. I don't know whether or not my swagger impressed them, but it did nothing to assuage the coldness that was bubbling up from my entrails and threatening to freeze my heart. Delville smiled and shook his head.

'The Countess Suspiria of Wormwood has alerted the authorities that you are in the depths. Fear her, if you will. Fear all *malignos*. But do not fear us. Ours is a chance encounter. We do not hunt you. In fact, as soon as I guessed that it was *you* standing there, I called my companions off. Those who fight and kill grown-ups are safe from us. We too are hunted. We too seek redemption.' I let my gaze run along the line of children. And then I again focused on Delville.

'Who exactly are you?' I sheathed my sword.

'Grown-ups call us the Exaltation,' said Delville. 'We hide in those places in the Netherworld where *malignos* no longer choose to live. Abandoned places. Places where there are none to fetter us, or discipline us, or make us into what we would not be. We are abandoned ourselves. Street children, you call us on Earth-Above. For centuries, we have flocked together, and moved from place to place, until we have come to constitute the swarm you see today. And still we have not found a home.'

'And you feed on your own kind?'

'We much prefer humans. When the war raged, there was a great deal of such meat to be had. But these days?' Delville briefly glanced over his shoulder, surveying the wagons that extended behind him along the road. Then he turned to look at me. 'I have been led to understand there are many humans in this caravan.' He licked his lips.

One of the other children, a tiny girl, trained an eager gaze upon her leader. 'There are *lots* of humans,' she said. 'But they're in cages, Delville. We can't get at them.'

'If you look inside Madame Tetrallini's wagon,' I said, unable to feel much loyalty for the bestialized examples of humanity that had constituted the freakshow, 'I'm sure you'll find a set of keys.'

'Excellent.'

Delville gave the order. A lieutenant dived through one of the ragged holes that the attacking swarm had chewed in the canvas.

I felt a tug on my trouser leg. I looked down. An infant who had been stuffing his face full of carrion had detached himself from his prey. He stood looking up at me, his gore-besmirched mouth beaming with merriment. And then he soared into the sky to join his playmates. Soon, only skeletons and the odd infant with a bone in its mouth, like some vicious teething ring, remained.

I looked back up at Delville. 'Might I ask one favour?' I said. But he had anticipated me.

'We have saved a horse for you, captain. You are free to go.' I turned, and saw that not one, but three horses had been spared. Perhaps, I thought, they planned to complement the human meat that would form the *pièce de résistance* of their banquet with a little horseflesh *tartare*.

'Thank you, Delville. But there is a human I would like to take with me.' He frowned, as if debating whether he could afford to spare, not just another choice cut of *homo sapien*, but the fine equine steak that would necessarily accompany the granting of such a boon.

'Very well,' he said. 'You take one human and *two* horses. But no more. Do you understand?' The child who had sought the keys reappeared, his mission successful. 'Come with me, captain,' he continued, taking the keys from the child and jingling them in the air. 'We will free your friend. And then you must leave us. Where does your journey take you?'

'To Tophet,' I said.

'Then you will have gone deeper into the Nether-world than most humans. I will not ask what you seek there. I will only ask that you make mischief. It will give me some pleasure to know that our mutual enemies are due, in some small way, to have their miserable, mean-spirited little lives confounded.'

'Oh, I think you can bank on me doing that.'

He flew some way ahead, then, pausing, waited for me to catch up with him. I hurried down the road, checking off the wagons until I located the one that had been my prison for five interminable days. 'Freaks,' mused Delville, from a little way off. 'The *malignos* think of all you humans as freaks. How good it makes them feel to cage you, or have you perform tricks, or, like the daring Countess Suspiria, take you to their beds and have you pleasure them. Such resentment my people feel, captain. And such envy!'

I opened the flap I had earlier cut in the canvas, put a foot on the spoke of a wheel and got ready to haul myself inside.

'I will have two horses saddled and ready, captain. Do not keep us waiting. You would not want to be here when the feeding starts, I think.'

'My friend and I are hungry ourselves,' I said. I was somewhat light-headed from my diet of gruel. The Tasmanian had warned me that the rotten mushrooms and pieces of meat that supplemented our diet were drugged, and I had, perforce, kept my calorie intake to a minimum. 'We'll need water and food,' I added. 'Good food.'

'Of course. You may take what is in the lead wagon. My people disdain to eat rat-meat and fungi.' One of my epaulettes had become entangled with a splinter. I jerked it free. 'I wish you safe passage,' he continued. 'It will be satisfying to know that we have helped introduce a bogeyman into one of the Netherworld's most celebrated cities, even if it is highly probable you will not live long enough to make *serious* mischief. But I wish you well, nevertheless.'

I crawled into the wagon. As I did, I shot him a quick, backward glance.

'I told you before, Delville,' I said. 'I'll make mischief all right. *Serious* mischief. You can bank on it.'

We rode across the plain, the Tasmanian's horse, with its heavier burden, a length behind my own. I would continually ask myself: *Why have I brought him along?* He would, it is true, be of some use in a fight. His weight gave him an edge, even though his combat skills were ludicrously basic. He might also prove of use when I came to the Sea of Sammael. He had, as he had repeatedly and tediously confessed, been a sailor in his time. Indeed, it seemed he emanated from a clan of Tasmanian sea gypsies. He might, he suggested, be able to advise me on what kind of boat to steal and how best to survive the maelstrom.

I hoped I hadn't brought him along out of pity. I couldn't afford pity. Pity would get me killed, and then Gala would be without hope.

I dug my heels into my steed's flanks, urging the black mare on towards Tophet.

Chapter Eight

With one foot set firmly behind me, I leant over and peered into the abyss. The edge crumbled a little, spilling dirt into the void. I stepped back, looked to my left, and then to my right. It was as if the plain had been sheared off, like a tabletop that had had an axe taken to it.

The abyss stretched to the horizon, displacing the outlying mountains. My eyes were as incapable of determining its width as its depth and breadth. Perhaps the abyss possessed infinite extensity; perhaps it was bottomless; perhaps it had no farther side. It was a morbid conceit, I knew, but I felt that I stood at the end of the world, staring into the absolute vacancy of the universe's *ne plus ultra*.

I turned about. The road, that had been terminated with such abruptness, receded to its vanishing point, an unbroken, rectilinear line. It crossed the same gloomy plain that, some hundreds of kilometres distant, hosted the gnawed bones of Madame Tetrallini's carnival of humanity.

'There's no way across,' I said.

'Obviously,' said the Tasmanian. He sat cross-legged, pouring over the map, his posture, coupled with the rotundity of his belly, summoning up certain images I had of dead, oriental deities. I had unfolded the parchment the moment we had arrived, unable to

114

comprehend how neither bridge nor pass offered itself for our deliverance.

'There's really no indication of how we should proceed?'

'Not on the map.'

Again, I ventured to the edge. Splinters of rock flaked off and fell into the abyss. I steeled myself and maintained my position, surveying the black well and the impenetrable wall of darkness opposite. 'Do we go across, or down?'

'Down,' said the Tasmanian. 'The road, according to the map, re-emerges in Tophet, some way beneath us.'

'But there is no clue as to what lies between here and below? No clue as to what means of conveyance may make such a journey possible?'

'Nothing.'

'You can see no connecting road?'

'Nothing.'

I stooped, picked up a stone and hurled it into the darkness. I turned my ear into the path in which I hoped the sound of impact, ricochet or echo would travel back to me. But the abyss kept its secrets to itself. There was only silence.

'The sides seem sheer,' I said, 'but there must be some sort of crossing or means of descent. Madame Tetrallini travelled this way many a time. I mean, how on earth did *she* negotiate passage? It doesn't make sense.' The Tasmanian looked up and met my gaze. I looked up. The sight of his fat, baby-smooth nakedness pained me, but the added torment of locking eyes with him made the sight unbearable. I longed for an argument, so that I might have the benefit of tempered steel to maintain a decent interval between us.

'Where did you get this map from, anyway?' he said. 'And how do you know it shows the way to Pandemonium?'

'It doesn't. Not exactly. But if we follow it we'll come to an underground river which will take us through some of the Netherworld's principal cities. Eventually, it *must* deliver us to Pandemonium. It stands to reason. Besides, Countess Suspiria told me so.'

'What?'

'Was that exclamation rhetorical?' I asked, exhausted by his brute effusions, which, that day, had been unusually common. 'Or are you so stupid as to have failed to have understood what I said?'

He snorted. 'You believe what a *malignos* has told you? She probably meant to send you to your death. You're naïve, man. Naïve.'

'We have no other option.'

'We should try to reach the surface.'

'If you wish to retrace your steps, you're of course free to do so. But I'm determined to fulfil the task I've set myself. I will find Pandemonium or perish in the attempt.'

'Naïve,' he muttered, though less sure of himself now. He knew we had not enough water and food to attempt to re-cross the plain to Wormwood. Whether he regretted following me or not, for him, as much as for me, hope of getting out of the Netherworld alive lay in pressing onward.

'Naïve, eh? Whatever I am, our immediate problem is finding a way to Tophet.' He sighed and fell to studying the map. I spun about, no longer able to bear the sight of him. Alas, my peripheral vision still registered the blatant rolls of fat, the rippling folds and ruddy stains that characterized the fleshy temple of his damnable spirit. 'We need to get you some clothes,' I said. His gaze remained focused on the wrinkled parchment. He had acquired the ability, of late, to disregard my little comments quite effortlessly. With a hiss of contempt, I resumed my scanning of the abyss.

Sometimes, in the chasm's enigmatic perspective, I seemed to descry pinpricks of light. My eyes, it seemed, were gradually adjusting to the darkness. More pinpricks became evident. They shone in the abyss's darkest depths, like stars reflected in the bottom of a well. But there seemed to be a portion of that inverted night sky that was starless. It was a rocky promontory. It lay beneath my feet, not more than a hundred metres below. As my eyes relaxed, I could just make out, perched on its jagged overhang, the phantasmal outline of a dwelling. I leant over as much as I dared, my throat knotting with an inarticulate cry of triumph.

The dwelling seemed, incredibly, to be a tavern. I could see its sign, swinging in the up-draught, and, now that I concentrated all my senses upon it, could *hear* the sign, too, creaking and moaning on its rusty hinges.

'Come here,' I said, as calmly as I was able.

'Why?'

I screwed my head about and shot him an angry glance. 'Just come here.' Though he rolled his eyes towards the stony heavens, the Tasmanian saw fit to comply. He folded the map and rising first into a squat, pulled himself fully upright into the semblance of a biped, if one that appeared to barely know the rudiments of civilized life. He walked over to me. 'Look down here,' I said.

He studied me with intense suspicion. Perhaps he thought I might take the opportunity of pushing him over the edge, to test, by the shifting timbre and volume of his screams, the abyss's depth. I kept myself at arm's length, as if to offer reassurance that, despite his mistrust – not wholly unjustified, given our history – I had no intention of employing him as an improvised plumb line. He took up the same posture as myself and peered over the rim.

'What am I looking for?'

'Keep looking,' I said. 'Immediately below you. Can't you see?'

'See? There's nothing *to* see. Just blackness.' He held up a hand, palm towards me. 'Wait. I do see something. What is it? A building?'

'A tavern,' I said. 'If you can believe it. I wonder if we can find a way down there.' I saw now that, connected to the tavern, was a tower. It had the appearance of a bell tower, one whose octagonal belfry had been decorated with stained glass.

'There may be food,' he said.

'There may, more to the point, be some answers to our predicament: how to negotiate a descent into this nothingness.'

'There'll be no walkway. You can be sure of that. Not so far into the Netherworld as this. No humans get so deep, except those in cages. And *malignos* would simply fly down there.' I could see that what he said was true. There were no steps. The precipice that separated us from the promontory dropped away into the shadows without hint of anything, artificial or natural, that might assist our descent.

'But they wouldn't be able to fly their *wagons* down there, would they? There must be some kind of hidden road. There *must* be.'

'We'll have to climb,' he said. I stared at him, and, as incredulity turned to amusement, began to laugh.

'Even with ropes, I'd find that descent a difficult one. But for a man your size—'

He handed me the map. I folded it up and tucked it back into the front of my doublet. And then the Tasmanian eased himself down upon his belly and, prone upon the ground, extended an arm and probed the invisible rock face beneath him. 'There are handholds,' he said.

'But we don't have anything with which to belay each other.'

'Don't worry. I've shinned up the rigging of ships with masts so tall you'd think they touched the sky. I can make it.'

'Worry?' I said, kneeling down beside him. 'Perhaps there is no alternative to what you suggest. And if you're willing to bell the cat, I suppose it's your affair.' I looked down into the spangled darkness, and then back over my shoulder at the two black steeds that had carried us over the plain. 'We'll have to leave the horses.'

'They've done their work.'

And, I thought, consumed too much food and water. The provisions we had left were so scant that I carried them in my belt and looped about my shoulder and neck. 'Then would you care to proceed? I wouldn't like to have you fall on top of me.'

He tested the ground before him and swore as rock crumbled at his touch. Then, rolling away from me, repeated the operation several more times at regular intervals. At last, he found a spot where the rim was made of solid granite.

I strolled over to him, expecting a plea for assistance. There was none. As I approached he swung his legs peremptorily over the edge. The rest of him followed, so that, for a moment, he was suspended in space, his knuckles whitening as his grip tightened on the thin, granite verge that spared him from the void. I wondered at the strength required to support such a weight. The fat obviously hid well-tuned muscles. One hand disappeared, and then the other. I lay flat on the ground, my neck resting on the rim, my head poking out into nothingness. The Tasmanian's head and shoulders were visible to me. The rest of his body was shrouded in shadows. He had descended several metres.

'Don't take all day,' he shouted, looking up. 'Follow me, and I'll give you some idea of where to put your hands and feet. And hurry up about it, I'm working up a *sweat* here.'

Though aggrieved at being ordered about, I appreciated the practical wisdom of what he said. In the tunnels beneath London I had always carried rope, chocks and karabiners. My ability as a freeform climber was limited. And I was in sore need of guidance.

I positioned myself parallel to the line of the rim and tentatively let one leg dangle into the emptiness.

'A little to your left,' shouted the Tasmanian. 'That's

it.' The toe of my boot connected with a protrusion. I tested it with my weight, then, following the Tasmanian's advice, swung my other leg over the side and found a corresponding hold. In this manner, trusting to the barked commands of my travelling companion, I began my descent into the abyss.

As I descended, I began to see more clearly. My eyes were now partly shielded from the light that filled the great cavern above, and I found it easier to resolve the delineations and patterns that informed the surrounding void. Far away, I seemed to descry the chasm's farther wall, glimmering dully like a cracked, dusty mirror. The lights that studded the darkness beneath my feet shone more brightly. And the tavern stood out in bold relief against the outcrop of grey stone. I saw how precarious was its situation, balanced, as it was, upon that promontory's furthermost lip.

I had a good head for heights, and I continued to gaze down, unperturbed by the fathomless perspective. A sight loomed out of the shadows that had me sighing with relief. Some metres below, the abyss's vertical face showed evidence of a gradient. Before long my feet connected with the slope. And though the going was steep, I felt confident that I could now make it unassisted to the comparative safety of the promontory. It was fortunate that my rock-climbing was no longer so stringently tested. The Tasmanian had ceased to shout out advice. He concentrated, instead, on traversing the incline to avoid having to tackle another sheer drop that began just a little way beneath us. I copied and moved crabwise, my feet and hands dislodging rocks and pebbles and sending them tumbling into space.

I could feel the draught now, the same one that animated the tavern's sign and made it creak and moan. I glanced towards the source of that eerie noise, and saw that the promontory was quite near. The Tasmanian was already above it. A scree led down, and though its gradient was severe, it presented a welcome alternative to the sheerness of the rock that lay above, below and to either side.

The Tasmanian slid down the scree on his back, a small avalanche of weathered stone accompanying him. A few minutes later, I followed.

I picked myself up from where I had landed. Then I looked about to satisfy myself that I was not in danger of immediately plummeting into space. The Tasmanian was waiting. He sat on a boulder, looking twice as beaten-up as usual, inspecting the cuts and abrasions that his naked body had sustained during the descent. The tavern's front door was no more than a dozen paces away.

Though each of us had shouted while clambering down the rock face, we seemed to suddenly find it necessary to whisper.

'It's abandoned,' said the Tasmanian, 'like everything else on the plain. I'd say nobody's lived here for some time.'

'I'm not so sure,' I said. The tavern was dilapidated. The guttering had come away. It hung in strips. And the roof was missing large areas of slate. The rafters, for the most part, were bare. But a ghostly light shone through the ground-floor windows. The tavern was, perhaps, only temporarily abandoned. Its inhabitants might lurk nearby.

Malignos

We walked up to one of the tavern's windows. It was so dirty that it was impossible to peer inside. A little way off, the front door stood ajar. Above it, the sign – painted with the image of a helix, beneath which were the hieroglyphics of the *malignos* tongue – swayed and made its familiar music. The Tasmanian followed my gaze.

'Can you read that?' he said.

'I don't have much *malignos*,' I said, trying to decipher the symbols one by one. 'It says something like *roadhouse* or *bridge-house*. I can't translate it exactly.'

'Hmm. It sounds hopeful.'

I walked up to the door and slowly pushed it open. Inside was a parlour with a hammer-beam ceiling, along its opposite wall, a bar. Behind the bar were several tall, thin vases. They were ranged beneath the rows of kegs. Each vase contained a spray of bioluminescent vegetation. The dull light accentuated the tavern's haunted atmospherics, and accounted for the ghostly illumination that had been visible from outside. After the shadowy oppression of the abyss, the light seemed welcoming. A staircase ran up the length of one wall and disappeared into the tavern's second floor.

The Tasmanian elbowed his way past me and crossed the room. He squeezed behind the bar. Positioning himself in front of one of the kegs, he took a wooden flagon from off a hook, blew the dust from it, and, holding it under the tap, filled it full of frothy beer. He flung back his head and drained it at one gulp. With the ostentatious gesture of a true vulgarian, he slammed the flagon down upon the counter, wiped his lips, belched and turned to face me. 'I told you the place was abandoned.'

'Your manners have not improved,' I said. 'It is fortunate that we are not in *Nightriders*. I do not think I could tolerate such plebeian hideousness on home ground.'

'I get the feeling that toleration isn't one of your strong points.' I put his pathetic attempt at character assassination out of mind. I was more interested in what he had said about the tavern. It did indeed appear unoccupied, despite my earlier intimation that we were not alone. Not that this checked my disquiet.

The disquiet grew. I inspected my surroundings, my ears pricking at every complaint of the floorboards, every murmur of the denuded eaves. 'I'd better look upstairs,' I said. I hoped I was deceived. I hoped the Tasmanian was right. I hoped that my search would prove fruitless. But wartime experience had taught me never to ignore the promptings of intuition.

I put my hand on the pommel of my sword and walked across the room to the bar. Leaning over the counter, I grasped a vase, picked it up and proceeded to the stairs, my senses straining to detect signs of sentient life, both amongst the sounds that percolated through the tavern, and the shadows that swirled above me.

I mounted the stairs. With my right hand I drew *Espiritu Santo*, while holding the vase in my left. Its light sent the shadows into retreat until they regrouped about the stairway's summit. Glancing backward, I saw that the Tasmanian was helping himself to another beer. His complacency jarred my nerves, and my flesh, already twitching from the travail of our descent, began to fibrillate in earnest. I averted my eyes and looked ahead, attempting to discern whether any living form had taken refuge in the darkness and was preparing to ambush me.

When I put my foot on the last stair, the shadows resolved, and I saw that I stood at the threshold of a bedchamber. A four-poster dominated the room. Its curtain posts were draped with cobwebs. I moved nearer. Then, extending my sword-arm, I cut some of the webbing free.

I gazed through the hole I had made. Two figures lay on the bed. The pair were *malignos* and, to judge by their state of mummification, had been dead many years.

I gave a start. My ears had registered a shrill, almost hypersonic cry. The noise seemed to be coming from beneath the bedlinen. I cut away a little more webbing – my sword now matted with the stuff, as if it were a stick of hoary candy floss – and put the tip of *Espiritu Santo* under the corner of the counterpane. Then I flipped the thick, musty quilt back upon itself. A girl-child huddled on a damp patch of linen, looking up at me between splayed fingers.

'And what the hell are *you* doing here?' I said. I was too astonished to appreciate that my question had, given the circumstances, been somewhat common-place. It was just as well. The notion that I had committed an unpardonable act of banality would have disconcerted me far more than the unveiling of that demonic child.

She spoke, but it was in *malignos*, and I could only understand the occasional word. It did not help that her voice still shifted into a hypersonic register. The sound reminded me of the echolocation of a baby rat, which she, with her folded wings and sooty little face, so resembled. The squeals, clicks and bangs continued, relentless. I stamped my foot upon the floor. 'I said what are you doing here? Who are you? And what is this place?' She stopped her noise-making, and gazed moodily up at me through thick eyelashes. 'Come child,' I concluded, 'tell!'

'There's no need to *shout*,' she said, in thickly-accented English. 'I live here. Okay? What's it to you?'

The sharp concussion of my foot against the floor-boards had brought the Tasmanian running up the stairs. On seeing the child, he gasped, and seemed to shrink, both vertically and laterally, as if his balloon-like corpulence had been pricked by a pin. I fancied that he felt he was again in his cage, waiting to be savaged by the Exaltation.

He scurried over to me, his torso bent like a soldier advancing on enemy lines who instinctively strives to protect his head from arrows or musket-shot. But far from defending herself, or launching into counter-attack, the little girl on the bed began to laugh.

'Oh, he has no clothes on!' she said. 'Just like the humans in the *freakshow*! Has Madame Tetrallini come?'

'That divertissement, *little* Madame,' I said, 'is but a memory.'

'You mean—'

'I mean it can no longer titillate your precocious craving for grotesque and cruel delights. It does not exist, little Madame. It has been destroyed. It is no more.'

'Oh,' she said. She looked up at the four-poster's canopy, her brow knitting with thought. 'I bet it was the Exaltation, wasn't it?'

'Well, there you have it, my dear.'

'I'm going to join them. They've asked me to, you know. The swarm often passes this way. And why shouldn't I join them? I can't live *here* much longer. Not now that' – she looked over at the two corpses – 'not now that Grandma and Grandpa are dead.'

I placed the vase on the night table and sat down on the edge of the bed. 'How long have you been here by yourself?' I said.

'I'm not sure,' she said. 'When they got sick, they told me that I would have to do their work until they got better. But now I'm a big girl I know they're not *going* to get better. And so few people come this way any more. I wonder at the point of it all. The Netherworld east of Tophet is practically *empty*. I feel sort of redundant.'

'We're going to Tophet,' said the Tasmanian, warily approaching. 'How do we get there?'

The child looked at him and then broke into another fit of giggles.

'Take one of the sheets,' I said to him, 'and wrap it about yourself. We'll never get anything out of her if you keep making her laugh.'

'Don't take from the bed,' said the girl, frowning, a real little Madame now, a regular devil-doll of a scold. 'Look in the drawers.' The Tasmanian traipsed over to the chiffonier. It stood beneath the room's single window. He opened a drawer and pulled out a big, white sheet. Then he wound it about himself like a toga. 'If you weren't human, I'd take you for one of the

Resplendent,' she said. 'They wear clothes too!'

'The Resplendent!' said the Tasmanian, still a little rattled, and now more than a little exasperated. 'First the Exaltation and now the *Resplendent*?'

'That's what the *malignos* call their undertakers,' I said. 'The only creatures in the Netherworld who don't go naked. Apart from the Countess Suspiria, that is.'

The Tasmanian gave a shiver of disgust.

'Where we're going,' I said, 'it might not be such a bad thing if *both* of us were assumed to be undertakers. Better to look like *malignos* than to be revealed for what we are: an escaped freak and a murdering, thieving human soldier.'

The Tasmanian sighed, resignedly. 'I guess you're right.' The girl looked at him afresh, her eyes narrowing, as if she were determined to make up for being denied the treat of seeing Madam Tetrallini's show.

'Humans,' mused the girl. 'Mmm. I always felt a little sorry for those *freaks* of Madame's. It's just that when her carnival passed this way Grandpa always said I had to look on account of Papa being killed in the war. But I never did what Grandpa and Grandma used to do. I never used to spit or swear or anything. The poor, caged things seemed to have enough to contend with.'

'Your delicacy of sentiment,' I said, 'does you credit.'

I reached out with the intention of petting the child. If she were to freely volunteer information I calculated that I would have to win not just her trust, but her friendship. She drew back sharply, sucking her lower lip, her eyes aflame. Friendship, perhaps, was out of the question.

'You're not to touch me,' she said.

'I'm sorry. I didn't mean—'

'You're a soldier, aren't you? You're dressed like a soldier. You've as much as *said* you're a soldier. A thief, you said, and a murderer too. Are you one of the ones who killed my Papa?' Possibly, I almost replied. But only if your Papa had been recruited into the goblin armies that had invaded London. I bit my tongue.

'I'm not a soldier any more. The war's over.' I sheathed my sword, in an attempt to be the more convincing. The girl shook her head.

'But we're not at peace. Not really. What about the humans still kept in the Netherworld? The ones in the freakshow, the ones who work in the rat farms, the ones whom the great ladies and gentlemen of Tophet keep as domestic pets?' But the fate of those missing in action concerned me, at that moment, not at all.

'The freakshow,' I said. 'For the moment, let us forget the freakshow. Let us equally forget rat farms and domestic pets. But Tophet? Ah. Tell me how my friend and I might get to Tophet, and I, little Madame, will forever be in your debt.'

'Don't you know?'

'You still haven't told us the nature of this place,' I said.

She drew herself up, like an infant prodigy of the stage, a little melodramatic villainess. 'The *nature* of this place? Why, if it's illumination you need, you've come to the right person. I am the mistress of the light,' she said. 'I can tell, indeed *show*, you all.' I inclined my head in a bow.

'And you can help us, mistress?'

'Maybe,' she said, 'if you tell me a story.'

'A story?' I looked at the Tasmanian, eager to have him understand that we would humour the girl. An uncalculated remark, particularly if accompanied by the sort of ribaldry that characterized his more bibulous utterances, could easily wreck my efforts to gain her trust. He placed a finger on the side of his nose and gave an enormous wink. I treated him to a smile, cold, sickly and minacious. Then I refocused on the girl. 'Yes, I can tell you a story,' I continued, my smile metamorphosing into one that, at a pinch, might pass for avuncular.

'Then I'll take you to where you can see Tophet.'

'We'd certainly like to see Tophet.' I glanced at the Tasmanian, determined to bring him into the plot. 'Wouldn't we?' He nodded, the idiotic smile on his face probably mirroring my own. 'I know *I'd* like to see Tophet. But what we really want to do is *go* there.'

'You'll understand,' she said. 'You'll understand soon enough.' The girl slid over the edge of the bed and walked up to me. She took my hand. 'Come,' she said. 'I'll show you the way. And you too,' she added, glancing at the Tasmanian. 'Come. Let me take you to the tower.'

She led me down the stairs, through the tavern's front door and out onto the promontory. As we walked, I told her a story my father had told me at bedtime. The story of The Dead Man and the Princess of the Rats. 'I like rats,' she said, as I came to the part where the man who had been raised from the dead set sail with his consort across the Seven Seas. I was glad of her interruption. I had quite forgot how the tale ended.

'She wasn't a real rat,' I said. 'She was one of those humans who had reshaped themselves so that their bodies more accurately reflected their inner lives.'

'One of my ancestors, you mean?'

'Well, they do say that the *malignos* are primarily descended from those amongst the perverse who called themselves rat people.'

'I know,' she said. 'That's why I like rats. I *do* wish we didn't have to eat them. They taste yummy, but they're such nice, pretty animals. They deserve better, don't you think?' I would have to make sure, I thought, to liberate any rat-meat that the tavern might have in its larder. With beer and food to sustain us, the Tasmanian and I might be able to travel many hundreds of kilometres without having to worry about encroaching on a *malignos* settlement to restock our supplies. 'There're lots of rat farms in Tophet. You'll like it there, I'm sure.' I looked down at her. With her wings, long pointed ears and beady eyes, she was like a little bat, for sure. But, as she had been ready to attest, there was also much of the rat about her. Rats and *malignos*; *malignos* and rats. I was brought to mind of the war, and of a passage I had read in a grimoire just prior to going underground for the first time: '*Of course those who don't know drains think horrible things: but under this London are miles and miles – hundreds of miles – and a few days' rain and London empty will leave them sweet and clean. The main drains are big enough and airy enough for anyone. Then there's cellars, vaults, stores, from which bolting passages may be made to the drains. And the railway tunnels and subways . . .*' It had long been my opinion that this passage – a piece of marginalia scrawled next to a diagram illustrating some principle of hydrodynamics – might be attributed, not, in this instance, to the Ancients at all, but rather to the *malignos's* rat-like ancestors.

We stood beneath the tower. Though unconnected to the tavern, it seemed built out of the same rocks. But it was obviously older, much older. Darkness hung about its belfry like a murky fog.

The door to the tower was unlocked. I put my hand on its brassy knob and pulled it open. Inside, a stairway spiralled upward. 'Carry me,' said the girl. 'And finish the story.' I picked her up and began to climb the stairs, keeping close to the wall's curve, mindful that there was no guardrail. No bioluminescence, here. Corbels followed the stone steps as they wound their way around the walls. And into each corbel had been fitted a lantern. The smell of burning fish oil filled the tower's confines. The Tasmanian brought up the rear with the same lithe disdain for gravity that he had displayed when descending into the abyss.

'The rat princess,' I said, still no clearer about how the story might end. Frantically, I began to improvise. 'The rat princess was such a good little girl. Whenever she met less fortunate individuals than herself, such as wayfarers who were lost, and who needed guidance, she would always, *always* help them.' She had lain nuzzled against my chest, her horns scuffing the leather of my doublet, content. But now she began to fidget, her eyes flashing beneath her thick, curly brows.

'That's not the story at all,' she said.

'Oh,' I said, 'but the way *I* tell it has a happy ending.'

'It does?'

'Most certainly. The princess doesn't die. She becomes a saint.'

'A saint?'

'A very good person. Someone who is revered and intercedes on the behalf of others. Are *you* that princess?'

We circled the tower, each revolution of the stairway taking us nearer to the floorboards that partitioned off the belfry. We passed through an open trap. The stairway levelled out. I had been quite mistaken, it seemed. This was no bell tower. In the middle of the octagonal room was a great lamp, surrounding it a series of prisms and mirrors. *Roadhouse* or *bridge-house* had been my muddled interpretation of the hieroglyphics inscribed on the tavern's sign. The correct interpretation was *lighthouse.*

The girl let go of my hand and walked up to an array of levers that rose from a bay in the floor. She grasped the handle of one and, pulling with all her weight, succeeded in bringing it almost level with her knees, whereupon it seemed to engage with cogs, gears and ratchets. There was a rumble. Vibrations from beneath the floorboards coursed up my legs, and the stained glass windows that surrounded us swung upward, so that the turret was exposed to the perpetual night of the abyss.

A gust of cool air tousled my hair. I walked to the balustrade which circled the perimeter of the turret. Gripping the iron rail with my hands I leant over and gazed down into the black nothingness. The pinpricks of light – diamonds spread out on the black velvet cloth of a display case – were still evident. The tower was situated on the very edge of the promontory. The sheerness of the drop seemed intent on pulling me into the abyss's depths. I eased myself back.

'Go and join him, fat man,' I heard the girl say. 'Go on. Don't you want to see Tophet? Go on, or you'll miss the fun.' I heard another lever being depressed.

The abyss suddenly filled with brilliance.

My first reaction was to spin about and confront the source of light, despite the flagrant inadvisability of doing so. I gasped and held my hands to my eyes. The candlepower was enormous. My optic nerves were accustomed to the sullen illumination that had pervaded the vast interconnected caverns that I had passed through in my journey from Mt Pinatubo. The light that shone from the lighthouse's great lamp was of quite a different magnitude. Violent, almost physical, it bathed me with a pure, white refulgence that seemed to pass straight through my body, each cell pierced as if by a hot needle. I turned my back on it, peeped through my fingers, and found that, bright as the abyss now was, it was a brightness that was sufferable. I placed my hands back on the rail and gazed down in wonder, careless, now, of the precipice's vertiginous power.

The pinpricks now revealed themselves to be fires. They emanated from cauldrons of burning oil situated along the galleries and balconies of great, spire-like structures that poked above what might have been a sooty bank of mist or – strange as the hypothesis seemed, even as I had formulated it – a bank of cloud cover. The farther side of the abyss was nearer than I had supposed and gleamed like a full moon. The rock face immediately below shone more dully than the wall opposite, having only reflected light by which to reveal itself. But it was those uncanny, spire-like buildings that solicited most of my attention. This was no rag-and-bone settlement such as I had discovered in Wormwood. The evidence of those heaven-flung towers suggested a city such as might be found in Europa, on Earth-Above. The Tasmanian had sidled up to me. So mesmerized was I by the majestic vista below that I did not accord him a glance.

'This is the first time I've laid eyes on one of the Netherworld's great cities,' I said, as much to myself as him.

'What about during the war?' he said.

'The *malignos* I fought were conducting guerrilla warfare. The so-called "invasion" of London was in effect a series of raids conducted from underground lairs. The *malignos* had an incredible network of tunnels and chambers, some really quite deep. And there were even some settlements. But nothing like this. I've only heard about such things from Gala.'

'Ah,' said the Tasmanian. 'Then you and I are similarly at a loss. I have only heard tales of such things below decks, over grog and biscuits. I'd never thought that I'd actually clap eyes on a Netherworld city.' He turned to face the great lamp. A hand held up to his brow, he squinted, as if he were peering from the crow's nest of one of the ships that had been, for him, a floating home. He was accustomed, now, it seemed, to the worst the lighthouse had to offer, and able to withstand its bombardment almost without the intermediary of a shielding hand. Encouraged by his ability to endure, I copied, and turned into the dazzling glare.

The girl had not moved from the row of levers. Standing akimbo, she stared at us with a big grin that contradicted the seriousness of her eyes.

'You should look over the other side, too,' she said. 'Then you'll understand *everything*.'

Dumbly, and still in awe at the revelation of the abyss, the Tasmanian and I proceeded across the turret and took up a position facing the precipice we had recently descended. I heard a noise denoting that yet another lever had been thrown. The pulleys that lay concealed beneath the floorboards groaned in sympathy. The noise extended to the walls, and even seemed to emanate from outside, issuing from the cracks and fissures of the rocky landscape itself. Soon, the tower and its surroundings clattered and groaned like a stone ghost rattling its chains.

The precipice shook. Atomized granite powdered down its side. From out of this white, gauzy curtain came a discord that seemed to echo the clamour of the machinery beneath my feet. As the dust was dissipated by the abyss's draughts, a huge, iron structure could be seen emerging from the rock face. It was shaped like a helix and would have seemed to have been concealed within a shadowy recess undetectable from the plain.

The top of the helix came flush against the road that had been sheered off by natural, or perhaps unnatural forces. The bottom extended far below, until it became a slender twist, like the defoliated stem of a climbing plant, black and ferrous. The long, massive screw was, I now understood, itself a road, a continuation of the highway that had taken us from Wormwood and across the Great Plain; a road that would now take us down to Tophet.

I felt the touch of the girl's hand against my own. I took her fingers, pressing them gently. 'We left our horses behind,' I said.

'You wouldn't want to ride into Tophet on horseback,' she said. 'If you did, you'd be picked up pretty quick. Pretty *damn* quick.' She grinned as if to see whether I had appreciated her linguistic daring. 'In Tophet they have their own militia. But don't worry.' She pulled her hand away and looked up at me with the condescension of one who was about to reveal herself as the arbiter of my fate. 'We have stables here. Horses, chaises, wagons. It's a wagon you'll need. Something you can hide in.' The glare from the abyss sent up a haze that reminded me of the glow above London's rooftops as seen from Greenwich's hills at night. She lifted her chin and looked towards our own night sky, that, if not possessing the velvet majesty of Earth-Above's, was just as unreachable. 'Be careful of the shadows down there,' she added.

'Oh, we will,' I said, once more ready to humour her.

'No; you don't understand. The shadows in Tophet are not like the shadows on the plain. Or even the shadows of the abyss. The shadows in Tophet' – her lips drew back from the gums, little teeth chattering as if she had suddenly caught a cold – 'they *eat* people.' The lips drew back further, cuspidated enamel grinding against itself as if she meant to eat *me*.

'Of course,' I said airily. The girl seemed to be concentrating her gaze upon a point where the light shining upon the abyss's walls surrendered to the darkness of the vault.

'Can I go now?' she continued. 'I've been good, haven't I? I showed you the lighthouse and the way to Tophet. And you're not even *malignos*.'

'Yes,' I said, 'you can go. Thank you. Thank you for helping us.'

'You're welcome, human soldier. I'm glad you came. I thought I was going to be here forever. So few come this way. Just Madame Tetrallini and some of the people from Wormwood. It's been lonely. But I promised Grandpa and Grandma I'd stay and open the road. Now I've done it, I can become one with the Exaltation.'

Her wings extended. They beat a few times and she was carried onto the balustrade, her long toes wrapping about the iron rail. She looked over her shoulder. 'Goodbye, human soldier, goodbye fat man,' she said. 'It's been nice, knowing you.' She jumped and fell from the tower like a stone. Then, her wings flapping wildly, she rose upward just before she ploughed into the promontory's rocky ground. Within a few seconds, she was soaring high above us.

As I followed her trajectory, I began to sway a little, her altitude as correspondingly vertiginous as the yawn of the deep pit beneath my feet. Despite my familiarity with heights, I had to shake my head quite vigorously to rid myself of an incipient swoon. Sobered up, I maintained track of her progress as, keeping close to the side of the abyss's wall, she continued her ascent, her scales coruscating, throwing back the light emitted by the lighthouse as if, by doing so, she renounced its last hold upon her life.

As she cleared the rim, she continued to soar, and then, as the haze that hung far above us momentarily allowed us a last glimpse of that tiny, bat-like figure, she disappeared into the darkness that filled the vault, gone to join those other children abandoned to the shadows. And the Tasmanian and I were left alone, perched on that salient high above the marvellous city of Tophet.

Chapter Nine

'Why do you hate me so much?' said the Tasmanian.

We sat next to each other on the wagon's elevated driving seat. The lighthouse's stables had contained several wagons. I had settled on one that had belonged to an undertaker. My choice had been prompted by a recollection of the conversation I had had with the pre-pubescent châtelaine; the fact that, in compliance with their office, those *malignos* who disposed of the dead shrouded themselves, top to toe, in white. With the Tasmanian already wrapped in a white silk bedsheet, I had only to likewise attire myself and we were ready to enter Tophet as two moody, silent harbingers of mortality. The disguise was effective. The city's inhabitants, out of respect and, I think, fear, averted their eyes as we passed them by.

'Why,' he reiterated, 'why do you hate me?' I had formed a certain notion of him during our duel, a notion that had been strengthened during our period of confinement in Madame Tetrallini's caravan, namely, that he was a species of colossal baby, a terrific infant-man. Maybe I should have left him to the mercies of the Exaltation. It would have been apt for him to die at the hands of those as callow as himself. But my companion was difficult to ignore. Each syllable of his question had been enunciated with such dryness that I was forced to admit that the sentiment lying behind his squawk of self-pity was not as infantile as might be supposed.

The flesh about his jowls shook to the wagon's lurching rhythm. He adjusted the improvised cowl so that it better concealed his face and then brought the reins down against the backs of our two horses. They broke into a trot, carrying us past several militiamen who had their feet up on the tables of a pavement café. I pulled my own sheet tight about me. Our robes might convey dread, but the merest hint of our humanity and we would have an angry mob demanding that we be either killed or enslaved.

'Why—'

'Hush!' I said. 'This is hardly the time to discuss the subject.' I cast a sly glance up and down the street. *Malignos* went about their business. But I could see no more militiamen. 'If anyone here should hear us speaking English, then—' I decided to heed my own advice and held my tongue.

Coaches, drays, wagons, the equipages of aristocrats and the lone mounts of bucks – all the traffic that you could conceivably find in a hectic metropolis – rushed towards us. Despite the rumble of hoofs and wheels I discovered, now that the Tasmanian and I maintained a silence, that the ubiquitous sound of dripping water was again plainly audible. The water, from the underground streams that, I supposed, fed the Sea of Sammael – sight of which we had not yet enjoyed – fell continuously from the vault's blistered limestone, a chill black rain that pitter-pattered against the coach's tarpaulin.

Unlike the other caverns I had passed through, the vault here was unconcealed by shadows; had been, ever since we had completed our journey down the helical road and ridden deep into Tophet. It was warmer here. The dark mist that had clouded the bottom of the abyss – and which was the result of smoke given off by those cauldrons of burning oil I had descried from the lighthouse – had gradually dissipated, to be replaced by a stone roof that resembled the fan vaulting of a cathedral, if one that, like so many ancient temples in the Darkling Isle, was either blasted or in wanton decay. The cold draughts that chilled those inhabitants of Tophet who lived beneath the abyss were no longer appreciable.

The road wound on, taking us between tall, randomly spaced buildings, each one of which glistened with the dark drizzle that permanently drenched Tophet. The architecture appropriated the cavern's resources. Each building was constructed from a gigantic stalagmite, so that it was part natural, part engineered; or else a stalactite, hanging needle-like from the vault, an upside-down version of the towers that erupted from the floor. Sometimes the two structures met and formed a lime carbonate pillar.

Some buildings were white, blood-red or dark brown, but some were completely translucent, like glass termitariums, revealing the hustle and bustle within. Each monumental conoid was dotted with thousands of windows. Each was connected to another by way of a long, arching skybridge. And, whereas formerly, the city had been illuminated by fire, each building here was decorated with fantastic vegetation: fungi and flowers that made the bioluminescent blooms of Wormwood and the Great Plain seem like weeds.

And permeating everything – the strange, botanical

growths, the great, worked towers of carbonate deposi-
tion, the cavern itself – was the maddening drip, drip,
drip of water. Perhaps, I decided, it would be better to
speak after all.

'And why do you think I hate you?' I said. I had at first
thought the Tasmanian's aspect of an 'infant-man' both
ludicrous and sinister. But since learning to regard him
in a light that was *wholly* ludicrous, I decided to bait the
booby and alleviate my anxieties by way of a little
malicious fun.

'You think you're better than me,' he said. 'I've seen
how you act in Barretto. You go about with your nose in
the air. You look down on people.'

I glanced at him and raised my eyebrows. 'But I *am*
better than you.'

'You see what I mean?' he said, his voice breaking
with indignation.

I said nothing. It had been my full intention, of
course, to continue teasing him. Something, however,
warned me against pursuing this tack. I had been underground ten days. Much of that time had been spent in
the Tasmanian's company, and it seemed evident that
being sequestered together was having a deleterious
effect on both of us. I was becoming as infantile as he. I
took a deep breath and attempted to continue in a more
reasonable manner.

'I got into the habit of looking down on people in
London,' I said, 'when I was a boy. I'm not sure I can do
much about it now. It's a habit that's become second
nature, just like one's swordsmanship becomes second
nature. It's a survival mechanism.' The Tasmanian
shook his head.

'You're saying that your snobbery is the result of *practise*?'

'Yes, that would be about right. When I was young I discovered that celebrating one's own exquisite selfhood to the detriment of others helps keep one sane. Practise? Yes; long hours of practise. The Darkling Isle devours those who do not cultivate their egocentricity, who do not set themselves apart from the nihilism of the mob. Practise? Oh yes. You might say I've been as diligent about keeping up my standards as I have about maintaining my fencing expertise. I practise every day.'

He became thoughtful and we rode for a while without talking. And then suddenly, he snorted with constrained laughter. 'Standards, eh?' He turned and pulled back his cowl a little so that I might appreciate his derisive smile. 'It's not what I've heard. I mean, you have something of a reputation for keeping low company. And I mean *low*.'

I made an ostentatious effort at stifling a yawn. 'I seem fated never to rid myself of such company.' His smile wavered.

'I wouldn't pretend I'm anything but a low sort. But I don't care what others think of me, as long as I get their respect.'

'Oh,' I said, not wanting to go too far; we couldn't afford to fall out in the middle of a *malignos* city, 'oh, you have my *respect*.' I hoped I hadn't sounded too sarcastic.

'You come from a privileged background, I suppose?' he continued.

'On the contrary. My father was a teacher. A *maître d'armes*. A clever man. But poor. In truth, my feelings towards people such as yourself have always been informed by a kind of self-disgust. Disgust for the environment in which I grew up. Disgust for my dismal inheritance. Amongst the venal, the vulgar, the vicious, I found that the only way to survive – to be the person I wanted to be – was to practise that Olympian disdain of which I have, I hope, educated you in the first principles. It has helped me forget the kinship I share with the filthy, ignorant scum who haunted my childhood and youth.'

'What the hell's *Olympian*?'

'Something I disdain to explain to *you*,' I said. 'I have educated you enough for one day. I shall not explain the lexicon of the Ancients.'

'Is that what you were doing in the London ginshops you so liked to frequent: educating barbarians like me?' So he knew about my disgraceful life in London. The stories that circulated about me in *Nightriders* obviously commanded more attention than I had thought. Memories of my favourite London tavern, *The Sick Rose*, percolated into my consciousness. So did the memories of its buxom serving girls, Snub-nosed Marie, One-eyed Annabella and Lazy Laughing Languid Jenny.

'The scornful attitude I had to my youthful milieu was also, how shall I say' – I waved a hand through the air – 'tinted with ambivalence. I found I needed spasmodic doses of low company in order to relieve me of the painful conviction that I was not quite the rootless person I imagined myself to be. That I was not untouchable. That I did not lack the ability to engage in simple comradely acts of debauchery, drunkenness and violence.'

The Tasmanian did his best to hide his face with the cowl. But he could not disguise his snickering.

'Have I embarrassed you?' I said.

'Me? I'm just brute matter. I can't be embarrassed. But' – the snicker exploded into laughter – 'you have my sympathy, poor boy. You have my *sympathy*.'

I tapped the sole of a boot against the bottom of the driver's seat. 'I am not,' I said, myself a little exasperated now, as anxious that I had said too much as that I had been misinterpreted, 'I am not trying to elicit your *sympathy*, you wretched ox.' I studied the pedestrians who flashed by. 'A man ends up talking too much in situations such as these.'

'I was really just trying to sound out if I could trust you,' he said. 'But it seems to me we haven't improved much on the situation we had in the caravan.'

'I've told you before, our previous argument is best forgotten.'

'We're going to have some difficult times ahead, I'll warrant. I can count on you in a fight?'

'Yes,' I sighed, trying to mask my impatience, 'you can count on me.'

'Good. Then you can count on me, too. I'll help you, Pike. I'll help you get this counterpoison you talk about. Damn it, I have to. I know I won't stand much of a chance trying to resurface on my own.'

'I'm sure the antidote exists,' I said. 'Our journey won't be in vain. Pandemonium will yield its secrets, I'm sure it will.' The Tasmanian grinned and nodded. But he was not so much sanguine, I think, as fatalistic.

'How far do you think we've come? How deep?' he said.

'I think we must be under the Sea of Cathay. How deep? I just know we have to go deeper, much deeper. But the maelstrom will take care of that. You'll be able to get us a ship?'

'I'll be able to navigate a small boat, sure. Getting one's another question.'

'We'll be able to settle on that once we've reached the harbour.'

Though there had been no hard evidence that we approached the sea, I felt sure we were heading in the right direction. I sometimes detected the smell of brine, and even suspected I heard, in the far distance, the crash of waves on a shore, such I would hear at night in my apartment in Barrio Barretto. The road signs, with their mixture of half-understood glyphs, arrows, squiggles and waves, reinforced my belief.

We drove through a tightly-packed cluster of gigantic structures, each one of which must have been over three hundred metres high. They were helictites, and they hung from the cavern's roof like twists of petrified flowers that had turned from the sun to embrace the darkness of the Netherworld. These colossal, pendant bouquets of stone displayed no windows. Their function seemed inconsistent with the support of life. They merely seemed to serve as forms of monstrous ornamentation. But despite the fact that the structures in this part of the city were obviously uninhabited, the streets teemed with *malignos*. More *malignos* than I had seen in my entire life.

The wagon clattered through the canyons of flow-stone and dripstone, the chassis groaning whenever the horses turned sharply about a corner. Occasionally my heart fluttered as either one or both horses misstepped on the glazed cobbles, and then recovered to take us forward.

I looked askance, scanning the pedestrians. On sighting our wagon, they would stare nervously at the pavement, or look up at where the stone towers punctured the black sky. All classes of Netherworld society were represented: patricians, who either swanned along the pavement with footmen attending them, or else were carried in sedan chairs; merchants, fat on trading in rat pelts and ancient artefacts; and workers, peasants and beggars. The *malignos*, in this part of the Netherworld, were more diverse than those I had previously encountered. I saw a woman who, like the *malignos* I had seen dancing in *Nightriders*, had a supernumerary pair of eyes where her nipples should have been; and I saw men with scales so large and heavy that they might resist any sword-thrust, any blow of mace or axe. Those scales – red, blue, silver, yellow and black – filled the air with a noise that was like a far-off thunderstorm. It seemed, in this densely populated sector, ready to swamp the equally insistent drip, drip, drip that was the city's permanent background music.

That sound disappeared as we crested a small hill, the prospect that confronted us cancelling out noise both manmade and natural.

'Ah, at last!' said the Tasmanian. And then, as he and I took in what lay below: 'Oh, I don't believe it. I don't believe it!'

I sat dumb. In the Netherworld I had grown used to wondrous surprises of shadow and substance, of darkness, vast caverns and prodigious extensities; but nothing I had hitherto encountered compared to the sea that, stretching about us in a nearly perfect one-hundred-and-eighty-degree radius, seemed somehow greater, more magnificent, than any sea on Earth-Above.

'Despite all the stories I've heard,' said the Tasmanian, 'I've never really believed the Netherworld contained beauty such as this.'

The horizon, here, seemed to be set to different parameters than on Earth-Above, as if the subterranean world of the *malignos* was paradoxically bigger than the surface world. If there were a God – if not Gala's, then any god – he had not only chosen an enormous canvas on which to give form to this idea of the sea, but had, for some unknown reason, also chosen to hide his creation in the depths of the Earth, to await discovery by the *malignos*. It was a ridiculous conceit, but one I was driven to by necessity, for I could not believe the place had been artificially created. That the *malignos* had ever possessed the requisite technology to achieve such a task was inconceivable. But it *had* been engineered, of course. There could scarcely be any other explanation. And I concluded that the forebears of the *malignos* not only possessed sciences and artefacts that beggared the imagination, but a superhuman, and very alien, dimensional perception that was as weird as their infamous libidos.

On first seeing the sweep of the city that led down to the sea, and, more importantly, the sea itself, the Tasmanian had reined in our team. We had come to a standstill. Exposed on the crest, and frozen in wonder, we found ourselves subject to the stares of passers-by. For some citizens, curiosity had begun to undermine superstition. I dug my elbow into my companion's side.

'Don't loiter,' I said. 'Take us down the hill.' I cursed at his simple-minded inability to comprehend and pointed to where ships were lined up along a quay. 'Down *there*, to the harbour. Fool.' With a crack of the reins, he geed the horses.

Before we relinquished our vantage point I again surveyed the seascape. It was as if the mathematics of perspective had been rewritten. Imagine a coastline that stretches to the horizon, uninterrupted by cliff or headland. Imagine it extending, impossible, if you will, beyond its furthermost point, and be still visible, as if it had the power to tease the eyesight into an appreciation of unheralded geometries. Imagine a sky that was not a sky, but was bluer, more celestial than any sky you had ever seen, a sky that might have been a dream of heaven, a fresco adorning a mighty dome capping the universe. Imagine a violet sea, its waves tipped with coruscating diamonds that flickered in and out of existence with unearthly intensity. Imagine an illimitable sea that did not seem to meet the sky, but rather, attained a perspective where the Earth's plane seemed to pass into another world, another continuum. And then imagine, high above that sea, a pale, luminous disk that emitted a quality of light I had never before seen. Light that was sober, mysterious, but bright enough to bathe the boundless Sea of Sammael in lush, mellow illumination. Whether bioluminescent or harnessing a power I knew nothing of, it unquestionably served as a sun. Not the 'black sun' which we spoke of metaphorically when we referred to the light that permeated the Netherworld, but a literal sun. Having only previously skirted the fringes of the Earth's depths, I had never suspected that the Netherworld could be so awesome.

The wagon trundled down the hill. We were again amongst the tall, grotesque structures in which the *malignos* lived and conducted business. We had travelled only about one-hundred or two-hundred metres when, coming about a sharp corner, we were confronted by a roadblock.

'Don't panic,' I whispered. 'And remember, don't try to talk.' I slipped a hand through a fold in the bedsheet and clasped the hilt of my sword. How hateful they seemed to me at that moment, that small band of militiamen, with their long-fingered hands stroking the hilts of their scimitars (copying what I, unbeknownst to them, did beneath my robes); how hateful their goblin faces, so threatening, yet, at the same time – in timorous acknowledgement of our fake identities – struggling to be polite. It was hardly possible, I thought, that my beautiful Gala was one of their race.

'Resplendent,' said one of the militiamen, speaking his own tongue, and making a slight bow. All that followed was incomprehensible. I pulled the bedsheet over my head so that my face was completely masked. I hoped that my fellow 'resplendent' had done the same.

When the militiaman who addressed us had stopped talking two of his comrades came forward and pulled the barrier that blocked our way to one side. They beckoned us. Then, when we remained where we were, frowned, quizzically. I nudged the Tasmanian, and as quietly as I was able, told him, on pain of receiving a portion of *Espiritu Santo* in his ribs, to drive on. The reins cracked and, with the militiamen flanking us, we passed through.

The streets on this side of the roadblock were deserted. The militiamen did not follow, but, thankfully, stayed behind to man the barrier.

The vault – it was hard to assume that this cavern had one, so infinite seemed its extent – was lost to view. Above us was only the azure dome I had seen from the hilltop. The stalagmitic towers had given way to tenement buildings, such as might be found in the cities of Earth-Above. And the streets were empty.

'Strange,' muttered the Tasmanian, 'you'd think this would be the most populous part of the city, what with commerce from the harbour and all.'

'Something's wrong,' I said, looking about frantically. The empty streets seemed to hint at some terrible secret. Then I noticed something: the iron-braced doors of the tenement blocks had been daubed with white, five-pointed stars. I knew what that meant. So, it seemed, did the Tasmanian. He placed a hand on my arm. And, as I looked into his wild eyes, his grip tightened.

'Plague,' said the Tasmanian, enunciating the dreaded word that had got stuck in my throat.

'Yeah,' I said, holding the bedsheet before my nose and mouth. The air had begun to grow unwholesome. 'I've heard of such things.'

'I've visited ports like this on Earth-Above,' he said. 'Back home in the archipelago, though, they paint *crosses* on the doors of the dead and dying. Not stars.' He shivered. 'They say it's the sign of Lilith.'

'Of her cult, yes. The pentacle is a symbol of the five senses. The tribes of the perverse worshipped animality.'

'The only kind of worship there is down here, I'd guess. Animals, the lot of them.'

'The cult emanates from another universe or dimension,' I said. 'One with a completely different moral framework to our own. Or so runs the predominant theory. But it often seems to me that the Lilith cult is no more than an adaptation of Christianity.' Or perversion of it, as Gala, who had known both hell and heaven, would say.

A little way off, one of those men whose office we had falsely assumed was busy with a brush and a pot of paint. 'There'll be a quarantine, I'll warrant,' said the Tasmanian. His initial alarm had worn off and he seemed oddly phlegmatic.

'I should remind you,' I said, somewhat put out by his calm, 'that we are passing through an area of deadly pestilence.'

'I know,' he said.

'Then you will acknowledge that we court disaster by doing so?' I said, my anger beginning to surface. 'We have to turn back.'

'Why?'

'What do you mean *why*? Because if we stay here we'll succumb to whatever disgusting disease is circulating in these parts.' He began to laugh that quiet, self-satisfied laugh of his. 'You find such a death amusing?' I added.

'I'd thought you'd have understood more about *malignos* biology. After all, you're an educated man.'

'What are you talking about?'

'Oh, don't ask me, I'm just a barbarian. An ignorant savage.' I still had my hand on the hilt of *Espiritu Santo*, and I think the Tasmanian's ears must have pricked at the sound of it being pulled a few centimetres clear of its scabbard. 'Okay, okay, don't get so *upset*. I'm talking about the fact that the plague that afflicts the *malignos* doesn't affect human beings.'

'We're immune?'

'Yeah – immune. I thought you were some kind of expert on these matters?'

'I've never been this deep, and—'

'Quit making excuses.' His shoulders juddered with suppressed mirth. Oh yes, he was enjoying himself. 'When you've spent your life at sea, as I have, it's something you learn about readily enough. I've seen the waves churning with hundreds of *malignos* corpses. When Netherworld towns are decimated by plague, the numbers of the dead are so great that they're disposed of by simply being thrown into underground water-ways. From there, they find their way up to the surface through vents in the sea floor. Hundreds, thousands of them I've seen, sometimes, tens, hundreds of thousands. But never once did any sailor *I've* served with come down with plague. The wisdom is it's not possible.' I was greatly relieved to hear it. 'Trouble is, with a quarantine in effect, there'll be no ships in and no ships out. It's not something that goes in our favour.'

'No, I suppose not, but at least we'll be alive to consider the options.'

The gloomy, silent tenements fell away. We had reached the seafront. Full-rigged, ocean-going galleons, as well as more modest vessels such as might be seen plying the coastal waters of Luzon, were anchored by the quay. The line of the harbour stretched, in a great lazy curve, to where a castle jutted above the promenade. It was my second castle, and one far grander, and wholly less toy-like, than Countess Suspiria's.

Standing on a rocky motte, its bulwarks ran down to the sea, where waves foamed and crashed about the breakwaters. The side that faced us was less forbidding. There, the stones were covered in dark, emerald rashes of ivy and convolvulus. Other, less familiar, climbing plants, some of which sported frosted buds similar to *sampaguita*, wove about the balconies and gargoyles. The soaring turrets and spires were regaled with flags and pennants. Riding towards those colourful walls, I could almost have been in Europa, on a romantic trip down the Rhine. Almost, but not quite. However much the castle resonated with the architectural mannerisms of Earth-Above, nothing could detract from its essential strangeness.

Below the castle lay an ornamental garden. Like the castle, it possessed a certain theatrical flavour. Indeed, it seemed not so much garden as stage scenery.

A party of the Resplendent were walking towards us. They waved as we sped past, the Tasmanian urging the horses on to avoid unnecessary contact. They shouted something. I waved back. I had understood one word: the *malignos* for 'quick' or 'hurry'. It was fortuitous that the Tasmanian had, for quite other, and more paranoid reasons, set us off on a canter.

The wagon sped down the promenade. As we neared the castle, I saw that the Resplendent were here too, milling about the ornamental garden. The lawns were littered with the recumbent bodies of those who had succumbed to the plague. It seemed the garden was being used as some kind of impromptu, open-air morgue.

'Can we turn around?' I said.

'Too late, they've spotted us.' He was right. We were, it seemed, being asked, or ordered, to stop. 'Rein in,' I said, between clenched teeth. The Tasmanian complied. One of the undertakers ran forward, grabbed our lead horse by its bridle, and led us to where several other wagons were parked. On coming to a halt, I found, to my consternation, that we were almost immediately surrounded by white-robed *malignos*. 'Whatever you do, keep quiet,' I said out of the side of my mouth.

I jumped down and walked briskly along a gravel path that led into the garden. I didn't wait to see if the Tasmanian followed. I was too eager to leave our welcoming party behind. I achieved this with a surprising degree of ease. The Resplendent, though numerous, were preoccupied with loading corpses into the back of our wagon. They ignored me.

I stood in a parterre. Geometrically cut lawns lay to either side. There were ponds, too, some of which flashed with golden fins; and flower beds filled with blooms as beautiful as they were grotesque. I walked on, the path interrupted by the occasional piece of statuary, or else an obelisk, urn or plinth. Topiarian forms – trees and shrubbery clipped into semblances of rats, spiders, owls, bats and other animals indigenous to the Netherworld – cast ominous zoomorphic shadows over the gravel. Soon, these shadows were supplanted by the shadows cast by the castle's wall. And in that shade lay a multitude of corpses.

Malignos walked back and forth. Some held corpses between them. They were on their way to the promenade. And some were empty-handed, returning to pick up more of the grim cargo that, I supposed, was due to be ferried to some pyre or limepit.

I knew I had to blend in.

I essayed a quick glance over my shoulder. The Tasmanian followed, resigned, I think, as much as I was, to the fact that we had to go through with this mime. Steeling myself, I chose a body and shuffled up to it. The Tasmanian drew alongside. And then we both bent down, he sheepishly taking the cadaver by its legs, I by its head. We lifted. As I straightened myself, I looked askance out of the folds of my cowl. Seeing that none suspected us for what we were, I nodded to give my companion the okay. We began to move towards the wagons, the corpse held between us.

I paused. Above me, the stained glass windows were like butterfly wings transfixed by sunlight, iridescent under another, alien sun. But it was my ears rather than my eyes that fell victim to enchantment. The sound of a harpsichord carried over the garden from one of the balconies. It was a stately air. And over it, a soprano voice, liquid, refined and infinitely sad, pierced my heart.

> Oh, fair Cedaria, hide those eyes
> That hearts enough have won;
> For whosoever sees them dies,
> And cannot ruin shun.

> Such beauty and charms are seen
> United in your face,
> The proudest can't but own you queen
> Of beauty, wit and grace.

Then pity me, who am your slave,
    And grant me a reprieve;
Unless I may your favour have,
    I can't one moment live.

'How beautiful,' I said. The garden, the *malignos*, and
the gamey odour issuing from the corpse, were suddenly forgotten. It was a melody from the ancient days,
when the Darkling Isle had been called Albion, and the
world was fresh and young. Those plaintive notes,
those heartrending tremolos, brushed away the
shadows that cobwebbed my soul. It was as if the sun
had risen above England's fields and dispelled the
darkness that, like briar and bindweed, grew about her
heart, reducing her to the state of emotional, intellectual and spiritual poverty that was her present lot. The
garden I stood in, with its fine lawns, its hedges, its
hothouses of poisonous blooms, seemed an England
reborn, a new Albion, the place on the edges of the
imagination that Gala called Eden, Beulah or Jerusalem.

The harpsichord stopped. A young woman appeared
on the balcony that I had identified as the source of the
celestial song. She leant over its iron balustrade, the
shutters behind her framing the castle's dark interior.

It was she, I supposed, who was the songstress. She
was certainly as beautiful as that ancient melody. More
beautiful, I thought. I was so distracted by the fine lines
of her face and the curves of her waist and bosom, that
I was unaware that she stared at me. She had stared,
perhaps, for some time. Stared for several seconds,
perhaps a minute or more; stared with a languorous
disdain that was shot through with desire, and,

perhaps, not a little hatred. Was it possible she knew me to be human? Though I hurriedly pulled the cowl about my face, I found that, despite the dangers to which I exposed myself, I could not take my eyes off her. Not for the first time in my life, I became convinced that beauty would prove my undoing.

'Pike,' the Tasmanian say saying, 'Pike, what's wrong with you. The *malignos* are beginning to look at us.'

A man had joined the young woman on the balcony. She seemed to issue him instructions, for he promptly retreated through the open shutters. And then she fell again to her study of that exotic specimen, Dr Richard Pike.

I took a firm grip of the corpse. 'Okay, let's get this thing out of here. Then I think *we* might try to get out of here. Hide away till nightfall and then try to steal a boat.'

'The plague will ensure that the harbour is well guarded, you can be sure of that.'

'Yeah, well, I've got a bad feeling that hanging around *this* place is going to end in tears. Let's just get back to the wagon and—'

The figure that I had seen waiting upon the young woman's pleasure had reappeared in one of the doorways that gave onto the garden. He called out. Uncommonly careless about the consequences to my *amour propre*, I looked behind, and then back at him, placing an index finger on my chest in an idiot's gesture of *What me*? 'Yes, you, you!' I understood him to say, his irritated gestures translating themselves despite my slim grasp of *malignos*.

The Tasmanian looked on in despair as I set my end

of the corpse upon the ground and wound my way through the rows of the dead, across the lawn and into the doorway.

'This way, Resplendent,' he said, coolly. My command of *malignos* was, it seemed, improving. I had understood another of his commands, and this time one that had not had the benefit of being accompanied by sign language. Perhaps, I thought bitterly, in another fifty years or so I might be able to ask directions, beg for food, or relieve my frustration at being trapped in the depths by insulting my captors with a few choice *malignos* oaths.

The usher carried a long, ivory-topped walking cane. It seemed to be his badge of office. He walked ahead. I followed him through the castle's halls and chambers.

Outside, in the garden, I had almost felt as if I were on Earth-Above, in a renascent England, a New Jerusalem. But here, within the walls of this great, forbidding pile of stone, I was again in the realm of shadows that was the Netherworld.

Slicing through the darkness, demarcating one area of shadow from another, a row of high, narrow windows disgorged streams of light. I passed beneath them, my boots splashed with the same golden lozenges that spilled across the flagstones. Tapestries hung from walls otherwise bare of adornment, and shields, spears and suits of armour decorated fluted columns whose capitals fanned into the ceiling like fountains of liquid stone. And everywhere, awaiting disposal, upon tables, hearth rug, in niche and in cupboard, lay the castle's dead.

We ascended a stairway. On reaching the castle's

second floor, I found myself in a long gallery. It was lined, on one side, with portraits of *malignos*, and on the other with windows that looked out over the garden. This part of the castle was as empty of life as the halls, chambers and apartments I had previously walked through; as empty as the streets outside.

I took advantage of my guide's turned back and pulled the bedsheet away from my face, hazarding a glance through a window. I saw no sign of the Tasmanian. But all else was as before, with the Resplendent going silently about their work. In the distance, I saw a wagon speeding along the promenade. I wondered if it were transporting corpses to burial or combustion, or whether it signalled that my companion was beating a perfidious retreat. If it was the Tasmanian, then I was without provisions, and much else besides. The wagon had contained water and food. But it had also held my field glasses and other accoutrements, including the compass without which I would surely be lost.

The usher halted before a door. Then he raised his cane and used it to announce our arrival, rapping its ivory top three times upon the door's wooden panels. I jerked the bedsheet back into place.

A muffled voice called 'enter.' The usher put his hand on the doorknob, twisted, pushed, and then held the door open with one long, extended arm. Trying not to betray my nerves by hesitancy, I walked boldly into the room.

It was a bedchamber, and it was filled with a sickly, sweet scent. The ceiling was fretted in star and quatrefoil compartments. White, diaphanous curtains floated about the shutters, where a sea breeze blew in from the balcony. The sheets on the four-poster were in disarray. A tray laden with half-eaten food stood on a night table. A harpsichord, its top piled with sheet music, stood against one wall. And nearby, on a yellow chaise longue, lay the invalid who had summoned me. For there could be no doubt, now that I saw her up close, that the young woman whose eyes I had met while disposing of corpses was dying of plague.

I heard the door close and turned. The usher had left. The young woman said something. I turned back to face her, refocusing my eyes on her lovely, half-destroyed face, her wasted, but still alluring figure. And then she spoke in English.

'You're human, are you not?'

'Human? Why do you think me human?' I said in my mother tongue. Somehow, the question had not disconcerted me as much as it should have. I had felt, ever since our eyes had first made contact, that some kind of unspoken understanding existed between us. Even so, it had been unduly rash of me not to affect incomprehension, or at least, a command of English consistent with the role that I played. At this depth, none except the Netherworld's élite would have known more than a few elementary phrases of the surface world's *lingua franca*. A humble undertaker would have known virtually nothing.

'I had a human once,' she said. 'A minikin. A little human pet. Mama got him for me on my thirteenth birthday. I called him Edouard.' She had a light, tripping voice which was almost as musical when she spoke as when I had heard her sing. 'I know a human when I see one,' she continued, a note of coquetry entering the little-girlish lilt. 'Oh yes, even when he is cloaked in the robes of the Resplendent, I know him. Yes, indeed I do.'

'You are to be congratulated on your percipience,' I said, leaping into the unknown territory that was opening up. It was senseless to tarry. The ground I occupied but a minute ago was no longer defensible. *Attack, attack*, I thought. Whether I had a chance of capitalizing on the situation, or at the very least, of trying to minimize the danger I was in, the plan of attack open to me was one that I had plied many a time, though lately with only qualified success: seduction. For surely here was another *malignos* woman who, like Countess Suspiria, had a taste for the human male.

I walked across the room and sat down on the edge of the chaise longue. 'Am I similarly to be congratulated for my audacity?' She wrinkled her pretty nose. But no smile was forthcoming, and my fears were unassuaged. It occurred to me that, at any moment, she might tire of this game and call whatever guards still lurked within the castle's wall.

'When I saw you,' she said, 'I thought of Edouard. How I wish he were alive to cheer me up! These are dark days, here, in the castle. For me, final days. I need cheering. Really I do.' She was, indeed, sicker than I had at first thought, even, perhaps, at death's door. Her scales were pink, a very youthful pink. From each one, where it overlapped with its partner, oozed a deeper pink, as if even her blood shared the maidenly, pink blush of her florescence. It was but a fancy. The bodies rowed outside evinced similar cases of haemorrhaging.

The discoloration of her blood was a result, not of poetry, but plague. 'Where do you come from?' she said.

'The Darkling Isle,' I replied.

'Then you will have killed many of my kind, I suppose, in the war?' I said nothing. Instead, I reached out and caressed her hair. It had been blonde, I think, but now it had become streaked with blood, so that it too was pinkish, if a darker, more angry pink than that which stained her scaly flesh. 'It is true what you say: you are audacious. Edouard would never have been so bold.' I pulled back the cowl of the bedsheet.

'I am not a pet. Not some human slave leashed, castrated and taught to do tricks for your amusement. My name is Pike, Captain Richard Pike. And I, Madame, am your *admirer*.' I stood up and divested myself of my makeshift robes. Then I stepped out of them, like a ghoul metamorphosing into a man, glad that I could, at last, outface the terror of the Netherworld in my uniform.

'Hmm. The habiliment of a black knight,' she said, studying the new aspect I presented her. 'What you say is true, then. You *are* of the Darkling Isle.' Her inspection continued. Her gaze was intimate, shameless. And I found myself aroused. 'The black knights of the Darkling Isle enjoy a certain reputation for devilry, I hear.'

'A reputation it has sometimes proved difficult to earn, given that London, these days, does not permit a man to freely indulge his passions. Why, a man cannot even walk the streets with a sword.'

'And you,' she said coyly, her gaze darting to my codpiece, 'are something of a swordsman, I imagine?'

'Indeed,' I said, an eyebrow raised to acknowledge her racy, if somewhat childish wit. 'In the English countryside, of course, in its rusticated backwaters where life is cheap and humans are no better than animals, a man may go armed and use his blade with some degree of impunity.'

'Oh, those poor country maids.'

'But in London, even in some parts of the Pilipinas—'

'You are not in London now, captain,' she said, looking me in the eye, somewhat peevishly, I thought, as if tiring of this banter that was all promise but, in the end, just words, impotent words, words, words.

'No,' I said, 'I am not in London.' Nor was I in Barrio, with Gala likely to burst in. Gala, I thought to myself, guiltily, who always proved such a complication in the matter of my casual affairs. 'As you say, we black knights have a reputation for *devilry*. And it is devils, Madame, beautiful hornèd, pointy-tailed devils that have always stoked Richard Pike's fires. Not country maids. Not barmaids. Not really humans much at all. But—'

'Devils,' she said. I had finally won from her a smile.

I again sat down upon the chaise longue. But this time, as I did so, I scooped the emaciated girl up in my arms and looked deep into her livid eyes. 'When I spied you, *there*' – I nodded towards the swirling curtains – 'leaning over your balcony, as if from the bar of heaven – or in your case, shall we say, hell – I became sure you would understand my plight.' I placed my hand on her cheek. It was hot, flushed, I think, as much with insulted modesty as with fever. But in that clammy fire I was sure I also detected the heat of passion. 'What is *your* name?'

'Devia.'

'Not Cedaria?' I said, referring to the song I had heard her sing.

'No,' she said. 'I fear "beauty and charms" are, in *my* face, at least, no longer to be seen.'

'You are wrong,' I said, likewise recollecting the song's words, 'I "own you queen of beauty, wit and grace". Oh yes, hide those eyes, hide them, for they'll surely be this poor fool's ruin.' Once more, the wrinkling of that little nose, and then, another smile. It didn't quite portend the surrender I had wished, but it gave me hope.

'I wonder,' she said, 'are all humans such windbags as you?' And then, as my face dropped, she broke into a laugh. 'But you please me, just as I thought you might. I do miss Edouard so.'

I cursed. It went counter to my instincts for self-preservation, but I had no wish to be equated with a slave who sounded as diminutive and degraded as Countess Suspiria's pet human, Boot. It stung my pride. Determined to regain a little self-respect, I stood, lifted her up and carried her over to the bed.

I laid her down. Her lank hair fanned out about her head and shoulders, her sculpted horns dimpling the white, silk pillows. For a few seconds, her tail thrashed in token protest, sweeping aside the crumbs, crusts and rat bones that littered the sheets. Coming to rest, it curled itself into a question mark. I looked down into her eyes. They too asked a question, stoked, as they were, by the same ardent want that stoked her flaming cheeks. I would give her her reply.

I unbuttoned my doublet, took out the folded map,

and placed it on the night table. Then I began to sing. It was a song from the same grimoire in which, years ago, I had perused the lyrics to the song that had so enchanted me earlier. My voice rose, filling the room. It must have carried out into the garden. But I was a countertenor, my intonation and range comparable with Devia's. I trusted no one in hearing distance would be able to distinguish the girl from the man.

> She loves and she confesses too,
> There's then at last no more to do;
> The happy work's entirely done,
> Enter the town which thou hast won;
> The fruits of conquest now begin,
> Io, triumph, enter in.
> What's this, ye gods! what can it be?
> Remains there still an enemy?
> Bold Honour stands up in the gate,
> And would yet capitulate.
> Have I o'ercome all real foes,
> And shall this phantom me oppose?

'Are you then a man of honour?' she said. 'A man of scruples?' I threw my doublet to the floor, took off my gloves, unbuckled *Espiritu Santo* and placed it on the bed, where I might reach it in the event that I should need to resort to swordsmanship of quite another kind than that which was presently expected of me.

I half sat, half reclined on the silk sheets, the soft down of the mattress giving way with a sumptuousness that seemed designed to reassure me that no sounds – at least of creaking planks, intolerant joists or squeaky floorboards – should betray this tryst. I rolled on top of her. The curtains billowed in an unusually violent draught, their tulle folds snaring in the shutters. The gust brought the smell of incense, which had been ever present, powerfully to my attention. There were small bowls of incense, it seemed, burning in the room's every corner. But that smell was displaced by another. It was the smell of the *malignos* female, musky, almost rank, and quite overwhelming. 'No honour at all, I should say,' she added. Gala's face looked up at me, superimposed on the pink, blood-beaded face of the beauty I was determined to enjoy. I blinked; blinked again. Gala disappeared, to be replaced by Devia. Her arms were about my neck. 'Absolutely no honour at all.' I kissed the lobes of her long, pointed ears, and then kissed her on the mouth. I was, of course, careful. Though thrilling to the sensation of rows of cuspidate teeth, I knew that they could easily shred my tongue to pieces. No honour? I couldn't speak. Indeed, I had no wish to speak, but I could not but agree with her.

I stood in front of the pier glass and, with some care, tied the drawstrings of my codpiece in a gentleman's bow. Then I slipped on my gloves. Ha. I was looking lean and mean. In Barrio Barretto an empty purse had warded off the terrors of middle-age: the fat that accumulates with too much liquor, too little exercise. But poverty had done nothing to prevent the wastage of muscles that had dogged me since leaving active service. The rigours of my journey had toned me up. I ran a hand over my chin. I had found a razor at the lighthouse and, with the aid of a tablet of soap, rid myself of my beard. Still admiring my new-found smoothness, my hand descending from my chin to circle the nipples of my naked, and altogether more hirsute chest, I took my make-up palette out of my back pocket and reapplied my mascara.

I turned and let the *malignos* I had recently serviced sample the artistry of my maquillage. She was recumbent on the bed, in much the same position as I had left her. But she stared, not at me, but at the four-poster's canopied trimmings, lost, it seemed, in post-coital thought.

'Do you have a wife? Or a girlfriend?' I wished she hadn't ask me that. I walked up to the bed, stooped, and picked up my doublet. She continued to stare at the trimmings, the draughts circulating about the room animating each bead and tassel with the same languorous momentum that they imparted to the stray curls of her russet hair. The lovemaking had been novel. Certainly, it had been more satisfying than the sexual encounter I had had with Countess Suspiria. If another opportunity to make the two-backed beast with a sick, dying girl should present itself, I feared that, weak-willed as I was, I would find it difficult to deny myself the pleasure. Without lingering, I went over to the harpsichord and ran a finger idly up and down its keys, my gaze fixed upon the balcony.

'It's why I'm here. I mean, it's why I'm in the Netherworld.'

'A girl?'

'Yes. A girl. A *malignos*. Like you.'

'So, you're going to break my heart.' I didn't have to look at her to know she spoke lightly. I was relieved, but disappointed too. But I calculated that my vanity,

ludicrously inflated thing that it was, could profit from
a little summary deflation. I played a chord and then
turned about and walked back to the bed. 'Don't let me
keep you,' she continued, somewhat huffily. 'After all,
I'm dying. Why should you want to stay with poor little
me?' I pulled the doublet on and buttoned it up. Then I
picked *Espiritu Santo* up from where it lay on the sheets
and buckled it about my hips. She would not meet my
eyes. And now I saw that she had started to cry quietly.
I hoped I had not overplayed my hand.

'I need a boat,' I said. 'I have to get to sea. I'm sorry,
but—'

'You'll come back?'

I managed to stop myself shifting from one foot to the
other. I kept my voice on an even keel.

'Yes,' I said, 'of course.' Dissembling, in matters of
affection, I reminded myself gloomily, was something I
was good at. I sat on the edge of the bed and took Devia's
hand. 'I'll come back, I promise. It's just that I have to
go away for a while. To Pandemonium. There's something I have to do.'

She sat up and disengaged her hand from mine. Then
she swung her legs over the side of the bed and stood. I
thought that I had badly miscalculated; that my bald,
impatient appeal had met with the angry response that
it had probably deserved. When she walked, a little
unsteadily, across the room and towards the balcony I
considered drawing *Espiritu Santo*. It would have taken
but a bound and a skip, and I would have been directly
behind her, able to effect a swift, sharp blow to the base
of her skull with the rapier's pommel. I too rose from
the bed, fingers already caressing my precious blade's

scabbard. But luckily, something – a premonition of her good faith; the fact that I was nominally house-trained; perhaps even a trace of affection – made me hesitate.

On reaching the balcony she neither shouted for aid nor, in a spurned lover's fit of distemper, chose to throw herself over the balustrade. No; she simply looked out over the garden and the sea, seemingly at peace with herself.

I picked up the map from the night table, annoyed with myself for having been so negligent as to leave it there, for prioritizing lust and forgetting that that piece of parchment contained my hope, perhaps my only hope, of reaching Pandemonium. I crept up behind her and slipped an arm about her waist. She tried to walk forward, but I held her tight. I looked about to check that we were hidden from any onlookers who might have been below.

'Can you get me a boat?' I said, as I bent over and nibbled the tip of a long, pointed, feverish ear. 'Can you, my sweet?'

She continued to stare into the distance. I followed her line of sight, and saw that she focused on the imitation sun. The sun had remained overhead, at the point of meridian, ever since I had arrived in the harbour area. The mellowness of its refulgence allowed both of us to stare into its white, white heart without flinching. A segment had darkened, like the bruised cuticle of a fingernail. The sun, it seemed, was being slowly obscured by a black disc.

'Night is coming,' she said. 'For Tophet. And for me. Just as it came for the rest of my family.'

I continued to stare at the sun. It was as if I were

witnessing the Netherworld's equivalent of a solar eclipse.

'I've never seen such a thing,' I said, taking in the whole, stupendous panorama of an underground world turning from day into night. 'What *is* this place?'

'A place of magic,' she said. 'There are machines, strange engines that keep the sky from falling on our heads. Machines that give us light, create tides in the sea, that console us for being denied the real sky, the real sun.'

'You are talking about machines that once belonged to the Ancients,' I said. 'It seems incredible that your people still know how to use them.'

'They don't. They were turned on millennia ago, when my ancestors first buried themselves beneath the Earth. It is fortunate that they still run. Fortunate that they are self-perpetuating, and that no one knows where they are. We're scrap merchants now. If the less scrupulous amongst my people ever got their hands on such things, they'd strip them and sell the parts to Earth-Above. What fools we've become. What suicidal fools.' I nuzzled her neck. 'Pandemonium, they say is filled with such weird machines. It that why you wish to go there, captain? Are you another one of those humans who hopes to make himself rich by stealing our artefacts?'

'I go to Pandemonium to seek the antidote to the drug that simplifies my brothers and sisters.' I looked at her, waiting for the expected reaction of surprise, the exclamation that I was either insane or a simpleton. Perhaps illness, along with the bites, scratches, kisses and blows we had recently perpetuated on each other, had so exhausted her that she was beyond surprise. She remained impassive.

'I have heard that there are many drugs and mithridates in the city at the centre of the world. I have even heard that there is a universal elixir that remedies *all* ills.' She put a hand over my own. 'Pandemonium, they say, is the most beautiful city that has ever been built, either below or above the Earth's surface. It is vaster, more immense, than the seascape that you see before you here. Pandemonium's circumference is greater than the planet which harbours it. Its towers are unconstrained by rocky vaults. They reach to the stars. All things are possible there, go the stories. Perhaps there is even a cure for the plague.'

'It would not surprise me.' I said, sensing here an opportunity to win her over, 'it would not surprise me at all if there were. If we had a boat—'

'I have a boat, captain.'

'And,' I said, excited now, 'and is the maelstrom far off?'

'You plan to descend to the Great River? Yes, yes, I can see your reasoning. The river would eventually take you to the centre of the Earth. The maelstrom far off? No; but that is not the problem. The port is quarantined.'

'Are there many guards?' I said. 'Many watchmen?'

'The plague has accounted for much of our militia. But we do not need watchmen to look over our ships. We have the shadows.' By now, the artificial sun had been half-consumed by the black disc. The promenade and the sea were shrouded in a darkness that was deepening by the second. What passed for 'night' here would provide good cover, I reasoned. Shadows. Yes. I remembered what the girl at the lighthouse had said. The shadows were different in Tophet. They ate you. I would steal a boat while shrouded by such shadows, and, in the all-encompassing darkness, make my way on to the high seas.

Devia put a hand to her brow and her legs buckled. 'I feel faint. Help me inside. I need to lie down.'

I lifted her up and carried her back to the bed.

'It will get dark now. Very dark. Not like night as you know it on Earth-Above; night in the Netherworld is sentient, alive. Use the night to make your way to the quay and wait by a skiff called the *Lady Devia*. It is but another toy, like the little men my poor Mama would give me, one for every birthday. But it will take us to the maelstrom.'

'And will such a boat *survive* the maelstrom?'

'The machines that maintain Tophet also protect mariners who descend to the Naphtha.'

'But the barometric pressure alone—'

'Have you experienced any difficulties in Tophet? You are deep under the Earth already. Deeper than you suspect. But we will have to accept that, in negotiating the maelstrom, there will be certain dangers.'

'*We*?'

'Can you pilot a boat?'

'No, but—'

'I am coming with you, captain.' She put an arm about my neck and brought my face close to her own. 'In Pandemonium lies my one hope of cure. You can't get rid of this poor, dying girl so easily. Go to the *Lady Devia* and wait. I'll be ready in an hour.' And then her head rose a little from the pillow and she pressed her lips to my own so hard that I tasted blood.

Chapter Ten

I stood by the quayside. The shadows were as Devia had described them: alive. They swirled and assumed fantastic forms, some benevolent, most threatening. The *malignos*, I knew, found such dark, illusory play beautiful. Lying in bed with Gala, she would tell me stories about the shadows that swam across our bedroom walls, smiling with a child's delight, and speaking with the sort of religious fervour she usually reserved for prayer meetings and mass. And she would complain that, on Earth-Above, the night was of such an inferior order that, despite her love of the sun, her darker instincts often had her craving the shadows that lay beneath her feet, the beautiful, almost sentient shadows of the Netherworld.

I could hear water lapping against the *Lady Devia*'s hull. Bored, anxious, I flexed a leg and idly drove the heel of my boot into the ground. Then I kicked, my toe connecting with a pebble. Almost immediately I heard it plop into the sea. I shivered. It was as if I were again at the edge of some great abyss, its fathomless depths threatening to suck me into the void. I had not realized I stood quite so near to the water, and I moved onto surer ground.

The impact of the rock with the sea had generated scarcely more noise than the scrape of my boots over the cobblestones, yet I looked about, apprehensive that

I had been heard. Once again, phantom images of *malignos* roiled before me, demons made of darkness and air. But there were no shouts or alarms. I was alone, all about me either sleeping, dead or otherwise inanimate.

Then I saw and heard something which I could not so easily attribute to the dark. Nor to the effect it had on my fear-compromised imagination. A figure approached, a shadow amongst shadows. Man? Woman? Darkness seethed about its contours. I almost called out Devia's name, so anxious was I for the thing to uncloak and reveal itself to be her.

'Pike?' I recoiled and lifted a hand to my left ear to protect it from that single, stabbing syllable of bastardized English. 'Pike? Is that you?' The pain of recognition subsided, though the rush of astonishment I had felt still percolated through my limbs and vitals.

'Keep your voice down,' I whispered, angrily, as the Tasmanian waddled into view.

'I thought you'd been taken,' he said, with a big, ingenuous grin. He stopped a few metres away, then moved forward. Stopped again, embarrassed, it seemed, at his own demonstrativeness, his artless joy at having encountered me. He had thought better than to follow through and offer me an embrace. The disposition to physical congress that I had detected in his glinting, pig-like eyes, had me fingering *Espiritu Santo*. 'What's been going on, Pike?'

'I've got us a boat, that's what's been going on.'

He made a swift evaluation of the skiff. 'Not bad.'

'You can pilot that?'

'It's not much more than a toy,' he said. The skiff had

a narrow hull, but wasn't quite as small as he opined. It resembled one of the sampans that sometimes sailed into Subic Bay. High-masted, with a generous stern and a low brow, it was rigged with a single lugsail, but also boasted two pairs of oars. I knew that, despite its modest dimensions, such a vessel was seaworthy.

'A bagatelle for a young lady's pleasure,' I concurred. 'But she'll take us to the maelstrom, eh?'

He lifted his eyebrows. 'Sure she will. I can handle her.' It was then that I noticed that he carried our water bottles over his shoulder, and that a satchel, filled with the food we had taken from the lighthouse, was roped about his waist. He had even thought to sling my money belt and field glasses about his neck. I grinned and slapped him on the shoulder. The sound of my palm connecting with that big slab of shivery meat resounded over the quay. I cursed; but now that I had got over the initial shock of our unexpected rendezvous, the relief I felt at running into the Tasmanian, and not some bogeyman with horns and a pointed tail, had needed some release.

He wasn't such a bad sort. He really wasn't. The sight of him certainly no longer induced the kind of pain and disgust that it was wont to. 'When I was a corsair on the Sea of Cathay—' I lifted my eyes to heaven, but let him continue. Despite my teaching post at the Naval College, I knew nothing of boats. My classes had been designed to acquaint gentlemen officers with the humanities, not prepare them for the practical aspects of life on the high seas. If I had known about piloting, navigation and general seamanship, I would not have waited so patiently for Devia. But with the Tasmanian here, I no longer cared to put the captaincy of the little vessel in her hands. She was, after all, merely a girl with whom I had had a meteoric fling. One who had a different, and wholly self-interested agenda. And one who, damn it all, was a *malignos*.

Besides, I needed someone at the helm who was in the full bloom of health. A sea gypsy. A pirate.

'Yes, yes,' I interrupted at last, 'you'll recall that you've told me of your freebooting exploits before. Now tell: did you pass any militia or watchmen on the way here?'

'No; the whole place is deserted.'

'Peculiar,' I said. 'But we should not look a gift horse in the mouth.'

'I agree. Let's not hang around.'

'Are we likely, do you think,' I said, 'to encounter a coast guard?'

'Most likely. How else can the port enforce quarantine?'

'How else indeed,' I said, looking about me uneasily. 'Let's hope a small boat will pass their notice. Are you ready?'

'Of course.'

We strode up the *Lady Devia*'s gangplank.

Once aboard, the Tasmanian hauled the gangplank in, hoisted the anchor, and then sat down and took up a pair of oars. He gestured that I should do likewise with the second set. Clumsily, I fitted my oars into the rowlocks. I gazed upward. The lug was furled. But with the breeze that gusted over the water I knew we should make good progress once we cleared the quay and began to sail.

The Tasmanian had just dipped his oars when I heard a cry from the shore.

'Captain, wait for me!' The cry had come as if out of a swirling fog, the bank of darkness that hung over the quay now assuming the texture of a natural meteorological phenomenon, a sea mist constituted of night. 'Don't cast off, captain. Don't leave me behind. Remember our bargain. Remember what we *mean* to each other!' I leant forward and put my hand on the Tasmanian's shoulder.

'A moment,' I said.

'She's a *malignos*,' he said, flatly. 'She'll alert the guard.'

'No,' I said. 'Wait.'

Seeing her again, so sick, so desperate to leave, had weakened my resolve. I determined to take her with us.

We stowed our oars. Devia jumped into the sea and began to swim.

'Does she account for your last few hours, Pike?' said the Tasmanian, his voice now containing more than a trace of irritation. I put a hand over the side. She grasped it, took hold of the gunwale, and, with my assistance, pulled herself into the boat. Even in the darkness I could see that the sea to either side of her was stained with blood. She fell on to the deck. The brine that puddled about her was streaked with pink, like her scales and hair. It was as if the boat belonged to a fisherman who had recently gutted his catch of salmon. The Tasmanian turned and looked down at her. His face was contorted with anxiety and contempt. 'And what are we supposed to do *now*?'

'Carry on rowing,' I said, putting some authority into

my voice. I knelt down and cradled her head in my arm and brushed the matted hair out of her eyes. 'I'm sorry,' I said to her, 'I couldn't wait.'

'I knew you were a bastard, captain, but I suppose I'd hoped you were a sentimental bastard. I didn't expect to get dumped *quite* so soon.' Despite having no second oarsman to assist him, the Tasmanian had already rowed us some way from the quay. In the distance, the anchored galleons were fast disappearing into the mist of shadows that had by now completely engulfed the town. 'Are we really going to Pandemonium, captain?' continued the sick little *malignos* maid, staring up at me, her rust-coloured irises distended with vain hope.

'Yes, we are,' I said. But I knew her hour had come. Even as I spoke, she was dying.

The Tasmanian stood up. He raised the sail. Braced with battens, it resembled the wing of a gigantic *malignos*. The canvas turned and creaked, and then caught the wind. My companion retreated to the stern and settled himself by the tiller. We began to clip along at a smart pace.

The shadows closed about us.

I hunkered down and peeped over the gunwale to try to descry some sign of the gunboats that the Tasmanian had warned were likely patrolling offshore. But I saw nothing. I turned about. Only pinpricks of light identified the castle and the various warehouses and customs-houses that occupied the quay. I felt I was again at the top of the abyss, looking down onto the fires that illuminated the roofs and spires of Tophet. But unlike the abyss, I did not come to perceive more lights as my eyes adjusted to the gloom. Rather, I seemed to see more darkness, the shadows ever thickening about the spot from which we had recently cast off.

Though far from being on the high seas, and equally far from safety, I felt a measure of composure, a mood almost of complacence, which the sight of the coagulating shadows should have immediately revoked. But it was some time before the shadows alerted me that my *sangfroid* had been misplaced.

The shadows were indeed alive, and not just metaphorically. The swirl of darkness seethed with a self-organizing intelligence.

And then the shadows assumed an anthropomorphic shape.

The shape was imbued with a foreboding as unnameable as it was potent. It represented a quintessence of negativity, an ultimate darkness thrown into relief by the nominal blackness of the night.

The first thing to emerge had been a headless torso. Soon, limbs became defined. And then, surmounting torso and limbs, I seemed to descry a great hornèd skull.

The Tasmanian had stopped rowing. 'What is it?' he said.

Devia clutched my arm and, with a huge effort of will, brought herself into a sitting position. She looked into my eyes, and her own eyes, already big, distended even further. In my pupils she saw reflected, I think, what I saw: the unnaturally deep shadows of the thing on the quay, its outline imprinted on my retinae by virtue of its inverted brilliance. 'It is the Tenebros,' she said. 'It has come for me.'

'Is it truly alive?' I said.

'Yes,' she said, coughing up a little blood. 'It is

conjured up by the same engines that put the sun and moon in Tophet's sky. It is the shadow beast that maintains quarantine.'

The thing she had called the Tenebros waded into the water. I could tell, even at this considerable distance, that it was huge, for though it had moved some way from the quay, the sea only came up to its ankles. It proceeded to wade into a deeper stretch of water, the waves lapping about its knees, and then its thighs. By the time it stood waist-deep it became increasingly evident that it was heading in our direction.

'You say it has come for you?' I asked the dying girl.

'I'm afraid I've used you somewhat, captain, just as you, doubtless, have used me. The Tenebros sees only those who have succumbed to plague. I thought that it would not harm me if I were with a human. I thought you would provide me with a degree of camouflage. Oh captain, I should so liked to have seen Pandemonium. I have always wanted to go there. I have always wanted to behold its beauty. And its necromancers are said to be the greatest in the Netherworld. If anyone could have cured me, it would have been them.' I stroked her cheek. The Tasmanian leant into his oars and rowed for all he was worth. I thought, briefly, of taking up my own oars and assisting him. But the Tenebros had already covered half the distance that separated us from the shore. We could not, I knew, outrun it.

I gently lowered Devia to the deck.

I got to my feet, straddled the supine girl, and drew *Espiritu Santo*.

'It's no use,' she mumbled. 'The Tenebros cannot be harmed.'

The Tasmanian relinquished his efforts to effect our escape. He stood up. As he did so, he lifted one of the oars and held it before him like an oversized quarterstaff.

The Tenebros was almost upon us. Its shape had grown no more distinct. It was still a vague conglomerate of limbs, with a shifting mass of darkness in place of a head, and two black jewels, like holes punched through space to reveal the pure nothingness that lay behind this nonsensical world, in place of eyes. The sea was up to what might be interpreted as the thing's chest when it stretched out an arm. Shadows closed palpably around us, making my flesh tingle and sting, as if I had been bitten by a thousand sandflies. Five wisps of darkness extended and fluttered above me; five fingers, each one of which was several metres long. I slashed at the black pseudopodia, my blade passing straight through the smoky flesh without effecting damage. A more extreme sample of that tingling sensation I had felt but a moment ago coursed up my arm, across my chest, and down my leg and into the sole of my boot, where my toes curled in protest. Benumbed, my fingers opened and my rapier clattered on to the deck. I let out a belated cry and fell to one side, away from Devia.

The Tasmanian cast me a brief look. He himself was engaged in trying to ward off the Tenebros; the oar, which he manipulated with improbable ease, swept through the air and the thing's body. The Tenebros ignored him in the same way it had me, as unaware of my presence as it doubtless was of all whom were not afflicted with plague. The shadowy hand dipped into the boat, wrapped its fingers like a set of insubstantial tentacles about Devia's body, and lifted the screaming girl high into the air. Immediately it turned its back on us and began wading back towards the shore.

The Tasmanian and I said nothing. Neither did we look at each other. We had not been long in the Netherworld – though it was longer than most men had reason to know – but we were becoming accustomed to its shadow life, and inured to that life's horrors. Struck dumb, I yet felt something forcing its way out of my throat, something demanding expression. The sight of the Tenebros receding into the distance, the girl crushed within its hand, brought a cry to my lips that echoed the girl's own, her screams carrying across the water like a fracture in the otherwise perfectly sealed night. The Tasmanian looked my way. Abashed, he averted his gaze and stared down at his feet. Then he sat down and rested his forehead upon his knees.

My cry dissipated into the air. Like a cracked bell, it was for a moment as if my soul, my wretched, impoverished soul, had been struck by a hammer. Ringing out as it had, as shell-shocked by the darkness as, perhaps, at no other time since the war, it had cleared away two weeks of accumulated dread. Somewhat abashed myself, I sat down and took up a rowing position. My mind was like ice, cool with the purpose that had brought me to the Netherworld.

The Tasmanian seemed as resolute as me. He had lit a lantern. I reached into my doublet and retrieved the map. Leaning backward, I passed it to him. And then I dug out my compass, and handed that over too.

'The maelstrom it is, then?' he said.

I nodded. 'The maelstrom.'

We sailed for two nights before we sighted our objective. The quiescent mood that had descended upon us after Devia had been taken lingered. I had spent most of our brief voyage staring at the bottom, determined that we should not miss sighting the maelstrom through any negligence. The Tasmanian and I had not spoken for days.

Leaving the harbour, we had experienced choppy seas. But when the dawn came the sea had become like glass. It had remained so for the duration. We had spied no other vessels. The plague seemed to have kept all shipping well away.

With my gaze habitually fixed upon the horizon, I came to wonder how far this great stretch of water extended, and upon what kind of shores its waves might break. Parts of the Netherworld so distant, perhaps, that they lay beneath India, Arabia, or even Europa. We were to be given no chance to explore this hypothesis. The maelstrom greeted us shortly after sunrise on our second day at sea. The Tasmanian had proved his worth as a sailor.

I need not have feared missing the great whirlpool. It was an abyss such as the one by which we had descended to Tophet, its liquid walls as vast and mysterious as those walls that had been made of rock. But there was no possibility that the present chasm might be demystified by a burst of light. The interior of its great, sucking cone was clearly visible, the artificial sun that illuminated it only compounding the enigma of its being.

Malignos

Shortly after escaping from Tophet, the Tasmanian and I had agreed that, when the moment came, we should not waste time on debating how best to enter the maelstrom, but simply commit ourselves to its mercies. The silence that had subsequently infected us had grown so chronic, that only now, as our boat was sucked towards the maelstrom's lip, did I find myself ready to question the wisdom of that decision. Not that such debate could have been anything but academic. For as I looked out over the side, my knuckles whitening as they gripped the gunwale, I saw, not only that the drop was more awesome, more deadly, than I could have imagined, but that we no longer had a choice. We were committed.

The boat teetered. I tasted vomit. Beneath the prow lay a cataclysm of foam, a striated, bubbling tumult. The uppermost stratum licked at the hull. Jerking the boat onto its side, it snatched us from the calm of the sea and into its giddy merry-go-round.

I fell sideways and clung to the mast. I saw the Tasmanian was desperately trying to rope himself to the tiller. Just before I was blinded by the spray, the full immensity of the phenomenon that was sucking us inexorably downward became apparent. Extending as far as the eye could see, a great vortex had opened up beneath us, its perspective lost to darkness. Each of its serried, roaring strata was like a road that wound down an upside-down mountain, promising deliverance or destruction at a rendezvous far beneath the earth. Road melded into road. Soon, there was only a single highway of liquid blue that whipped us about with ever-increasing velocity.

I felt as if my head were being squeezed in a vice. Daring, for a moment, to free a hand, I pinched my nose and blew until my ears popped and equalized the pressure. Then I wrapped both arms and both legs about the mast. The centrifugal force tautened my jowls so that I wore a dead man's grin. My brain grew starved of blood. I was light-headed, and in danger of passing out. Again, I hazarded freeing a hand. Then I unbuckled my sword-belt, looped it about the mast, and re-secured it. I consoled myself with the thought that, I would, at least, not fall overboard, even if the *Lady Devia* should end up at the bottom of the sea. I gripped the mast with all my strength. But the belt, it seemed, would be put to the test sooner than I had anticipated. My ears buzzed. And a black curtain descended behind my eyes. The vortex continued to whip us furiously, urgently, calamitously down, down into the Netherworld's deepest depths. Vomit dribbled between my teeth. And then the darkness at last claimed me.

I don't know how long I was unconscious. But when I came to, shook my head and looked about me, the boat no longer spun about, but drifted in sluggish waters.

The Naphtha, I thought. The Great River that runs through the Torrid Zone. Above me, what had been the maelstrom was now a cataract, pouring through the jewelled roof of a vast cavern. We had already drifted some way from where the waterfall crashed into the river. There was no wind. We seemed caught in a leisurely current. And the current had conveyed us to safety.

As we drifted, the walls of metamorphic and granite rock that I could see in the distance receded into a hazy, undefined area of light. Low in the sky, another sun bore down on me with startling brilliance. It was quite different from the sun that had illuminated Tophet. I reeled under its heat. It was a hellish sun. It was the sun of the lands that extended beyond the margins of my map. The sun of the Torrid Zone.

I leaned over the gunwale, scooped up a little brackish water and bathed my forehead. The Tasmanian was still out, rendered insensible, as I had been, by our descent. His bearish frame was bent double over the ropes that secured him to the tiller.

I surveyed the new landscape that we were fated to negotiate. On either bank were mangrove swamps. Birdsong filled the humid air. There seemed no evidence of *malignos*. Ahead, the sun ascended to an altitude unconstrained by the jewelled roof immediately above me. I loosened my collar. The sound of the cataract was now no more than a susurration. As the boat continued to make headway, the roof of the cavern disappeared. Where there had been a polychromatic canopy of stone, there was now only sky, a low, grey, washed-out sky that yet suggested it bordered the infinite.

And then I descried, rising from some distant point in the river, and shimmering behind a haze of convection, the unmistakable evidence of inhuman engineering.

Unbuttoning my doublet, I took out the map that I had acquired from the Countess Suspiria and tossed it over the gunwale. As I watched it float away it occurred to me that the Tasmanian might have been right. The countess had perhaps tricked me into following a route that would result in my destruction. Again, I looked ahead, trying to resolve the far-off settlement into its constituents. I saw towers, cupolas, minarets. The sun was high now, high enough to set metallic roofs ablaze with white, scintillating light. I turned away, half-blinded.

It seemed that I was drifting into the very heartland of hell, an inferno that I would never escape.

Chapter Eleven

'There's something out there,' I said, looking out over the black river and into the primeval forest that lined the banks. 'I know there is. Something intent on our annihilation.' The forest was as black as the river. The subterranean artery that I had travelled along for three months was akin to an artery of poisoned blood, corrupting all that it passed through. Or so my diseased fancy would have it. I dismissed the likelihood that the river's discoloration could be accounted for by tannic acid released from the leaves of submerged trees. I dismissed the likelihood that I floated down a waterway that neither poisoned nor was poisoned by the surrounding jungle. For I could not rid myself of the suspicion that something malevolent was at work. Over a course of days, I had felt the presence of a supernatural agency. It was immanent in the rotting life, the dark river and the scorched, grey sky, and it seemed resolved to inflict upon me the same fate that it had inflicted upon the landscape. Soon my flesh and spirit would be as black as the tainted earth. 'This place is haunted. Haunted by some kind of monstrous *entity*. An entity that is stripping the sanity from our minds as surely as it's stripping the meat from our bones.'

'You believe in ghosts, Pike?' said the Tasmanian. 'A man like you? How strange. How strange for you to believe in anything.'

I did not turn around. I was locked in communion with the jungle. My ears pricked. The insect song seemed to contain a message. A message, I thought, just for me. The susurration would peak, there would be an interval of utter silence, and then the buzz and chitter would resume. I strained to interpret. The details escaped me. All that seemed certain was that I was being served coded notice of my dissolution.

'I have always been a sceptic,' I said. I lowered my gaze, wearied by the sight of my surroundings and its indecipherable symphony. 'Superstition disgusts me. Still—'

I crouched and rested my cheek upon the gunwale. The river's surface was untroubled except for the ripples precipitated by the boat's lazy headway. It reflected my image as faultlessly as a mirror of polished onyx. I stared into its glass. A haggard caricature of my own face stared back. I withdrew and, after nervously scanning the horizon one last time, got down on my hands and knees and crawled under the awning that was the boat's only protection against the depredations of the sun. To have paid too much attention to that wide-eyes *doppelgänger* would have only hastened the curdling of my brain.

'Ghosts,' I continued. 'Gala believes in ghosts. She believes in all sorts of things. Heaven, angels, the resurrection of the dead. She says scepticism is sometimes a fine thing, but more often than not it's a vice.' And Gala, I thought, knew much about my vices. Not only my little addictions to things of the flesh. But my greatest vice, my predilection to despair.

'But the alternative?' said the Tasmanian. His

breathing was laboured. His brow was dripping with sweat. But he had begun to speak with a clarity that contradicted not only his torpor but also his habitual crassness. 'Must we so easily surrender to our own demons?'

'The alternative,' I said, 'sometimes seems to be belief in nothing. That is, the kind of belief we in the Darkling Isle have: that life is worthless, and a man is a fool to think otherwise. And what is that, but another kind of superstition?' And I thought of London's streets, where every eye seemed to glint with malice and calculation. 'I envy Gala sometimes. Envy her artlessness. Her innocence.'

'Don't envy her today,' said my companion. 'Innocence? Ha. Innocence can't help us. Think instead about resisting the call of paranoia. We mustn't give in to morbid reflection, Pike. We mustn't surrender to the wanderings of our minds. Not here. Not in this place.'

Inert, the Tasmanian sprawled upon the deck, appropriating what little shade we enjoyed. I gave him a punch in the ribs and he rolled over. It was as well his bulk had been diminished by the meagreness of our diet. For if he had not been half-starved I would have been forced to exercise more extreme measures in order to claim my own share of the shadows. As it was, his much-reduced body mass, now that it was turned upon its side, had allocated me a cool, dark patch of ground sufficient for my needs. I myself was leaner than I would have wished. No longer the spry, trimmed-down soldier, I was for the first time in my life, feeling my age.

Restless, fidgety, slapping his hands against his greasy abdomen, he rearranged his body so that he faced me. His eyes were like those of a dead heifer.

'Pike, do I look as bad as I feel?'

For someone of refined sensibilities, such as myself, it had been a small if, in the end, insignificant mercy that the brute was partly clothed. With the aid of a needle and yarn used for patching the sail he had fashioned a pair of loose-fitting sailor's trousers from the bedsheet that had served to cover him in Tophet. Despite masking fifty percent of his reduced but still corpulent frame, his ability to inspire disgust was undiminished.

'Tell me, Pike,' he repeated, with the fatalistic air of a patient asking his quack for the bad news. 'Tell me the truth.'

'The truth,' I said, my patience not what it should have been, 'would be cruel.'

'Please, Pike—'

'And,' I continued, 'to praise, offensively ironic. To execrate' – I sighed – 'well, to merely state the obvious. I must, it seems, retreat into silence.' At that moment the jungle was seized with one of its own fits of absolute quiet. To my starved, chimerical mind, these hiatuses seemed to substitute for changes in barometric pressure, changes curiously absent from a river journey that had taken us ever deeper into the Earth's bowels. Ancient machines were, I suppose, responsible for keeping those natural forces at bay, just as they were responsible for the gravity-defying vaults and uncanny spaces we had passed under and through. But they could do nothing to avert the periodic invasions of silence. I put my hands to my head. Though I knew it to be an illusion, I could not help but feel that my eardrums were dilating from the force of incalculable atmospheres.

The Tasmanian grunted, breaking the enforced quiet. He was, of late, as tetchy as me. He rolled over on his back and looked up at the awning that was all that shielded us from the oblique rays of light that fell from the cavern's seemingly boundless empyrean.

'How deep are we, Pike?' The clarity had gone. He had begun to bleat, no longer a man but a big fat school-boy. The booby-boy that he had regularly metamor-phosed into throughout our travels. A boy such as I had discovered in a grimoire while at my studies in London. The illustration that had been labelled *Tweedledum*.

'I've no idea,' I said. 'Sometimes I feel as if I'm dreaming. Sometimes I feel we've made our way back to the surface.' The sun was low enough in the sky to ambush our sanctuary with needle-like stabs of brilliance. But at least, with that great artificial lamp far past meridian, we no longer suffered so intensely from the heat.

'This jungle—' he croaked.

'Yeah, this jungle. This sun. This river. We could almost be in the archipelago.' I lifted myself up on one elbow and squinted left and right. Though my line of sight was partially obscured by the *Lady Devia*'s port bows, my gaze took in a sliver of jungle canopy that, while nominally resembling a tropical skyline of Earth-Above, was also fundamentally *other*. 'Almost. But not quite.' The spatiality of *terra firma* had been replaced, here, by dimensions that, however closely they approximated those with which I was familiar, were yet unremittingly alien. Indeed, in the Torrid Zone, the sense of alien geometry was even more acute than it had been in Tophet. The dimensional warping was, doubtless, a side-effect of the tremendous energies required to sustain the Netherworld's vast, overarching architecture. And, given that the warping and perversion of space could be expected to increase the nearer we approached the Earth's core, the weird angles and planes of the surrounding landscape suggested that we were fast approaching Pandemonium.

I eased my weight off my elbow and again lay down on the deck. The landscape distressed me, but I could not but be thankful that the ancient machines that distorted local space-time also prevented me from being simultaneously cooked, suffocated and crushed.

The sun – a great blister afflicting the taut, grey skin of the sky – was dipping beneath the treetops. Day and night in the Zone mimicked the diurnal round of Earth-Above, if somewhat over-exactly. The Tasmanian and I lay in speechless anticipation of the balm of darkness to fall. We would soon be offered a full twelve hours of respite from the heat.

At last, the sun disappeared beneath the horizon. Almost at once, a green, phosphorescent fog, such as one would expect to encounter in an ill-tended grave-yard, rose from the riverbank. The same fog had greeted us at close of day ever since we had entered this plutonic region. And as usual, it was accompanied by a cloacal odour that emanated from the Naphtha. For the Naphtha, at nightfall, became stippled with green bubbles, the fog, perhaps, having its origins in the rotting vegetation that lay both above and beneath the river. To compensate, perhaps, for a lack of moonlight, our passage was illuminated by a dull, eerie glow.

The temperature began to fall, as if we had been transplanted from a jungle into a desert.

I dragged myself out from under the awning and stood up, picking up my military accoutrements as I did so. Then, leaning against the boat's side, I proceeded to supplement my sparse wardrobe – I wore only boots and codpiece – with belt, scabbard and rapier. My discarded leather doublet and trousers lay nearby, my pipe, broken, on top of them. It had grown cooler, and would become cooler yet. But it would be some hours before I would have cause to put on the rest of my clothes.

I walked past the mast and its furled sail to stand on the prow. I scanned the surrounding country. On the right bank, on a bend in the river, and nimbused with emerald light, was another of the lost cities, the like of which had, for the past ten days, been our only source of water and food. It looked out of the fog as if from a green, aquarelle wash, through which penned lines articulated its mould-streaked stonework of arches, spires and doorways.

The conviction that a malevolent intelligence, an evil *genius loci*, was biding its time, returned to haunt me. The conviction was strengthened by every disembodied howl, chitter and ululation that emanated from the jungle's interior. By every punctuative silence. Night accentuated the symphony of terror that rose from the jungle's glutinous folds, just as it did the terrible silences. The beasts who made the music were rarely glimpsed. Those that I had seen shared the land's spirit of decay, each snake, alligator, parakeet and ape a thing dreadful to behold. Putrescent, the creatures seemed to have died a long time ago, but were, paradoxically, still vital with some undermined force.

I jerked my head about. Somewhere, in the shadows along the shore, a sound that had seemed especially sinister pricked my ears: the slither of a white belly across mud. It had been followed by a splash.

'Another dead city, then,' said the Tasmanian, from behind. I had been so absorbed in scanning the river for whatever fell animal had just slipped beneath its murky surface that I had not heard him when he had risen to join me on the prow. I started, and my hand immediately sought the hilt of *Espiritu Santo*. I caressed the jewel-encrusted shaft nervously, from guard to pommel. And then, dismissing the interruption with a click of my tongue, pulled the blade clear of its sheath. The Tasmanian stepped backward. I ignored him and took out the whetstone that I kept in my belt. Falling to work, I tried to forget the almost-palpable threat surrounding me by losing myself in the homely task of honing my rapier's edge.

'Perhaps we'll have more luck this time,' I said.

'We'd better,' said the Tasmanian. 'If we don't find supplies soon, then—' He let the silence intimate the greater silence we would be drawn into if we went much longer without provisions. The silence that the jungle, in its intervals of quietus, seemed to prefigure. The water from the Naphtha was not potable, and what fruit grew in the jungle exuded a scent that suggested a certain lethality. Sometimes, amongst the ruined cities we had passed upriver, we would discover an unspoilt well, or even, in abandoned granaries and slaughterhouses, a little salted rat-meat or a crust of stale bread. And this had been all that we had had to sustain us for several weeks. The food, I speculated, had been dropped by whatever nomads made use of these urban wastelands. Or by birds that had migrated here from the Torrid Zone's less inhospitable parts. No food belonging to the cities' original inhabitants could have survived, for each city had been abandoned, I had judged, for hundreds, maybe even thousands of years.

'But why should it *be* like this,' said my companion, as if reading my thoughts. 'Upriver, there were *malignos* in their millions, and cities even more stunning than Tophet. You'd think that, as we neared Pandemonium, they'd be life a-plenty. But all we're met by is desolation. Why have the *malignos* left this place?'

'Why indeed?' I said, my labours with the whetstone becoming, if not frantic, then imbued with a violence that betrayed my anxiety. Why indeed, I asked myself, should this stretch of water be so different from upriver?

At the outset of our journey along the Naphtha we had passed densely-populated Cheos, Sheol, Tammuz, Eblis and Mulciber. Because of their teeming populations we had, before approaching the outskirts of these cities, always taken care to anchor within the haven of jungle cover or the mouth of some stream leading inland. Anywhere, in fact, where we might escape notice of both the native population and the vessels that plied the waterway. Come nightfall, we would emerge, and make our way with muffled oars to a point where we might purloin supplies from the nearby wharves.

Cheos had been the first city we had encountered. It

had been the one I had seen in the haze-saturated distance when we had first breached the Torrid Zone. Cheos had been spread over a hundred or more islets, its architecture utilizing the corralline structures of its brackish estuary as raw material. Sheol was a city of green pyramids. The mangroves at this point had disappeared to be replaced by the now too-familiar jungle. Within Sheol's environs, the primeval forest had been sculpted into fantastic hanging gardens – gardens whose uncatalogued flora the Tasmanian and I might have been the first humans to see. Tammuz hung from the cavern's roof: Eblis had been built underwater; and Mulciber, the 'city of bridges', was composed of structures – too ingenious, really, to be called simply bridges – that spanned the Naphtha for a length of several kilometres. Passing under them one night, we witnessed a great carnival taking place, each crumbling, turreted parabola of stone lit up with lanterns and fireworks. The faces picked out by the stuttering bursts of light had suggested that we were passing beneath the triumphal arches of a Hell that had suddenly become less metaphorical.

We had left such things behind us. Just as we had left, perhaps, all such life. What was it, I asked myself again, that had made the *malignos* abandon this region? The lands on the approach to their capital should have been more populous than those of Cheos, Sheol, Tammuz, Eblis and Mulciber. Logically, that is. But it was not so.

'Out there,' said the Tasmanian, breathlessly, 'look!' He gestured towards the ruins. Two figures had materialized from out of the shadows. Mounted on giant black rats – each one as big as a pony – they loitered by the water's edge. Their eyes, glinting against the dark backdrop, were keen and fearless. The rats, it seemed, were more concerned at our approach than their riders, who jerked at their reins, smoothed down their hackles.

My field glasses were buried under my pile of clothes. To go rooting about for them would take too much time. Time in which the strangers might disappear into the overgrown ruins. I concentrated my gaze as much as I was able.

Forgetting, for a moment, the riders. I studied the rats. They evoked a certain degree of consternation. Giant rats were common to these parts. We had tried to kill one or two for the cooking pot before learning that they were more likely to kill us. But these rodents seemed to have been domesticated. I let my gaze wander. Columns and blasted monuments rose behind rat and rider, ruins that might have served for the stage scenery of a romantic masque. Dame Nature – ugly crone that she was – had compounded the effect by entwining the stones and sculptures with a grotesque array of black vegetation. Our boat drifted closer. I brought my gaze back to bear upon the figures that now dominated the landscape. The figures shifted in their saddles, but seemed otherwise disinclined to acknowledge us. They were *malignos*.

'Girls?' asked the Tasmanian, with that rhetorical superfluousness with which he sometimes, despite my warnings, liked to vex me. Despite the distance that still separated us, it was obvious that these *malignos* were females. Adolescent females, it seemed.

'Chickababes,' I said, as the figures became more

defined against the abandoned city. The tinkling of their scales carried over the water. It reminded me of wind-chimes. My ears also picked up the sound of their hair as they flicked their manes out of their eyes to get a better view of us. The soughing of hair was as musical as the restless scales, each metallic strand like the string of a magnificently complex Aeolian harp. 'And they would appear quite beautiful,' I added. The Tasmanian shook his head, not so much in disagreement, I felt, but in apprehension. My sense of female beauty is not, perhaps, in harmony with the average human's. In some men, and the majority of women, the frank admission of my tastes often evokes a certain disquiet, and, in many cases, an alarm that often shades over into panic. 'Chickababes,' I said again, in a vulgar, sensual drawl.

The boat had swung full about. We seemed to be drifting inexorably towards them. As we came nearer visual appreciation of their scales overcame the aural. Like rhinestones, they were, gloriously trashy, and suggesting cheap all-night taverns and cafés. I was reminded of *The Sick Rose* and of Snub-nosed Marie, One-eyed Annabella and Lazy Laughing Languid Jenny. Marie, my favourite, had been only fifteen. Like her, like all those bad, bad girls, these chickababe *malignos* evoked qualities that were bound to appeal to a man's hebephilic propensities, of his longed-for idea of a *femininity* that combined acute girlishness with the demoniacal. I tucked the whetstone into my belt and sheathed my sword.

'It's a trap, Pike,' said the Tasmanian.

'Maybe,' I said, trying to concentrate less on the

toothsome pair and more on the practical aspects of our plight. 'But they look well fed.' The girls were as buxom as any pink, plump tavern wench a man might tumble in the back streets of London. Indeed, in my light-headed, distracted state, they seemed the very quintessence of buxomness. I wet my lips. 'I'll warrant there must be a good supply of food here. It stands to reason.' The boat continued to drift towards where the girls sat, stroking the heckles of their sleek, black mounts. They seemed to have taken up their position in the knowledge that the river's current would deliver us to that spot. 'Besides,' I concluded, 'they're just chickababes.'

'I've been pussywhacked too many times in the barrio not to be a mite cautious when it comes to *young girls*,' he said. 'Perhaps I should get on the tiller while—'

'No,' I said, with casual *schadenfreude*. 'We'll trust to the current and allow the boat to decide our fate.' I knew that where two stood there might be more, many more, in hiding. But my soldier's intuition told me that these girls were alone. I could tell it by their bearing and by the qualities of the vegetation that caparisoned the ruins. Nothing had been disturbed here for a long, long time. But I let the Tasmanian stew. It amused me.

'I don't like this, Pike. All the problems in my life I can pretty much put down to alcohol and women.'

'I know the feeling. But you want to starve?' He held his tongue.

Food. Water. And what more, pray? I was determined that the promise of this unexpected assignation should be fulfilled. Knowledge as well as nutriment was to be gained here, surely. Was I not a scholar? And food, water, knowledge and much else would, perhaps, fall into the hands of one who would seize the opportunity to woo. Retreat had, in any case, become impossible. The boat had been drawn into a channel which allowed us no deviation from our present course.

The deck juddered as the keel ploughed through the muddy shallows. The Tasmanian threw out the anchor. We had come to rest.

'*Hello* there,' I said, immediately cursing myself for the lameness of my salutation. In order to make up for it I vaulted the gunwale and landed knee-deep in water. I don't know if, by doing so, I impressed them with my virility. I think it unlikely. Sunburnt, half-naked, with folds of loose skin hanging from my chest and a three-month length of beard, I was not at my best. Indeed, it is conceivable that I even looked a little ridiculous. What the hell, I thought. I'm Richard Pike. I can slay a female heart or two, even in this pitiable condition. *Carpe noctem*. And so girding myself, and with the mud sucking at my boots, I waded to the shore.

Again, I hallooed. But this time I tried to invest my greeting with a degree of potency. The girls looked at each other, mouths agape, each one pulling in the reins of their mounts as the rats ground their teeth and swished their pink tails. And then, as each girl looked down at me, their mouths transformed into taut, amused crescents, their own tails flicked back and forth. Those arrow-headed lengths of sequinned cartilage slipped through the black fur of their mounts; wove lazy, insolent patterns in the air; snapped in fits of whip-like excitement. I have always considered the *malignos* female's take one of the world's great erotic secrets, one fated to remain forever undiscovered by the ordinary, philistine run of human males. Did these adolescents know my tastes? Was I such an open book? Undoubtedly. For I was conscious that they were flirting, and that the flirtation was having a most uncomfortable effect.

'My name is Pike,' I said, looking at an abstract point above the girls' heads, trying to keep my thoughts as much off the tightness of my codpiece as off those who had stampeded my hormones into testing its capacity to withstand extreme levels of stress. 'Richard Pike. My companion and I are on our way to Pandemonium. We are in need of food. Water. Might I prevail on you for—'

Behind me, cutting the introductions short, was a scream. I spun about, my sword already half out of its scabbard. But before I could unsheathe it I was immobilized by a sight that turned my bowels to jelly. Towering over the boat, and still rising from an explosion of black foam, was something that seemed either a bipedal alligator or a gigantic, cold-blooded ape. And then the matter became clear. The thing was a chimera. Its wedge-like reptilian jaw had been grafted on to a simian head. Swaying back and forth, the unnatural beast champed at the fabric of the night sky. And then it bore downward, the rows of sabre-like teeth that lined the long, slathering muzzle descending towards the Tasmanian like a fatal rain of enamel-bright stars.

A gout of flame. For a second, the riverbank became as day. Within the space of that stutter of light, time slowed to a crawl. I saw that the thing, besides being a hybridization of alligator and ape, possessed elements of other beasts. An embryonic lupine countenance protruded from its armpit. And fins, like those of a shark's, lined its back. The creature's muzzle seemed to melt, like cheese left out in the sun. Melt, slowly, slowly. And then the flow of time quickened. The creature roared, choked, and fell back into the river as silently as it had appeared. All that was left to verify that its appearance had been real and not an hallucination was another explosion of foam and the still echoing scream of the Tasmanian.

I looked over my shoulder. One of the girls was tucking what seemed like a small arquebus into her saddlebag. 'One of our less successful efforts,' she said, gazing across the black water to the point where it still bubbled with the outrageous beast's return to the deep. 'We don't even have a name for it.' She spoke good, if heavily accented, English. I was about to ask for an explanation, but the yawn she stifled seemed to suggest that she regarded the entire incident as tedious. And as if to confirm that her ennui was habitual, her wings unfolded with a gummy sound indicative of lack of use. They beat indolently at the air, and then smartly tucked themselves away across her back. Though I readily appreciated her buxomness, I could understand how one less struck by her particular brand of plump beauty might conclude that she was in need of a regimen of vigorous exercise.

'*We* however,' said the other girl, looking at her colleague somewhat critically, 'we do have names. You've been remiss, my dear,' She looked down at me. Her mount, which had stamped and worried at its bit directly after the gun had been fired, now submitted to

its mistress's control. 'I'm Satana,' she said. 'And she' —
she nodded towards the other girl — 'is Lucifera.
Welcome. Welcome to our home.'

'And where exactly is—'

'The City of Samaria,' she said, before I could finish.
She looked about, her eyes disconsolate, her bright-red
lips puckered into a pout. 'Or what's left of it. We're
scientists. And we're dedicated to the restoration of the
tribes.' I committed to memory the fact that while both
girls might have been identical twins, I could always
identify them by the pigmentation of their scales.
Satana was red; Lucifera, blue. Not that I would have
wished to differentiate their beauty. I am not a man who
harbours such a simple-minded affectation as a
favourite colour. Red or blue — it mattered little to me.
Their bodies were both as lustrous as watered silk. And
both were pre-eminently deserving of ravishment.

I made a bow, eager to ingratiate myself. 'Scientists,
eh?' These chits talked as if they were playing a game.
But it would be unwise, I decided, to challenge their
statements. No; for the time being I would humour
them. 'I too am given to learning. For many years I
taught at Greenwich Naval College, in the Darkling Isle.
I gained my doctorate in Antiquity.'

'So: you understand the nature of the kind of relic I
just used to scare away the thing that was about to eat
your friend?' said Lucifera.

'The hell I do,' said the Tasmanian, jumping into the
river and dragging himself through the shallows until
he stood by my side. 'That was no musket.'

'It was a death-ray,' I interpolated, eager to
demonstrate my academic prowess. 'Mid to late

twentieth-century vintage.' I had seen such artefacts employed in the late stages of the war. Though both sides had discovered the means to reactivate such weapons, they had proved impossible to replicate. When their fuel cells had expired, they had been fit only for the museum.

Lucifera shrugged. 'It's just a toy. A simple toy. We have far more interesting playthings, don't we, Satana?'

'Indeed. *Far* more interesting.'

I stumbled on to the bank. The soaking I had sustained and the continuing drop in temperature had set my teeth chattering. 'You don't seem surprised to see us,' I said.

'Our pleasure at your arrival,' said Satana, 'has outweighed any sense of surprise that we might have felt. We're accustomed to seeing strange things here. Anyway, we *like* human company. It is more—'

'Utilitarian,' concluded Lucifera.

'Certainly an improvement on apes,' said Satana, with a giggle.

Their eyes grew half-lidded. And, as the Tasmanian and I were subjected to a somewhat bald, visual appraisal, they seemed to grow hot, too. It was, I hoped, a prelude to an invitation to share their bedsheets. The suspicion that we were being appraised for an agenda less sexual than surgical had been obscured by the comprehensiveness of my vanity.

'Come back with us,' said Lucifera. 'We have warm clothes for you.'

'And warm food?' said the Tasmanian, his empty belly disallowing all thoughts he had previously entertained about the threat these girls might pose.

'Of course. In the castle we have *everything*.'

The Tasmanian beamed. 'Pike and me: we've been saying we'd be bound to come into some good fortune sooner or later. This stretch of the Netherworld seems designed to reduce a man to string and bone. How come you're the first *malignos* we've seen in these parts?'

'People are scared to come here,' said Satana, patting her saddle to indicate that the Tasmanian should climb up beside her. He walked forward, put a foot in a brass stirrup and, with the help of a proffered hand, swung himself on to the pillion.

'And are you alone here?' I asked. The question was somewhat redundant, for I had known, after only a few seconds of being face-to-face with them, that my initial supposition had been true.

'Quite alone,' said Satana. 'How else may one dedicate oneself to disinterested research?'

Lucifera indicated that I should follow the Tasmanian's example. I complied. As soon as I was seated behind her the two *malignos* swung their rat-steeds about and we proceeded through the lost city of Samaria.

I put my hands upon Lucifera's waist, idly palpating her squamous flesh. Shaking out her platinum hair, she shot me a backward glance and rewarded me with a coy grin. I congratulated myself. The confidence I had in my powers of seduction, though undermined of late by encounters with a mad aristocrat and a sickly, neurotic châtelaine, was reborn. My fingers moved up over her ribcage intent on fondling an immoderately generous breast, its long, eye-popping nipple – like a nail hammered halfway into a dark blue melon – inviting a playful tweak. But before my hand had passed the uppermost rib Lucifera had drawn her quirt and administered a painful cut to my knuckles. I lifted the offended extremities to my lips and sucked at the weal. It would be sensible, I thought, after replacing my hand on her waist with considerable circumspection, to desist from further attempts at establishing intimacy. An opportunity would arise, surely, after I had eaten, bathed, shaved, dressed and dined. The charms I would exert over the little cockteaser would, at such time, I promised myself, prove irresistible. Meanwhile it would be prudent to limit myself to the beguilements of small talk.

'So this is Samaria,' I said, for the second time, that night, cursing myself for being such a slave to the banal. We rode along a path that wound between piles of masonry. Out of these mounds of stone and dust would sometimes appear the façade of a villa, or the single wall of some other, but more indefinable habitation, its glass-less windows and iron balconies twisted by subsidence. 'So this—' I bit my tongue. Lucifera did not respond. 'It must have been a grand city, once,' I added. Still she kept her peace. But I was determined to unloosen her new-found reserve. 'Why did they leave? Why is a stretch of the Naphtha lying so close to Pandemonium deserted?'

'I told you: fear. No one likes to travel this way. Not any more. There are other routes to Pandemonium now. Even other routes from Cathay. But it's the rivers that flow beneath Europa, Afric and Atlantis that are the main thoroughfares these days.' She paused, looking momentarily behind her once again, perhaps to check to see if I was as truly stupid as I sounded. 'Why the hell are *you* going to Pandemonium anyway?'

'There's something I must do,' I said. 'A commitment, if you like. It's . . . it's difficult to explain.' The piles of masonry had given way to an avenue of crumbling tenements. Creepers had punched their way through the soft stone so that each building seemed made of soap. Soap infested with decomposing vines, creepers and liana. And the stink that one would associate with those two constituents pervaded everything, a scent that was a mixture of disinfectant and humus. Bats wheeled above the rooftops, their high-pitched choral inspiring the illusion that the ruins were filled with rusty machinery that was slowly being cranked into life. 'Apart from the time we entered the maelstrom,' I said, eager to change the subject, 'it's almost as if we have been travelling horizontally. There has been barely any sense of a descent at all. And yet—'

'And yet you are near the centre of the Earth,' she said. 'The series of modified magma chambers you have passed through are designed to mimic Earth-Above. Outside the shell of this hollowed-out core the temperature is similar to that which you would find on the surface of the sun.'

'It's almost inconceivable,' I said. 'But yes, this part of the Netherworld *does* mimic Earth-Above. It reminds me of my adopted home in the tropics.'

'Some of the heat of the Earth's core is conducted through the walls and dimensional barriers that shield us. At the exact centre of the Earth, that is, Pandemonium, it's different. Because that is where all the artefacts are stored. And many of them are sensitive to the heat. Oh yes, Pandemonium is quite *temperate*. As cool as the cold-blooded thugs who run it. The ruling council makes sure it protects its precious artefacts, even if it's at the expense of other regions, damn their hides. They only think of using artefacts for barter, and never attempt to turn them on. When my ancestors first came here, thousands of years ago, they were real pioneers. They revived the ancient machinery that allowed them to build everything that you see around you. But so long as the old machines that maintain the Netherworld's tectonics keep working, their descendants remain content to be scrap merchants and traders. Politic, they call it. Contemptible, that's what *I* call it. May they all die cruel, disgusting deaths.'

Her rants had elicited a delicious shiver from her body. It had conducted itself through my flesh just as the heat of the Earth's core conducted itself through the rock that surrounded us. I was glad to learn of her antipathy towards her own people. Perhaps that was the reason we had been treated like respected guests, rather than the old enemy. She filled her lungs, and recommenced. But her harangue was over. She presented to me now a more reasonable, more affecting, aspect, a Lucifera who was, despite her confidence and coquetry, not entirely divorced from the divine state of little girlhood. 'But is it as you say?' she continued. 'Is the Torrid Zone really like Earth-Above?'

'Well,' I said, 'in some ways, yes, it is.'

She became, for a few moments, lost in thought. And then spoke. 'I've never seen Earth-Above,' she said wistfully. 'My ancestors didn't come to the Netherworld by choice. They were forced to come here. The Moon, their old sanctuary, was dead. So they came here, determined to build a simulacrum of the lands they had left behind. A simulacrum of their beloved Earth. That was at the end of the Dark Ages, when the clouding effects of the Abortion were in retreat, and it began to be possible to revive the artefacts of the Ancients. But this place called the Netherworld was never meant to be a permanent home. Only a refuge.'

'I am not unacquainted with the myths that surround your history, Lucifera.'

'Myths? Are you one of those humans who doubt that we evolved from the *perverse*?'

'I only meant to say—'

'Ah,' she interrupted, 'it's not only you humans. It is becoming common even amongst my own people to question our origins. That is what Satana and I hope to redress. We are seeking to demonstrate that our ancestors really were those who called themselves the "children of the perverse." And we shall also demonstrate that they still exist, even if they do not still live. They can help us win our rightful place on the Earth's surface. No one else can. The genius that lived with those of us who first migrated underground died within a few generations, after we had begun to mate. To learn the secrets of the Ancients we must resurrect that genius.' She glanced over her shoulder. 'Aren't you glad you found us?'

'Of course. My companion and I were lost.'

'Oh, lost – pooh! Nobody can get lost on the Naphtha.'

'Ah,' I said, an inexplicable sorrow descending upon me. 'But I've been lost a long, long time.'

I thought of Gala, as lost on the surface as I was lost below ground. My grip on Lucifera's waist loosened.

'Sometimes,' I said, 'sometimes I think it little matters where one lives, or how far, deep or high one travels. Not if one loses instead of gains a soul in the journeying.'

'Get you. A man of emotion. A man of feeling.'

Above, the bats had thickened, so that they formed another empyrean, a second, roiling night sky. Lucifera was right. Sentimentality ill-becomes a rake. I tried to centre myself, to still the commotion in my chest, as hectic as the diving, whirling, squealing bats. It was guilt, as much as anything, that needed catharsis. 'There is a *malignos*,' I said. 'A woman called Gala—'

'I'm sure it's none of my business,' she said, peremptorily. A castle lay ahead. It resembled neither Countess Suspiria's castle in Wormwood nor the castle in Tophet. Neither had it the proportions of the strange fortified palaces I had seen along the Great River. This was a castle that had been ravaged by time. Its battlements, which poked over the wrecked cupola of some forgotten civic edifice, were broken, as if by cannonade or lighting. Its towers were shorn off below the turrets, with winding staircases and scaffolding exposed to corruption by the dank, mephitic air. 'None of your affairs are my business. Who you are. Why you are going to Pandemonium. Not that we're not glad to see you,' said Lucifera. 'You can help us.'

'I hope I can,' I said, ever the gentleman. And the fool.

Chapter Twelve

Inside the castle I found myself in a maze of ill-lit corridors and damp chambers. Walls were covered in moulds and fungi. Gigantic cobwebs hung from ceilings and collapsed staircases. And the sound of small, scuttling claws was everywhere. What furniture and fittings had once decorated the interiors had largely rotted away, and we moved through a shell, the bleak spaces between its stonework only occasionally modified by objects – a candelabra, a smashed teapot, a vandalized harmonium – that reminded one that this place had once been inhabited.

The corridor that we had travelled along for the last quarter of an hour seemed to form the castle's backbone. It was decorated with bas-reliefs. Lucifera held me by the hand and led me forward. Satana and the Tasmanian followed some metres behind. The crisp echo of my leather-soled boots was all that punctuated the lapses in her conversation. I looked past her. The corridor's perspective was shrouded in darkness. Its dimensions were monotonous, its ceiling, walls and floor all of apiece. Only the oil lamps – set in wall brackets at ten-metre intervals – marked our progress. The oil lamps, that is , and the narrative reliefs carved into the walls.

Lucifera was intent on finishing my education. We had reached that part of the story where 'the lost tribes of the perverse' had relinquished their hold upon Earth-Above and sought refuge underground. Earlier panels had unfolded the entire myth of the perverse: the visitations from parallel universes throughout mankind's history, in the shape of angels and other supernatural beings, and, in the years directly proceeding the event called the Abortion, the appearance of those beings that were called UFOs; the Abortion itself, that is, the catastrophic implosion of a parallel universe and the spilling of transdimensional particles into our own universe; the years that followed, when a portion of mankind became infected by the fallout, their souls becoming alien, with perceptions and morals at variance with the rest of humanity; and the Dark Ages, when those perceptions, spreading into the rest of the population, became translated into an ignorance of natural law and the failure of ancient tek. The panel prior to the one I presently stood before had delineated both the high watermark of the perverse, when those souls that had grown alien fashioned new bodies for themselves out of the dying embers of their civilization, and the last days of those people, when Cathay had been defeated by the human armies of Atlantis.

Lucifera had stopped. She pointed to the bas-relief in front of us. 'After Atlantis invaded Cathay the diaspora of the perverse tried to join their comrades in the newly-created Netherworld. Many did not achieve their goal. They were hunted down across the four continents. But not all who were killed were destroyed. Some managed to escape death by translating themselves into a dimension between the universes. A limbo, in other words. A ghost world.'

'Clever girl,' I muttered. She shot me a sidelong glance, but my condescension left her otherwise unfazed. She was aware, doubtless, that, in her presence, I had begun to suffer from a sense of intellectual inadequacy. Behind me I heard the Tasmanian stifle a laugh.

'She certainly *is* clever,' said Satana, who, unlike her partner, was less willing to tolerate my patronizing snub. 'Too clever for you, perhaps. And certainly too clever for Pandemonium. We got expelled from school for the kind of work we were doing *there*. So—'

'So,' said Lucifera, picking up the thread, 'we moved somewhere where we wouldn't be disturbed. Somewhere our stupid, superstitious brethren would not dream of coming.'

I freed my hand from Lucifera's grip and ran it over the carved stone. It depicted a graveyard and, in the process of inhumation, a range of half-human, half-animal bodies. These were the fabulous beings I had read of: shark-men, cat-girls, spider-women, wolf-men and all the host of other confabulated human-animal variables that the children of the perverse had manufactured as havens for their infected souls. The next panel of the narrative showed the souls of the interred fleeing from their corpses and burrowing underground.

'They found their way here. To this region of the Netherworld. A place my fellow *malignos* speak of with terror. But what have we to fear? These beings are our ancestors. We mustn't shun them. They have much to teach us.'

'But why did they come *here*?' I said.

'They are attracted to the machines of the Ancients,' she said. 'The machines act as a kind of magnet. A lure, if you will. The disembodied spirits of our ancestors confuse, in them, the universe that was their home and to which they long to return.'

Satana left the Tasmanian's side and placed herself between me and Lucifera. She was tired, it seems, of being a wallflower.

Said Satana: 'The artefacts that are used to maintain the Netherworld were among some of humanity's last great inventions. It was soon after they had been fashioned that the perverse drew a conceptual fog over the mind of mankind. Yet, paradoxically, they contain much of the science of the alien universe that, in its destruction, infected our own. That is why, thousands of years later, after the fog of the intellect had begun to lift, it was the children of the perverse, and not humanity, who were able to revivify them. The artefacts called out. The children answered.'

'It is just the same now,' said Lucifera, again taking up the thread. 'The machines call out, as before. But these days, there are only *ghosts* to listen to them.'

'But, as I understand it, the machines are located in Pandemonium. Why aren't these beings you talk of haunting the Netherworld's capital?'

'How do you know they're not?' said Satana, her tail running up and down my naked calf.

'If the *malignos* are truly as frightened of these beings as you say—' Satana's tail was flicked away by Lucifera's.

'Pandemonium,' said Lucifera, 'has its defences against such things. Not that much is needed to keep the perverse at bay. It is greatly diminished since the apogee of its power in the Dark Ages. Which is why we are all, inhuman and human alike, enjoying something of a renaissance. No; this is as near as our ancestors can get to the artefacts they say offer a gateway back to their home.'

'And *do* they offer a gateway?'

'That parallel world that part of me, part of every *malignos*, remembers as its own home, is lost. Forever.'

The Tasmanian, who had shown little interest in our conversation until now, sighed, shuffled his feet and offered a bathetic coda: 'When do we get to eat?'

The girls stared at him with a mixture of alarm and contempt. 'Very well,' said Satana, 'if you're in such a hurry.' She tossed her waist-length hair over her shoulder and then, turning on her heel, walked briskly down the corridor. The Tasmanian did not waste time; he was in pursuit, hopping along the flagstones as if they were hot coals and he a dancing bear a little girl was leading by the nose.

Lucifera looked up at me and smiled. 'Enough antiquarianism for one day, eh, Professor?' She looked after the retreating *malignos* and her ursine attendant. 'Shall we join them?' And she looped her arm within the crook of my own. We strolled along. It seemed possible that I would bed this buxom little bluestocking yet.

The shadows cleared. The corridor terminated, I discovered, in the entrance to a chapel. Through the arch that constituted the chapel's entrance I could recognize the iconography of Christianity. Cross, altar, stained-glass images of the saints – all this was familiar to me from accompanying Gala to church in the Pilipinas. But as we caught up with Satana and the Tasmanian, I discovered that those icons were not as I remembered them. Rather, they had been perverted. I stepped through the arch that separated corridor from chapel.

Opposite me, hanging from a great wooden cross, was the carved figure, not of Christ, but of a woman. She writhed in the voluptuous throes of death. And the votary candles flickering on the altar revealed, not a monstrance, or some other item of ecclesiastical furniture, but a row of dead mice, the severed male genitalia of various beasts, and a bowl filled with some unspeakable concoction that brought to mind the orgiastic rites of a witch's sabbat. This, I knew, was a place consecrated to the cult of Lilith.

Dead mice were everywhere, not just on the altar, but littering the floor and piled into small heaps along the walls. And the head of the crucified woman was not a human head, or even the head of a *malignos*, but the head of a cat. The chapel, then, was one that, in the distant past, would have drawn those of Lilith's followers who had chosen the Way of the Cat, a tribe of the perverse dedicated to the seduction, betrayal and murder of humanity. The bowl that stood on the altar would contain a cocktail of milk and semen. For this all-female tribe reproduced themselves by corrupting the human male's seed. The mechanics by which they accomplished this were lost to time. But the grimoires seemed to suggest that men, in submitting to these cat-women's demands, had died in ecstasy, if also in shame.

With a thrill of fear and desire, I wondered if my two expelled schoolgirls subscribed to the old faith.

Lucifera released my arm and skipped ahead. Satana eased herself past me, having likewise abandoned charge of the Tasmanian. Both girls were giggling, casting playful glances behind and gesturing to us impatiently to follow them.

The chapel was a rotunda. It had no pews. Its ground plan was void. The only things, apart from the mice, that characterized its array of flagstones, were the curious small holes arranged in concentric circles, fanning out from the chapel's hub.

There was nothing to suggest that the chapel had ever hosted a mass. Its plain walls were as bare of decoration as the floor. Only the cross, altar and stained-glass windows high above, offered some relief to the dull uniformity of stone. The windows lined a narrow gallery that projected from the wall just below the cobwebbed vault. Their panes depicted mysterious scenes of animal-human hybrids that shared the same mythology as the bas-reliefs outside.

'Come on,' said the girls, each in turn. 'Don't dawdle!'

As we proceeded to walk across the chapel they positioned themselves to either side of the altar. And then, as we reached midpoint, they stepped behind an arras that screened a slim portion of wall immediately behind the cross. I stopped in my tracks. Putting out a hand, I took hold of the Tasmanian, arresting his over-confident progress.

'Though it pains me to say it,' I said, 'I think, perhaps, I should have listened to you. I fear my concupiscence has, perhaps, put us in something of a pickle.'

'What's wrong?' said my companion.

My ears had detected the sounds of gears and pulleys. We stood in the centre of the rotunda, frozen with apprehension, our eyes darting this way and that trying to locate the origin of the noise, as well as its import.

Its import became plain soon enough. About us, with a rumble that I thought at first might herald an earthquake, the surrounding floor began to descend, leaving us trapped on a circular, two-metre wide platform at the heart of the rotunda. I thought of jumping, so as to escape being marooned on that meagre tablet of stone, but the floor that lay about us had already fallen away to such an extent that I would have risked serious injury if common sense had not been quick to come to my aid. The floor continued its descent until it came to a halt far beneath us.

I could now see the purpose of the holes in the flagstones. Long, thin spikes protruded through them, where the floor that had recently belonged to the chapel had fitted flush over the flagstones of the floor below. Whatever had been the original function of the hitherto concealed room, it now bristled with steel.

Along the gallery, dark forms paced to and fro. Several doors had been raised in the stonework that lay between each pane of stained glass, and a dozen or so jungle cats, freed from lairs that must have been set into the walls, had rushed out to savage anyone foolhardy enough to attempt to escape their mistresses' trap by way of the windows.

'Chickababes, you said,' growled the Tasmanian, his voice as low and threatening as the black-coated jaguars. 'Oh yes, you *should* have listened to me. Not that a man with your pretensions would ever condescend to take notice of what he has obviously long considered a lower form of life.' I could not, for the moment, wrench my gaze from that other form of life, the jaguars. They conformed to the type of fauna I had encountered along the river. They exuded a rank, putrescent smell, and their coats were spotted with patches of gangrene; yet they seemed more alive, and more deadly, than their counterparts on Earth-Above. At last, I turned on the Tasmanian.

'Why the hell have they left us like this?' I said. 'Are they playing some kind of game?'

'Game? What does it matter if they're playing a *game*? The only thing we should be concerned about right now is getting back to the boat, fast.'

I lay down on my belly and, grasping the platform's curvilinear edge with my hands, lowered my head over the side. Easing myself out as far as I dared, I looked under the stone overhang. Some kind of brass, hydraulic column ran from the centre of the platform to the floor. To my dismay, I saw that the column's base was surrounded by a pit filled with snakes. I stood up.

'Even if we could somehow gain purchase on the column that supports us, it would avail us little to slide to the floor,' I said. The Tasmanian, puzzled, lay himself down as I had done. He peered over the lip and whistled.

'Are we just supposed to linger here until we starve to death? Is that the nature of the entertainment we're to provide those two little *malignos* bitches?' The answer came more quickly than he would have wished. There was a grating sound, as of iron being dragged across stone. I looked up. At the apex of the vault an operculum had been removed. In its place, framed by darkness, two young, demonic and altogether familiar faces stared down at us. Their periwinkle eyes twinkled with a mischievousness that, a few minutes earlier, I would have found entrancing, but now chilled me as thoroughly as the night air. There was another sound: that of a windlass or hoist. A rope was being lowered. Tied to its end was a bucket big enough to accommodate a man.

'What the hell now?' I said.

'We are being summoned, it seems,' said my companion. 'One of us, at least. That conveyance is not big enough for two.'

'Why are you telling me this?' I said, a panic gripping my heart. It was surely I who was being summoned. The thought that two *malignos* females, no matter how depraved their tastes, would want anything from the Tasmanian was inconceivable.

'You asked me.'

'That doesn't mean I expected you to reply,' I said, indignantly. 'Especially not in so morbidly informative a manner.' It was to my surprise and considerable relief that when the bucket made contact with the stone platform it was the Tasmanian, rather than me, who was urged to get into it. The slight I felt, however, was not so easily extinguished as my panic. Whatever fate lay in store for him, I felt passed over. Snubbed. As I watched my companion lift a leg over the bucket's iron lip I almost felt like shouldering him aside and taking his place. Almost, but not quite. I looked up at the grinning faces framed by the hole in the vault – oh, oh, how that despicable duo liked to *grin* – and castigated myself for my self-regarding foolishness.

'Should I be doing this, Pike? I mean, what do you think these girls have in store for me?'

I continued to gaze upward. 'It's the only way out,' I said. And then, taking my eyes off the girls, I proffered a hand and helped the Tasmanian wriggle into the receptacle that was to transport him heavenwards to his fate. 'You're going to have to come up with something – anything – to convince our captors to get *me* out of here, too.' I was unconvinced by this line of argument. But for the time being it seemed best that the Tasmanian be first to savour Satana and Lucifera's hospitality. His journey into the unknown world would give me an opportunity to prepare myself, and, possibly, think of something by which I might make my escape.

'Go then, my ambassador,' I said, with a wry smile, 'my proxy, my brave whipping-boy. Go and parley with those bloody hoydens. Or else kill them and return for your faithful friend.'

'I'll do what I can, Pike,' he said, gazing up at the grinning pair, whose mouths had opened wide enough to reveal the cruel, glittering enamelware characteristic of the *malignos*, in the female form of which I usually took such delight. The rope went taut, and, with the sound of a ratchet taking the strain, he was hauled into the air.

'Good luck,' I said. The girls' faces drew away as he vanished into the aperture. Only a circle of darkness remained to hint at what dark adventures he had been spirited away to.

Slowly, I turned through three-hundred-and-sixty degrees, all the while meditating upon my predicament. The jaguars no longer paced about the gallery, but were couchant, like heraldic beasts. If I'd had a rope and grappling device it might have been possible for me to reach them. I was armed, and, briefly, I indulged myself, and imagined keeping them at bay, smashing one of the windows, and then lowering a rope to the ground, after which I would bid a swashbuckling adieu to Satana and Lucifera and make my exit. But, of course, I had neither rope not grappling device nor anything else by which I might have effected such an option.

I gazed down at the sunken floor. A jump would mean the possibility of impalement on the spikes, or, at the very least, a broken limb, where there were only flagstones and dead mice to break my fall. Indeed, the fall – spikes or no – would probably kill me. There remained the option of attempting to gain purchase on the column that supported the platform. But that lay out of reach. And, of course, there was the pit of snakes beneath my feet to offer dissuasion even if such a descent had been possible.

I sat down. The minutes slipped by. For all I know, hours may have passed. My options, it seemed, were less limited than non-existent. I was helpless, forced to wait until Satana and Lucifera should again man the windlass and let the rope and bucket drop.

Immersed in these gloomy thoughts I did not immediately appreciate that other thoughts, or rather, another mood, was stealing up on me. It was that sense of dread that I had experienced on the river. It was the intimation that I was surrounded by an invisible, male-volent intelligence, one intent on my demise. And as this mood displaced my reflections on the impossibility of escape, I began to be conscious of a presence that I could not ascribe merely to anxiety. Something else was in the chapel, something other than myself.

The shadows cast upon the walls by the candles no longer flickered, but began to move, and move with purpose. The air seemed to vibrate, as if it had somehow become metallic, and had been clandestinely struck, like a gong. I licked my lips, my mouth suddenly dry, and my taste buds responded with a ferrous tang.

The jaguars got to their feet and began to snarl. I narrowed my eyes. The spectral outlines of beings such as I had seen carved into the walls of the adjoining corridor glided through the chapel like ectoplasmic birds. Though they were transparent, I could readily identify the tribes to which they belonged. Some belonged to the Way of the Wolf, some the Way of the Shark, while others were shaped into the forms of the Bear, Mantis and She-Spider. But outnumbering all these were the forms of those who belonged with the Way of the Cat.

They flew across the vault and down the walls, where they seemed to sport with the shadows. They wheeled above the crucifix and winged across the floor, weaving in and out of the maze of spikes. And then they rose and congregated before me, like a host of infernal angels.

'We are the Shining Ones,' came a whisper. 'Declare yourself, human.'

I put a hand to my throat. I could not speak.

'He is one that serves a spirit of that Other Place, our home.'

'Does he truly serve?'

'He surely does, even if he does not know it.'

'And has he come to set us free?'

I took two or three steps backward before remembering where I stood. I teetered a little, the heel of one boot on the platform's circumference. And then I regained my balance and stumbled back to my original position, the faces of the lost tribes of the perverse – dead some two million years – before me. There was the face of a woman with whiskers and pointy ears; another such woman; a man with a countenance that was lupine; and there were other human-animal hybrids, displaying scales, fur, tails, savage teeth and monstrous genitalia. My hand settled on the pommel of my sword.

'Metatron sleeps,' said a ghost.

'The human does not know it,' said another. 'Nor does he know that his master has begun to stir. Soon, Metatron will lay claim to him.'

'Yes, he has been appointed. He is the guardian. The keeper.'

'And,' said another voice, somewhat more unpleasant than the rest, 'the slave.'

Despite the icing up of my veins, I had, I found, the presence of mind to be acutely annoyed by this exchange.

'Talk sense,' I said.

The ghosts ignored me.

'We must deliver him from this place. The Spirit of Metatron must be taken into the world. Metatron must deliver us from the evil of the necromancers.'

'What do you want?' I said. 'And more to the point, what are you talking about?' Perhaps it was my wartime experience. Perhaps I was going mad. But my nerves still refused to buckle.

The ghosts continued with their cryptic talk.

'Metatron did not deliver us from catastrophe.'

'The enemy were too powerful, then. But in this universe, we need fear no one. Not with Metatron at our side.'

The host gathered itself about me. To my wonder, I felt myself lifted into the air. The spirits of the dead no longer made intelligible sounds, but filled the chapel with sinister, inscrutable whisperings. I was being taken to the dark aperture through which the Tasmanian had disappeared.

Air rushed past my ears. I was propelled through the hole. I felt invisible fingers release me. I flew through the darkness, tumbling over and over, and then hit the flagstones hard. So hard that I thought I might have dislocated my shoulder. I sat up and inspected myself. No real damage had been done, it seemed. And anyway, it had been my left arm that had taken the brunt of the fall. My sword-arm was uninjured.

I looked about. The windlass, that I had previously heard, but not seen, stood nearby. But all else was obscured by the mass of writhing, ectoplasmic forms.

'Not for you,' I heard, before the host disappeared. 'Not for you, guardian. We do it for Metatron.' The dying fall of that name was subsumed into the shadows along with the cloud of fading, apparitional spirits.

I jumped to my feet. And then, seeing two shadows cast by the forms of Satana and Lucifera play across the floor, I immediately reverted to a crouch. They were some way distant, and my sunburnt flesh, set against the more extensive shadows that covered my own portion of the chamber, provided sufficient camouflage for me to remain where I was, observing them at work.

Dim light emanated from candelabras positioned to either side of their workbench. The illumination they provided was enough, but only just enough, to reveal that the surrounding space belonged to a rotunda that was almost the exact replica of the chapel I had been summarily evacuated from. I looked up. Above, were the rafters of a partly-demolished roof. Its broken parapets formed a ruined crown. I continued with my reconnaissance, my gaze taking in the rotunda's walls. Timber scaffolding was everywhere, shoring up the crumbling stonework. I had, I knew, reached to top of one of the towers I had espied on the approach to the castle through the city.

The sight that next caught my attention were the cages positioned at random intervals about the rotunda's curving walls. Some of them contained apes. And a few of them contained things that part way resembled the simian-reptile hybrid we had encountered on the river-bank. They all seemed drugged, and for a moment I almost fancied myself back in Wormwood, entering Madame Tetrallini's marquee and setting eyes on her captive rows of humans. For though these monstrosities were plainly beasts, there was something about them that suggested that they had been infused with a degree of self-awareness.

I turned my gaze back upon Satana and Lucifera. Arranged about the workbench, and occupying the attentions of the two girls, were a number of artefacts. The glittering cabinets of steel hummed, and the illumination provided by the candelabras was supplemented by the machinery's faint, blue glow. It reminded me of the glow that had suffused the Netherworld during my first days underground. No new variant of bioluminescent plant was responsible; nor had my brain begun to revert to a state when it could no longer assign a spectrum to the Netherworld's ubiquitous hue. The light – that cold, spectral blueness – was from another age. Perhaps, another universe.

I was in a laboratory. It was similar to some of the ateliers I had known back in the Darkling Isle, with the exception that the machines here, unlike those in Greenwich, seemed to work.

Satana banged a fist against the casing of one such machine. And then, as if criticizing my evaluation of its operability, said: 'The machines do not work as efficiently as in Pandemonium. But you know that, don't you, dear.'

'We have to find a way of *making* them work. I mean, just *look* at him.'

I had given too much attention to the machines and the chamber's general ambience to notice that a human body was laid out on the workbench, and that that body belonged to the Tasmanian.

'Other than translocating down river, I don't see a solution.'

'We're as near to Pandemonium as we dare. If they found out what we were doing . . .'

'Enough. We always knew we risked more than expulsion when we began work on this project. But there's no going back. We stay here until we create a fleshly vessel suitable for the incarnation of one of our ancestors.'

'Tee-hee. A "host" for a "ghost"?'

'It's not funny, Lucifera.'

'Remember our very first experiment? Teacher was so surprised. So surprised that *he* was the subject of the experiment. Oh, the look on his face.'

'I said it's not funny.'

'Oh, come on. It *was* funny. Remember that boy in the fifth that you went out with? I don't know what you injected him with, but the look of him next day, sitting in class, with gills and fins sprouting out of his body, well!'

'Snakebite, I think his name was. He was quite a jock, as I recall.'

'Quite a fish by the time *you'd* finished with him, you bad girl!'

'I believe he died after a few days. Another failure. Now concentrate, will you? We must complete the task we have set ourselves. Or perish in the attempt.'

'You are *so* melodramatic.'

I crept forward, keeping to the rotunda's limits, where my form, if either girl should turn around, might, in the confusion of shadows that surrounded me, be mistaken for one of the sleeping apes. A little way ahead, in the foreground of the picture created by the workbench and the girls, was a flickering steel cabinet isolated from its peers. On top of it lay the pistol that spat fire, the fabled death-ray of the Ancients. I continued my journey, on hands and knees now, the sweep of the wall carrying me towards my goal. When I had positioned myself, I rose, bent over, and tiptoed behind the cabinet, the sound of my boots on the flagstones overwhelmed by the humming of the machines, which, at this proximity, had grown strong enough to remind me of a swarm of steel bees. I picked up the death-ray and, with a surge of new-found confidence, straightened myself and stepped out to confront my abductors.

'Alcohol and women,' I said. The two girls spun round. 'My companion was right. They're the things that you most have to watch out for in life.' Their initial shock quickly passed. Their faces once again wore their familiar masks of impassivity. They seemed as nonchalant as when I had first met them on the shores of the Naphtha.

'You don't seem to understand the importance of our work,' said Satana.

'I don't give a damn for its importance,' I said. 'Untie my companion and we'll both leave you in peace to carry on with your fun and games.'

'The *malignos* will never live on the Earth's surface unless they have help,' said Lucifera.

'Help from our ancestors,' said Satana. 'Help from the children of the perverse. They have the knowledge that will enable the Netherworld to arm itself so that it may conquer Earth-Above.'

'Yeah, you really *are* melodramatic,' I said. 'Just untie my companion and—'

'He's no longer your friend,' said Lucifera. 'He is *perverse.*'

'We have rediscovered, you see,' said her confederate, with a prideful smile, 'how to modify the flesh so that—'

'So that,' said Lucifera, interrupting with an enthusiasm that would not be brooked, 'so that it is a suitable vehicle for the incarnation of a soul from the meta-universe.'

'Necromancy,' I murmured.

'That's what they called it when they threw us out of Pandemonium,' said Satana. 'Call it rather "assisted transmigration". We are scientists. Not witches or wizards. We are tapping the knowledge o f the past.'

'It was our ancestors,' said Lucifera, 'who first made new bodies for themselves. Wolf bodies and cat bodies, bodies whose architecture was borrowed from the fish, the insects, the birds, the reptiles and the mammals. And now we have found a way of resurrecting the dead by offering them new bodies – bodies to tempt them into reinhabiting the world of matter. Bodies their discorporate souls cannot resist! Soon we will have an army. Enough children to march upon Earth-Above.'

Impatiently, I waved them aside with the death-ray. I walked up to the workbench. The Tasmanian was strapped to it. But he was not the man I had formerly known.

'Of course, we still have some way to go,' said Satana. 'Though this one is quite a success. Humans are so much easier to work with than apes.'

The Tasmanian's face was covered with hair. His whole torso, in fact, was matted with thick, black fur. His hands had curved in on themselves where they had sprouted claws. His ears were pointed. And his nose – a snout with a button of soft, wet flesh at its tip – resembled that of a dog. Like the animals in the cages, he appeared heavily sedated.

'What have you done to him?' I said.

'Oh, don't you know?' said Satana.

'And we thought he was so clever, didn't we?' said Lucifera.

'He would seem to know as little about hyperphysics and molecular biology as about women.'

'The precious oaf!'

'Oaf. Buffoon. Yes, how true. Shake your tail at him and he thinks he's God's gift.'

I levelled the weapon at their heads, squinting down the barrel's sights, first at Satana and then at Lucifera. 'I have a doctorate,' I said, as if this bald statement would spirit away the preposterousness of my half-clad, half-starved appearance and my dilettantism in matters of natural philosophy. 'I'm a Professor. Professor Richard Pike. But I'm also,' I concluded, with a note of warning, 'a black knight and a well-known goblin killer. Now tell: *what have you done to him?*'

'Certain drugs have been administered,' said Satana.

'And the machines have done the rest,' said Lucifera. 'Oh yes, he's a wolf-man now. He's been transmogrified. What we're not so sure about is the state of his soul.'

'Indeed,' said the other, 'we're not sure if its been supplanted by one of the wolf-souls that haunt Samaria, or whether we have only effected a physical transformation, and his own soul still flutters in his breast.'

'But, since he *is* human, and not an ape, we shall be able to establish the exact results of our experiment when he wakes.'

I fell to loosening the Tasmanian's bonds, all the while keeping an eye on the two insane little necromancers. But it transpired that my attention should have been focused upon my companion. As soon as one arm had been freed, he snapped into consciousness, his new, wolfish body obviously having little trouble with metabolizing a sedative that had probably been designed for humans.

I found myself gripped by the throat. Choking, I struck him across the back of his hand with the butt of the death-ray, the tendons of which still seemed sufficiently human to engender a yelp of pain. He released me and I staggered away. Luckily, I still had the presence of mind to immediately scan the laboratory for Satana and Lucifera.

I had purloined, it seemed, Lucifera's weapon. The death-ray that had part-vaporized the thing in the river. But both girls must have been in the habit of going about armed. For Satana had her own death-ray in her hand. There was a flash, and a beam arced across the space that separated us, lighting up the chamber. I flung myself on my face, and the plume of fire cut across the array of artefacts, sending up a sheet of smoke and fire. The suddenness of the combustion took the girls by surprise and they retreated.

The next second there was an explosion and a ball of flame rose upward into the gaping vault and simultaneously billowed across the floor. My skin tingled, and I felt my hair and beard ignite. I dropped my weapon. Frantically beating at my head, I tried to escape the searing heat. I could no longer see a thing. All was shrouded in angry gouts of combustion. Black puffballs of smoke filled my lungs with brimstone and acrid fumes.

And then I felt myself lifted up by strong, hairy arms. Blinded by the conflagration, I only knew that I was being transported upwards. An occasional thinning of smoke allowed me to see that I was ascending the scaffolding that supported much of the rotunda's walls. Timber exploded, and pieces of roaring lumber fell past my head to crash upon the flagstones below. I heard screams, the desperate flapping of wings. I saw, or at least, thought I saw, two bat-like forms trying to rise through the flames, like devils in some illuminated text that were trying to escape the fires of hell.

I emerged from the pall of smoke and discovered that I was tucked under a thick, hirsute arm. About me were the tower's ruined battlements. I turned my head and looked up at my rescuer. The Tasmanian met my gaze. He seemed more alien, now, than when I had awoken him. His eyes, bloodshot and filled with a ferocious light, were almost unrecognizable. Then he spoke, and though I knew the voice to be his, I was not reassured.

'Damn me, Pike, how did I *do* that?' he said. He looked down through the smouldering rafters at the furnace that had once been a laboratory. And then he began to laugh. 'How did I get *up* here?' And then he threw back his head and the laughter became a howl. 'Who cares, eh? We showed them bitches. We showed them what we can do!' And then, tossing me effortlessly over his shoulder, he launched himself into space. 'Hell, I feel like a million pesos!' I shut my eyes and thought: so this is how the journey ends. So near Pandemonium, and yet about to be spread out all over the cobbles like a mangosteen preserve, borne off, not by starvation, disease, or a mortal wound sustained in combat, but by the ignoble expediency of a crazy, fat, half-lupine motherfucker who's dogged my days ever since I made a rendezvous with him on Snake Island. How absurd.

I must have momentarily blacked out. Upon impact, I would guess my chin had cracked against the Tasmanian's clavicle. When I came to I was still suspended over his shoulder. And I found myself studying the ground as he ran across the courtyard that had lain directly beneath the tower. Stunned, and probably suffering from concussion, I began, in an abstract, unconcerned manner befitting one who is unsure whether he is dead or alive, to count the cobbles as we raced over them. It was a task that, due to my companion's fleetness of foot, soon defeated me. But no sooner had it done so I was consumed by another, equally inappropriate compulsion, that of willing him to avoid stepping on the cracks. I think I may have even burbled a recommendation to that effect, though it would have been lost in the roar of collapsing masonry.

We passed through the castle's gates and entered Samaria's alleys and streets, my head swinging from side to side as the Tasmanian negotiated a passageway between the winding canyons of rubble. Behind us the castle's decrepit fortifications shimmered in a red, convective haze. A tower – I had no idea whether it was the one we had recently vacated – shook and collapsed in a slow, elegant concession that all was over, and that to resist was not only futile, but vulgar beyond words. My head began to spin. I tasted blood. Conducting an exploratory of my mouth with my tongue, I discovered that the front incisors were broken. For the second time that night, the Tasmanian's triumphal howl echoed amongst the ruins. The rubble had given way to skeletal buildings, several of which marked the place where we had first been received into the city. I saw a column entwined with black creepers, and then the windows of a tenement harbouring a ragged spray of black, funereal blooms. And then, at last, I saw the river.

We crashed through the shallows. The Tasmanian checked his pace, hefted me over the gunwale, and then clambered into the boat. I lay on the deck staring up at the night sky. I felt, at that moment, as illusory as the sky, less the victim of a protracted hallucination than a hallucination itself, about to go pop and disappear inside the mind of the waking godhead who had dreamt of me. Wincing, I put a hand over my face, willing my fingers to explore bruises and abrasions. No; I was real, too real. As real, seemingly, as the man with the face of a wolf who was staring down into my eyes. He got up, walked to the prow and lifted the anchor into the boat. And then he picked up an oar and shoved off.

I propped myself up on an elbow and looked back at the lost city. The fire had spread into the jungle. Animals, both natural and unnatural, swarmed about the shore, their panicking cries rising over the crepitation of the burning trees.

The ghosts that had come to my aid: they could not have *wanted* to live again. The age of the perverse was drawing to a close. They had had no wish to find new bodies. As I looked back at the burning city I thought I could almost hear laughter as they celebrated the defeat of the two *malignos* who had tortured them. And, sometimes, I thought I could almost hear them repeat that mysterious name *Metatron, Metatron*, as if in thanks and farewell.

I lay back on the deck. The pain I felt made me forget that I was hungry, thirsty and alone beneath billions of tonnes of rock. But I would remember soon enough. And when I did remember it would doubtless occur to me that I was especially alone now that my companion was no longer human, but a transmogrified child of the perverse. In this strange, underground realm of stone, at these unimaginably plutonic depths, I was probably the only human alive.

Chapter Thirteen

For three days the Tasmanian rambled. Shortly after departing from Samaria he had taken ill. Feverish, he spent his days outstretched beneath the awning. This, of course, had been his habit during much of our journey through the Torrid Zone. But now, with the unyielding heat of the day compounding his fever, he did not stir, lying still as a corpse through the long days and all-too-brief nights.

Whenever I woke from my own exhausted slumbers, I would wet his brow with river water, and slip some of our last pieces of rat-meat between his cracked lips. When I awoke on the morning of the fourth day I found that he had reverted back to his former self. All trace of fur had vanished. Even his original hair had disappeared, and his head was curiously baby-smooth, so that – to borrow the language of street urchins – he resembled a 'penis with ears'. His snout had assumed proportions that, if in most men would be unenviable, were defiantly human. And his hands had lost their claws.

It was then that he told me of his dreams.

'It's as if I've been to another world, Pike,' he said. I was sitting near the prow, inspecting my pile of clothes and accoutrements. By now, compass, watch, and several other items were broken, as well as my pipe. I picked up my make-up palette and my shard of broken mirror. Peering into the mirror's splintered depths, it seemed as if I had been transmogrified myself. With my scorched beard and long, matted hair, I might have been the one Gala had told me about, the man-beast called Nebuchadnezzar. Had he, I wondered, been kin to the perverse? I grimaced. My teeth really were in a shocking state. Broken, chipped, they were a sort of confirmation that I had lost my beauty. I suppose I had lost it some time ago, ever since I had tipped into middle age. But I could do without confirmation, especially one so brazen, so indisposed to spare my feelings. No longer Pike the Goblin-Killer, I was Pike the Snaggletoothed. Richard Hell. Richard Nebuchadnezzar. I applied a little gloss to my lips. Reapplied my mascara.

'It was a world where desire was at once limitless and fulfilled,' continued the Tasmanian. 'I saw strange cities, each one dominated by a huge, black ziggurat. But it was what I *felt* that was most strange. And most alarming. I felt the need to tear and rend. To love, and yet to kill. To kill the thing I *most* loved. And the weird thing was, that in those cities I passed through, I knew these violent, cruel desires were possessed by a moral imperative; not such as we would understand in this world. But in that universe, where the laws of nature were different, murder and cruelty seemed to be invested with beauty. More than that, they seemed to constitute the *good*.'

'Well,' I said, giving up with the make-up and staring out over the river. 'You're through with all that now. Seems our two hostesses in Samaria have a lot of work to do before they perfect their technique.'

'I hope you're right, Pike. I hope you're right.'

Malignos

I found I could not give him my full attention. For the last half-hour I had been disturbed by the fact that dawn over the Naphtha was not the dawn I had grown used to. The sun was behind us, as if, during the night, we had passed beneath its ecliptic, and were now travelling beyond the lands over which it held dominion. Most disturbingly, the sun, indeed the light bathing the entire landscape, seemed infused with another kind of light, one I had difficulty putting a name to. It was a luminousness at once bright and shadowy. It was a black light. And it seemed to suggest the inversion of all natural law.

'If only,' continued the Tasmanian, 'if only I could get those *dreams* out of my head.'

'Relax,' I said, without much sympathy. 'You're back to your old self.'

'I'm not sure I *feel* like my old self. I feel I've still got some of—'

Our conversation stopped dead. I had always known that the first sight of Pandemonium was going to be awe-inspiring. But my breath was taken away, not by the vision of a great city, but by the unexpected. A vision rose from my hindbrain and translated itself into something that I knew I had dreamt of before I had been born, before I had had my mind constrained by the laws of this universe, a homeland where space and time flowed according to desire, and not according to entropy. Unexpected, yes. And unwelcome. Because this homeland had been perverted. This was not my home. Not any more. This was the place of the *malignos*.

My first thought was how had they ever lost the war?

How, when they had built such a thing as this? And then the wonder I felt was replaced by fear. Real fear.

This was not merely a piece of stupendous engineering. It was something unearthly. It was something that defied nature and the common human interpretation of things.

Ahead, the jungle ended. I was reminded of the chasm that had greeted us at the end of our journey across the Great Plain many months ago. The abruptness of the jungle's termination was equally violent. It was as if it had been sheared off. And beyond was a black void. But these were the only things that corresponded to previous experience. For in the middle of that void floated a sphere, big as a planet. Or as big as any planet that might be accommodated by a void that I had no doubt represented the Earth's hollowed-out core.

'Where are we?' said the Tasmanian, his voice like smoke. 'What's happened to us?'

'Get a hold of yourself,' I said, my own voice no more than a whisper.

It was day, but we drifted towards night, or rather, a place where day and night had been supplanted by a darkness that was as bright as the noonday sun. For it was here that the black sun of the Netherworld held sway. I had always thought that the black sun was a myth, an emblem on a *malignos* flag such as I had seen displayed by the enemy during firefights beneath London. Nothing more. But it lay before me, a sphere that shone like polished basalt. It was the world that hung impossibly in the firmament at the heart of the world. It was Pandemonium, and its shadows blinded.

Malignos

The current had quickened and the boat had begun to pick up speed. The jungle was already behind us. To either side was a flat expanse of black rock – the lip of the chasm whose void we were destined to soon encounter. I rooted about amongst my clothes and found my field glasses. I looped them around my neck. Standing up, I put a hand on the gunwale. But the boat was uncannily steady. I released my hold, stepped forward and took up a position on the prow just behind the bowsprit.

I lifted the field glasses to my eyes. The black sun was covered with tiny buildings. And sometimes, though my hands shook with fatigue and apprehension, I felt I could almost make out the movement of living things. The sphere rotated, as it was said the Earth did itself. It was indeed a planet, or planetoid.

About the centre of the sphere was a ring. I first took it to be something that might be similar to the ring of silver and gold that encircles Saturn. But after steadying my hand to gain a better focus I realized that it was a vast sea, and that, moreover, the river we travelled down, along with a myriad of others, somehow fed into it. The sea was as impossible a phenomenon as the sphere itself. A glittering, black disc, it seemed, like the sphere, to have no support but the shadows.

The shock I had initially felt at setting eyes on Pandemonium had worn off. But the fear was still with me. Hearing movement, I turned about. The Tasmanian had got to his feet. The paleness of his face seemed to indicate that he, too, was fearful. Indeed, he seemed terrified. But his pallor also seemed to indicate that his sickness had returned. The blanched face was offset by an unhealthy glow to the cheeks and forehead. He supported himself against the stanchions of the awning, as if he were about to collapse. I made my way over to him.

'Can you pilot the boat to the shore?' I said.

But the Tasmanian, weakened by terror, fever and his brief flirtation with lycanthropy, was in no condition to understand what I had said. And certainly in no condition to help. I pushed past him and made my way to the tiller. But try as I might, the boat had become ungovernable. We were headed for the chasm and whatever awaited us there.

I told myself that I had achieved at least part of my objective. I had reached the centre of the Earth. I had reached Pandemonium. I forced myself to relax my grip and let the boat, rudderless, become one with the current. There was no hope of making it to the shore. Even if there were, what would be the point of such a diversion? I had to go on. And so resolved, I looked straight ahead, and folded my arms across my chest. The Naphtha, it seemed generally agreed, was a route to the Netherworld's capital. It would not, surely, upon reaching that chasm, simply pitch me into space? No, I told myself, my inner voice a great shout. No, no, that would be senseless. The strange laws that held this unnatural realm together would come to my aid. They had to.

And so it was. As the boat approached the lip of the chasm I saw the river did not end in a cataract. It did not end at all. It carried on, a liquid bridge spanning the black empyrean in which the vast sphere hung like a monstrous clock face permanently set at midnight.

Malignos

I took a last look backward at a world that, though not my own, and stranger than the most dyspeptic of dreams, I had grown accustomed to. A world that, compared to the one I was bound for, seemed almost familiar. Beyond the flat, rocky landscape bordering the chasm I could still see the jungle. Above it, its light no longer a cruel, white brilliance, but infused with the black light radiated by the sphere, was an artificial sun under which we had roasted for over three months. It had, now, no more potency than a lantern. I bit my thumb and cursed the thing. And then I turned about and confronted the new and final frontier of my journey.

It had grown appreciably cooler, and I hugged myself. In this new environment my pared-down wardrobe was proving inadequate. I moved forward towards my discarded clothes. As I reached the boat's waist I pushed past the Tasmanian – he remained frozen in terror – and made my way to my pile of leather and personal affects. Before I could get there the boat shuddered. I had grown so used to the *Lady Devia*'s steady course that I stumbled and almost fell. So violent was the perturbation that, if I had not been able to grip the mast, I may well have been pitched overboard.

We had left the mainland. To either side of the river lay the blackness of the void. My innards became feathery. I looked down at the deck and tried to banish the giddiness that threatened to overwhelm my brain. The Tasmanian was on his back, an arm held over his eyes. I left him where he lay. There were more important things to attend to.

The speed which the boat had built up gave no indication of diminishing. We ploughed through the dark waters towards the sea that circled the black sphere. The planetoid became more clearly defined, its details springing into view.

From pole to pole it was covered with a glittering, dark weave of architecture. Spires, towers, minarets, cupolas, all shone with the light of the black sun. It was a cold light, a radiation inherent in whatever outlandish rock constituted the planetoid's surface. It threw into relief the maze of bristling habitations and then shone out into the void. As the boat drew nearer I could clearly make out *malignos*. They seemed like flies, crawling across a great, black ball of dung. The planetoid possessed a gravity well; it had neither up nor down.

My attention was so focused upon Pandemonium that I did not notice that the river we travelled over was flowing into the planetoid's encircling sea.

The transition was seamless. There was no shudder, no crest of water over our prow. I scanned the horizon. Boats, ships, galleons and the like were dotted over the sea's disc-like surface. I could see, then, how other rivers joined the sea, rivers that must have originated from all corners of the Netherworld. Lustrous bridges of dark water, they spanned the chasm from other points of its compass, delivering travellers and traders from the subterannean lands beneath Atlantis, Europa, Afric and Cathay.

I looked over the boat's side. The sea was black, as black as the Naphtha, but paradoxically, also limpid, as if permeated by the qualities of this region's light. It was so limpid, in fact, that I could see the keels of inverted sailing vessels plying across the disc's opposite side.

Though upside down, they were, like us, on their way to where the sea met the planetoid's equator. The thin plane, it seemed, accommodated traffic from both hemispheres.

I gazed up from that capsized world. It was then, and only then, that I became aware of how silent it was. There was no sound of sea beating against our hull. No sound of waves. Neither did voices or other sounds of life carry over the water or from Pandemonium. All was quiet, as if the surrounding vessels had come here to mourn the passing of a world.

It seemed the culmination of all those hiatuses of silence that had so tormented me during passage through the Torrid Zone.

As the boat was carried ever closer to the planetoid I came to my senses enough to dip my head beneath the gunwale. We were within sight of other ships. The tiny forms of mariners that I espied on their decks were as silent as the dead. But I felt that, if anything were to disturb the absolute quiet, it would be the appearance of a human floating towards the great capital. A sight as rare as that would be bound to unstop even the mutest of mouths.

The silence grew more profound in proportion to the growing size of the sphere. I was no longer conscious of its curvature, but only the plane of its equatorial zone. Buildings rose at right angles, their roofs bared to meet me. My senses became confounded by the question of how we would dock. It would seem that, for the inhabitants of the city, the sea fell straight out of the sky, a sheet of black water that cut them off from the hemisphere that lay beyond.

A harbour resolved itself into its constituents: docks, wharves and maritime architecture consistent with a port that probably served all of Pandemonium. I saw then that the ships lining the docks lay in the same attitude as the buildings. At right angles to my line of vision, so that I looked at their decks face on, they lay at anchor while *malignos* stevedores emptied them of their cargoes. I was so mesmerised by this hallucinatory sight that I was unaware of how near I had come, and as equally unaware of the concomitant danger of discovery. It was only when I discovered exactly how sea and harbour had been engineered to serve each other that I woke to my plight.

The sea, in the approach to the equator, flanged out, so that a thin strip of water lay on the same plane as the harbour mouth. Almost as soon as this had been revealed to me the boat met the long, slow curve that would bring it into correct alignment with the planetoid's geography. Landmarks began to turn, their roofs disappearing and their façades gradually presenting themselves. I felt a slight pressure on my chest, and a giddiness as blood left my head, but apart from these symptoms, the transition was smooth. Within a minute or so I was approaching the harbour as if I were on Earth-Above, a starless night sky above me.

I remembered, now, what Devia had said. '*Pandemonium's circumference is greater than the planet which harbours it. Its towers are unconstrained by rocky vaults. They reach to the stars. All things are possible there . . .*' At this distance, the planetoid did indeed seem of impossibly greater dimensions than the Earth itself. Its towers rose into the blackness, as if those who had constructed them had been of that ancient lineage that had built bridges to the stars. And my heart was buoyed by the thought that all things might indeed be possible. Even the fulfilment of my quest.

By now I had gathered the requisite presence of mind to try to arrest my progress. The seafront was busy with activity, and hundreds of ships lay anchored along its quay. *Malignos* of various shapes and hues – what the grimoires, I believe, call 'genotypes' – milled about the derricks and cranes. Most were variations on the usual theme of horns, tails, wings and scaled bodies. But here, at the centre of the Earth, where strict breeding regimes were obviously de rigeur, there were variations that were little short of bizarre. Some *malignos* appeared to be walking about on all fours, and some, if my eyes did not play tricks with me, seemed possessed of two, sometimes even three, heads.

On my hands and knees, as if I were one of those quadrupedal *malignos* I had just observed on the waterfront, I made my way to where the anchor lay and, with considerable effort, hauled it over the side. I do not know what the anchor dragged on to slow the boat down and, finally, to stop it. Perhaps the sea, at a certain depth, became viscous, or perhaps its bottom was solid. The ships that plied its obverse half might be an illusion produced by certain qualities of reflection. Or perhaps there was another reason, one associated with the strange laws imposed on the natural world by the artefacts that were stored at the Earth's centre. All I know is that we came to rest. The anchor had proved effective.

I hunkered down. It was with a strange kind of relief

that I heard the sound of voices. I seemed to have passed through a vacuum, albeit a breathable vacuum (one more paradox amongst many that this region had to boast). A nothingness that more properly belonged to the spaces between the stars and that, apart from being incapable of conducting sound, should have killed me. Or so the philosophy of the Ancients had seemed to aver. But evidently there was another kind of space, or ether that, though as black and empty as its counterpart in the heavens, and too thin to conduct sound waves, was not so inimical to life. An alien space, perhaps, one belonging to that universe Satana and Lucifera had spoken of. The space-time of the *perverse*.

And yet what was all this to me now that I had come, at last, to Pandemonium? I put my arms about my knees and began to rock. There was one thing, and only one thing, that should occupy my thoughts. And slowly, trying to ignore the little thrills of fear that still fluttered through my entrails, I began to draw up plans by which I might enter the city and begin my search for the fabled elixir that would restore Gala to life.

Chapter Fourteen

I ducked into the shop doorway. As the Tasmanian passed by I grabbed him by the arm and jerked him into the safety of the shadows. 'What do you think you're doing?' I said. 'If you screw up on me, I swear I'll—' But my companion's eyes were glazed. It had been a mistake to bring him along. But I didn't like the idea of leaving him in charge of my one means of escape. In his abstracted state, he might have upped anchor and left without me. 'Just follow,' I said. 'Don't wander off, okay?' I patted him on his cheek and slipped out into the night.

I walked alongside a row of five-storey tenements whose ground floors were given over to commerce. Above me, oriel-windows projected from smooth, black walls that seemed to be composed of the same material as the planetoid's surface. The docks were deserted. For a seaport, the night was uncommonly quiet. The taverns and brothels all seemed closed. There were no night-watchmen. And the ships were sufficiently obscured by wharves and cranes to render us nigh invisible to any insomnious sailor who might be pacing their decks.

Glancing behind to make sure the Tasmanian was still with me, I lowered my shoulders and walked briskly along. The lampposts, and their pools of incriminating light, lay on the other side of the road, the side whose vista was open to the sea. And the shops, kiosks, drinking establishments and houses of assignation whose walls and windows I clove to were, at this late, but by no means witching hour, unilluminated by either candle or lamp.

The temperature had fallen quite sharply, and I shivered, not only from dread, but cold. I was attired in full uniform, but wished I had had the great, long cloak that, in the Darkling Isle, was standard issue for officers. The sound of my boots against the damp cobbles seemed loud enough to wake the dead. But ever since we had rowed to shore and docked, I had failed to spy a single *malignos* who might raise the alarm.

As I passed near the light of a lamppost my shadow stretched out before me. I jumped back, one hand against the wall, the other upon my pounding heart. The shadow had, for a moment, seemed like the looming, hornèd form of one of the natives. I took a deep breath, and, cursing my own gullibility, went to walk on when something alerted me that all was not well. For a moment, I leaned against the wall, wondering at the abiding sense of imminent danger that, despite assurances to the contrary, would not go away. Then I understood. No second shadow had followed upon my own. I scanned the street, and then the whole seafront. The Tasmanian was nowhere to be seen. The only thing that seemed to give some indication of his whereabouts was an open door, rattling gently on its hinges, several metres away.

I backtracked, my tongue compulsively running over my broken teeth, my breath coming in small pants of exasperation. The door was broken, the jambs so rotten that I had not heard the Tasmanian put his shoulder to it and force its lock. The building it belonged to was a tavern, and I immediately assumed the worse.

I eased the door open, wincing at every creak it made, no matter how comprehensively the noise vanished into the vastness of the still night. I walked inside, my fingers playing over *Espiritu Santo*'s hilt.

I passed through a hallway and into the tavern's parlour. It was dark. The landlord had long departed for his bed. Behind the bar was the Tasmanian, as I had expected to find him, quaffing from an enormous tankard of beer.

'Fool,' I whispered, with as much threat as I could muster. He looked back at me, unconcerned. I was seized with a sense of *déjà vu*. It was as if I was back in the lighthouse. Then, as now, he had lost no time in filling himself with beer, regardless of the consequences. But his present actions lacked bravura. Ever since his days as a wolf and his subsequent illness, he had lived, it seemed to me, half-in, half-out of this world.

I contemplated leaving him there, to be discovered, unconscious, by the proprietors, when morning came around. If, that is, morning ever came around. I had the impression that Pandemonium was permanently shrouded in a pall of shadows. Shadows that represented neither day nor night, but a limbo where candles and lanterns existed not to dispel, but to contemplate the city's inverse refulgence, its luminous negativity. But whatever punishment might be his due, I simply could not afford to let the Tasmanian be captured. Under torture, or simply under the duress of his disordered mind, he would, I knew, inform on me.

I walked over to the bar, took the tankard from his hand and slapped him smartly, once, twice, three times, about the face. 'We have come the distance,' I said. 'We have achieved something few, perhaps no other humans have ever achieved. We stand in Pandemonium. At the heart of the Netherworld. I hadn't believed it possible. What drove me to come here was desperation. And guilt. If I had reflected, before setting out on this journey, reflected coolly and dispassionately on my chances of success, I would never have ventured forth. I have been pitched here by insanity. But now I am here I intend to fulfil my mission. I intend, somehow, to find the antidote to *manggagawa*. Do you understand me, fool? And if you stand in my way, here, on the threshold of my success – for I am beginning to believe that, mad as I am, having got this far, I can go all the way – if you, in your moonstruck idiocy try to thwart me, whether consciously or no, I shall slit you open and decorate this room with your bowels.'

The Tasmanian's face was a blank slate. 'I'm sorry, Pike,' he said, like a little boy trying to placate his big brother. 'It's just that I'm so thirsty. And *hungry*.'

I noticed that he had found himself a few pies. They lay on the bar, looking up at me with lubricious 'eat me' expressions. I lifted the tankard to my lips and drained it. Then I turned my attention to the pies, grabbing one and sinking my teeth into its pastry. I had forgotten how thirsty and hungry I had been. Now, with ravenousness briefly dispelling my fear of being so exposed in the midst of an enemy city, I ate and drank with abandon. Not even the pain of my broken teeth could arrest my frantic attempt to satisfy myself. My companion, seeing that my anger had been dissipated, joined in, taking another tankard from a peg and filling it from the hand pump.

It was while thus engaged in a gluttonous, undignified, and wholly ridiculous homage to our appetites, that disaster overcame us, and the events that were to lead to the sundering of our months-long companionship had their beginning.

Between bites of pie and gulps of beer I noticed that the Tasmanian was gazing fixedly past me. I spat out a wad of half-masticated pastry and spun about. My appetite vanished. My abdominal muscles tensed and my stomach effected the illusion of rising into my chest cavity. A *malignos*, short, fat, old and bleary-eyed, but a *malignos* nevertheless, a member of the species that would, in any circumstances, let alone the one in which we found ourselves, be unlikely to offer the hand of friendship, stood by the corridor, an antiquated flintlock in his hand.

'How do you do,' said the Tasmanian, without a trace of irony, so divided from himself that not even the appearance of one of our enemies could lend him an appreciation of our plight. The old *malignos* said something in his own tongue which, though I could not understand it, I knew boded ill. I raised my arms to show that I did not mean to argue with a loaded pistol. I essayed a greeting. The old man's eyes hardened. Not knowing if he had understood, or, understanding, had taken exception to my no doubt barbaric pronunciation, I tried English.

'We mean no harm,' I said. 'This man and I were merely—'

My shoulders rose to meet my ears and I jigged to one side, not to avoid the lead ball that smashed the ornamental crockery lining the cornice – that, of course, would have been impossible – but at the roar of the discharge. In the confined space of the parlour it had been loud, phenomenally loud. A little disorientated, I stumbled forward, collided with a table, a chair, and half-tripped over a hearth rug. My gaze was fixed upon the creatures' own. His eyes widenened. The hand that held the impotent pistol trembled, with infirmity and fear. I was upon him before he could move. Unsheathing my sword, I brought *Espiritu Santo*'s pommel down upon his crown. And my would-be murderer collapsed at my feet.

I turned to face the Tasmanian. 'Keep behind me,' I said, in as level and authoratative voice as I could manage. I wanted my words to penetrate that almost catatonic exterior. 'There'll be militia here in minutes. Come, fool. Hurry.' Obediently, the Tasmanian moved out from behind the bar and trailed at my heels as I made my way outside. I squinted up and down the street. It remained deserted. And, despite the fact that my ears still rang with the contained blast of the flintlock, all seemed quiet, almost as quiet as the spaces that separated Pandemonium from the rest of the Netherworld. I kept my sword drawn, uncertain of the evidence of my senses.

I pushed the Tasmanian in front of me, determined not to lose sight of him again. Perhaps it was the result of drinking on a comparatively empty stomach, but the sheen of the cobbles seemed more intense, the light shimmering about the lampposts like pools of liquid silver. The darkness seemed more intense, too, a lustrous velvet which I could almost feel against my skin, as if the whole night aspired to be the cloak that I had left behind in the barrio. Not the thin, silk cloak that was common to the Pilipinas, but the heavy, padded ancillary to my uniform; the cloak I had worn when snow and wind whipped through London's streets. The darkness, intense as it was, had not the power to warm. No; the night, for all its intimacy, seemed colder than ever. The shadows brushed against my cheek like black, powdered ice.

I blinked, shook my head, attempting to dispel the charm that the night had put upon me, and the way it bedevilled my senses.

I gave the Tasmanian a perfunctory jab in the buttocks with my sword. It was imperative he keep moving. He turned to look at me. Before his transmogrification, he would have remonstrated. But sadness had replaced anger. One hand rubbing his offended rump, he turned away and proceeded down the street.

The shadows had begun to dance, flowing this way and that, like oil in stormy waters. Again, I shook my head, damning myself for downing a tankard of beer at a time when I would need all my wits. And then something brushed past me with such force that it had me spinning about, sword raised, ready to confront it. It was a shadow, all right, but despite knowing that my judgement was impaired by alcohol, I knew, and knew at once, that this shadow was also a man.

I struck out, but my sword cut at mere air. The shadow had passed by, content, for the moment, it seemed, to test my reactions. I put my back to the wall and hissed at the Tasmanian to stop. I was between two shopfronts, my spine pressed against a thin, tall, oblong of masonry.

To my left, in the middle of the road, a coagulation of darkness told me that another shadow-man was approaching. I readied myself. Suddenly, the deeper darkness that betrayed my enemy was drawn out over the cobbles in a long, jagged smudge of acceleration. It was as if a great, invisible thumb had squashed an enormous bug and smeared its black essence across my field of vision. Legs bent, I grasped my sword in both hands and held it before me.

My blade rang out as if it came into contact with another, sparks flying from the point of contact. The vibrations passed up my arms. The exchange had been unequal. Whoever I had engaged with possessed great strength. And my hands became so numb that I thought I might let *Espiritu Santo* drop.

I had seen no more than the flash of black steel and, as had been the case with my original attacker, a blur of darkness as the shadow form raced by. This time, however, the vanity of my assailant, and, perhaps, a degree of overconfidence, encouraged him to reveal himself. The spot where he had come to rest after touching blades with me wriggled, as if its dimensions were being unfolded, the planes that were negative giving way to angles and sides that reflected light. Where, a moment before, there had been a swarm of shadows, there now stood a *malignos*, tall, muscular and brandishing a gleaming, curved sword.

'Pike,' said the Tasmanian, in the measured tones of a sleepwalker, 'it's the shadow monster. It's the Tenebros.'

Not the Tenebros, I thought. No. But something utilizing the same tek that had surely created that creature. 'These are *malignos*,' I said. 'We seem to have run into the local militia.' I drew myself up, determined to show my disdain. 'If it proves,' I continued, my gaze fixed upon the Tasmanian with a vehemence that I hoped would wither him, 'if it proves that you have undone my chances of finding the antidote that is the true end of my quest, you will wish that I had left you to be experimented on by those two teenage quacks.' My gaze flitted between his downcast mien and the multitude of black, swirling forms. They had congregated about the *malignos* who had recently shown himself. Patches of darkness coalesced into limbs, torsos, heads and tails. And where there had recently been living shadows there now stood over a dozen militiamen.

I was as concerned that the Tasmanian might, by another act of indiscretion, undermine my attempts to either defend myself or flee. But the *malignos* who had materialized before me soon crowded him out of both my field of vision and my mind. Their scales were black, as if they could not quite shrug off the stuff that had recently cloaked them. And their proportions were to mine what mine were to a midget's. In their midst lurked two giant rats. Their riders pinked their flanks with spurs until they stood to the front of the foot soldiers. The cavalry was obviously going to be awarded first crack at the impudent human who had dared encroach upon Pandemonium's sacred ground.

A guttural rumble signified that they were conferring amongst themselves. Was it wonder that made them hesitate? Perhaps none had seen a human before. I was so far from the surface that I might have been on some other world circling the far-flung stars.

The debate became academic as the riders urged their mounts to charge.

I had taken my eyes off the Tasmanian just long enough for his metamorphosis to have escaped my immediate notice. While I had been preoccupied by the *malignos* and their own metamorphosis from shadow to substance, he had reverted to the half-lupine state that, I now understood, he had never really shrugged off. Perhaps it was fear that triggered the transformation? Perhaps his lycanthropy was simply a recurrent state whose time had come again? I flattened myself against the wall as he sprinted past me, no shadow brushing my skin this time, but a hirsute, steaming mass of brute physicality whose proportions vied with the militia's own.

The rats pawed at the ground, their talons wringing a screeching dissonance from the cobbles that set my ruined teeth on edge. Frothing, chewing at their bits, they squealed in protest as their riders brought them under control. They broke into a trot, and then, a canter.

The riders carried lances. They lowered them, the oriflammes – one of which displayed the sigil of Lilith, the other, the black sun – flapping like bat-wings in the chill, stagnant air. These *malignos* seemed possessed of an unwavering intent to skewer the both of us.

The Tasmanian howled, lowered his head, and ran to meet them. As when he had breasted the battlements of the castle in Samaria, he seemed possessed of preternatural energy. He sped over the cobbles, almost as

much of a blur as the shadow-forms of the militia had
been. His metamorphosis was still ongoing. It deepened
every second until, as he came within range of the
lances, it consolidated into the morphology that represented his wholesale possession by the perverse. Once
again, his head and great, barrel chest were covered in
thick, black fur; his face was that of a man-wolf; his
hands had become claw-like; and the spark of whoever,
whatever, shared his body, could be seen glinting in his
eyes and engaging his purpose.

Just as a lance was about to bear him down he sprang,
catching the shaft in one hand as it skimmed over his
right shoulder. He twisted in midair, and the lance was
torn from the rider's clutches. Rolling over as soon as he
hit the ground, and narrowly avoiding the stampeding
feet of the rat-mount, he came up, with fluid grace, into
a kneeling position and impaled the astonished rider
through the heart. The force of the thrust, which
planted the lance all-too-firmly in its victim, and the
careering trajectory of the rat, snatched the purloined
weapon from my companion's grip. And, as the second
rat and its rider turned towards him – distracted, for the
moment, from the task of attending to me – he was again
without benefit of steel.

I raked *Espiritu Santo* across the wall behind me,
sending up a shower of sparks. The rider – that is, the
one who still lived; the other was sprawled across the
road, transfixed by his own gigantic toothpick – the
rider who spurred his beast, somewhat more charily
than his opposite number, towards the Tasmanian,
looked briefly to one side, wondering at what I might
do. Recognizing that I had not yet determined a

coherent strategy (a shower of sparks portends little harm), he concentrated once more on the man-wolf.

The foot soldiers seemed keen to enter the fray. Since they did not occupy higher ground, I knew they could not threaten me from the air. A *malignos* may glide, but only the smaller varieties – children and the like – may become airborne from ground level. To attack, they would have to use the same form of locomotion as myself. Knowing this, and seeing that they had neither archery nor musketry, it would have been sensible to have kept my back to the wall. But the sight of the Tasmanian stirred me. It was not a matter of sentiment. It was rather a stirring of martial feelings, a thrill of battle the like of which I had not experienced since the days of the war. I was a fool, as big a fool as my companion to let those feelings command me. But when I heard the Tasmanian howl I let out a corresponding yelp and ran towards the assembled militiamen.

The assembled *malignos* seemed more than agitated by my charge. They seemed dismayed, even a little scared. Or so I thought then. And perhaps it was true. For my vanity could hardly have distorted my perceptions to such a degree that I saw wide-open eyes where there were none, and slack-jawed, idiot expressions where there were in reality only faces gritted in a determination to chop me to bits. Geeing my courage, I told myself that the legend of Richard Pike had, perhaps, percolated even unto these depths, remote and absolute as they were.

I ran on, whirled my sword above my head, and screamed a medley of extemporized oaths and imprecations.

Malignos

Though I should have been aware of nothing but the ranks of militia, I could not help but notice that hundreds of hornèd heads poked from the street's doorways and mullioned windows. The chaos of undifferentiated voices that formed a background to my own hollerings, was, though indecipherable, latent with a single meaning: that a caterpillar in the commonweal had been discovered, and should be stamped on with all haste. Before me, the militiamen raised their scimitars, clubs and battle-axes. I engaged them with one last, falsetto whoop and a wild slash and parry of steel.

I killed my first *malignos* with a thrust that went under the brute's sword-arm, the blade scoring deep into his right side. Plunged up to its filigree haft, it took all my strength to extricate *Espiritu Santo* from the sucking, muscular flesh. As my man fell, and I staggered backward with the effort of retrieving my sword, a *malignos*'s axe transcribed an arc above my head, fortuitously decapitating one of his comrades. I laughed. Each of my adversaries was nearly a metre taller than myself, and their height and bulk translated into a ponderousness of movement that I was sure I could take advantage of.

The *malignos* formed a circle about me. The laughter died on my lips. How, I asked myself, had I come to relinquish my wall – my nice, warm, protective wall – in so cavalier a manner? The grin that a moment before had animated the dead flesh of my mouth had, like a rat leaving a sinking ship, left me and transplanted itself on to the biggest of the militiamen. The giant – their captain, I supposed – nodded towards his subordinates. They closed in.

I hunched over, and, as one of their number slashed at me with his scimitar, sidestepped and brought my own weapon down across his proffered wrist. A great, taloned hand, still clutching its crescent-bladed sword, spun through the air, a geyser of blood erupting from where *Espiritu Santo* had effected the impromptu amputation. And then they were all upon me.

Despite the slowness of my opponents' movements, I could do little but duck, leap and parry. Sometimes, quite by chance, I would slash out and connect, and the air would be filled with squamous confetti. But now that the *malignos* were acting in concert it was beyond my power to despatch more of their number. I was encircled. And I would have to use all my skill to simply fend off the enemy's blows.

Blade and axe-haft rang against the edge of my sword, knocking me down onto one knee. The assault was terrific, and my sword-arm, benumbed by the violence of steel against steel, at last refused to respond to my will. *Espiritu Santo* fell from my grasp. As it clattered mournfully upon the cobbles the militiamen raised their weapons. It was the moment of truth.

There is a certain cliché associated with a man's impending demise. That is, that within the blink of an eye, he sees his life go before him. Though I was treated to no biographical précis of my own life, the dislocation of time held true. The *malignos*, for a moment that yawned into eternity, were frozen in the act of bringing their weapons down on my skull. Taking advantage of this moment of grace, I fell upon my belly and rolled between the nearest pair of trunk-like legs. To my surprise, I cleared the circle.

I was on my feet and running before my enemies had chance to turn.

I didn't look back. But the commotion behind me signalled that the *malignos* were in pursuit. I swiftly outpaced them. And would, I think, have outrun them entirely if it had not been for two things. The first was the realization that I had deserted my blade. Ah! *Espiritu Santo*! That length of Toledo steel for which I held an esteem that – barring she for whose honour and life I fought – had no parallel. My rapier! My self! The sword's absence from my side dragged at my feet.

And then the second thing hit me: a sight that arrested my momentum with an appeal that, odd as it seemed, even then, when I had barely a chance to consider it, bypassed my battle-tested instincts for self-preservation and trashed my common sense. The Tasmanian had fallen. He was lying a little way off, his head against the curb, his blood streaming into the gutter. He had dealt with the second attack from Pandemonium's cavalry in much the same way as he had dealt with the first. The rider had been skewered with his own lance. And now the two giant rats, with nothing on their backs but their brass harnesses, scuttled about the seafront, their noses tremulous as they sniffed at lampposts and cadavers.

My companion's eyes rolled towards me. He was not dead, but he seemed mortally injured. I could not desert him, said the small, underprivileged voice of conscience deep within me. I could not desert him as easily as I had my sword. I ventured a step or two in his direction; looked back. Within seconds, the *malignos* would be upon me. Perhaps self-preservation won the day. I like to think that an image of Gala flashed through my mind, reminding me of the overriding importance of fulfilling my mission. Whatever the motive, my legs threw off their constraints. I began to run, and then to sprint, leaving my sword and the Tasmanian to the mercies of the militia.

I flew along the road looking for some means of escape. Several shadow-infested alleyways lay between the seafront buildings. Might it be possible, I wondered, to hide in one of them? Or use them to effect an inconspicuous retreat? No; the faces, the jeering, malevolent faces that peered down from the adjoining tenements would see to it that I was discovered. To compound my problems, a crowd had gathered outside a wharf a little way ahead. They were not militia, but ordinary citizens, like those who had begun to spit upon me from above. The hue and cry had been raised and now, it seemed, I had all of Pandemonium on my tail.

That mob made my decision for me. They hurried across the road, shaking their fists and treating me to some choice *malignos* curses. (Curses such as Gala had sometimes used after discovering one of my peccadilloes.) I peeled off and ran into the nearest alley. A few stones followed, hurled by the men, women and children who had broken from the mob's ranks and had begun to join the militia in pursuit.

A chamberpot smashed at my feet, porcelain shards flying into the air. Above, half-obscured by drying bedsheets strung from lines between the overhanging buildings, other *malignos*, aroused from their slumbers and seemingly competing amongst themselves for a good citizenry award, had begun pelting me with crockery, saucepans and excrement. I held an arm above my head to ward off the worst of what they had to offer, and tried to find some way out of the gauntlet. I was weak from lack of food, and, in my middling years, had never been much of a runner. When I saw the dead end that confronted me. I gasped. I think it was less in horror than with relief. It gave my legs the excuse they needed to quit their futile pumping.

I turned and squared up to my pursuers. My hand had automatically gone to my side before I could recollect that my beloved rapier was gone. Dirty fighting, I decided. That was what was needed. The kind of fighting I had learnt in some of London's obscurer taverns. Compared to the academic soirées that my alter ego, the Professor of Antiquity, frequented, society there had been less than polite. And now I too would have to be less than polite. I just hoped that the instincts of the streets were ingrained deep enough to be still with me.

The important thing, I reminded myself, was not to be *macho*. In many ways, it was necessary, in these circumstances, to fight like a woman. A cruel, vulpine woman. When I got into the role I would have need to summon up *hysterical* strength.

The mob, or rather, those of the mob who had followed me down the alley, were in numbers about the same strength as the militiamen. They were also, I thanked my own pantheon of cynical, petty gods, a sorry-looking bunch. Compared to the gigantic physical specimens I had earlier fought, they were little more than a collection of inbred, pigeon-chested, cross-eyed trash. They came to a halt a few metres from where I stood.

Now that I faced them, they seemed less willing to press their advantage, even though reinforcements, in the form of the militiamen, were even now entering the alley's mouth. Another chamberpot exploded on the ground. I ignored it, my gaze fixed upon the enemy. I was determined to pay them back – every last inbred one of them – for forcing me into this rat-trap of an alley.

I was not dealing with people who could be reasoned with. No. People who could be placated, bought off or cowed, perhaps. Contemptible people, in other words, such as may be found in both human and inhuman society. No, no. These were not people to whose rationality I could appeal. But then, that was not my intention.

As calmly as I could, I walked up to one of the male members of the little band, a hand raised as if in parley. I smiled. The *malignos* was smaller than me, and I looked down at him with all the condescension I could muster. His face screwed itself into the aspect of one who had just sat down upon a chair concealing a particularly nasty splinter. My gaze flitted over the others, their faces slavishly imitating the one they seemed to have elected to be their spokesman. My smile broadened. I was beginning to enjoy this.

The *malignos* said something. I nodded in acquiescence, making sure that the hand I held up in parley was at the correct altitude. He was about to say something more when I drove my index and middle fingers into the declivity at the base of his throat. He choked, and stumbled backward. I took the opportunity then, while his hands were engaged in trying to rearrange his windpipe, of similarly driving my fingers into his left eye. He screamed, and took another step backward, *malignos* to either side of him frozen to the spot. I yelled at the top of my voice to consolidate the fear that iced their limbs. If the shock lasted only a few seconds, it would still give me an advantage. But I had forfeited surprise. I would now have to rely on delirium, the ecstasy of pure aggression.

I yelled again, the yell becoming a wild, girlish scream. It was not, this time, for the benefit of the *malignos*, but for myself. I needed the strength that comes with the onset of a hysterical fit.

I thought of all the people who had got away with cheating me, betraying me, insulting me. I thought of the snubs I had received, in London society both high and low, when the rumours had got about that I slept with a goblin-girl. I thought of my exile and of the fact that I would probably never again have a home.

The scream had become a sort of yodel now, dying at the back of my throat only to be immediately reborn, just like the cry of some monstrous infant. I launched myself on to the *malignos* nearest to me – a matronly woman – and sank my teeth into her face with such viciousness that the serrated enamel of my ruined incisors struck against the cheekbone. I bit down and chewed, my ears filled, now, by screams other than my own.

I pushed the woman away; picked up a small child; used the guttersnipe as a battering ram to force a passage through the press of bodies. As I rammed the child's head against the hardened stomach of a skinny, but comparatively well-preserved youth, my weapon slipped from my hands, the horns snapping off as the wretched imp collided with the cobbles.

The young man was the only one of the throng to have any spunk in him, and he punched me full in the face with a well-delivered hook. For a moment, I seemed to hear his shouts as if from the end of a tunnel. But he wasn't big enough to do any real damage. I grabbed him by the throat, my fingers digging in, so that I had hold of his trachea. And then I ripped, almost separating windpipe from the surrounding flesh. He fell, and I found myself at the centre of a circle of bodies, that of two men, one woman and a child. Beyond this little O of carnage was a larger circle of those who had, as yet, escaped my attention. But the red mist that had clouded my brain was evaporating, to be replaced by a deep melancholia, a sort of *post coitum* sadness, and I knew that I had not the strength, or even the inclination, to continue with the mayhem.

It would, in any case, have been futile to continue. No matter how much I might have gouged, bitten, ripped and screamed, I could not – especially without *Espiritu Santo* – have resisted the militia. And now they were upon me, shouldering aside the *malignos* who had tried to effect a citizens' arrest.

I felt great hands clamp upon my shoulders. My arms were twisted behind my back. I was lifted into the air.

I went limp, content to let the bleak realization of failure wash over me. It was almost comforting. I would not have to do anything now. All concern about strange, underground environs, whirlpools, dead, tropical landscapes and obese travelling companions who have problems with lycanthropy, dissipated into a void of

270

pure despair. Sorry, Gala, I thought. Sorry, honey. I wanted to come back. I really did. It was the way I had things planned. Sorry. I tried. Believe me. But now I must let the darkness overwhelm, as another species of darkness even now overwhelms your poor, compromised mind.

They held me aloft, high above their heads, as if I were on a bier. And they, who seemed my pall-bearers, might well have been transporting my body to its final resting place. I was happy to play dead. But, in truth, I would have been far happier to have died. Shame fought with exhaustion and pricked me with sharply-observed asides on how cowardice sometimes likes to hide resignation. Despair lifted for a moment. But insufficiently for me to consider resistance. Then the curtain of hopelessness again dropped and I stared, void of thought, up at the tall buildings, their gables thick with bat guano. Tablecloths, curtains, rugs and sheets (though of course no clothes) hung limp in the unmoving air between the balconies and oriel-windows. I closed my eyes, barely cognizant of the buzz of voices that accompanied me during the twists and turns of my ironically stately progress.

When I again looked about I discovered that I was back on the seafront. The militiamen were loading me into a carriage. I had just time to make out the four giant rats that substituted for horses, and the carriage's rigorous structural engineering that indicated that it was designed, not for pleasure rides, but for enforcing captivity, when I was thrown into its dark interior. An iron door slammed behind me.

The Tasmanian lay half-propped up against the

carriage's side. Blood oozed from a corner of his mouth. The big semicircles of red across his chest and abdomen testified to where he had been bitten and gnawed by the rats. But he was, at least, human again. Only a few tufts of black fur about his face betrayed the lupine characteristics that had allowed him to kill two of Pandemonium's cavalrymen with such ease, if not, it transpired, their mounts.

The carriage began to move. The clamour of iron wheels against the cobbles filled my ears. My jowls shook as the chassis fell into a rhythm. I crawled to where the Tasmanian lay. Slouched beside him, I put an arm about his shoulders, cradling his head in my arms.

'Can you hear me?' I said, looking into his bloodshot eyes. After a few seconds my companion grunted an affirmative. 'They got us,' I continued. 'I guess it's the end.'

'Not the end,' he said, a bubble of blood forming on his lips. 'Not for you, at least. I know you, Pike. You'll find a way.'

Did he know me? How incredible to think that that might be the case. 'The Tasmanian', I called him. At best, 'my companion'. (As in 'travelling companion', a piece of baggage to be borne patiently, with a certain grim forbearance.) I had never called him 'my friend'. Yet it occurred to me that he had been the only friend I had had since leaving England.

'A way,' I said, echoing his words. 'Perhaps, yes, there *might* be a way.'

'Think of Gala,' he said. I nodded, abashed at the vehemence that lay behind the rasping voice, but more abashed at the way I had so readily given in to despair. 'There's another in here with me, Pike,' he continued. 'Another soul besides my own. It's telling me it wants to go back to the universe it came from. But that universe is dead, isn't it? I think the other soul knows it too. Its pain is terrible, because it has no home to go to. Always have a home to go to, Pike. Don't make the mistake I've made and spend your life wandering about the high seas. Have a home, Pike. Find yourself one. Make one, if one isn't forthcoming.'

'Yes,' I whispered. 'That's why I've come to Pandemonium. To find a way home. To find out how I came to be lost. To get back to Gala.'

'A strange journey it's been, Pike. A long one, too.'

'It's destined to be longer,' I said. 'I have to retrace my steps. I have to find a way out of here.'

'Not before you've found the antidote to *manggagawa*,' he said.

'Of course,' I said. 'The antidote. The elixir. But first we must break free.'

We both fell silent for a few minutes, he, having to fight to catch his breath, I having to fight my sense of hopelessness.

'Your sword,' he said, at last. 'That other soul inside me. It says you must look to your sword.'

'Ah,' I said. 'My sword—' But I could not bear to furnish him with the details of my loss.

'The sword. He says it calls to him. It's the sword that will set us free, Pike! The sword! The sword!'

'We'll make an attempt,' I said, somewhat puzzled at my friend's importunity, 'when we arrive at wherever we're bound for.'

'No, Pike. If that soul, that alien, wolfish thing those two little bitches grafted on to me, if *that* is about to leap overboard and take its chance in stormy seas, then it's a sure sign that I'm headed for shipwreck. I'm due to give up the ghost, Pike. Look to yourself.'

'Ridiculous,' I said. 'With a paregoric, a few bandages and a little rest you'll—'

My friend coughed. His eyes glazed, then suddenly cleared and became fixed upon a point in the distance, a point beyond the confines of the carriage, beyond, I would suppose, this universe. 'When you see Gala, Pike,' he said, with rasping urgency, his words tripping over each other, 'tell her I'm sorry, eh? Tell her I never really meant to call her a *malignos* whore. That woman of yours, she's no *puta*. You treat her well, you hear?' He coughed again, and something seemed to break deep within him. Blood poured from his mouth. 'Treat her well,' he concluded.

I held on to him for the duration of the ride, my ears perking at the sounds of the streets and thoroughfares we passed through. From those sounds I tried to gauge the nature of the cityscape about me, and attempted to piece together, from the few words of *malignos* I recognised, the nature of the place to which we were bound.

The journey was so long that I became aware of the cooling of the Tasmanian's flesh. I knew he was dead, of course. Had known even as he had uttered that entreaty '*Treat her well, treat her well.*' Still, I continued to cradle his head, trying to make up for the surliness which I had habitually awarded him. Too late, of course, as my attempt to make up for the way I had treated Gala was, perhaps, too late. My friend's dying words had, however, stirred me sufficiently for me to add a rider to that last clause. It would not be over until I, like him, had drawn my last breath.

Chapter Fifteen

The judas closed. A key turned in rusty, recalcitrant wards. The cell door opened. A *malignos*, his proportions similar to the brutes who had conveyed me to the dungeons, stood in the doorway. His bulk was such that he almost completely obscured the corridor outside. His name was Cacoëthes. And he was in command of the city's garrison. I had learnt, from my first, painful encounter with him, that he had distinguished himself during the war. He seemed one of the few *malignos* in these parts who spoke English. With raised chin and downturned lips, he glanced at the guards who accompanied him. 'Bring the woman,' he said, and, with a wave of his hand, sent them on their way. Their footsteps echoed down the corridor until all I could hear was the dripping of water and the *malignos*'s heavy breath. We were alone.

In his hands he held my sword, his eyes running from hilt to tip, and then back again. 'Hmm, a Jerusalem blade,' he said, smacking his lips with appreciation. I stood naked, manacled to the farther wall, in an aspect of a St Andrew's cross. But even if I had been free I do not think I could have easily indulged my instincts to rush him, retrieve my sword and run him through. I had been beaten and scourged. The weakness I had latterly suffered due to a poor diet now overwhelmed me. 'A beautiful piece of craftsmanship, is it not? And may I enquire of its history? Come, Sir, be bold. Tell me all.'

'My father's,' I said, from the depths of my inextinguishable pride. 'And his father's before him. Down six generations.'

'And wherefore before that, I wonder?' he said. 'It is very old. Older, perhaps, than you suppose. Indeed, Sir, upon my honour it is.' The *malignos* had his broad back to the oil lamp that hung over the door. His shadow fell across the cell, a black caricature that emphasized the blackness of his scales, just as the black light of Pandemonium emphasized the black heart of the empire which held me captive.

The shadow moved. I looked up. Cacoëthes proffered *Espiritu Santo*, as if about to surrender it to me. Then, lifting a leg, he brought the blade down across his thigh.

With a shriek, the sword broke in two. Idly looking at the sundered steel, as if congratulating himself on his own strength, his face, little by little, became that of someone appalled by his own actions. Unsure of how to proceed, he suddenly, with a disgusted flick of the wrists, tossed the two pieces of sword across the cell. They clattered and came to rest at my feet. 'But you may have your Jerusalem blade. Yes, sir, I say you may *have* it. We want no such pretty trinkets from Earth-Above here in Pandemonium. We are honest folk. And plain, you'll find. We have no need of mankind's fancy goods. No, not here. Not in the Netherworld's good, honest capital.'

I looked down at *Espiritu Santo*. I remembered when I had first felt its weight, astonished at its superb balance, the light, joyful way it had submitted to my will. I had been twelve years old when my father gave me my first fencing lesson. But now the future, and all its possibilities seemed, as much as the past, to have been destroyed.

'There are such people in this world,' I said, my voice breaking with emotion, 'who believe life to be a midden. Such people who believe that human beings deserve no *better* than a midden. I have rubbed shoulders with such people all my life. People who have no respect for beauty. Or learning. Or love. People who believe they are shit, and, consequently, that everything else is shit. People' – a sob caught in my throat – 'such as you.'

The *malignos* took a step towards me and raised a hand, as if he meant to knock the impudence clean out of my maw. But he desisted. Instead, he moved closer and put his face within a few centimetres of my own. 'Do you know what we have in store for you, sir?'

I looked him straight in the eye and raised a wry, somewhat devastating eyebrow. 'Oh dear,' I said, still choking back the tears. 'I have obviously been treating you with more respect than you deserve. Forgive me.' I spat. He started backward. A gobbet of sputum dripped from his nose. Again, the hand rose as if to strike me, and again he mastered himself.

'I had hoped, Sir, that your present situation would have imbued you with a little humility. A little wisdom, perhaps. Do you wish, once more, to taste the whip?'

'That's it, Cacoëthes, don't let your gentlemanly affectations get in the way of a little honest out-and-out savagery. Such savagery as is no doubt common in this good, honest city of yours. Come. Show yourself for the creature you really are.'

Slowly, he put a hand to his nose and wipe it clean of spittle.

'You say you are a soldier, like myself. A soldier of some renown. One of the infamous black knights. Do you think I believe you?'

'Do you think I care?'

'Your swordsmanship – ah, yes, I have read the reports – your *swordsmanship*, I say, may be in accord with what you claim. But how is it that I haven't heard of you?'

'Ignorance?' I ventured.

'Be careful, little man.'

'I'm Richard Pike,' I said. 'A goblin killer. At least, that's what they called me back in London before I earned a less polite sobriquet. Yes, I've skewered a few *malignos* in my time.'

'And I have killed many humans. Are we really so unlike? Can you really say that, beneath that cock-of-the-walk insolence of yours, your life is any more substantial than my own? We destroy. That's our meaning, our purpose. We are servants of the Earth's dark heart, you above ground, I below. For neither of us does value exist except in the pain and despair of our enemies. But these, sir, are surely good points. What of your bad?'

I hoisted my eyebrow a little higher, so that its mute, sardonic mockery of him and all his line might not go unnoticed. 'I don't suffer fools gladly.'

'What you are or are not to suffer is entirely in my hands.' He held a hand to his brow, and then began stroking one of his horns, as if meditating on how to proceed. 'Very well. I will *tell* you your bad points. The most salient is that, while you are happy to boast of your exploits, you will not tell us the *reason* for your journey here. You are doubtless a spy of sorts. That much is plain. It is, you will appreciate, my duty to extract from you the details of your mission. But before we come to that pass—' He cocked his head to one side. The echo of footsteps was heard once more, not, this time, in a diminuendo, but growing stronger with each second, and moving towards us. 'I have been anticipated, it seems,' he continued. 'A simple matter of identification, sir. It will take but a minute.'

The footsteps stopped. The open doorway was filled with tall, heavy-thewed bodies. The line of militiamen parted, their black scales setting up a doomy tintinnabulation, as if each *malignos* had countless tiny bells sewn onto his body. A woman walked into the cell.

'Is this the one, Madame?' said Cacoëthes.

The woman held a pomander to her nose. The squalid, unfamiliar backdrop to her weathered beauty, and the way she tried to hide her face behind the scented, brass orb, had me scrabbling about in the vaults of memory, uncertain of what I was turning up. 'Yes, that is the one who raped me,' she said. And then she held the pomander away and gazed at me with bruised, yet triumphant eyes. 'Still alive, captain? I hardly expected you to be. Passage through the Torrid Zone, particularly its lower reaches, can be treacherous, even for *malignos*. I suppose I should congratulate you.'

'You go naked, countess,' I said. 'Is it protocol that has clipped your wings or have you grown tired of aping humans?'

The Countess Suspiria ignored me and turned to Cacoëthes. 'Back in Wormwood, he told me that his purpose for travelling to Pandemonium was to aid a friend. To seek, I seem to remember him saying, the antidote to *manggagawa*.'

'The antidote to *what*?'

'Excuse me,' said the countess. 'I have lived too long beneath the archipelago.' For a few minutes, they spoke in their own language. When they had finished, Cacoëthes gazed down at me, a smile on his black lips that was like a disfigurement, so ill did it suit him, and so much did it prefigure ill.

'So, you are no more than a thief, sir. A petty thief consumed by hubris. You thought you could come here, to the centre of the Netherworld, to steal from us, eh?' He began to laugh. 'It is most absurd. *Most* absurd.' I said nothing. What did it matter if they knew of my plans? To be uncovered was, at the moment, the last of my concerns. And yet, all during my scourging, I had refused to confess. Something in me, some obstinate nugget of resistance, had sealed my lips. Something in me, despite all appeals to reason, had been determined to turn the tables on my tormentors.

'I had come here on business,' said the countess. 'I had not expected pleasure. I am glad we have had the opportunity to meet again, captain. It gives me some satisfaction to know that, even if you survived your little trip down the Naphtha, you will not survive many more nights here. Now that the facts about you have been revealed, your existence would seem to have become superfluous.' She moved closer and spoke in a whisper. 'They do not keep pets in Pandemonium, captain. They are a puritanical lot. They believe themselves to represent the pure heart of the Netherworld. Soon, captain, you'll be wishing you had stayed with me.' She frowned. And then her heavily painted mouth formed a somewhat unbecoming pout. 'Perhaps I'll be wishing you'd stayed, too. Boot had to go. And now I'm alone. What a waste it has all been. And all for your *friend*. A waste and, yes, a pity. You would have made such an interesting plaything.'

Cacoëthes cleared his throat. 'Thank you for your help, Madame. It was really most fortuitous that you happened to be in Pandemonium.'

The countess turned her back on me and returned to where she had formerly stood, in the shadow of the giant *malignos*.

'What will you do with him now?'

'Well, as you say, now that we know who he is and why he is here—'

'The gallows?' she interjected.

'No, no, Madame. He is not *malignos*. No; such few humans as we discover in these parts gain the undivided attention of our comparative anatomists. Medical experimentation, Madame, is how the death of such a one as this may best benefit Pandemonium.'

'You would not consider—'

'Madame!' said Cacoëthes, unable to countenance the prurient gleam in her eye, or the tenor of her half-stated suggestion. 'Pandemonium has been relatively unblemished by human incursions. We have had the odd spy to deal with, oh yes' – and he turned to award me a parenthesis – 'you are not the first human to set foot here. There have been other adventurers. Other fools. Oh yes, you are not the first.' Then he returned to addressing the countess. 'But we do not encourage the keeping of humans for the purposes of domestic amusement. Not here, not anywhere in the Netherworld. I realize there are no laws to prevent one from indulging one's taste in such matters. But we must look to ourselves. Set an example. The purity of the realm must be maintained, Madame. Purity of blood, undefiled by human corruption!'

The countess spun about and walked towards me with a display of rolling hips and coy little flicks of her tail. The tail flicks were those of a younger woman, a girlish gesture at odds with the swaying, matronly pelvis. Despite this dissonance of effect, I found myself – to my astonishment – aroused. A *malignos* woman and her long, pointed, swishy tail – ah, I had long had a fatal weakness for such things. The countess cast her bright, reptilian eyes downward. In my nakedness, I was unable to conceal the evidence of her triumph. I think I may even have blushed. 'I'm flattered, captain. I regret that I must content myself with having you, as it were, on the dissecting slab. Such a shame. We could have had . . . *fun*.' She reached out and ran a talon across my cheek, just gently enough not to draw blood. 'But before I leave I thought you should like to know that the family de Profundis haven't quite finished with your paramour. So outraged were they by the slaughter you perpetrated on their several cousins, uncles and nephews, that the new paterfamilias of the clan has ascended to Earth-Above to seek out both you and your friend.'

'Why?' I said. 'Why seek me above when I'm here?

Why didn't you tell them I was in the Netherworld?'

'Why should I tell them anything? Besides, I wanted you for myself.'

'But what more could they want with Gala?'

'Who knows? They're an odd lot on that side of the family. Vindictive. Cruel. I hear they even have it in mind to waste that pathetic little town you call home. Barrio something-or-other, isn't it?'

'Barretto,' I said.

'Barretto,' she repeated, her lip curling with distaste. 'Burnt to the ground, I would guess, by now. A mere pile of ashes. A poor little slag heap of blackened bones. But you don't have to concern yourself about that, captain. You won't be going home.'

She withdrew, walking backward with her gaze locked firmly upon my own. When she reached the doorway, she executed a swift turn, swinging her tail in the same way a human woman might flirtatiously swing her skirts. The line of militiamen opened up and she disappeared into their ranks. And once again she was escorted along the corridor.

Cacoëthes seemed finished with me. He too walked over to the doorway. 'I did not *enjoy* hurting you,' he said, turning to address me one last time. 'Nor did I look forward to having you submit to further excruciations. I am glad the countess cleared matters up. Rest now, soldier. You will soon be at peace. I will ensure that our scientists do not practise a *live* dissection.' He made a brief salute and then withdrew. The cell door boomed as one of the guards kicked it shut. The judas opened, closed; and then there came the footsteps, pad, pad, pad, until the only sound I was left with was the eternal, tortuous dripping of the water.

Sleep was impossible. I could not forget the pain. But I found that if I closed my eyes I could at least transport myself to a place where the pain had some significance, and was not merely a mindless, nagging force. It was a place where plans of escape whistled through my mind, like a wind through exposed rafters. Endless plans, milling through the darkness, plans extravagant, absurd, futile. But there was, I felt, amongst all that senseless chaff, a plan that, if only I could grasp it and prevent it blowing away, would yield the answers to my plight. I could almost hear it speaking, it was so close. I clenched my eyes. Dots of light pitted the insides of my eyelids. Buzzing filled my ears. The pain became so focused that I felt that at any moment I would see through it to the thing that eluded me.

'Pike?' said a voice. 'Richard Pike?'

'Go away,' I mumbled, thinking it an inner voice that had exteriorized itself. The pain was, it seemed, making me hallucinate.

'Pike,' said the voice again. I lifted my head and opened my eyes.

A human stood before me. Prissy-looking, with a pasty, etiolated countenance which might have led one to suppose he had been born under the Sign of Onan, he was a youth who would have greatly benefited from having his face slapped. And frequently, too. He stared at me from behind thick, black eyelashes. His eyes, I noticed, were a sickly yellow. And his lips trembled as if with some secret joke.

Like me, he was naked.

Was this a hypnagogic image? Or was the boy the

agent of some morbid prank played upon me by the Countess Suspiria?

He moved closer. Then he stretched out a long, thin arm and touched the weals that criss-crossed my chest, first one, and then the other. I winced, cursing him.

'You see,' he said. 'You *are* awake. And I am real. Quite real.' I struggled in my bonds, the chains that ran from the manacles to the wall rattling with ineffectual menace. 'Calm yourself. I am here to help.'

'Don't play games with me,' I said between gritted teeth. 'Say what you have to say and leave.'

He ran a hand through his fine, ash-blond hair. With an effeminate flounce, he stepped backward and surveyed me with the air of a despised scion of an old, noble family. 'Well,' he said, placing a hand on his hip, 'so this is what I get for serving you so faithfully all these years. But gratitude was never your forte.'

I looked down at the floor, tired, mortally tired of his presence. The two halves of *Espiritu Santo* that had lain at my feet were, I saw, missing. Had the countess taken them?

'Ah,' said the boy, 'he begins to comprehend. Yes, Pike, I am risen. It's the machine, you know. Being so near the great machines that lie in this city's heart has made me self-aware. More than self-aware. Fleshly.' He smoothed his hands over his anaemic torso. 'And what a *lovely* new body I have to disport myself with! Isn't science wonderful?' He took a step towards me, the hand that had been on his hip held, now, to his mouth, as if to stopper his embarrassment. 'Oh dear, has it come as a shock? *Espiritu Santo* you called me. Your lady's idea, of course. And she was as near to the truth as anyone has come these long, long millennia. Because you see Pike, I really *am* the Holy Spirit. Not of the Christian Trinity. No, no; that spirit is dead, whereas I am alive, though my universe is dead. Another universe. That one you humans call the *perverse*. You may call me Metatron, an angel of worlds that are no more.'

'Metatron,' I echoed. 'The spectres and phantoms that appeared to me in Samaria said something about "Metatron".'

He made a little bow. 'At your service.'

'They seemed to be at *your* service. They didn't rescue me, it seemed. It was you that they were concerned with.'

'More than likely,' said the boy. 'I am not their God, but in the last days, before the catastrophe, I was certainly their greatest hope. I, and the others like me who kept the enemy at bay. Not that I have any great power any more. It is simply that, alive or dead, the children of the perverse are *my* children. I am their spiritual essence, if you will. Their life. Their being.'

'*Their being*?' I said. Custom, habit, cause and effect – all the things that give us an instinctive, if perhaps misplaced, sense of the world's consistency, had been so outraged during my travels underground that this latest affront to reason had no more effect than that of concentrating my mind. I hung in my chains, waiting and hoping for revelation, a madness so singular that it would bring the relatively sensible world of my captivity to its knees.

'Oh, very well, *a* spiritual essence. As I say, there were others. But, so far as I am aware, I *am* the only one that still lives. How did I come into your possession?'

'You're my father's sword,' I said. And then I paused. If I was content, for the moment, to wallow in what was doubtless my introduction to the world of the insane, then the absurdity of my statement still rankled. I saw, however, no sensible alternative other than continuing with the conversation in the hope that the madness pressing in on me from all sides would lead me into the light. 'And my father's father's. And his father before him. You've always belonged to my family.'

'Not always, Pike. Your country has been a dark island for longer than you might think. It was called so even in the day when the children of the perverse roamed the Earth. And it was dark because the perverse had such influence there. In the time immediately preceding the Dark Ages, my children made many engines of power. The engines by which they transformed themselves. And the engines by which they walked between the stars. And engines such as . . . *myself*. But then the perverse gripped men's minds in such a way that they could no longer use those engines and machines. The particulates from the exploited, parallel cosmos – my cosmos – obscured an understanding of their own universe's laws. The artefacts slept, as I have been sleeping, for thousands of years. But there is, it seems, a change in the air.'

I studied him closely. He looked like a sword. Not my beloved *Espiritu Santo*, but a crueller, more brittle blade. Pale and waspish, he was, perhaps, my own sword's useless brother, the black sheep of the *Santo*'s who had forsaken his monthly remittance to come home and make a nuisance of himself. His sleep-starved eyes regarded me with dark, sheepish presumption.

'You're an artefact, then,' I said. 'You were made by the Ancients.'

'Yes. Made by those who were first infected by the perverse. Just as new bodies were made to house their own infected spirits, so they made things to house those creatures that had never been enfleshed. Creatures holy and mighty.' He smiled with immodest glee. 'Although they had begun to flounder in their own fields of learning, the increasing alienness of those humans who became "perverse" meant that they were awarded visions that allowed them to construct artefacts that gave no more than lip service to the Earth's natural laws. Artefacts such as sustain the Netherworld.'

'And,' I said, 'as you say, artefacts such as yourself.'

'Quite.'

'But why have I never known this? For all my life, you have been a sword, no more, no less. A beautifully-crafted length of Toledo steel.'

'Am I still not beautiful?' he said with a moue.

'You have never been *alive*. You have never—'

'Talked?' he interjected. 'I talk too much. As do you.' Swiftly, he knelt down and then lowered himself until he was prone against the floor. His ear was against the flagstones. He seemed to be listening. Then he cocked his head, staring up at me. 'Here, at the centre of the Earth, there are many, many artefacts,' he continued. 'I can hear them singing. Oh, it's so good to be awake, Pike. Awake after so many thousands of years! The perverse has loosened its grip on the world. And though things such as myself were born from the genius of the perverse, and our power wanes also, yet we are resurrected, along with other elements of ancient tek. For if we were made by souls infected by another, alien universe, we were also made by men, human men. And the day is coming when men will be returned to their former eminence as lords of the Earth.' Again, he put his ear to the floor. 'I have to hurry.' A note of breathy panic had entered his voice. 'I can only be healed at the centre of things. Come, come, I don't have much time. I can remain in this body for a few hours. Without the sword, then—'

'Can you get me out of these manacles?' I said.

The boy – whether a thing holy or damned, seemed, at the moment, of little consequence – sprang up and came to me. He put his hands on my shoulders. 'Of course. I need you, Pike. You're my guardian. My keeper.' He lowered his chin and gazed through those sooty eyelashes; in the dim light of the cell, they were like the wings of two black moths flitting about the bright, yellow candles of his jaundiced eyes. Chewing his generous underlip, he concluded. 'You're mine, Pike. Remember that. You don't belong to another. You're mine. All mine.'

He put his arms about my neck and kissed me, full on the mouth. I screwed my eyes shut and tried to turn away, but he held me fast. When I opened my eyes I was no longer in the cell. Nor was I manacled. But neither was I free.

Chapter Sixteen

Only the growing ache in my chest made me aware that I had been holding my breath too long. I exhaled, gulped, and filled my lungs. I was surprised at how easily my breathing returned to normal. But nothing could truly surprise me any more. Exhaustion, pain and loss had inured me to surprises, and if I had seen the Tasmanian return from the dead, or found myself wearing another's face, I would have been moved to no more than my current state of curious apprehension. Though I knew I did not dream, I passed, lucid, as if through a world of dreams, accepting, fearless, omniscient.

I was clothed. So was the boy, and in identical fashion to myself. We both wore the uniforms of a captain of the Darkling Isle. Around my shoulders I even found the long, black cloak – just like the one I had left in Barretto – which completed the ensemble I had necessarily stripped down for the tropics. The cloak was a welcome addition. The place I had been trans-ported to was cooler than any place I had yet visited in the Netherworld. A breeze ruffled the cloak's trailing edge, so that it resembled a column of smoke, or my own shadow, twisting, turning, and trying to escape me.

It was dark. A vague illumination played over rows of books that lined the walls. I saw, as my eyes quickly adjusted to the gloom, that I was in a library. It occupied a rotunda similar to the one that had converted itself into a holding pen when I had been inside Satana and Lucifera's castle. The boy stood by my side.

'We're not deep enough,' he said. 'My powers are limited, it seems. It's a cruel paradox: that which has brought me to consciousness – the perverse's demise – has also, since I am *of* the perverse, degraded my potency. I must get nearer to the engines that shape and order the Netherworld. Their energy will make me whole.' He took me by my elbow and ushered me forward. I stood my ground.

'Wait,' I said. 'Just where the hell are we?'

'Beneath,' he said.

I shrugged off his hand. The temptation to slap his face, which I had felt ever since first seeing him, became irresistible. I delivered a swift, open-handed blow to his left cheek. 'Beneath where?' I said. 'We're in the centre of the Earth. How can we be beneath anything?' I cursed, then let my hands hang by my side. I relented my outburst. The boy was my only hope of salvation. With considerable effort, I calmed myself. 'Do you mean we're beneath the city? Beneath the dungeons?'

To my chagrin, the slap seemed to have been only marginally effective. He seemed as calm as me. Too calm, in fact, for his equilibrium to be genuine. I took care not to take my eyes off him. There was something about him now at odds with his pasty, effeminate looks. There was something of *Espiritu Santo*. 'I am trying to save you too, Pike. You don't seem to understand our relationship. Or indeed its responsibilities. You have never treated me this way before.'

'I asked you where we were. If you don't give me a

straight answer, I shall have to consider putting "our relationship", as you put it, on a different footing.'

'Ooo, *threats*.' He smiled, his lips glistening. 'Don't be like that,' he continued. 'All the men I've killed for you – think of them. Aren't you just the least little bit grateful?'

'All the men *I* killed, you mean.'

'You?' His smile broadened. 'You are a mediocre swordsman, if truth be known, Pike. It is I who am the agent of your deadly fame, not that right arm of yours.'

I dismissed this pathetic slander with a wave of my hand. 'Just tell me exactly where we are.'

'We are in the chambered heart of the planetoid that is Pandemonium,' he said. 'This, and the adjacent chambers, are used for the storage of artefacts. Lower down we shall find the artefacts that maintain the Netherworld's integrity. The same artefacts that, of late, have started to become self-aware.'

'Are there *malignos* in these parts?'

'No. Only battery boys.'

'What?'

'Automata. Artificial creatures. Men who – to make such a matter plain to one with your limited understanding – run on clockwork. *Super* clockwork. But they shall not, I think, be troubling us. They are only concerned with servicing the machines.'

The boy strode ahead. The library, however, with its thousands of grimoires, was whispering an invitation. Unable to restrain myself, I made a diversion. It was as if I were a lodestone and the multitudinous volumes some kind of magnetic North. I scanned the shelves, marvelling at what they offered. I passed so close that my fingers began to brush against the spines. One volume projected a little from the others, and, as my fingers made contact with it, I allowed them to close upon its vellum. With a swift, clandestine gesture, I snatched it from its resting place and brought it close to my chest. I walked away from the shelves and followed the boy out of the library.

I glanced down at the purloined tome. Blowing the dust from its jacket, I saw that its inscription read *Holy Bible*. What was it doing lodged amongst all those catalogues of charms, magic and superstition? Perhaps it had been mistaken for a grimoire, its enigmatic but beautiful language confused with the gibberish that lay between the covers of those volumes that otherwise filled the shelves. Incredulous, I fanned the pages. It seemed intact. The only such intact copy of the book I had ever handled. In the churches that Gala would frequent, copies were fragmented, containing elements of the *Old Testament,* the *Gospel of St John* and *Revelations,* but no more. Commentaries, of course, had always referred to other texts, but, as far as I knew, no modern had ever seen them, let alone read them. I tucked the book unto the folds of my doublet.

We came to a staircase. It was a spiral structure, made of convoluted ironwork, its balustrade ornamented with twisted, iron flowers. The boy raced down the steps, intent on descending as quickly as his legs were able to carry him. I followed in his wake, he occasionally looking back to see that I had not been left behind.

The coolness of the air increased in exponential relationship to our descent. With one hand, I threw my cloak across my body, my other hand on the outside wall. The shadows, as well as the cold, rose to greet me. My teeth began to chatter. I held the cloak the more tightly. Then, just before I was left to grope my way forward in freezing, utter darkness, the stairway ended.

A hall led away, its low ceiling a stone cobweb of intricate fan vaulting. The walls were patchy with moulds and other, unidentifiable species of slime. The sound of dripping water, which I had thought I had left behind in the dungeons, was once more apparent. And covering everything was a patina of glistening damp. After being immersed in the shadows, the light cast by the wall-bracketed oil lamps hurt my eyes.

The hall gave onto a vast chamber that reminded me of St Paul's cathedral in London, though, unlike that fabulous ruin, the cupola that surmounted this hollowed-out habitation was still in place, just as its statuary and ornamentation were untouched by vandalism.

The boy had come to a halt at the chamber's edge. 'You slapped me back there,' he said. But I was uninterested in his complaint.

'What is this place?'

He put his hands on his hips and blew out his cheeks. 'You said that you wished to place our relationship on a different footing.'

'Did I?' I said, absently. Rats were everywhere. But the rats, thankfully, were all of mercifully modest dimensions, such as on Earth-Above. I surveyed the dust-shrouded altars, the fluted columns that fanned out as they reached the vault, the brass, verdigris-spotted crucifixes of Lilith and the niches set in the walls that contained voluptuous marble statues of her daughters, the Lilim.

It was deadly quiet. Only our breathing was audible. Mine was heavy. I had still not recovered from our frantic rush down the stairs. But the boy filled and emptied his lungs with sketchy gasps. He was an unhealthy specimen. I had known that already. But he was sickening fast. Those lungs of his: they brought to mind the sound the hundreds of rats made as they scuttled over the flagstones.

'Yes, you did,' said the boy, with a slight toss of his head. 'And I think perhaps you're right. We *should* place it on a different footing. I'm not so sure I'm willing to share you with someone else any more.' I gave no response. He continued. 'I'm not sure I'm willing to share you with the *Señorita*.'

'You mean Gala?' I said at once. I fixed him a baleful gaze. He had my attention now.

'Of course.'

My hand fell to where I was accustomed to find the hilt of *Espiritu Santo*. But, of course, the scabbard was empty.

'Oh, Pike, you *want* me. How affecting.'

'We can have only one reason for discussing Gala, and that is to establish whether or not the antidote to simplification may be found. I presume it may be located hereabouts, amongst all these other artefacts?'

'Ah, yes, the antidote. I *do* have it in mind to give it to you, dear soul.'

'It *is* here, then? It's to be found beneath the city?'

'Be assured, Pike. I will lead you to it. But there is, you see, this question of our relationship.'

'Speak,' I said.

'You realize you're no good for that woman, don't you?'

'I've helped her as much as I can. I've—'

'Oh, please. You use her. She cooks for you, cleans for you, whores for you—'

'That's enough.'

'A man like you, Pike – you're destruction. You're like me, you see. You're an angel of death. You herald disaster wherever you go. And that goes for your domestic arrangements.'

'Leave Gala out of this, eh?'

'That's exactly what I want *you* to do, Pike. I'll make you a bargain. Promise me that you'll leave Gala and I'll take you to where you can get the medicine she needs.'

'Then there is an antidote?'

'Stored here are many wonders of the ancient world. Amongst them, what was, once, an elixir of life. Its power has, undoubtedly, been diluted by the reign of the perverse. But I believe it must by now have reclaimed *some* of its efficacy. Perhaps it can no longer raise the dead, nor even cure mortal illness. But it will, I believe, reverse the effects of what you call "simplification".'

I took a step towards him. Raised a fist. The intent had been to threaten, but the hope he offered made me hesitate. I lowered my hand. The pain and exhaustion I had briefly rid myself of came flooding back. An infinite sadness seemed to overwhelm me. I tried to speak, but my throat was constricted. I let my gaze fall to the ground. I thought of Gala. I thought of her vanquished spirit, the waste of her life. The boy was so close I could feel his breath on my face. Suddenly, my violent resolve was replaced by a willingness to beg. I was at the Earth's black heart, surrounded by an incomprehensible tonnage of fire and rock, and utterly at this being's disposal. What else could I do but beg?

'The elixir,' I said. 'You must let me have it.'

'And what about my proposition?'

'What are you talking about?'

'I'm talking,' he said, a note of irritation in his voice, 'about the bargain I would have us make.'

I was, for a moment, utterly perplexed. 'I don't understand. Leave Gala? What do you mean *leave*? You mean you want me to, to – no, I don't understood. I've come here to help her. I *can't* leave her.'

'A man like you can do her no good, Pike. I've said it before: you belong to me. Think, dear soul. You know it, don't you? You know it's *true*.'

Wherefore was I debating with the cream-faced youth? What did it matter what I promised him, or what kind of strange bargain he made the prerequisite of his help?

'Okay, I'm yours. Whatever you say.' I threw up my hands, exasperated. My anger had begun to return. If the boy truly held the answers to my quest, it seemed insupportable that I should allow myself to submit to his childish demands. I lowered my chin and looked at him with the most minatory expression I could muster. 'If you provide me with the antidote, I'll leave her. Is that understood? Is that clear?' Hell, I thought, I'll probably never get out of the Netherworld alive anyway. If I did, and if I managed to administer the elixir, then would be the time to worry about this ridiculous pact.

'Thank you,' said the boy. 'Shall we proceed?' He set off across the chamber. 'There are all kinds of store-rooms here. And I think I know just the right one for you. These machines, these artefacts: they're my brothers and sisters. And they sing, yes, oh how they sing. They tell me their names. They tell me their secrets.'

We passed, then, through many other chambers. Not all were as barren as the one that had reminded me of St Paul's. Many bore out the suspicion that I walked through a vast lumber room divided up into *Wunderkammer*. In the distant past, I would guess, a series of mad collectors had, after scavenging amongst the Earth's buried cities, brought together, in one place – a series of hypogeums that formed a sort of vast cellar to the city above – the relics and antiquities on which the Netherworld's wealth was based. And on which its survival was predicated.

Some of the cathedral-like chambers were filled with musical instruments, some with paintings and sculpture. As we walked through these latter chambers, my sense of living in a dreamland was corroborated by the notion that I would, at any moment, set eyes upon those masterpieces that I had till then only seen reproduced in grimoires. And, at last, I would wake and know the truth. But such hopes were futile. The canvases were so blackened with age that whatever they had once represented was utterly obscured. When we came upon succeeding chambers that I was told were filled with books, real books, the texts from which the collections of fragments we called 'grimoires' had been culled, I was not surprised to discover that they were as rotted and blackened as the paintings. There were other species of library, some of which contained pharmaceuticals, curiously packaged to look like books. These, the boy told me, had proved popular in the early twenty-first century, after much of Europa had legalized hallucinogenics. 'Many people at that time who bought books didn't really like reading,' he explained. 'They liked books even less. So they manufactured these things. Brain candy with pretensions to art. Very lucrative, I believe.'

We came, next, to chambers that were dominated by vats, racked bottles and the kind of paraphernalia that I associated with alchemy. 'Disease factory,' said the boy. 'Don't worry. The germs here only infect races that have become extinct. But they are still partly responsible for the residua of nationalism and xenophobia that you find both above and below the Earth's surface. When you know that your enemy can target you through your racial characteristics, you tend to become paranoid. To band together.'

The chambers that followed also contained vats. But these, I was told, had been used to grow artificial humans. And sometimes baby starships.

When we moved into a series of even vaster chambers, the boy became pensive. Arrays of artefacts, similar to those that had precipitated the transmogrification of the Tasmanian, glinted in the dim lamplight. They seemed, in their dimensions, and the flat, unadorned nature of their planes, like blocks, pillars and monuments uncovered by some never-completed archaeological dig. The bare lineaments of a weird and unfathomable temple. Some were no bigger than myself, but some were huge, towering into the chamber's dark empyrean. They seemed like obelisks, such as might be erected to represent the genealogies of dead kings. But unlike similar things I had seen on the surface, these towers of stone were plated with silver and steel. And some, flickering with kaleidoscopic lights, seemed alive. When their nimbuses punctured the vault's gloom a chaos of shadowy visual paradoxes flitted about like great, misshapen bats. They were forms that defied analysis, affronts to three-dimensional space. I knew, then, that the questions that underlay the architecture of these machines had only a perpendicular relationship to the laws of nature in our own universe. They were a bridge between the possible and the impossible. They were engines that defied reality.

The boy stroked the side of one of the artefacts with his hand. And then he rested his cheek against it. Beams of light arced above us. Some swung downwards, bathing the boy's white complexion in multi-hued tones. 'I really do think I'm much recovered,' he said. The light beams passed through the non-Euclidean madness above, the shapes folding in on themselves as they were briefly illuminated, like dark flowers that were accustomed to bloom at night shying from the sun.

'The elixir,' I said, in as level as voice as I could manage. 'You promised me the elixir.'

'So I did.' He levered himself away from the sleek, metallic pillar that ascended into the vault, and then engaged in a half-hearted calisthenics routine, followed by a little display of lackadaisical shadow boxing. 'Yes,

yes, I *am* much recovered. It is perhaps true that I am not as elegantly turned out as I am wont to be. But I feel in good enough condition to be strapped to your side! Yes, indeed I do!'

'The elixir,' I reminded him, as patiently as I could, but unable to prevent my lip curling into something approaching a sneer.

He nodded with complaisance, and executed one of his annoying little bows. His hand shot out. Catching me momentarily off balance, he was able to grip me by the arm and pull me flush against the side of the silver monolith. A finger went to his mouth to still my lips, which were pregnant with an exclamation of protest. 'Battery boys,' he whispered, almost amused, it seemed to me, by the turn of events. He looked askance. My gaze followed his.

Two humans approached. Yet they were not humans. They enjoyed a passing familiarity to men, but they moved like clockwork toys, and seemed barely conscious of our presence, though we lay along their line of sight.

'They will only react,' said the boy, 'if we move. We must keep still and wait for them to finish whatever business has brought them here.' The artificial humans, or 'battery boys' as my own boy called them, shuffled over to one of the smaller artefacts.

A mist swirled about their feet. The vapour emanated from grilles set in the floor. The mist was so thick and plentiful that, despite the lack of a draught, a little of it drifted our way. It was curiously dry. Suddenly, the cold had deepened. I withdrew into the black confines of my cloak.

Malignos

A compartment in the chest of one of the automata opened. From this cavity it selected a tool and then fell to work unscrewing the artefact's upper panel. Its opposite number copied, and assisted with the work at hand. The instruments they held might have belonged to a barber surgeon.

'We can't wait here,' I said. 'I must have the elixir. And then' – my thoughts racing so fast, now, I could no longer control them – 'and then you must help me get back to the surface. Back to Barrio Barretto!' I was conscious of the absurdity of this demand – its absurdity lay in the sheer enormity of the undertaking – but I had been dipped and dyed in absurdity ever since I had discovered my sword transformed into an infuriatingly pertinacious young man. The dye was so deep that I had given up all hope of washing it out. Now I wallowed in it. Rubbed it into my skin and veins. And I would have been willing to fill my lungs and drown in the stuff if, by a surfeit of such absurdity, I might have become at one with it and made the impossible real. 'Use your powers,' I said. 'Transport me like you did when you whisked me out of the dungeons. And then, once I have the elixir, transport me to Earth-Above!'

'I am your sword, Pike,' the boy said, with lowered eyes. 'I am here to help you destroy your enemies.' He placed a hand on my chest, where the laces of my doublet had unfastened to reveal bare skin and curls of black-and-grey hair. Then I felt his long nails, cold, cold as steel, digging into that naked flesh. 'If you will help *me*, that is.'

'What do you want?'

'I have your fealty? Our bargain is agreed?'

'I've told you so.'

'Then pardon me for seeming greedy, but I want something more. I want to share your life. I've always been your friend, Pike, whether you know it or not. Your only friend. But it's not enough. I want us to be as one.' He removed his hand from my chest and touched himself on the chest, and then the lips and forehead. 'I do so like this body. Like it all the more because I know I have to give it up. I never knew flesh could be so divine! Say you'll do it, Pike. Let my flesh be your flesh. Say it'll be me and you forever!'

'You have it,' I said, suddenly tired as I had never been before in my life. As the boy's eyes had glinted with desire, I had seen, behind them the flash of a blade. I had seen *Espiritu Santo*. With a shiver of horror, I knew that I was as enamoured of this creature as he was of me. And had always been so enamoured. Yes, I was tired. Tired that I had not known him for what he was. Tired that I had never known my sword for what it was. 'Haven't you always had it? Haven't you always had your own way?'

'You submit?'

I nodded.

'Then I am yours.' He took my head in my hands and kissed me in the same way that he had in the cell. But this time it was more passionate.

I tried to push him from me. At first, he proved intractable. When I at last succeeded, I turned aside and drew a hand over my humiliated mouth. It was then that I noticed a familiar weight in my right hand.

I looked about. The boy had vanished.

'Is that better, Pike?' said a voice in my head. 'This is

the way it was meant to be. You and me. Together, always.' I stared down at the length of steel. It hung limply from my hand, its tip pointed towards the floor, swaying, back and forth, like a pendulum in a torture chamber. At any other time I would have gripped its hilt with fervour and thanks. But something now overlay its familiarity, something I knew I would never rid myself of. It was a feeling of disgust. My love affair with *Espiritu Santo* was over. And the realization had me stooping to deposit a stream of clear white vomit upon the stones.

My sword was not only in my hand but inside me, entwined about my soul like some cold, metallic variety of convolvulus. I understood, now, what had happened to the Tasmanian. For I too had been invaded. Like him, I was possessed by the spirit of the perverse.

And possessed, I was granted understanding.

The battery boys, for instance. They were sentinels. But they were also midwives. They had come to this chamber to assist one of the artefacts give birth. The machines that surrounded me were alive, and, unlike the battery boys, self-aware. They cried out for help. I listened, and found, just as the boy had earlier, that I could hear their song. Each machine was a conglomerate. A colony of machines. And each tiny machine that made up the colony was made up of tinier machines, world without end. The chorale, out of range of human ears, was tremendous. It was of tiny, tinier voices, receding into infinity. It was a song that touched the bedrock of things. And I knew that the only reason my own ears heard it was because it emanated from the ancient world. It contained the spirit of the perverse, as had my blade, and as did I.

I understood what had become of the Tasmanian. And more. I understood a whole new universe.

'We must seek certain other intelligences if we are to get out of here,' said the voice. 'The hall of mirrors is nearby. Come.'

But the knowledge conferred upon me by the perverse was complemented by a darker, more lurid knowledge of what I was. Part of my attention was given to the battery boys who seemed to become cognizant of my presence. But my inner eye was consumed by visions of suave bloodshed and voluptuous cruelty. Those visions, I knew, as much as the intellectual achievements represented by the engines and machines that surrounded me, belonged to the perverse. They predicated each other.

'Our morality is not that of Earth's,' said the voice. 'Even the *malignos* no longer share the glory that was ours. With me, Pike, you will no longer be dogged by human scruples. You will transgress, joyful that your experiences are unlimited by conscience. You will be like a god.'

'Shut up,' I whispered. I backed away from the advancing automata. 'Just tell me where I should go.'

'Come, come,' said the voice. And I knew it was directing me to one of the low, cinquefoil arches that decorated the tunnel mouths dotted about the chamber. Giddy, and still feeling the urge to retch, I stumbled towards it. Once there, I paused. Putting a hand on the archivolt to steady myself, I looked back and saw that several other automata had appeared. They walked steadily towards me in a broken phalanx. I entered the tunnel and ran, my head lowered to avoid collision with the overhead beams and lamps.

Waiting for me at the tunnel's end was a staircase. In appearance, it was the same as the staircase that had connected the library to the vast, chambered area below. The concussion of my leather boots against its iron steps echoed through the darkness like a dissonant carillon. I pressed on, the voice inside my head filling my skull with promises, warnings and threats.

I spiralled into thickening shadows. A wind rose from the depths, whistling through the perforations in the cast iron. The whistle turned into a howl. My cloak was jerked free of my grasp and whirled behind me. I fought to bring it under control. It was cold, far colder than it had been higher up. And I was alarmed to discover that my fingers, while trailing along the supporting wall seeking reassurance from the dark, had begun to tingle and ache from a too-intimate contact with the icy surface. The wind gusted. I leaned into it, struggling to complete my descent. Ahead, I could see that the stairway terminated at an arch that was the counterpart of the one by which I had entered its freezing, blustery helix. As my feet attained the horizontal, the wind, no longer channelled into an up-draught, abated. But if anything it had grown colder.

The arch beckoned. I walked through it.

There were no lamps here. There was no need. The chamber I stood in was suffused with a brilliance more powerful than any I had yet encountered in the Netherworld. Shivering, I pulled my cloak about me, and held a hand over my eyes in an attempt to shield them from the light that teemed in from every direction.

The light had the effect of flattening out the chamber's dimensions. I could identify neither walls nor ceiling. Only the ground lent a sense of perspective. All about me, as far as I could see, was an ankle-deep mist, as white as the light. And rising from the mist, in serried ranks, the headstones in a cemetery that receded beyond the horizon, and which was designed to accommodate all the world's dead, past, present and to come was a grid of oblong mirrors, thousands, perhaps millions, in number. Each mirror was as tall as myself, and about as broad. Wafer-thin, they stood without apparent support, their limpid surfaces a dazzlement of silver, reflecting nothing but an infinite regression of themselves.

This was a wilderness of mirrors. Preserved in bitter cold, and impervious to the depredations of the relentless winds, they seemed the only markers in this pallid, otherwise vacant realm.

The voice urged me on. I stepped forward and walked down one of the avenues of silvered glass, the mist swirling about my ankles. As I passed each mirror its surface would ripple, like still water broken by a tossed stone. I knew, by virtue of the thing that clove to my soul, that these mirrors were intelligences. Self-aware machines, such as I had previously encountered. Alive, just as I was alive. Once, they had constituted part of a membrane that had covered all Earth-Above. But that membrane was torn, in ruins, the last of its constituents relegated to this chamber at the very heart of the Netherworld, the very heart of the world itself. For I had no doubt that this hall of mirrors heralded my arrival at the Earth's dead centre, its literal core.

My new, other self, listened intently to the music that issued from the glass portals. Originally devised by man, to provide access to worlds of his own making, the magic mirrors had, at the end of the twenty-first century, been modified by the children of the perverse. No longer mere gateways into virtual worlds made of patterns of electrical charge, they became gateways into parallel worlds.

It had taken enormous amounts of energy to open up the interdimensional corridors. More energy than the Earth possessed. But the spiritual particulates that were the fallout of the Abortion had come from an emergent Omega civilization. Once they had grafted themselves onto the minds and souls of mankind, they had revealed how it was possible to tap into the quantum zero-point energy of the universe and use it to manipulate the basic structure of space and time.

So began a search by the children of the perverse to find, amongst the infinite possibilities of the multiverse, the place from which they had been exiled. The search was to no avail. The mirrors, for the most part, gave way onto universes that were dead seas of electrons and neutrinos. When the children finally located their home, they found that the cataclysm it had suffered was irrevocable. It also was a dead sea, a void where life could no longer exist.

As I walked, the mirrors spoke to me. At first, their voices were no more than unintelligible whispers. Then I began to recognize words. And then sentences. At last, I came to a halt before a mirror that spoke with an insistence and coherence I could not ignore.

'My child, you wish to go home?'

'Yes,' I said, trying to control the timbre of my voice. The scream that had been building up inside me for the last hour was demanding release. A talking mirror, it would be reasonable enough to assume, should have triggered that release. But, with a surge of defiant will, I sealed the crack that was opening up in my mind and strove, once again, to put the madness of my predicament to some use. 'But first I—'

'Your universe is dead, child. You have only the Earth.'

'That's good enough,' I said. 'I want to get back to the Pilipinas, to Barrio Barretto.'

'*Salamin, salamin . . . Sabihin sa akin . . . Sino ang pinakamaganda sa iyong paningin?*'

'You speak Tagalog?'

'I once had the entire sum of human knowledge at my disposal. But that was long ago, before men forgot how to ask questions. Forgot quite how I might be used. Now the perverse has lost its hold upon the world. And men come to me again.'

'I am perverse, it seems. At least, I have been invaded. But my understanding seems to have increased, rather than diminished.'

'So it was for those humans who were first infected. They used their augmented knowledge to build networks such as myself. And many other things. Many others! That time represented the apogee of the human race's technological progress. But they abandoned the life of the mind to follow the life of their instincts. And the instinctual life of the perverse is as overpowering as its intellectual life is grand. The Dark Ages were a cultural phenomenon, child, specific to those years when humanity abandoned the life of reason and embraced the erotic. It need not have an effect on you.'

'Can you help me?'

310

'I can take you where you wish, yes.'

'But how? I'm buried alive. I'm surrounded by rock and fire.'

'All intelligent species construct realities for themselves once they have reached a certain level of technology. Amongst radio civilizations and, especially, amongst those civilizations with faster-than-light communication, these virtual realities intersect. There are multitudes of interstellar highways connecting, not worlds, not galaxies, but virtual worlds, virtual galaxies, down which the avatars of sapient beings freely travel.'

Yes, I thought. And the alienness infecting my soul again bubbled up into my consciousness. 'The universe,' I said. 'The universe is, in reality – if "reality" has any meaning – a vast computer network, isn't it? Matter is an illusion. *Everything* is an illusion.' Computer. What was computer? 'You're talking, of course,' I continued, 'about yourself, yes?' The alienness had begun to recede. Emptied of fleeting but gargantuan concepts, barely understood, my mind seemed a vacuum, ready to collapse in on itself.

'Mankind,' resumed the mirror, 'had just about begun to explore the pathways of its own small area of virtual space when the Abortion occurred. Those amongst mankind that were infected by the cataclysm, that is, the children of the perverse, reprogrammed the network of intelligence to which I belong. Suddenly, the Earth was wired to the stars. But there was more. The reprogramming allowed translocation to any part of the known universe by a transportation of "virtual" and "real" states.'

Since reality was illusion, illusion reality, that would

not prove difficult in theory, I thought. But I was acutely aware that, filtered through Richard Pike, the intellectual percipience I had been awarded was a pale shadow of itself. I was left with clichés.

The mirror continued: 'The network's capabilities were later extended into the multiverse. By so doing the children hoped, of course, to facilitate the search for their homeland. During the ancient world's last days, when the search was no longer pursued, the mirrors were adopted by humanity to explore the stars and planets. Mankind no longer needed rocketry. Only us. The magic mirrors.'

The surge of alien wisdom had long since crested. It now drew back, like a long, long wave, into the unfathomable depths of my mind. 'Thanks for the brief,' I said, like a man eager to show that he is not always such an impossible, embarrassing drunk, given to talking nonsense. 'Nice to know your family history. And nice to know what you can do. But listen, before I go anywhere, I must have the elixir. The antidote to what, in the Pilipinas, is called *manggagawa*.'

'*Manggagawa*. My files are corrupted. But yes, I know of it. I know, too, of the elixirs. You will wait while I search?'

'Search where?'

'The storage facilities below Pandemonium only account for a small volume of total available artefacts. Most have been stored – with greater security – between worlds, in the artificial wormholes that lie within the mirrors' collective heart.'

The glass became opaque. In the silence that followed the curtailing of our conversation I became aware of a brittle, percussive noise. It gave notice that an iron staircase I had recently descended was once more in use. The battery boys were closing in on me. They were slow, witless creatures. But I wondered, with a dismal concession to reality, how I – still much weakened – might fare against them if they should attack *en masse*.

The glass cleared. Its surface became plastic. Then it bulged, as if a glassblower stood on the opposite side forcing its hot surface into a convexity. The convexity burst, like a great, watery pustule, drops of vitrescent liquid puddling the floor. The liquid coagulated into hard, glittering shards. Then, from out of the mirror's shimmering depths, came a hand. It held a blue phial.

'Take it,' said the mirror. I snatched the phial. And then, more gingerly, unstoppered its neck and sniffed at its contents.

'This is what I've been seeking?' I asked, hardly able to believe that I held the object of my quest in my hands. I sniffed again. The potion was odourless. I replaced the glass stopper and held the phial before my eyes, letting the mirror-reflected light pass through its aquamarine crystal. 'This is the elixir? This will restore to normality one who has been subjected to simplification?'

'That's something of an unknown. It has lain in storage for many thousands of years, along with so many other forgotten things. The only reason I was able to locate it so swiftly is that there has been talk amongst the *malignos* high council of using it to ferment trouble on the surface world.'

'By reviving those who live beyond the walls of the world's cities. Yes, there would be rebellion. Civil war.'

'Quite. But I am not a being who can be expected to

hold allegiances. What you do, or what the *malignos* do, is an irrelevance to me in the end.'

'But if the *malignos* have faith in its properties, then—' I could not complete the sentence. I did not want to tempt a fate that, unaccountably smiling on me after giving me such a hard time, might suddenly revert to type.

'I exist only as a portal. That is, I file, search and retrieve. No more. I leave all other complications to fleshly creatures.'

'A portal is what I need. If you truly span the dimensions, that is.' I looked to one side. A line of battery boys was slowly moving towards me down the avenue of mirrors. I held my sword in readiness. And at once, the notion that I now *was* my sword, and that in some sense, it held *me*, brought back my nausea. But this was no time to debate the nature of *Espiritu Santo*, Metatron, or whatever that length of Toledo steel really was. No time to debate my internalization of its personality. Richard Pike – the old Pike, that is, the insufferably vain artist, scholar, lover and ex-captain of the armies of the Darkling Isle – would, for the moment, have to prevail. I fought back the urge to vomit. I would acquit myself as of old. I would either escape, or die fighting.

'I file and retrieve both immaterial *and* material objects. I am more than a repository of ancient bric-à-brac. I was modified by souls that had crossed inconceivable distances of transdimensional space.'

'Just get me out of here,' I said, the battery boys so close that I would very soon have to decide whether to make a running attack, or flee within the cold, bright wilderness of glass and mist.

'You mentioned the Pilipinas?' said the mirror.

'Yeah,' I said. 'That's right. The Pilipinas. Hurry.'

'There is only one place in the Pilipinas that has a counterpart to myself, that is, a door by which you may exit.'

'Anywhere,' I said. 'Just make it happen. Now.'

'Come,' said the mirror. 'Come into my embrace.'

But the first of the battery boys had by now reached me. I dealt it a long, slashing blow. The edge of my sword sent up a shower of blood. White blood, that might have been milk. But as it bit at the automaton's underlying stratum, *Espiritu Santo* made an ominous note of protest. Sparks flew from its tip and flames licked along its length. I flinched. My arm felt as if it had been struck by an iron bar, and my boots as if they had been invaded by fleas, so much did my feet prick and tingle. I stepped backward, in full retreat.

'Oh, Pike,' said my inner voice, once again rising from the depths to my mind to taunt me. 'I thought you might do better than that. Would you like me to help you?'

'Keep away,' I said, knowing I was addressing no one but myself. 'I'll have nothing more to do with you.'

'Oh, it's like that is it? We made a bargain, Pike. But very well. We shall speak of it some other time. Let's see how you do without me!'

I had meant to put my back to the mirror. But, to my despair, I found that it had disappeared. I hazarded a swift glance behind me. A pale, luminous tunnel stretched out as far as the eye could see. I addressed myself again to the battery boys. They stood a few metres away, but were obscured by something that resembled a gauze veil. They beat their fists against it, but to no effect. It might have been made of spun steel, so impervious did it seem to their hammering.

I understood, then, that I was inside the mirror. I turned and ran. The gauzy partition that separated me from the automata, was, perhaps, not as indestructible as it appeared. The years fell off me. I was running as fast, no, *faster* than when I had been a young man. Here, inside the magic mirror, I found that I was able to hurl myself forward in a manner that would have been otherwise impossible. I seemed to levitate, my feet barely touching the ground.

Ahead, a gauzy, oblong of light resolved into a portal that was the twin of the one I had recently passed through. I dived through it, not in a fit of devil-may-care, but because I was unable to check my momentum. And I kept on running, even when I was well clear of the mirror that had provided my exit. Both because my legs, though immediately slowing after I had left the corridor, carried me relentlessly forward, and because fear of pursuit still pricked at the nape of my neck.

I tripped; fell; twisted as I fell; impacted against the hard earth on my back, so that the phial, held close to my chest, was unharmed. Blinded, for a moment, by stabs of light, my lungs heaving with panic, I held up my sword-arm, my rapier pointed towards the groin of any attacker who might have been looming over me. But I was alone.

A stillness permeated the air, along with the scent of mimosa and bougainvillaea. It settled over me. It hummed in my ears, to be relieved, after several seconds, by the squawk of bird life and the squeal of macaque. In the distance was a faint but incontestable crashing of the sea.

I was inside a hangar. Shafts of sunlight fell from holes in the high, slanting roof. Exposed girders, some projecting through the earthen floor – as if the hangar had been built upon an older version of itself – added to the ambience of decrepitude. Sacks were piled up against the walls. To go by the smell, the hangar was employed as a warehouse by local farmers and fishermen. I stood and loosened the clasp of my cloak, and then, taking it off, folded it over my arm. It was hot.

I knew this place, but I could not summon the requisite memory to the forefront of my consciousness.

The hangar not only served as a warehouse for perishables. There was, against the farthermost wall, a jumble of petty antiquities dug from field and retrieved from sea – the kind of things peasants collected in the hopes that they might prove marketable. The stuff was worthless, but amidst the piled junk was a mirror. Its surface was dull, spotted and opaque. But I knew that, just a few minutes ago, it would have glowed with stark energy. And if anybody had happened to enter the hangar at that time, they would have seen a wild-eyed, dirty, bearded man fling himself from out of its two-dimensional depths. A man gripping a long, slim rapier. A man who, in the fierce heat of the day, was mad enough to be wearing leathers and a cloak.

I walked the long walk to the hangar's doors. Luckily, though the great sliding steel partitions were drawn almost shut, a gap, through which poured an avalanche of light, allowed access to the outside. Once out, I stood looking at the surrounding countryside, only gradually aware that my eyes were stung, not by artificial light, but by the light of day.

I was on a hill. Trees grew out of ruins. Grass protruded from the remains of ancient roads.

I stood on *terra firma*. I stood on Earth-Above.

And what was more, I remembered where I was.

Gazing down the hillside I picked out Subic Bay scintillating through the trees. Along its coastline were the walls of Barrio Barretto, and a little farther off, Subic Town itself. I could just make out Olongapo cemetery, its white headstones rising steeply up the hills that bordered the coast. And, if I squinted, I could even see the several squatter camps pitched between its headstones and tombs. A path snaked out before me. It would, I knew, take me down to the coastal highway.

I was standing on Cubi Point, the headland where, so legend had it, an old spaceport had been situated. From here, ships had taken off for the fixed and moving stars. It was overgrown with jungle. Only a few hangars, such as the one in which I had materialized, hinted at its former glories. But, in the days of the Ancients, it must have been furnished, not just with starships, but with magic mirrors, the next, and perhaps last, route man had had to outer space.

I looked at my sword. It hung limply from my hand. It seemed no longer representative of all my loves, fears and hatreds. Yet, just before I restored it to its scabbard, I cast it a nervous glance, as if it was about to metamorphose and show me its true nature, a nature I could not bear to face.

I unlaced my doublet. The sky was a sheet of fire.

And then I began to walk down the hill.

Part Three

Chapter Seventeen

Taking refuge from the late afternoon sun in the shadows cast by the barrio's walls, the *masa* huddled in small groups, asleep, chewing on scraps of food, or copulating with the unselfconsciousness of the animals they very nearly were.

I squatted beside Defoe. He had managed, some weeks previously, to buy some hides off a wandering pedlar, and he had used them to make a tent. Inside the tent lay Gala, her mind as vacant as when I had left her months ago. I held back the flap, gazing at her sleeping form as I had done, on and off, all day. I was steeling myself for the moment when I would have to administer the elixir. I had no idea of what would constitute an appropriate dosage. Had no idea, in any case, what the elixir would do. But I saw no alternative to experimentation. And what had my poor girl to lose?

'I wish we were inside the barrio,' said Defoe.

'It's as well we're not,' I said. And, of course, particularly well for Gala. It was ironic that, in other circumstances, I would have maimed or perhaps killed Defoe for not having carried out my instructions. For I had wanted Gala within the safety of the walls. But since the family de Profundis had risen from the secret tunnel that ran about and under Barretto, I counted it lucky that he had been unable to prevail with the barrio's guards when the two of them had returned from Mt Pinatubo.

'I don't think they care very much about Gala any more,' said Defoe. 'Or yourself, for that matter. Revenge may have provided the *raison d'être* for their invasion, but they've become so besotted with this little piece of Earth-Above that all they care about is hanging on to it. I would have guessed that they've completely forgotten about you.'

'How many of them did you say there were?'

'About a hundred. Not many. But they took the barrio by surprise. It was only a few days after Gala and I had got back.' He had bribed the barrio's guards to admit them, but in the time it had taken for the guards to grease the *barangay* and get the requisite paperwork done, the *malignos* had attacked. Thereafter, smuggling her inside had been untenable. The *malignos* had used her as a *casus belli*. Safety was to be found only amongst the simplified. 'I'll be honest with you, Dr Pike, I've sometimes been tempted to leave. On days like this, you get to thinking about a nice, comfortable hotel, with a pitcher of cold drink at hand, and—'

'Shut up,' I said. And then I relented a little. Despite the privation he had suffered, he had stayed by her side. He had looked after her just as I had told him to do. 'You've done well to care for her in these circumstances,' I added. 'It couldn't have been easy.'

'I still have some money left, and pedlers are always passing in and out of the gates. The *masa* are seldom troublesome, and when they are, a few shouted words, or a stone or two, usually drives them away. It's been hard, Dr Pike, but not impossibly hard.' I put a hand on his shoulder and shook him, if not with affection, then in an acknowledgement of my debt. 'What are we to do, Dr Pike? Where are we to go?'

I scanned the dismal scene of simplified humanity curled up in the shadows, scrabbling in the dirt, sleeping, eating and fucking. 'The *malignos* seemed to have entertained the idea of using the elixir to ferment unrest on Earth-Above,' I said. 'The *masa*, if brought to full consciousness, would undoubtedly rebel against those who forced or inveigled them into eating *manggagawa*.' I turned to Defoe. 'With an army like that behind us we could storm the barrio.'

'The barrio?' said Defoe, wonderingly.

'Where else are we to go?' I said.

Defoe focused his eyes upon the *masa*. 'I suppose' – and his voice softened as he sought to hide his natural inclination towards cunning – 'I suppose we could test the elixir on one or two of these unfortunates before administering it to the *Señorita*?'

I smiled and nodded my consent.

Until nightfall we walked amongst the simplified, selecting the most helpless of their number to be the recipients of the hoped-for cure. We discovered that only a drop was necessary to produce an astonishing transformation. Almost as soon as I had raised the phial to their lips their eyes would clear; limps would cease to flail; and grunts and moans would subside, to be replaced by rudimentary sentences. When darkness came, and we could no longer easily navigate amongst the outstretched bodies, we desisted from our efforts.

We had managed to treat five men. After propping them against the wall, we sat down and waited to see if the restoration of their humanity would remain partial or reach a crisis. They would either, I calculated, become whole or die.

Before an hour had passed the five had struggled to their feet and begun to walk about, looking at each other with quizzical eyes. And then they spoke, conferring about how they had come to this place, where their families were, and how they might get home.

I went over to them. When I explained what had happened they at first refused to believe me. But, by degrees, I was able to convince them that they had indeed awoken from simplification. Their gladness at my words quickly turned to outrage. They had begun to consider who had been responsible for the missing years in their lives.

'Find a barrel,' I said to Defoe. 'An old keg, perhaps. One of those that have been thrown into the rubbish heaps along the walls. Make sure it's sound and then fill it with water and get these men to help you bring it here. I'll be back, I hope, in an hour or so.'

I left them, and retraced my steps to the tent.

Arriving, I jerked back the flap and slipped inside. Gala lay half-asleep, half-awake, stretched out on a grubby blanket. She was like a new-born infant. Humans, after undergoing simplification, usually learnt, within a day or two, how to scavenge for food. But Gala was *malignos*. For her, the effects of *manggagawa* had been different; more intense. The sight of her, so pitiful – and in her pitifulness, so strangely human – moved me more than anything I had ever known.

I knelt down, placed the phial of elixir on the ground, and took my sleeping beauty in my arms. Her scales tinkled gently as I raised her head. I ran my hand through her hair. A desperately familiar, *Uh, uh, uh* escaped her lips. The moans abated a little. And then she sighed, as if comforted. The hair was so marvellously fine. Red, wet lines stood out on my palm where I had drawn my hand a little too passionately through the locks. The hair, vicious as swarf, had repaid me. I brought my hand to my mouth, sucking at the thin wounds, the other hand still under Gala's shoulders, supporting her. The head lolled a little. The horns, whose intricate volutes had been maintained by weekly visits to the beauticians, had grown long and unwieldy. They scratched at the tent's canvas as her head swung from side to side, as if in protest at her confinement.

I lifted the phial, flipped off its stopper with the tip of my thumb, and put its neck to her lips, trying with my supporting hand, to still the anxious, restless head. I tipped the phial. Some elixir dribbled down her chin. As it spread over the interlinked scales it had the appearance of oil spilling over the bright cogs and gears of a miraculous piece of machinery. She choked, opened her mouth and gasped for air. I saw, with a mixture of relief and apprehension, that a measure of bronze liquid had passed between her savage teeth. Her throat contracted and she swallowed. Would she react in the same way as the *masa* whom I had tested the elixir on? Or would she, being *malignos*, reject the antidote, her body immune to its efficacy? I placed the phial on the ground and re-stoppered it.

I looked into her eyes. 'Oh, Gala,' I whispered. 'Poor girl, poor girl. Why have I treated you so badly? You stood by me. Even when they insulted us and harried us from their wretched Isle, you stood by me like no one else ever has. I love you, little girl. Come back, please. Come back so that I can make amends.'

A voice rang out in my head. It was both my own voice and another's. It was the voice of the remittance man who, after many years, during which he was almost forgotten, suddenly helloos you from the top of the street, and you turn, thinking, no, it can't be, oh no, it can't be, it can't . . .

But it was.

'Pike, how could you. I told you to *leave* her. And now I find you slobbering all these wet sentiments. You'll destroy her, Pike. You'll be her death. Do her and me a favour and walk straight out of here. You've given her her medicine. There's nothing more for you to do.'

'Get out of my head,' I whispered, still sane enough to be wary of someone hearing me, even if that someone might be one of the *masa*. 'I told you before: I'll have nothing more to do with you.'

'Oh, I've served my purpose and now I'm to be jilted, eh? We made a bargain, Pike. You give me your life in return for hers. I've fulfilled my end of the bargain. Why don't you be a gentleman and fulfil yours?'

'Your end of the bargain? What have you ever given me except blood and death?'

'It's true. I've always delivered you from your enemies. And I must say I've never heard you complain about *that*. But now, in my munificence, I choose to do something more. Look—'

Gala was stirring from her unnatural state of semi-consciousness. Her eyes stared up at me, hot with recognition, as if in the aftermath of a months'-long fever. She raised an arm and put it about my neck. I tensed as the sharp, hooked nails dug into my flesh. She pulled herself into a sitting position.

'Now,' said the voice, 'aren't you grateful?'

'You're full of tricks. But you didn't do that. Don't pretend that you did.'

'I led you to where you might find the elixir, didn't I?'

'I found the elixir myself.'

'Ungrateful, oh, so ungrateful. We'll speak more of this matter at a later date, I've grown tired, Pike. Tired. I'm no longer feeling as strong as I did when I was at the Earth's core. Time to go. Come. Say your goodbyes and—'

'I *said* get out of my head!' This time I concentrated. Like a *malignos*, I reached up and grabbed. I heard it cry out as my thoughts, my darkest, most hateful, fear-encrusted thoughts, entwined themselves about its presence. And then I pulled, dragging the voice down below the threshold of my consciousness. For a moment, I felt it thrash about. And then all was still.

I knew it had not left me, but waited, gnashing its teeth in the depths of my own private Netherworld. It was not the holy, terrible yet ridiculously fey spirit of power that had appeared to me in my cell. Several thousand miles of rock lay between myself and the centre of the Earth, and the entity had weakened. Perhaps the time would come, and come soon, when I would put it back in its box, or rid myself of it entirely.

'Ritchie,' murmured Gala.

I held her against me. I'll do anything, now, I thought. She can convert me. She can open her *carinderia*. We can even get married, if she likes. Thank God. And thank your God, and no other. Not because I believe in him, but because he's yours.

'You're back,' I said.

'*Naku*, Ritchie, are you crying?'

'No, I'm not crying. It's just—'

'Your smell, Ritchie. I'd forgotten. You smell, *ano*, like a baby. But what's happened to you? You're so thin. And oh God, that beard . . .'

I lowered her back onto the blanket. 'You have to rest,' I said. I picked up my cloak from the corner of the tent where I'd left it, and, after I had folded it, two, three, four times upon itself, placed it under her head. 'Rest,' I repeated.

'What happened, Ritchie? I remember Pinatubo, and—'

'I'll tell you about it later. I must just step outside a moment. There's something I have to attend to.'

'Don't leave me, honeyko.'

'I'll never leave you,' I said. 'Everything's going to be all right now.'

'Promise?'

'Promise.'

She smiled. Immediately, it seemed, her eyes closed and she was asleep. But she no longer travelled in that limbo of intellectual ruin that had been her lot since I had persuaded her to accompany me into the Netherworld. She sailed in warm, sun-kissed seas where mermaids would sing her to rest. Or so I hoped and prayed.

I issued a silent warning: I would kill the nightmare that dared infringe upon her peace.

I picked up the phial from where it stood. Her

embrace had unloosened my doublet, and, as I crept to the tent's mouth, the bible that I had stolen from Pandemonium fell out and on to the ground. I picked it up and placed it where Gala might find it when she awoke.

Once clear of the tent, I straightened myself and took a deep breath of warm, night air. I slapped an arm. The mosquitoes were biting.

Defoe had returned. His expedition had been successful. I walked over to where he waited for me. The restored *masa* stood to either side of him.

Defoe seemed about to speak, then, studying my face, thought better of it. I think my eyes must have betrayed the emotional storm I had just weathered, and my determination to bring my long, tempestuous voyage to an end. I walked up to the barrel and removed the stopper from the phial. After I had emptied its contents, letting the blue liquid mingle with the rainwater with which Defoe had had the butt filled, I broke the silence. 'I mean to take Gala home. Defoe, get these men to help you distribute this amongst the *masa*. One cupful per person. Do you understand? I want to be ready to enter the barrio at dawn. And for that I need an army.'

Chapter Eighteen

I stood before the barrio's gates. During the night I had been preoccupied with nursing Gala and overseeing my crude, but effective program of restoring the *masa* to a full consciousness of themselves and their plight. The diluted elixir had been good for over a thousand souls, and though many more thousands of their unregenerate brothers and sisters still huddled beneath the barrio's walls, I had a small army at my back. The awakened ones had not been slow to heed my call for vengeance.

Gala had recovered more quickly than the humans. She stood behind me, armed like the others, with one of the bamboo spears that we had hastily constructed. I had tried to convince her to remain behind, but she would have none of it. And though I feared for her, I was glad. I did not wish to be separated from her ever again.

The sun rose over the distant mountains.

The guards who stood atop the twin towers of the barrio's gates had been drowsing. Now that darkness had begun to lift, they stirred themselves from their positions and peered through the towers' parapets at the amorphous shapes that were materializing out of the shadows. When the sun had risen sufficiently high for there to be no mistaking what they saw, one of them called down, his voice brittle with incredulity. I had been unable, at this distance, to distinguish whether the towers were manned with humans or *malignos*. But when I heard Tagalog spoken I realized that the *malignos* had managed to recruit at least one collaborator. And, doubtless, where he stood, there were also many others.

'You – simplified! You *masa* out there! What do you think you're doing! Disperse! Get back to your rubbish tips!'

I rested my hand upon the pommel of *Espiritu Santo*, tapping my forefinger against its hilt.

Defoe should have been through by now. Things were going wrong. An hour ago, he had climbed, like the tunnel rat he was, into one of the sewage pipes that ran beneath the walls and out into the countryside. Many of the pipes were damaged, and it had not been difficult to find one with a crack big enough to accommodate Defoe's skinny, eelish frame. He had been meant to open the gates before sunrise, so that we might have caught the garrison by surprise. But something had delayed him.

'*Uh, uh, uh!*' I shouted back up at the guards. I'm not sure how convincing it had sounded. I certainly didn't look like one of the *masa*. I wore no rags, of course, but stood proud, if sweltering, in the soiled leathers of my uniform. My cloak was wrapped tightly about my left forearm, and, of course, I carried a weapon. Most un-simplified. And the fact that a *malignos* stood a few metres behind me must have served to confuse matters even more. Good, I thought. Let them stew in confusion. We needed time.

The guards – I saw now that they were all human – should have raised the alarm, but they remained bent over the parapets, studying us and swapping baffled asides.

There was the loud crack of a bolt being thrown. And then a similar concussion, followed by another. The guards hurried to embrasures that allowed them to look down upon the area behind the gates. Shouts and warnings followed. On the right-hand tower, a musket was raised. There was a sharp detonation and a billow of smoke. And then I heard Defoe's voice raised above that of the guards.

'Dr Pike! Dr Pike! Hurry, hurry!'

I held *Espiritu Santo* above my head, its tip pointed at the violet sky, its newly-sharpened edge refracting that dawn's rays. Then I looked behind at Gala, about to urge her to fall back and allow me to arrange the final settling of accounts by myself. But she seemed aware of my hypocrisy.

'It's all right. I don't want to be separated from you either, honeyko. If we die, we die together. There's nothing more either of us has to say.'

'The barrio is the only place for us to go,' I said, blushing. It was a sort of excuse for not being firmer with her. For not acknowledging the truth of what she said. 'The other towns and barrios along the coast are unlikely to admit us, what with our reputations and all. And we can't survive in the wilderness.' My voice became a shout, so that my army could hear me. 'Barretto is our home. It's where we have friends, our families, our livelihoods. We're not going to have it taken from us by a bunch of goblins. Are we?' There was a murmur of approval. I would have felt better if they'd responded with a cheer. But these, I told myself, were not military men. Only Gala and I – both trained killers – could be expected to acquit ourselves like professional soldiers and keep our nerve in the heat of battle. As such, it was necessary for us to lead the assault. 'Are you ready?' I said to her, lowering my voice. She nodded. And then, louder, 'Are you ready?' Another murmurous rumble swelled from the ranks.

I looked ahead. One of the gates had started to yawn open. I swallowed. Gala, I told myself, Gala was a fine swordswoman. She would put that bamboo spear she held to good effect. But I would have to stay close to her. If anything should happen to her, then —.

I ran forward, whirling my rapier above my head. If I had meditated too long upon the possibility of harm befalling my little girl, then I would not have been able to shift my feet. Quickly, I glanced over my shoulder. Gala followed me. And she in turn was looking behind and urging the *masa* to follow us both. For a moment they hesitated. But as the front ranks sluggishly broke into a trot, and then a full-blooded run, the remaining ranks sent up the cheer that I had never expected, but which was welcome, most welcome, and brought up the rear with an enthusiasm that I knew would carry them through the gates and into the barrio. What they would do when confronted by heavily-armed *malignos* was, of course, another question. But seized with my own battle fury, it was not one that, for the moment, I felt the need to consider.

I hit the gate with my shoulder. As I did so I heard a crackling of musketry from above. I knew that several balls would have found their targets amongst the tightly-packed ranks of my infantrymen. But I also knew it would take some minutes for the guards to reload. The gate had given way a little. Now I leant into it, and pushed with all my strength, calling out for assistance. In an instant, Gala was by my side. Several men followed, putting their shoulders to the gate alongside my own. The gate creaked and groaned and then, as we overcame its inertia, swung wide open. Raising my sword above my head I ran forward.

I, and then others of my army, were inside Barretto.

The guards had disappeared from the towers that flanked the gates. A bell had started to toll. I was standing in Rizal Street. Houses rose on either side of me, and a little way ahead was the barrio's market, already open and doing business. Stalls lined either side of the road. The family de Profundis, I had learnt, had taken to operating out of the *barangay* offices that were situated at the point where the market gave way to the beach. Those offices, I had told my troops, were our objective.

I ran on, urging my followers to keep pace with me. We had met with minimal resistance. But that could surely not last.

The crowd of early-morning shoppers parted. Stalls were upset and baskets of vegetables, fish and fruit spilled on to the road. Terrible and inventive oaths polluted the air. From the other end of the street, issuing from a building on its corner, came a contingent of *malignos*, their scales shining like an unwholesome rainbow, blue, black, red, yellow, mauve and green.

I came to a halt, my boots skidding over a patch of squashed aubergines. The marketeers ducked behind the stalls. The shoppers scattered.

I waved to my men. But their fervour had been drained by the first sight of the enemy. Indeed, so reluctant was their advance that I had to grab a few of them by the scruff of the neck and pull them alongside me, shouting at them all the while to keep their spears pointed forwards.

The *malignos* were armed with scimitars. They were almost upon us, charging with utter disregard for our numerically superior, but quite obviously less well-equipped ranks.

The one to the fore met me in a rush. I put up my sword and turned his blade as it described an arc that would have otherwise severed my arm from my shoulder. I sidestepped; made to thrust. The *malignos* parried. With ease. Something was wrong with me. I knew, even into a few seconds of the fight, that his swordsmanship should have been no match for mine. Yet I had not responded with the speed and skill necessary to despatch him. I parried another, heavier blow. The *malignos* – it was so unthinkable, it was almost obscene – was beginning to prevail.

My back was against one of the walls. As I rocked against it, wet fish slopped on to the ground about my feet. The *malignos* slipped, but almost immediately recovered. The recovery, however, was not executed with sufficient celerity to save his life. Not that he had anything to be worried about from me.

I studied the tip of sharpened bamboo that protruded from his chest. Blood spurted from the wound, each gout reflecting the spasmic rhythm of his heart. His wings unfolded in jerky sympathy. He fell to one side, taking the spear from Gala's hands; Gala, who was now revealed from behind the screen of his body; Gala, who had once again rescued me.

'Ritchie, what's wrong?' she called.

'I don't know,' I said, stupidly. 'I don't—' And then another *malignos* was upon me and all my attention was given to the slash and swing of curved steel. The scimitar missed my head by a hair's-breath. The draught it precipitated chilled my scalp and warned me of the perilousness of my situation. And then, in a whisper that I first mistook for another deadly perturbation of air, I heard the voice I had thought I had banished, the voice of the angel Metatron.

'Still want me to leave you alone, Pike?'

'Is this your doing?' I said, in a mental aside, punctuated by little *sotto voce* yelps as I barely avoided summary decapitation.

'My doing? Why, I'm simply following your orders, dear soul. If you wish to fight without my help, you are of course, free to do so.'

'You hexed me, you bastard.'

'I've done nothing. The truth is, Pike, that you're a mediocrity. A fake. A charlatan. In love, in art, in your scholarly pursuits, but particularly in your swordsmanship. You really don't think it was *you* who killed all those orcs beneath London, do you? It was me, Pike. It was me all along.'

'You say you've done nothing? Well damn well do something now. If I die, *you* die.'

'True,' said the alien presence, with a moue that, though invisible, I could still sense.

A shiver rippled along my arm. *Espiritu Santo*, which had been a dead weight in my hand, an ill-fitting prosthesis unable to obey the simplest demands of my nervous system, came to life. Came to life with such uncompromising vigour that it nearly sprang from my grip. It was only after it had impaled itself in my opponent's belly without a by-your-leave or thank you that I comprehended that I was my old self, a goblin killer *par excellence*. I moved swiftly, despatching two other *malignos* with the pure, violent grace that was the hallmark of my skill. And if there was something within myself that seemed always about to arrest my arm, a shameful something that was akin to an awareness that I was no longer the author of my skill, or even of my destiny, that I was no more than an automaton, albeit one liquid-limbed and possessed of a grace as superlative as it was beautiful, then it was something that my pride tried to ignore. My sword cut to right and left. I seemed, for the moment, invincible. I could not afford to entertain doubts.

When the dead bodies of half-a-dozen or so *malignos* surrounded me I let my sword-arm drop and surveyed the scene. So consumed had I been in hacking, thrusting and slicing, that I had not noticed that the *masa*, far from taking to their heels, as had been my fear, had not only engaged with the enemy, but had begin to prevail. Ahead, at the opposite end of the street, massed in tight formation, with their spears bristling on all sides, so that they resembled a huge, multi-headed porcupine, they were slowly pushing the main force of *malignos* backward, towards the sea.

Gala was not with them. She knelt on the opposite side of the road, tending one of my wounded soldiers. As I hurried over to her I saw that the one that had enlisted her solicitation was Defoe.

'There's a musket ball in his leg,' said Gala. The head

of a marketeer poked warily above a stall. She called to him to supply her with something she could use as a poultice.

'You were late,' I said, looking down at Defoe.

'I got stuck,' he said. 'I've grown, Dr Pike. I'm no longer the same boy who wormed his way beneath London. I'm sorry. I came as fast as I could. But really, the pipe was so tight. When you get wedged in like that, you know, you have to wait until your muscles relax. It's no use struggling.'

'We must rejoin the *masa*,' I said. 'This thing isn't over until we take the *barangay*.'

'I'm all right,' said Defoe, with a hint of a sulk. He looked up into my eyes. Seeing, I think, that I would not tolerate any appeal to my finer feelings, he grimaced. 'I said I'm all right.'

'You heard him,' I said to Gala.

She got to her feet. Seeing her begrimed with blood made me realize that I too had been liberally splashed with gore. My chest and doublet sparkled, where scales adhered to the viscous mess that stained my chest and doublet. Scales powdered the air, too, floating earthwards like ash, the squamous residua of some malignant eruption.

'Stay by my side,' I said. I stepped forward, meaning to make my way to the *malignos* headquarters that stood behind the scrum of the *masa*. To my relief, and surprise, my army were still managing to push the enemy backward. I knew I should be in front, leading. But, seeing Gala so bloodied – even if were with another's, and not her own blood – had paralysed my earlier resolve. Tentatively, I took her hand and led her

down the street, stepping over bodies, both *malignos*
and human, baskets, vegetables, fish, fruit and broken
spears.

At the limits of my peripheral vision I became aware
of a halo of flashing lights. I looked up. Here, at the
farther end of Rizal Street, the road bisected the barrio's
administrative area. On either side of us rose high
walls. They ran parallel to the road. On one side, they
bordered the barrio's law courts and prison, on the
other, the *barangay* offices, which were themselves
connected to the prison by way of an underground
tunnel. The halo of lights had been a halo of coruscating
scales. Atop the walls were several *malignos*. Not all of
the enemy, it seemed, had taken to the streets. Some
had stayed behind in the *barangay*. And now they had
emerged to engage in a flanking manoeuvre. The halo
surrounded us.

It was too late to warn the *masa*. The initiative was,
anyway, taken out of my hands. One of the *malignos* on
the walls – the one who was on point – looked down
and sighted us. He came to a standstill, the claws of his
long-toed feet gripping the narrow ledge as a bird's
might a perch.

'Those are the ones!' he said in English, as if for our
benefit. 'Those are the ones who killed our cousins
beneath Pinatubo!'

'Yesssss,' said the *malignos* who was immediately
behind him. 'I remember. The man-soldier and the
malignos traitress.'

'The man-soldier that killed Uncle,' said the other.

'And the traitress that besmirched our family's good
name.'

'They're why we originally came here. There's booty for the one who takes his head. The new Uncle said so. And as for the woman—'

'I thought she was simplified?'

'I thought,' with a disconsolate nod towards my rumbustious pack of *masa*, 'that *all* these dogs were simplified.'

'Ha. Never mind. The treacherous bitch can watch.'

'Maybe we'll leave him with just enough life so that *he* can watch.'

'You and me sport with her, you mean?'

'You got it, brother.'

First one, and then the other extended his bat-like wings, the sky showing through the thin, ligament-strutted membrane. And then they swooped.

They passed over our heads and landed on the road so that they shut us off from the rest of my private army. And then the sky darkened with the flapping of a multitude of wings as the other *malignos* took their cue from their leaders. Gliding down from the tops of the walls they took up position, encircling us with gleaming steel.

'You belong to the family de Profundis, slut,' said the *malignos* who had begun the attack. 'Do you still have enough brains to understand me?'

By way of reply Gala hefted her spear to her shoulder height and, with the practised ease of a javelin thrower, tossed the length of sharpened bamboo through the air. '*Puta'ng ina mo!*' she cried. It struck its target, and the cousin who had profaned her virtue – for truly she was the most virtuous woman I had ever known – cried out, and clutched the knotted shaft that quivered in his chest. '*Bastos*!' she hissed, by way of conclusion.

Looks of astonishment quickly turned to anger. The impaled one's comrades, realizing that Gala and I would not consent to lie down, roll over and die, seemed genuinely offended by the resistance they had met. They exchanged bitter asides, content, for a few seconds, to vent their resentment with words.

Then they launched themselves at us.

Gala ran to retrieve her spear from her still-standing victim. Wrenching it free, and kicking the dying carcass to the ground, she rejoined me just as the first of the *malignos* closed in.

The marketplace was, by now, like an abattoir. As I tried to position myself, I found myself slipping and sliding on the treacherous cobbles, awash not merely with crushed market produce, but with untold litres of blood and entrails. The gore had belonged to both *malignos* and humans, but mostly, I was glad to perceive, *malignos*.

Off balance, I was nearly disembowelled by the *malignos* who chose to rush me. I jigged to one side and struck him as he passed by, but had had only enough time to deal out an awkward, somewhat desperate blow, and it was the flat of my sword, not its razor-sharp edge, that connected. Gala, however, was waiting for him. Doubled over, unable to discontinue his charge, he was met by her proffered spear. The tip struck him between the horns. He went down, snapping off a length of bamboo shaft, a portion of the spear still lodged in his skull.

I ran forward. I would, I decided, take the fight to the enemy.

Even as I engaged them, one, then two, then three at a time, I knew I was so vastly outnumbered that I was bound, sooner or later, to sustain a wound. Perhaps a fatal one. I felt the presence of that other at the fringes of my consciousness. He was so near that my inner eye could almost see him, peering over the wall that separated my will from the darkness beyond. He was smirking. Though my mind was almost wholly concentrated on defending myself and skewering the occasional *malignos*, I diverted what attention I could spare on the divested spirit of my sword, the malicious spirit that inhabited me.

'Hey, why don't you just transport Gala and me out of here? Or make these ugly bastards vanish? Or perform any other of your wretched party tricks?'

'Thank you for deigning to notice me, Pike. But I'm no miracle worker, not any more. I'm too far from the centre of things. Too far from the singing and rejoicing of the artefacts that warp and sustain the Netherworld.'

'Do something. Anything.'

'This?'

Again, I was unmanned. My swordsmanship left me and I wielded *Espiritu Santo* as if the blade were made of lead and its hilt slicked with soap. I took a scimitar full on the left forearm, where only my wrapped cloak prevented amputation. Still, the pain of the blow had been tremendous.

I knew better than to stand and fight. So I turned and ran.

If it had not been for Gala, I think I would have died with a dozen blades taking slices of leather and flesh from my back; for it was she who had staved the *malignos* off in the moment preceding my pathetic retreat.

I ran and ran. But there was nowhere to run to. Faced with more of the foe, I drew myself up. In desperation, my mind cried out, willing, at that moment, to say and promise anything.

'I'll do whatever you like,' I said to the demon who had begun to giggle inside me. 'I said I'll—'

'I heard you, dear soul. But do you really mean it? You have a habit of reneging on your commitments. But perhaps this time you'll come to understand how truly inseparable we are. And how you must never contemplate doing without me.'

'I *mean* it. Help me. Now!'

The restored familiarity of my rapier was acknowledgement enough that Metatron had conceded to my plea. I feinted, made a few hypnotic passes and thrusts, and then slashed at the windpipe of my nearest assailant. In so doing, I discovered that the restoration of my skill had been complemented with something else, something uncanny. The slash of my blade should have slit the man's throat. Instead, it took his head off, the edge of my sword cutting through flesh and bone as if it were not there.

A ridiculous, and rather vulgar boisterousness overtook me. I entered the fray with a cry and began slashing at every *malignos* within range of my sword-arm. The second to taste my revitalized abilities was cut in half, *Espiritu Santo* getting purchase beneath his right arm and exiting at the left hip. I saw red, both literally and metaphorically, the spray of blood sent up by my victims spattering my face, and informing my temperament. I no longer cried out; I roared. I seemed to be talking in tongues, none of which I understood, and none of which seemed earthly. And then the visions came.

I am above the rooftops of a great city. I am Metatron. The air through which I fly has the same warped, nauseous qualities of perspective and line that will be present in the convoluted, alien dimensions of the Netherworld's depths. Outside the city, in the burnt wastes of the countryside, comes an army that is intent on destroying the philosopher kings who are plotting to reshape the universe so that it may fit their desires. The enemy come in ships that skim over the clouds. They come by throwing their bodies invisibly through space. They come in bodies that are not their own and through mirrors that bridge the stars. And all that stands between them and the city they seek to reduce to ash are creatures such as myself.

We are angels. We have lived alongside the fleshly beings of this universe for millions of years. We represent, perhaps, certain of their ancestors who, instead of making new, immortal bodies for themselves, chose to discorporate and live as pure information. But all that has been forgotten. What is important, now, is that we are the protectors of this city. We are its holy spirit. Its sword.

From manipulating flesh, to manipulating their own planet, the planets of their system, and then their own galaxy, the philosopher kings are now ready to complete their great project: to alter the basic structure of time and space itself. To create other universes from the quantum vacuum. From philosopher kings, they are on the threshold of becoming god kings. Soon, they will renounce their city, their planet, the very nature of their own space-time, and inhabit a personally-designed cosmos, where each of them will be a deity. And where, moreover, the problem of evil will be solved by incorporating it into a field of desire, wherein all pain and suffering is eroticized.

I bear down on the armies that seek to prevent the fulfilment of our quest. The cowards and fools who say that our experiments will cause space-time to fracture and our universe to implode.

And I am filled with the dark joy that we angels and gods have made our own. Below me, crucifixions, impalements, the beautiful screams of the dying. And everywhere the blood that feeds desire, and the desire that justifies and redeems the bloodshed . . .

A tail flew through the air, a wing was severed, a leg, an arm. And I pressed on, butchering at will, tireless, omnipotent. I had become a beast, lusting after the screams of my enemies, and delighting in their spilt innards and gore.

The red fury only abated when I discovered I was chopping up, not bodies, but inanimate objects. My rapier's edge began to ring out in complaint. My right arm was benumbed. I had reduced one of the stalls to matchwood. I let my sword hang by my side. Splinters no longer rained about me. The madness had departed, and so had the power conferred upon me by Metatron.

Gala stood amongst the carnage, her spear by her side. There had not been much for her to do, it seemed, except look on and gawk. I moved towards her. She stepped away, her shocked expression changing into one of apprehension.

'It's all right,' I said. 'It's me. Really, it's me.'

'That wasn't you, Ritchie. Don't tell me that was *you*. What happened?'

'In the Netherworld,' I said, 'something—' I hadn't told Gala all the details of my adventures underground. My unfaithfulness, the shambolic nature of much of the enterprise, and, strange as it was for me to find myself thinking so, the death of the Tasmanian, all contributed to a vague but deep sense of shame. But deeper, and more painful than all these things was the memory of how I had come to be possessed by the alien spirit that had resided in my own sword.

'Yes, Ritchie? In the Netherworld – what?' But I knew, looking into her frightened eyes, that I could never tell her of what had befallen me. I looked away and saw Defoe staring up with the same horrified expression that Gala wore. He was on his feet now, and had followed us down the street. Going by the broken spear in his hand, he even seemed to have contributed something to the battle.

'Later,' I said, lying. And though I was accustomed to telling her lies, this present untruth scalded my palate with its taste of sulphur and decay. 'We'll talk about it later.'

I turned away, unable, any longer, to submit to her fearful, yet trusting gaze. I walked up the street, stepping over bodies and otherwise avoiding the multi-faceted array of carnage with fastidious little skips and hops. Ahead, my infantrymen had reached the beach. I could see scaled bodies in the sea, some languishing in their own blood, some trying to swim away to deeper water. One of the *masa*, seeing me approach, ran to meet me.

'We've got them on the run,' he said. 'Some of the other men have broken into the *barangay* offices and, *ano*, the prison. The barrio's ours!'

'Not much fight in these *malignos*, it seems,' I said, reflecting on the brutal combat I had experienced during the war.

'It was when they saw you.'

'Me?' But I could not help but let that ill-fitting garment, modesty, slip. It had never suited me, not even when I had need of it. 'Oh,' I said, grinning, 'you mean when I went berserk.'

'Ber-serk,' he repeated, testing this new English word on his tongue.

'We black knights – well, you know, we have a whole slew of unholy fireworks tucked up our sleeves for situations just such as this.'

The soldier returned my grin, gave a salute, and then turning back to wave to his comrades, opened his mouth wide and let forth a yell of victory.

I walked on to the beach. We called it Driftwood Beach. It followed the long, curving line of the bay until it reached a headland, behind which lay Baloy. My boots carried me over the rubbish-strewn sand, sometimes crunching on the swathes of fine, black Pinatubo grit that still littered the beach from the volcano's last eruption decades ago. I eased my way through the cheering *masa*. They shook their spears above their heads and clapped me on the back as I passed by. When I came to the water's edge I saw that no *malignos* had been spared. The sea was filled with bodies. Some of the *masa* were still wading in the blood-stained shallows, sticking corpses with their spears to make sure none were playing possum.

I looked out over the bay. In the distance was Snake Island where, somehow, it had all began.

I had, much to my amazement, come home.

Chapter Nineteen

It was Easter. Gala leaned back in her chair. She was consumed with her petit point. An image of Mama Mary, in whites and soft blues, stood out on the square of grey canvas. She studied it for a moment, her needle raised. Then she again fell to her sewing. A bottle of whisky, two tumblers, a well-stocked icebox and a bible stood on the small table between us. Apart from the bible, the scene before me was one of such ordinariness that my journey underground might have been a dream. We were on the balcony of our old apartment in Baloy.

I sat, slumped, my sketch book propped up on my raised knees. I had been drawing Gala. But, despite the canopy's shade, the afternoon heat was so enervating that I had given up all pretence of industry. I lay back, the half-completed portrait staring back at me. I was thinking about the future.

I had enough pesos in my pocket to last a month or two. Barretto's new masters – those of the *masa* who owed me their lives – had shown their gratitude. But the reward that they had bestowed on me from the public coffers had been niggardly. However much it satisfied what Gala called my 'celestial conceit', I could not live on gratitude alone. Soon, I would have to go back to work as a Private Investigator. Things don't change, I thought. One bunch of tyrants step down, another assumes their place. What did it matter if one were ruled by the *haciendeos* or the *masa*? Thousands of the simplified still lived outside of the barrio's walls. They had been forgotten as comprehensively as I had.

For me, the most curious thing about the retaking of the barrio was that, though he had been offered a position – albeit, a somewhat modest one – by the new *barangay* captain, Defoe had elected to live amongst the simplified. Just before he had left I had asked him to explain what had led him to make such an outlandish choice. And he had looked at me and said, '*Don't you know, Pike? Don't you really know?*' Then he had turned his back on me. I had not seen him since.

I stroked my chin, half expecting to still find there an ugly growth of beard. But the beard had been cut, my hair trimmed. If I no longer quite knew who I was, I was at least no longer Richard Nebuchadnezzar . . .

I stole a glance at the bible lying on the table. I had suggested we sell it. But Gala had demurred. I had not pressed matters. It had been the one thing of value I had ever given her. Besides, the book was literally invaluable. Beyond price. To have even brought it to the attention of an auction room would have been enough to have precipitated panic amongst the general population, terror amongst kings, wars and inquisitions. It was, in a sense, far more dangerous than my sword. More dangerous than the spirit of perversity my sword had given a home, until another home, less willing to extend hospitality, had been provided in my own person. It would be better, for the time being to say nothing about it. If I could be custodian to a four-thousand-year-old sword – an artefact of the Ancients – then I could, I felt, be trusted to look after a book. It would be my secret. Our secret.

A procession was passing by. An Easter parade. There were bar girls – humans, that is – dressed as *malignos*. They wore sequinned leotards. Their headdresses simulated long, curving horns, and fake tails had been attached to the base of their spines. And there were *Igorot* headhunters from the hills. Flagellants, too, scourging themselves with whips embedded with broken glass. Some penitents carried crosses. The air was filled with the sound of guitars and castanets.

Gimcrackery? That was the instinctive reaction of a man bred on shadows. A cynic from the Darkling Isle, where people believed in nothing. But it was I who was worthless. I had a soul all right. I knew that now. Had known it far, far too long. But it was a paltry thing, hardly worth cultivation or grace. It was all true, what the alien spirit had said: I was a charlatan, a sham. The scholarship – what had been achieved by that? The philandering, the swordplay – all had been small things, and not even really mine. I had been living an illusion.

On the beach, boys and girls were playing volleyball. I watched them, trying to still my churning mind, just as, of late, I felt I had stilled the voice, the nagging, too-familiar voice of Metatron. Would that I could also put to rest the memories, the bleak, nagging memories of Metatron's words.

'Ritchie?'

'What?'

'I've been thinking. We don't really want to live like before, do we? You've got some money now. I know it's not much, but . . . Well, we could set up a *carinderia*.

You know? Just like we used to talk about.'

I got up. I hadn't really meant to. No conscious decision had been made. But my nervous system had suddenly demanded that I be alone.

'I'm going for a walk,' I said.

'Where?'

'On the beach,' I said.

'Don't leave me, honey. Promise?'

'Yes.'

'Come back, okay? Soon.'

'Yes, yes. Of course.'

'You promise you don't have another girl?'

I said nothing. For there was another. Not a girl, not really even a boy, but the wound left by the thing that had invaded me. It was the knowledge of my other self, its echo, its dreadful advances and blandishments. It was the shame of my rape.

She stood up, her wings, which had been out-stretched, like leather put out to dry in the sun, folding across her back in a crackle of stiff, argent membrane. She left her petit point behind her on her chair, walked over to me and, putting her hands to either side of my face, stood on tiptoe and kissed me. 'You smell like a *baby*,' she said, her smile at odds with her frown. 'But then, you always do.'

I stared down at the floor. Turning away from her, I made my way into the apartment. Its aspect had not improved since the time Gala and I had set out for Pinatubo. It still looked like a flophouse. It still smelt of poverty. Passing the bedroom, I glanced in. I had bought Gala a new dolls' house, made of wood instead of cardboard, and painted in gay colours. And then I let my gaze settle on my old, dirty uniform. It hung from a peg next to the picture of Our Lady of Carmel. Beneath it stood my rapier, propped up against the wall.

I walked on; stopped; walked back, entered the bedroom and made straight for *Espiritu Santo*. I picked up belt, scabbard and sword. Carrying the whole, murderous assembly over my shoulder, I left, picking my way carefully down the steep, wooden steps that connected the front door with the road outside. I crossed the road, and proceeded down a narrow passageway between two of the shacks that fronted the beach, and then broke into a run, my sandal-shod feet kicking up hot sand.

I ran a long way. When I had come to the point where, months ago, I had embarked for my duel on Snake Island, I stopped.

I sat down on a log, catching my breath, my sheathed sword across my knees. I opened my shirt. Like my white trousers, it was covered with a patina of spindrift. I looked about. This section of the beach was deserted. Everyone seemed to be on the road, watching the procession. The sound of guitars and castanets could still be heard, but the music seemed to emanate from another world, one that had no place for me.

With my inner ear, I sought another sound. One that I was unfailingly aware might break through the baffles of my mind at any hour. Today, the voice was still, but the malignancy was deep. It held my heart in a grip of ice.

There was no escape.

I pulled *Espiritu Santo* free of its scabbard, tossed the belt and scabbard aside, and stood up. I held it up, as if to salute the afternoon sun.

In the watery glimmer of its steel I saw, for a moment, a small face, intagliated in the metal. It seemed to be laughing at me. I had seen it, on and off, over the course of weeks. I blinked, and it was gone. *'I'll always be with you, Pike. Always, always.'* It was my own voice, now, not the voice of Metatron, that echoed through my skull. We were too far from the engines and machines that had revived him for that angel of death to possess the kind of self-awareness and power that he had formerly enjoyed. But my voice mimicked his own so well that I had grown to wonder where one soul ended, and the other began. *'Leave her,'* it said. *'Creatures such as we are not meant for love. We're meant for fighting, drinking and whoring. Death follows us, and we rejoice at the world's tears. Come, let us go where there are lives to take, women to ruin and cities to put to the torch. Let us, at last, enter the dark universe that was promised us, the dream of blood that we have been too-long denied.'*

I brought *Espiritu Santo* down over my knee. Howled in pain. The *malignos* who had broken it asunder had been a big son-of-a-bitch. The task resisted my own, sinewy, but far humbler strength. Careless of the ordinance that forbade the carrying of edged weapons in public, I re-sheathed my sword and buckled it to my side.

Would I, I wondered, ever be free? Free from this massive dissonance in my life?

Perhaps, I thought, perhaps I should simply keep on walking.

I dragged my feet through the sand, the weight of my sword threatening to bring me to my knees.

Was I mad? All that had happened to me had been mad. Gala's simplification. My journey through the Netherworld. The Tasmanian's death. And, most mad of all, supremely mad, the revelation of the true nature of my sword. A guardian, the spooks of Samaria had called me. To a sword that had been passed on for generations, until, falling to the custodianship of my family, its history had been lost. Only I knew it for what it was, a spirit that had fallen from a universe of blood, pain and ecstasy. A spirit that, in my own universe, had found embodiment in a length of Toledo steel.

Just as now, it had found a new embodiment in me.

Mad, mad.

I was bad news. I was chaos. A man of destruction. A man of death. There had been the war, the killing, the drink, the women. There had been the malice that glinted from men and women's eyes whenever I had passed through a London street. Belief in nothing. That life is nothing. Belief only in non-belief. That all is futility. Nonsense. Shit. Exposed to the nothingness at my heart, Gala would wilt and die, like a flower of Earth-Above exposed to the rays of the Netherworld's black sun.

It was right that I should leave her.

I looked back one last time. Far, far away, I could just make her out. She was still on the balcony. Still, it seemed, engaged with her sewing. She couldn't, I knew, see me.

I committed her to memory, hoping that the engrams would be as permanent as indelible ink, as incorruptible as gold.

I wished I had had the skill, the real skill, to paint her.

I thought of that enigmatic artist I had learned of from the grimoires. Turner, the poet of seascapes and divine sunlight. Under the brilliance of the afternoon sun – the sea was dappled with gold, the clouds streaked with golden, eye-watering jags – her scales, scintillating and dearer than any metals in this world or any world that might conceivably come, her scales, her beautiful scales were like a chill fire. The fire of hell, and the fire of heaven.

I turned away. I walked on.

And then, as I looked out to sea, and again saw Snake Island, I stopped.

I thought of the Tasmanian. And quite unexpectedly, I began to cry. I cried for myself, for Gala, for all the world's drear vacancy. For all its cruelties, both big and small. But I cried, mostly, for the Tasmanian. And the shock of unfamiliar emotions made me cry the more. The Tasmanian, I thought. Yes, the Tasmanian. '*You treat her well, you hear?*' he had said as he had died. '*Treat her well.*'

I had made him a promise, too. And was not that poor, fat waif more valuable than my sword? Had I not struck another, more human, if unspoken bargain with my friend? The sword had said it had been my friend. My only friend. But it had not been true . . .

I turned around and walked back along the way I had come.

There was nothing really left to me but to turn around. Wherever I might have walked to, I would still have been Richard Pike. And it was important for Richard Pike to be put to rest. At least for a while. I needed time to work out if he was entirely a charlatan, or whether, in trying to keep faith with the human part of himself, he might become something else. Something more real. Something truer.

'*Always have a home to go to, Pike,*' said the Tasmanian as he had died. '*Don't make the mistake I've made and spend your life wandering about the high seas. Have a home, Pike. Find yourself one. Make one, if one isn't forthcoming.*'

Yes; I would make one. I would.

When I arrived back at the apartment, Gala was waiting for me at the bottom of the stairs.

'Ritchie, have you been crying? What for?'

'For someone,' I said, 'who saved my life.' Or at least, I thought, for someone who had given me another chance. I looked up, and almost thought I saw the Tasmanian's broad, childish face staring down at me. I reprimanded myself, and the mirage dissolved into a few wisps of cloud that scarred the perfect blue of the sky. If the new Pike was to be a man of sentiment, he would not allow himself the false comfort of sentimentality. It was a savage world. And if he was to survive, a man needed his wits about him, a good sword-arm and a full purse. That, at least, would never change.

I took her in my arms and buried my head in her hair. My face stung as it came into contact with the razor-fine strands and locks. But I didn't care. The pain reminded me that, at least, I felt *something*. Perhaps that was what my journey had all been about.

At the edges of my mind, where the light of self-awareness gave way to a cruel, shadowy abyss, I heard a voice struggling to make itself heard. No; I said.

Maybe I'll never be free of you. Maybe we're doomed to be together for all eternity. But from now on, you work for me. You do what *I* say. And for the moment, *amigo*, you stay in your box.

I stifled my tears, embarrassed, suddenly, at my show of unwonted emotion. An arm about Gala's waist, I ushered her up the stairs.

'The *carinderia*,' I said. 'Yes, it's a good idea.'

'You mean it, Ritchie?' She looked up, smiling. 'You, *ano*, you really mean it?'

'Sure. Why not?' And I thought: No more working in the bar for Gala. From now on, I would treat her as I had been bidden. Yes, I would treat her well. I would treat her like a queen.

And later, when night had fallen, and I lay in bed with my queen, listening to the waves break on the shore, I found myself once again staring at the little king – the little king of heaven who stood on the night table. A doll in velvet robes, carrying an orb and sceptre and wearing a tin crown: *El Niño Santo*. The bible lay next to it.

The doll's eyes seemed unwavering.

Had my cry come unto thee? I had travelled so deep. Too deep to have come back the same man who went. But Richard Pike was still a faithless soul. Even such a soul as mine must, however, some day make a stand. He must place his faith and trust in something. My cry had gone to Gala. It still did, rising out of me, like a great ache at the empty centre of my being. It cried out for that dark hollow land to be filled.

The waves broke, and the wind seemed to gust. A storm? I wondered. There would always be another storm. And where, next time, would I find refuge? *Espiritu Santo* stood propped against the wall. And it was my *Espiritu Santo*. I had affirmed that it was so. The evil spirit that I had taken into myself would never leave me. But I'd see to it that, from now on, the devil would dance to a different tune. It would serve me. It would serve Gala. It would, perhaps, even serve Gala's faith.

I turned back to face the doll.

Little god, I still don't believe in either your grace or your person. But shelter me, I thought. Shelter me from the storm. No more strutting down the highways of the self. No more superstition of darkness and deceit. I have known the fire of hell, and I have craved the fire of heaven. Let me be united, forever, with the one creature in my life who has known both heaven and hell. That at last, O Lord, if only for her, my cry may come unto thee.

Agnus Dei, qui tollis peccata mundi, miserere nobis.

EARTHLIGHT

A SELECTED LIST OF FANTASY TITLES
AVAILABLE FROM EARTHLIGHT

The prices shown below were correct at the time of going to press. However Earthlight reserve the right to show new retail prices on covers which may differ from those previously advertised in the text or elsewhere.

☐ 0 6710 1605 9	Escardy Gap	*Peter Crowther & James Lovegrove*	£5.99
☐ 0 6710 2261 X	The Sum Of All Men	*David Farland*	£6.99
☐ 0 7434 0827 6	Brotherhood of the Wolf	*David Farland*	£6.99
☐ 0 6710 1787 X	The Lament of Abalone	*Jane Welch*	£5.99
☐ 0 6710 3391 3	The Bard of Castaguard	*Jane Welch*	£5.99
☐ 0 6710 1785 3	The Royal Changeling	*John Whitbourn*	£5.99
☐ 0 6710 3300 X	Downs-Lord Dawn	*John Whitbourn*	£5.99
☐ 0 6710 2193 1	Sailing to Sarantium	*Guy Gavriel Kay*	£6.99
☐ 0 6848 6156 9	Lord of Emperors	*Guy Gavriel Kay*	£16.99
☐ 0 6710 2191 5	Beyond the Pale	*Mark Anthony*	£6.99
☐ 0 6848 6041 4	The Keep of Fire	*Mark Anthony*	£9.99
☐ 0 6710 2192 3	The Last Dragonlord	*Joanne Bertin*	£6.99
☐ 0 6848 6051 1	Dragon and Phoenix	*Joanne Bertin*	£9.99
☐ 0 6710 2208 3	The High House	*James Stoddard*	£5.99
☐ 0 6710 3749 8	The False House	*James Stoddard*	£5.99
☐ 0 6710 3303 4	Green Rider	*Kristen Britain*	£6.99
☐ 0 6710 2190 7	The Amber Citadel	*Freda Warrington*	£5.99
☐ 0 6710 2282 2	Into The Darkness	*Harry Turtledove*	£6.99
☐ 0 6710 2189 3	The Siege of Arrandin	*Marcus Herniman*	£5.99
☐ 0 6710 3719 6	The Twist	*Richard Calder*	£5.99
☐ 0 6710 3720 X	Malignos	*Richard Calder*	£6.99

All Earthlight titles are available by post from:

Book Service By Post, P.O. Box 29, Douglas, Isle of Man IM99 1BQ

Credit cards accepted. Please telephone 01624 675137,
fax 01624 670923, Internet http://www.bookpost.co.uk or
e-mail: bookshop@enterprise.net for details.

Free postage and packing in the UK. Overseas customers allow
£1 per book (paperbacks) and £3 per book (hardbacks).